Praise for The Unladylike Adventures
of Kat Stephenson:

'A blend of *What Katy Did?* and *Pride and Prejudice,* this book
manages to appeal to a modern reader. Burgis has written
a winning formula...' **writeaway.org.uk**

'A more substantial foray into the Regency world of Austen
and Heyer than that of Meg Cabot; albeit with elements of
J. K. Rowling thrown in for good measure...'
The School Librarian

'An excellent book and as it is the first of a trilogy, there is the
promise of more reading pleasure to come.' **thebookbag.co.uk**

'Fizzes with magic and intrigue and kept me glued to the page
from its dramatic opening.' **Chicklish**

'Regency romance and fantasy adventure all in one,
this is a satisfying read and a promising beginning
to a trilogy that is sure to be popular...'
School Library Journal

A Reckless Magick

A TEMPLAR BOOK

First published in the UK in 2012 by Templar Publishing,
an imprint of The Templar Company Limited,
Deepdene Lodge, Deepdene Avenue, Dorking, Surrey, RH5 4AT, UK
www.templarco.co.uk

ISBN 978-1-84877-485-8

MIX
Paper from
responsible sources
FSC® C020471

Printed and bound in Great Britain by CPI Group (UK) Ltd, Croydon, CR0 4YY

The *un*Ladylike Adventures of Kat Stephenson

Book Three:

A Reckless Magick

Stephanie Burgis

templar

FOR JENN REESE AND JUSTINA ROBSON, KAT'S TRUE GODMOTHERS

CHAPTER ONE

1804

DESPITE WHAT EITHER OF MY SISTERS MAY SAY, I ACTUALLY possess a great deal of common sense. That was why I waited until nearly midnight on the last night of our journey into Devon before I climbed out of my bedroom window.

Luckily, my family was staying on the first floor of the inn, so the rope I'd brought along in case of emergencies was more than long enough. Luckier still, I knew a useful secret: it's much easier to sneak out in the middle of the night when you can make yourself invisible.

I landed on the grass with a thud that sent the rope jerking hard against the window's edge. It was the moment of truth: I held my breath, watching the darkened window and searching for the faintest sign of an outraged older sister awake and ready to use all of her considerable powers – even scandalous witchcraft – to try to force me back to safety.

Nothing. My shoulders relaxed.

Not for the first time, I blessed my sister Angeline for the fact that she slept like the dead. If our older sister Elissa had been the one sharing a room with me, the noise would have woken her in an instant, and then there would have been goodness only knows how much commotion and offended propriety.

It was the first time I'd actually been glad that she was gone.

Elissa was one of my favourite people in the entire world, and ever since she had moved to London with her new husband last autumn, I had missed her every single day. When it came to matters of propriety, though, she was the prissiest female I had ever met. And there was nothing in the world quite so *im*proper as magic.

That was one of the reasons I loved it so much.

Grass tickled my bare feet as I took a deep, exhilarating breath of cold night air. My magic-working buzzed in the back of my head, strong and steady.

I was on a mission, and for once, no one in my family was going to stop me.

I turned round, letting my eyes adjust to the darkness. I'd landed to one side of the sprawling old timber-framed inn, which backed onto a hill dotted with trees. By the top of the hill, the trees thickened into a true forest, dark and full of secrets. We were only a mile away from the sea, the closest I'd ever been to it in my life, and I could smell a hint of salt in the air, exotic and intriguing.

To my left, the thatched cottages of the village below stood dark and silent. To my right, the trees whispered to themselves in the shadows and a cool breeze ruffled my hair with the promise of adventure.

I knew exactly which way to go.

There was no one in sight, but I held my magic-working steady to stay invisible as I hurried past the stable block and up the hill, towards the darkness of the forest. *Can't see me, can't see me, can't see me...* The night around me might look empty, but I knew what I'd seen earlier that day – and the day before, at the last inn we'd stopped at – and, most telling of all, outside our own ramshackle vicarage back in Yorkshire.

I was being followed, and I didn't care for it one bit.

I waited until I was deep into the trees and nearly fifty yards beyond the inn before I let the magic-working slip. *Ha!* My mysterious follower could spend the rest of the night lurking about the inn, for all I cared. But he couldn't possibly have seen me leave... which meant that I was free.

For the next five days, until Angeline was safely wed, I would have to be as proper, prim and ladylike as a saint, for my sister's sake. Her terrifying future mother-in-law, Mrs Carlyle, was already on the lookout for even more reasons to despise my sister, and I wasn't about to hand her any. But we weren't at Hepworth Park yet, and I had Guardian practice to do.

I knelt down on the damp grass in the centre of a moonlit clearing. I closed my eyes and felt the breeze on every inch of my skin.

Air, surround me. It was a silent command, with all the power of my will behind it. I sucked in my breath and felt the cool night air draw in around me. My hands rose up from my sides...

And a familiar voice spoke from just three feet away.

"I thought that was you I heard clambering about," said my brother, Charles.

"Oh, for heaven's sake!" My eyes flashed open. The magic-working fizzled out before it could even take hold.

Charles was standing beneath the nearest tree, his blonde hair rumpled and his coat and waistcoat both unbuttoned. He looked as if he'd been out for a night of wild dissipation – which, knowing Charles, was probably the truth.

"What on earth are you doing here?"

"I could ask you the same question," Charles said. He reached out one hand and pulled me up with effortless strength. "Not really the done thing, y'know, Kat, wandering around the wilds in the middle of the night."

"No, really?" I glared at him. "Well, it's lucky you were here to enlighten me, then. We all know what a model of propriety *you* are!"

Charles shrugged. One of the most infuriating characteristics of my older brother was his utter refusal to be drawn into any argument. "I reckoned you might not have thought it through," he said.

"You..." I shook my head, gaping. I couldn't even finish the sentence.

Charles thought *I* might not have thought through my actions carefully enough? *Charles?*

It was too ridiculous to even bother with a defence. Instead, I eyed his rumpled clothing. "What were you up to, anyway? And how did you find me?"

"I heard you knocking about in the next room," he said. "When I looked out of my window, I saw the rope dangling down. Well, I was pretty sure Angeline wouldn't be crawling out, so..."

Curses. I'd remembered to make myself invisible. If only it had occurred to me to make the rope invisible as well.

"What were you even doing in your room at that hour?" I said. "Don't you usually drink till dawn in inns like this?"

He looked absurdly offended. "Dash it, Kat. I've been

as sober as a judge since last September. You know that."

I blinked at him. "I do?" I tried to cast back my memory. It was true that I hadn't seen Charles foxed for a surprisingly long time – but I'd assumed that was only because he hadn't managed to escape Stepmama's clutches. As far as I could tell, the only things he'd ever learned at Oxford, before he'd been sent home for bad behaviour, were how to drink until his brain turned to porridge and – and now that I thought of it, this might be related – how to lose horrific amounts of money in pointless card games.

"I've changed my ways," he said. "I'm practically a saint nowadays. Didn't you even notice?"

"Erm..." I tried to think of a diplomatic answer.

It was too late. "Might've known," he said, shaking his head. "Sisters always notice when you do something wrong – oh, yes – but when you finally try to mend your ways..."

"I'm sorry," I said. "You're right, I should have... Wait." I narrowed my eyes at him. "Didn't you sneak out to play cards at the pub last month? And the month before, when Stepmama took Angeline to Harrogate to buy her wedding clothes? And—"

"That hardly counts!" Charles looked like an offended judge. "I didn't drink while I was there. And anyway, I won every time."

"So?"

"I always do, nowadays," he said, and slumped against the nearest tree trunk. "It's taken all the fun out of it. So I've decided to give up gambling, too."

Brothers were completely baffling.

I sighed and brushed the grass off my skirt. "Never mind. As long as you're here, you can make yourself useful."

He almost knocked himself out against the tree as he

lurched backwards. "Devil take it, Kat, you know I don't get involved in your magical nonsense."

"It isn't nonsense." I advanced on him purposefully. "But if you'll just help me, I can get it done much faster."

He was flattened against the tree trunk now, staring at me with as much horror as if I were aiming a loaded pistol at him. "I mean it, Kat. You and Angeline can play at witchcraft all you like, but I know what magic's like now, and—"

"This is not witchcraft," I said, "and it isn't wild magic, either, so you don't have to act like such a frightened kitten about it. Just because your idiotic university friends got you into that mess last autumn—"

"If you'd nearly been sacrificed to a blasted Roman goddess, you wouldn't be so calm about it either," said Charles, and began to edge around the tree. "Look here, I can see you're actually doing fine on your own now, so—"

"I saved you from being sacrificed," I said. "Remember?" I grabbed his coat sleeve before he could get away. "Tonight is my last chance to practice before my initiation. Half the Guardians in the Order don't even think I ought to be allowed in, just because Mama practised witchcraft."

Well, that wasn't quite the whole truth, actually. In the old days it had only been Mama's past that had made the rest of the witch-hating Order of the Guardians disapprove of me, but nowadays, the fact that I'd stripped the hereditary Head of the Order of all his magic powers – and his wits – had just as much to do with it.

I'd done that to save Charles's life, though, and that was something I could never hold against him or pretend to regret – not even to win an argument.

So I skipped that part of the explanation and only said, making my voice as sweet and plaintive as possible,

"Do you really want me to make a fool of myself in front of all of those important people?"

I knew exactly the moment that I won. Charles's shoulders sagged even before he spoke. "Fine," he said. "But considering the whole lot of them would be drummed out of Society if anyone found out they were practising magic..."

"I know, I know, I know." I dragged him back to the grass where I'd been sitting before. "Sit down here."

He eyed me warily as he lowered himself to the ground. "This isn't going to hurt, is it?"

"Don't be absurd." I sat down across from him, raising my hands. "You'll enjoy it, I'm sure." I closed my eyes and focused. *Air, surround me.* "Everyone wishes they could fly."

"I beg your pardon?" Charles's voice sounded more like a squeak.

I couldn't spare the energy to answer him.

Pressure was building in the air around me, much stronger now than the first time I'd tried. I lifted my hands slowly, cupping the night air. It felt thick and tangible against my palms, like butter. Higher up, it pushed against my chest so hard, it hurt to breathe.

I'd never done this before. My tutor, Mr Gregson, had told me that it might not be possible for me to do it yet without help. He'd even told me, meaning to be kind, that I wouldn't need to – that the other Guardians would understand if I left out that part of my initiation next week, as I'd had to wait so long to receive my proper training.

The very thought of leaving anything out set my teeth on edge. Oh, the other Guardians would certainly understand if I did a half-baked initiation. They would understand, and they would titter behind their hands, and then...

"Kat?" said Charles. "I say. Are you in pain?"

Oops. I'd been gritting my teeth so hard, my head hurt. I unclenched my jaw and let out my held breath in a sigh. *Focus.* The air had gone thin in my hands again as the magic-working fizzled out.

I took a deep breath and forced my shoulders to relax. *Air, surround me.*

I could do this. I was a Guardian by birth, just as my mother had been. It was the only connection to her that I had left.

To save Charles, I'd had to sacrifice my most cherished possession: Mama's magic mirror, her own inherited portal to the Guardians' Golden Hall. Even though I'd never known my mother, I knew it was the decision she would have wanted me to make. But the rest of the Order didn't agree with me. Not at all.

One portal was passed down in each Guardian family. One, and only one, to be protected and valued above all else. I didn't know how many generations had used Mama's mirror before I'd inherited it, but when I'd thrown it into the bubbling waters of Bath to complete the rite of wild magic and save Charles's life, I had, in the eyes of the Order, forsaken it in the most outrageously careless fashion. As far as they were concerned, I'd shown disdain not just for my portal but for the Order itself... and that didn't bode well for my initiation.

Oh, they couldn't refuse to admit me, not after I'd saved Britain from invasion by the French and saved the Guardians from the scandal of their own Head's treason. But in order for my initiation to take place, I would need a new portal... and to hear all the grumbling, you'd think I was demanding the Crown Jewels. It had been eight months now since I had lost Mama's mirror, and just as

Mrs Carlyle had made excuse after excuse to delay my sister's wedding, the Order had made excuse after excuse for why the time was never exactly right for me to finally be granted a new portal and initiated.

Perhaps I shouldn't have been surprised – after all, everyone had been outraged by Mama, too. First the Order had expelled her for secretly practising witchcraft, and then she'd scandalised all of England by letting the secrecy drop. In the eyes of Society, there was no crime worse than publicly practising magic of any sort – and the other Guardians in the Order weren't the only ones who still sputtered with fury and disgust whenever Mama's name was mentioned.

But I'd agreed to join the Order in the first place not only to fight malevolent magic-workers, but also to restore Mama's reputation as a Guardian. I might have had to give up her mirror, but I would be dashed if I'd let the snobs who'd expelled her for her curiosity and courage look down their noses at me during my own initiation ceremony.

I deserved a new portal. And I would prove it.

I cupped my hands and lifted the air in them. Power buzzed through my body, rising upward. I felt the night around me in my grasp.

Air, support me.

At first I thought it was only my imagination. Then I felt cool air brush underneath the skirts of my dressing gown.

I opened my eyes. Charles was staring at me, his mouth wide open...

And I was hovering a full inch above the ground.

I had to bite my lip to keep myself from laughing with sheer delight. Serious, mature magic-workers wouldn't laugh when they did magic. I tugged at the air. It lifted me two inches higher. The cool night breeze billowed the wide sleeves of my dressing gown around me like a pair of muslin wings.

I couldn't hold back my laughter anymore. It burbled up from my chest and overflowed. I tugged myself half a foot higher and met my older brother's astonished gaze. It only made me laugh harder. "If you could see your face right now—"

"Well, what do you expect of a fellow?" But Charles was grinning too now, and looking astonishingly like the brother I used to know before Stepmama sent him off to boarding school. "Come on, then, Kat, follow through on your promise. You're not going to sit up there all night on your own, are you?"

"Absolutely not." I closed my eyes and felt through the darkness. "Ready?"

I could hear Charles's grin in his voice. "Do your worst."

Air, surround him—

A twig snapped just ten feet away, as loud as a gunshot in the silence of the night.

My eyes flared open. I twisted around in mid-air.

A dark figure stood between the trees, watching me.

CHAPTER TWO

MY JAW DROPPED. UNFORTUNATELY, SO DID MY FOCUS.

I tipped forwards and crashed straight to the ground, hitting a massive knot of tree roots with my left shoulder. *Ouch!*

I didn't have time to moan over my injuries. I rolled over and pushed myself to my feet. The dark figure was already gone. Curse him! Charles, on the other hand, was heading towards me.

"Kat, are you..."

But I was already running. "Don't worry about me." I yelled the words over my shoulder. "We have to catch him!"

"Well, dash it, Kat, you can't just... Kat! Wait for me!"

I didn't bother to respond. I needed all my energy for the chase.

I dived between tree trunks and jumped over tangled roots, powered by fury. My mysterious follower might think himself amazingly clever for tracking me all the way across England this past week, but I would be damned if he'd get away with spying on me as I prepared for my own initiation ceremony. I wouldn't let him go until I finally found out what the devil he wanted from me.

But that was easier said than done. On my way here, I'd had time to carefully find my way through the darkness to the moonlit clearing. Now that I was running at top speed, every pointed tree branch in the forest seemed to aim directly at my face or arms, and every single one of them found its mark. I was scratched and panting by the time I burst out of the trees at the top of the hill, looking down over the inn and the village beyond.

The hill was empty. The stables were dark. There wasn't a single person in sight.

I let out a groan of pure frustration.

Whoever my mysterious follower was, he was a fast runner – and a quiet one too. If it hadn't been for that telltale twig snapping under his feet, he could have watched me and Charles all night long, and I never would have known.

What an utterly horrible thought.

I wrapped my arms around my chest and looked down at the stables that stood between me and the inn. Narrow, darkened windows stared back up at me like hollow eyes.

I was not afraid, I told myself. Certainly not. Only cowards eavesdropped and spied and ran away when they were spotted, and I could never be afraid of a coward.

But when I heard a crackle of breaking twigs behind me, I spun round so fast, I nearly fell over.

It was only Charles, emerging from the trees and brushing grass off his trousers.

"Blasted tree roots," he said. "I think at least one of them tripped me on purpose." He looked around, frowning.

"So, where is he? Whoever he is."

"Gone," I said, and ground my teeth together. "We were too late."

"Huh." Charles straightened his jacket. "You can't say much for his manners, can you? Lurking about in the woods to spy on people. Not what you could really call gentlemanly behaviour."

"Oh, for heaven's sake." I relaxed just enough to roll my eyes at my brother. "I can't believe you're huffing about gentlemanly behaviour. Aren't you the one who keeps getting sent home from Oxford?"

"That's completely different," Charles said. "Having a bit of fun—"

"You mean, doing stupid amounts of drinking and gambling, and taking on every idiotic prank that your friends dare you to—"

"It's not *ungentlemanly*." Charles lifted his upper lip in a sneer. "As you would understand if you were a gentleman."

"Ha." I started down the hill towards the inn, shaking my head. "If being a *gentleman* means..."

My voice dried up in my throat. I froze, five steps out from the shelter of the trees.

Something was tickling at my senses; something I'd been too busy to notice while I was arguing with Charles.

"What the devil?" Charles stumbled into my back, knocking me forwards. "Blast it, Kat, will you make up your mind? Are we going or staying?"

"Shh," I hissed.

My whole skin was tingling with awareness. I turned in a slow circle, peering through the darkness.

Moonlight cast a faint glow on the grassy hill, sweeping down to the stables and the inn and the thatched cottages beyond. There definitely wasn't anyone in sight.

But we were still being watched. I was certain of it.

I breathed deeply, all my senses alert. If he was using witchcraft to hide himself...

No. Every witch had a signature scent that lingered in the air when they cast a spell, and I smelled nothing but the fresh scent of grass and leaves, mingled with the salt of the ocean in the distance.

The trees rustled behind me, full of secrets. I thought my watcher had come out of the woods ahead of us... but had he really? Or was he still standing in the shadows, only a few feet away, listening to our conversation?

There was only one way to find out.

Clenching my hands into fists, I spun round, lunged forwards...

And Charles's arms closed around my waist from behind. To my utter shock, I found my feet rising high off the ground. My six-foot-tall brother had scooped me into the air, pinning my arms against my sides.

I was almost too startled to be outraged.

"What – on – earth – do you think you're doing?" I panted. I twisted and kicked against him, fighting to break free.

"I'm saving you from yourself," said Charles. He held me with maddening ease, no matter how hard I struggled. "Someone needs to, don't you think?"

"Of all the idiotic, dunderheaded...! No. Wait." I took a deep, calming breath and stopped struggling. Turning my head round as far as I could, I gave Charles my most calm and mature and reasonable smile. I had practised it before, in mirrors and on Stepmama, and I knew how well it worked. "The thing is," I said, both calmly and sensibly, "there happens to be something that I have to do right now, so if you'll just let me down for a moment, I'll—"

"Go charging into the woods after some lout twice your size?" Charles snorted. "I think not."

"How did you know – ?"

He shrugged. "I do have eyes, Kat. And you aren't exactly a blank slate, you know."

It was too absurd to be borne. This was Charles, for heaven's sake. Charles! For the past six years, ever since Stepmama had first sent him to boarding school, he'd barely seemed to remember that he even had a family. Why did he suddenly have to notice me now?

"I am a Guardian," I said. "Remember? You don't have to protect me from anything. And if you're trying to act like an older brother now—"

"I *am* your older brother," said Charles. He heaved a long-suffering sigh. "It would be pleasant if, for once, just one of my sisters would recall I am the oldest in the family, and take my guidance."

If I hadn't been so angry, I might have let out a shout of laughter.

"Just try telling Angeline and Elissa that," I said. "Really. I'd like to hear what they'd say. But in the meantime, if you're finished play-acting..."

"Sorry, Kat." He turned and started back down the hill, his long legs striding confidently forwards despite all of my exertions. "I'm sure you're a terribly powerful magic-worker and the whole world trembles when you let out a roar... but I'm still not letting you go flinging yourself into trouble anymore."

I kicked his leg, hard, on purpose. "Of all the people to preach at me about getting into trouble!"

"I've been spending an awful lot of time thinking, since last September," Charles said. "You did save me, after all. And you were right – I had been acting like a fool for a long time before that. But believe it or not, I'm not the kind of fellow who'd just ignore a thing like nearly getting killed, especially" – he grimaced – "when I had to be rescued by my infant sister, of all people. And besides, that showed me just how out of control you've become."

I gaped up at him. "I beg your pardon?"

He frowned as sternly as a judge. "Running around Bath at night, by yourself? Throwing yourself into battles with people twice your size? If I don't step in now, you're bound to get yourself killed or cause a public scandal before you even turn fourteen."

"*I'll* cause a scandal?" I took a deep, soothing breath, to keep myself from screaming. "Charles," I said. "I appreciate your concern. But of all the people to give me a lecture!"

"Trust me," said Charles, "I may have ruined all of my own prospects, but I won't stand by and let you ruin yours. Obviously Stepmama can't handle you, and now that Angeline's leaving, you'll have no one else keeping any reins on you at all. So from now on, I'm going to look after you myself... whether you're sensible enough to like it or not."

"Oh Lord," I moaned.

I subsided against him in limp horror. The whole world seemed to be whirling around me as he carried me down the hill.

I'd spent the last few weeks trying not to think about how on earth I was going to cope without either of my sisters once Angeline married Mr Carlyle and left me behind for the first time in my life. But it had never even occurred to me that there was a far, far greater threat in store.

The Charles I had known for the past three years, who had slept through every Oxford lecture and gambled the whole family into debt... well, he had been a problem, to say the very least.

But a brand-new Charles, wide-awake and determined to take charge of my life?

That was an absolute, unmitigated disaster.

I craned my neck to peer back over his shoulder as he carried me down the hill. No one moved out of the shadows of the trees. But I could still feel hostile eyes watching me all the way to the inn, and it made me burn with impotent fury.

Soon, I promised myself. Soon I would hunt down my mysterious follower, and I would show him I was a force to be reckoned with.

Just as soon as I managed to escape Charles's 'protection'.

CHAPTER THREE

THE NEXT MORNING I WOKE UP TO AN ALL-TOO-FAMILIAR SOUND.

"Katherine Ann Stephenson!" Stepmama's shriek could have shattered glass... or eardrums.

I groaned and pulled my bedcovers over my face. I had stayed up far too late, the sunshine through the bedroom window was far too bright, and I was nowhere near ready to face Stepmama yet.

I'd barely settled the covers over my eyes, though, when she snatched them off again. She was already fully dressed in a forest green travelling gown, and her cheeks were flushed with rage. "Explain yourself *this instant*, young lady!"

Angeline groaned beside me and pulled her pillow over her head. "What's Kat done this time?" she mumbled into the pillowcase.

Humph. So much for sisterly loyalty. I would have glared at her if I'd had the energy, but the bright light was hurting my eyes too much. Stepmama must have opened the curtains, too. "Please," I said, and put my hand over my eyes. "I'll get up soon, I promise. Just ten more minutes..."

"I'm not going anywhere until you explain how you came by those scratches on your arms and hands, young lady." Stepmama pulled my hand off my eyes, then gasped. "*And* on your cheek! What in heaven's name were you doing last night?"

Oh Lord. My late-night dash through the woods was coming back to haunt me. "Um..." I blinked up at her, trying to think through the sludge of exhaustion in my brain. *Be creative. Be creative.* "Ummm..."

Stepmama dropped my hand and collapsed onto the chair beside the bed. "I dread to think what Mrs Carlyle will say."

The mention of her future mother-in-law acted like a lightning rod against Angeline's prone figure. "Mrs Carlyle?" She yanked the pillow off her face and jerked upright , her thick, dark braid of hair swinging like a whip. "What about Mrs Carlyle? What's happened now?"

Stepmama gestured wordlessly at me. Angeline turned. She stared.

For once in my life I genuinely wished for an ordinary, non-magical mirror, just to show me my own face. From the way Angeline and Stepmama were both looking at me, I might as well have been an exhibit in a travelling fair.

I took a deep breath and lifted my chin. "I have a perfectly reasonable explanation," I began.

"Oh, dear Lord," said Angeline. "I don't think I can take one of your explanations, Kat. Not before I've had my morning tea." She dropped her head in her hands, massaging her forehead. Her voice was muffled by her fingers. "Exactly how far are we from Hepworth Park?"

"Less than ten miles," Stepmama said in her Doom voice. "It may take longer than usual because of the perilous road, but we'll still be there by noon."

"Damnation," said Angeline.

For once Stepmama didn't even scold her for her language.

I squirmed. In the heat of last night's chase it hadn't even occurred to me to worry about Angeline's dragon of a future mama-in-law. It was true, though – my arms were scored with deep scratches that could never be covered by the short puff sleeves of my gown, and I could feel my face stinging, too, where sharp branches had caught me.

"Can't you fix this?" I asked Angeline, touching one hand to my face. Angeline had laid claim to Mama's old diaries of witchcraft. "There must be some spell you could cast—"

"If you utter even one more word on that topic, I shall swoon," Stepmama announced. "Kat, don't you dare tempt her to such madness. Angeline Olivia Stephenson, if you so much as chant a single syllable—"

"Have no fear, ma'am. I'm not entirely a fool." Angeline dropped her hands and looked me in the eye. "For heaven's sake, Kat. Don't you even remember that horrible round of gossip last September? It took ages to persuade Society that I wasn't a witch. Do you really, truly think it would be a good idea for me to cast a spell right now, right here, less than ten miles away from Hepworth Park? Only four days before my wedding? When we could be absolutely certain that any observers would be ready and eager to spread the gossip where Mrs Carlyle and all of the wedding guests could hear it?"

"Um..." I gulped, thinking back to last night. "I... hadn't really thought about it that way."

"Obviously." She rubbed her eyes, yawning. "So. Tell us everything. What were you doing last night to come by those scratches?"

I bit my lip. If the two of us had been alone, I might have told her... or then again, I might not. Even Angeline might not completely understand why it was so important for me to prove myself to the other Guardians. Ever since she had discovered that Guardianship, unlike witchcraft, was only inherited by one member of each generation – and that I, the only one of us who had never known Mama, was the one who had inherited it from her – it had been a decidedly awkward subject between us.

And after what she had just said...

No. I would keep last night's Guardian practice a secret, I would find and deal with my mysterious follower, no matter how hard Charles tried to stop me... and then, after the wedding was safely past, I would tell Angeline all about it.

Long after the wedding was safely past, I amended, as I saw her expression shift into sudden horror.

"Please," she said. "Please, please tell me you didn't go down to the taproom last night and start a fight."

"No!" I gaped at her. "Of course I didn't."

"There's no 'of course' about it," said Angeline. "You're covered in scratches and..." Her eyebrows rose as she focused on my bare shoulder, where I'd landed hard on tree roots. "Bruises, too. You either fought in a taproom brawl or made a tiger angry. And considering we're at a provincial inn with no tropical jungles in sight..."

"The taproom?" Stepmama looked ready to swoon at the very thought. "Katherine, you wouldn't. Would you?"

I crossed my arms and glared at them both. "You have no faith in me at all."

They looked at each other and traded a meaningful glance. It might have been the first time I had ever seen Angeline and Stepmama agree about anything.

"She had an accident," Angeline said. "A terrible accident."

"Yes." Stepmama drew herself up. "Perhaps... a farm cat gone feral, who attacked her."

"What farm cat?" I said. "We haven't stopped at any farms."

"Shh." Angeline didn't even bother to glance at me. "It was lucky she didn't lose an eye."

Stepmama nodded. "Needless to say, the cat has been disposed of."

"Disposed of?" I stared at her. "That's horrible!"

"That," said Stepmama, "is the only thing preventing you from being sent straight back home, young lady. If you wish to be allowed to attend your sister's wedding, I suggest you commit that story to memory and stop arguing."

"Fine." I rolled my eyes. "But if I ever do get scratched by a cat, I'll remember not to tell you about it."

"Trust me, Kat," said Angeline. "If a cat does scratch you, we'll assume it had its reasons."

"Humph." I narrowed my eyes at her. What I needed was a really good, sizzling retort, the kind that Angeline could toss out as naturally as breathing.

But she spoke before I could come up with one.

"Can you promise me one thing?" Her dark eyes were fierce with worry as she leaned towards me, looking so vulnerable I had to blink hard to make sure I was seeing her properly. Angeline almost never let herself look vulnerable to anyone. It was all part and parcel of her 'I am so strong, no one can ever hurt me no matter how hard *they try'* attitude; the same attitude that had kept her proudly snarling in response to every humiliating snub thrown at us for our mother's blatant witchcraft, every absurd new excuse Mrs Carlyle had invented to delay Angeline's wedding and every long-awaited visit that Frederick Carlyle had been forced to cancel on his mother's orders.

It was the same maddening attitude that made my sister almost never ask anyone for help, no matter how badly she might need it... and *that* made it almost impossible for me to refuse her anything when she trusted me enough to ask.

Now she took my hand and said, "Can you absolutely promise me that no one who saw you last night will carry the gossip to my wedding party?"

I swallowed hard. I had never broken a promise to either of my sisters. I never would. But Angeline had been as tense as an over-strung harp ever since we'd first started planning for this wedding. If I told her about my follower now, she might just snap.

And really, whatever mischief or malice he might be planning, it had to be more significant than mere gossip to make him pursue me all the way across the country. So truly, if I looked at the matter in just the right light...

"I promise," I said, and let out the breath that I'd been holding.

Relief softened my sister's eyes. She squeezed my hand. "Thank you, Kat. I knew I could count on you."

I squeezed her warm hand back and hoped that she was right.

I couldn't let myself think about it for long, though, or my guilt would start to show. Angeline was expert at ferreting out my guilty secrets. So I dropped her hand and slid off the bed, my bare feet landing with a thump on the hard wooden floorboards.

"Is Elissa here yet?" I asked Stepmama as I scooped up my dressing gown from the floor where I'd left it.

The morning air was uncomfortably cool – I could see grey clouds through the window and the promise of rain coming later in the day – but I was already feeling better at the very thought of my eldest sister's arrival. It had been one hundred and twenty-three days since her last visit, and that was one hundred and twenty-three days too long for me.

Stepmama had been busy looking pained at my unladylike treatment of my clothing – after six years of living with her, I could interpret that particular expression and repeat the familiar lecture in my sleep – but now she just sighed and held out a folded letter. "I was about to explain, if you hadn't made every other thought fly out of my head!"

Angeline rolled across the bed and snatched the letter before I could take it.

"Not fair!" I jumped for it, but she held it over my head. I hated being the shortest person in my family.

"Stepmama was handing it to *me*," I said, and glared up at my sister.

"It's about *my* wedding," Angeline said, and curled her lip at me.

"Girls!" Stepmama heaved a martyred sigh from her chair. "Katherine, please remember you are thirteen years old and only four years away – heaven help us all – from being presented in Society. Angeline, you are about to become the mistress of a grand estate. Would you please have the goodness to behave like one?"

"You see?" Angeline gave me a superior look. "*I am*

about to become the mistress of a grand estate. Stepmama said so."

"Ha. Well, you aren't yet. And if you try snatching any letters from Mrs Carlyle—"

Angeline's lips twitched. "It's a good thing she's even shorter than you. It'll make it even easier to hold them out of reach."

"Oh, my heavens!" Stepmama moaned. "Kat... Angeline... my poor head – you mustn't even dream of..."

I met my sister's eyes. We both started laughing at once, drowning out the sound of Stepmama's protests.

"Oh, Kat." Angeline looped an arm around my waist and pulled me down with her to the bed. "I am going to miss you so much. Do you know that?"

The laughter died in my throat, turning into something hard and knotted that made my eyes burn. I wasn't going to cry. I was *not*.

But if I let myself think about losing the second of my sisters, I might not be able to stop myself.

"Open the letter," I said, and swallowed down the knot in my throat. "You might as well read it, now that you've got it."

"Fine." Angeline kept her arm around me as she unfolded the letter and spread it across both our knees. I leaned into her shoulder as I read, and I breathed in the familiar, comforting scent of my sister. We'd sat this way so many times over the years. I knew exactly where my head fitted against her shoulder, exactly where her dark hair tickled against my cheek. It didn't seem real – it didn't even seem possible – that in less than a week, she would be settling here in Devon for good and I would be riding back to Yorkshire without her.

When my vision blurred, I set my jaw and blinked hard.

But I still couldn't make out what the letter really meant – and for once, it wasn't only because Elissa had the tiniest handwriting of anyone I knew.

"'Physician's appointment'?" I read aloud. I'd read the letter twice already, and Angeline was still frowning down at it without speaking. "What physician's appointment? Do you think she's ill? But no, she can't be, or she wouldn't still be planning to come to the wedding. So what do you think it means?"

"Oh Lord. Who knows?" Angeline tossed the letter onto the bed with a sigh. "Only Elissa would think it was too improper to tell us why she needed to see a physician."

"It must be important," I said, "or she wouldn't have delayed the trip for it. She knows how worried you are about meeting the Carlyles."

Angeline lifted her chin. "I am not worried about meeting the Carlyles," she said. We were still sitting side by side, though, and I felt her whole body stiffen as she spoke. "Just because Mrs Carlyle has summoned the whole extended family to meet me, and they've probably spent the last eight months wondering why on earth she allowed the match..."

"*And* your younger sister looks as if she's been mauled by a tiger," Stepmama supplied.

Thank you, Stepmama. I scowled at her. Angeline didn't answer, but I felt her spine tighten another notch.

I thought longingly of Elissa's beautiful new travelling carriage, and how impressive it would have been to arrive at Hepworth Park in that instead of in our hired carriage, which looked every year of its age, especially with its peeling brown paint.

I thought of Mr Collingwood, Elissa's sweet, doting husband, who was wealthy and well-bred enough to impress even the most sneering of aristocratic in-laws.

I thought of Elissa herself, so graceful and elegant and self-possessed in every circumstance, so talented at smoothing over difficult situations.

"Didn't you say the road to Hepworth was perilous?" I asked Stepmama.

She groaned. "The road that leads directly from London to Hepworth is fine – one of the finest in the country, apparently, because the Carlyles see to it. But from our direction – why, according to the innkeeper, it's quite the most dangerous road in Devon. Narrow, full of treacherous stones, running along the side of a cliff... if I don't have a migraine by the end of it from sheer terror, I shall count it as a miracle."

"I wouldn't worry about it," Angeline said. "He was probably just trying to impress you."

"Maybe," I said. "But maybe not." I frowned.

Angeline frowned too as she looked at me. "What?" she said. "I know that look, Kat, and it never signals anything good. What exactly are you scheming now?"

"I don't know," I said. "Not yet."

But I hoped the innkeeper was telling the truth.

If the road really was that perilous, we would have to go slowly. And if we went slowly, that would give me time to come up with a truly stunning plan.

"Don't worry," I said, and took my sister's hand in mine. The bright red scratches on my skin stood out like flames warning me of danger ahead. Still, I smiled at her as reassuringly as I could, and put all my confidence into my smile. "You'll make a brilliant first impression on the Carlyles, even without Elissa here to help. I'll make sure of it."

CHAPTER FOUR

THE INNKEEPER HADN'T BEEN EXAGGERATING. THE ROAD was truly terrible.

Unfortunately, I'd left out one important point from my calculations: it is impossible to think up a brilliant scheme when your teeth are trying to rattle their way out of your head.

"So," Angeline said. She was clinging to the strap on the carriage wall, but her shoulder still knocked against the corner of the window as she spoke. "The innkeeper claimed this road was a bit rocky, did he?"

Charles laughed without opening his eyes. Stepmama only groaned, covering her face with both hands. Papa, seated across from me, was still doggedly trying to read his book, but he had started to look disturbingly green. I kept a careful eye on him in case I had to move out of the way fast.

My only consolation was that the innkeeper had been

telling the truth about something else, as well. This strip of road ran just above the ocean, hard against a grassy cliff. From the window I could see a wide swathe of bluish-grey water stretching on and on into the horizon, a full hundred feet below us.

It was an astonishing sight. In fact – I grimaced as my head banged against the back wall – if only I'd been able to focus on anything but the rattling of the carriage, I might even have found it beautiful. As it was, though...

A loud crack sounded underneath us. The back of the carriage dropped with a thump, too fast for me to react. My head bounced off the back of the seat. Papa's book flew out of his hands and slammed into my lap. Then I was flung forwards against him.

I put out my hands to catch myself on his chest just as the carriage slewed around. Suddenly I was falling onto Angeline instead, a tangle of legs and arms inside the wildly swerving carriage...

And we were all heading straight for the edge of the cliff.

For a moment the bottom of the carriage scraped over the rocky surface of the road, vibrating as though it was going to shake itself to pieces. Then the whole carriage flipped.

High, animal screams filled the air – the hired horses shrieking outside. I saw their hooves flash past the window as we toppled. Stepmama was screaming too. As the world spun around us, I had just enough time to wish that I knew how to swim...

The carriage landed on solid ground with a thump that juddered straight through my bones.

When my vision cleared, I found myself lying on top of Papa, breathing hard. He lay on his back against one of the carriage doors, Angeline kicked herself loose from Charles beside us, and the moaning weight sprawled half across me was Stepmama.

Blue sky shone through the opposite window high above us. Shards of glass lay scattered around us, glinting like diamonds in the sunlight.

Breath shuddered through my chest. I felt as light-headed as if I were floating.

There was a rap at the side of the carriage. The hired coachman called through, his voice hoarse.

"Mr Stephenson? Mrs Stephenson? I can't help you out. I think my leg's broke."

"Ah... that's all right, then," Papa called back. "Er, do look after yourself."

"And the horses!" Stepmama added. She was already brushing the glass off her gown, muttering to herself, "Of all the disastrous – ouch – ridiculous – ouch!"

"I'll get us out of here," I said. I started to push myself up, nudging her aside.

Papa cleared his throat underneath me. His voice sounded thin and strained. "Er, if you wouldn't mind – ?"

"Sorry, Papa." I moved my elbow off his stomach, still thinking furiously. I could certainly reach the handle of the other carriage door, but after that... "I think I can—"

"Out of the way, Kat," Charles said. He straightened and pushed the door wide open, then swung himself up and out of the carriage with perfect ease. "Come on, Angeline." He reached back inside to pull her out.

"I could have done it," I muttered to him a minute later as he helped me out onto the dusty road.

"'Course you could have," Charles said.

But I didn't trust his tone at all.

I narrowed my eyes at his back as he pulled out Papa.

Didn't he even remember who had saved him last autumn?

Then I looked past him, and my stomach gave a sickly flop. We'd missed the cliff edge by less than three feet. Beyond it there was a long, green drop to the water below – and something I hadn't seen from my earlier vantage point at the carriage window: sharp, jutting rocks at the water's edge. I imagined our carriage being thrown against them, and I swallowed hard.

Luckily, I didn't have time to dwell on might-have-beens. The coachman was sitting a few feet away, still hanging on to the horses' reins as they whinnied and stomped in place. His face was chalky pale, and his right leg was bent at an awkward angle. I hurried to his side, trying not to look at the cliff edge as I skirted it.

"Let me help you with the horses," I said. "You should be resting."

"That's all right, miss." He managed a wan smile. "I'd rather see to them meself, if you don't mind, especially this close to the edge. Right miracle it was that I didn't go over the side meself when we fell over."

"How did it happen?" I looked back to where the rest of my family was assembling in the middle of the rock-strewn dirt road. There were no houses or farms this close to the coast, only another tall wall of grass-pricked white rock stretching high above the twisting, curving road. *No one to ask for help*, I thought, and grimaced.

"The back wheel, it was. Come loose somehow and snapped straight off. I could've sworn... Never mind." The coachman shook his head.

"Sworn what?"

"Nothing, miss." His smile looked even more strained this time. "Never you worry about it. I was only imagining things. Would you mind seeing if your father or your brother are free to have a word with me about the horses?"

I looked hard at him. He was still pale with pain, and sweat rolled down his cheeks... but there was definitely more to it.

I could have sworn that he was hiding something. But whatever he knew or suspected, he wasn't about to share it with a thirteen-year-old lady.

I was so, so tired of being treated like a delicate young lady rather than a sensible human being.

He really was in pain, though, so I gave up for the moment and walked over to pass on his message to Papa. Papa, of course, was even less likely to know anything about horses than I was... but as far as I knew, the only thing Charles had ever done with a horse was gamble on it, so Papa would have to do.

As Papa hurried over to the coachman's side, I joined Angeline and Stepmama in surveying the wreckage. Charles had wandered off to the cliff edge and was frowning over it, kicking pebbles off the side.

"It was the back wheel," I reported. "It came off."

"No, really?" Rolling her eyes, Angeline pointed to where the wheel lay discarded on the road, several feet back. "Somehow, even I had managed to guess that much."

I shrugged irritably, looking back at Papa and the coachman. Papa had just beckoned Charles over to join them, and the three of them were frowning in the direction of the back of the carriage. Needless to say, it hadn't even occurred to any of them to invite me over. If only Angeline would just once let me have a good look at Mama's diaries of witchcraft, instead of hoarding them all to herself! I'd only ever managed to learn one of Mama's spells, and it certainly wasn't the one I most needed.

A spell to eavesdrop would be infinitely useful, especially right now.

I sighed.

Angeline met my eyes and smiled wryly. There was only one small cut along her cheek from the broken glass, but the left shoulder of her pelisse was ripped, her left hand was bleeding from several different shallow cuts, and her thick, dark hair had escaped half its pins. "Not quite the first impression I had planned to make on the Carlyles."

"It is an absolute disaster," said Stepmama. "We can hardly even ask the coachman to carry the news to Hepworth Park with that broken leg."

Angeline rolled her eyes at Stepmama even as she leaned over to wrap a handkerchief around her own hand. "Indeed. What can he possibly have been thinking to insist on breaking his leg only to inconvenience us?"

Stepmama's face tightened. "Very amusing, I am sure," she snapped, "but has it occurred to you yet that we are going to have to walk all the way to Hepworth Park, coating ourselves with yet more dust along the way?"

"I could—" I began.

They both turned to me with eyebrows raised in identical looks of disdain. I set my teeth.

"Fine," I said. "*I* couldn't, because it would be terribly improper, but *Charles* could ride to Hepworth Park on one of the carriage horses and tell them what's happened."

"Charles?" Angeline looked ill. "I think not."

"No," Stepmama agreed, and shuddered. "Certainly not."

"But—"

"We are trying to make a good impression on my future in-laws," Angeline said. "Remember?"

I felt a twinge of guilt as I looked over at Charles,

listening so seriously to the coachman. "He is getting better, you know," I said.

"Hmm," said Angeline.

"He hasn't got drunk since last September," I offered.

They traded another look.

I ground my teeth.

"Fine," I said. "What do you two propose?"

Before either of them could answer, Charles took the horses' reins. Leaning heavily on Papa's arm, the coachman limped to the back of the carriage. They bent down together to inspect it.

"Oh, thank goodness," said Stepmama. "Perhaps it's fixable after all."

I blinked at her. "By Papa?" She must have hit her head harder than I'd realised.

I had every respect for Papa – especially when it came to a matter of scholarship, or a crisis involving ancient Greek. Even when it came to physical courage, my quiet, socially petrified papa had shown surprising depth from time to time.

But when it came to practical matters... well, Stepmama of all people should have known better than to suggest anything so nonsensical.

Angeline said doubtfully, "Perhaps, if the coachman is *very* skilled at giving directions..."

But they were already straightening away from the toppled carriage, both frowning harder than ever. And I didn't need an eavesdropping spell when Charles called back to them from his position by the horses.

"Well? Was it intentional or not?"

"Ha!" I knew the coachman had been hiding something!

Papa winced, lifting one hand as if he could push back

Charles's words. It was too late. Stepmama had already stiffened, like a hunting spaniel picking up the scent of prey.

"*What* did Charles just say?"

The coachman murmured something to Papa. Papa shook his head, his shoulders slumping, and turned to Stepmama. "My dear, I didn't mean to worry you or the girls."

"Too late for that," said Angeline. Her voice was perfectly calm, but she looked every bit as dangerous as our stepmother. "I take it this wasn't actually an accident?"

"Well..." He looked back to the coachman for assistance.

"Someone sawed halfway through the axle, ma'am," the coachman said. "I checked the carriage myself last night when we first come into the inn, and there weren't no damage then."

"Someone at the inn," Stepmama breathed. "Oh, my heavens. Robbers! It must have been. They intended us to break down so they could spring upon us. We don't even have a pistol to defend ourselves! George, you and Charles must immediately—"

"Robbers, ma'am?" Angeline frowned. "Don't murderers sound rather more likely? If they knew where we were going, they must have known how rough this road was, and how close it ran to the cliff edge. The innkeeper did say it was notorious, didn't he? The rocks on this road were certain to work the rest of the axle loose, and then—"

"Don't be absurd." Stepmama stared at her. "Who would want to murder any of us? Your father and I have no enemies."

Oh Lord. I felt as if I'd just been punched in the stomach.

Stepmama was right. She and Papa didn't have any enemies...

But I did.

I opened my mouth. No matter how much it might horrify my family, I had to tell them about my mysterious follower.

Before I could, hoofbeats sounded in the distance. Not just one horse but several, judging by their thunder. They were still hidden by the curve of the road and the wall of rock that rose above it, but they would be upon us in a matter of moments.

Stepmama looked positively green. "The robbers who sabotaged the carriage," she said. "George... Charles..."

The coachman dug into his coat and pulled out a surprisingly large truncheon. "Step back, ma'am."

"I say, hadn't we better change places?" Charles said. "No offence, I mean, but with your leg as it is..."

"You three had better stand behind us," Papa said to Stepmama. "Angeline, Kat..." An expression of pain crossed his face as he looked at us. "I do hope you will take shelter with your stepmother?"

"Don't be absurd." I rolled my eyes and dug my feet in as Stepmama tried to pull me away. "I'm not about to hide like a coward."

"I'm afraid Kat is quite right," said Angeline. "I beg your pardon, sir, but scandal or no, if it comes to either letting ourselves be murdered for our non-existent jewels, or else fighting back with the powers we have—"

Stepmama gasped. "Don't you dare even consider—"

But before she could finish her command, or threat, the horses were upon us.

CHAPTER FIVE

TWELVE HORSES ROUNDED THE CORNER AND SWEPT TOWARDS us along the cliff road, all of them huge and glossy black. Six of them were pulling the most magnificent carriage I had ever seen.

It was a deep, freshly painted burgundy, gilded with gold trim and with a gold crest on the doors. Two grim-looking outriders rode beside it, holding guard. A liveried coachman plied the reins, and a second coach, painted a subdued dark brown, followed close behind.

"I don't think they're robbers," I said. But my voice was drowned by the thunder of hoofbeats rushing towards us.

The first coachman pulled his horses up only just in time, before they could trample Papa. They cascaded to a halt, stomping and blowing air out from their nostrils. In the corner of my eye, I could see Charles gaping at them in outright awe. I couldn't blame him.

Stepmama was gaping too, but not at the horses. As a

footman sprang down to lower the burgundy carriage's steps, Stepmama swung a desperate look around – from Papa, his cravat torn and his face covered with nicks from broken glass, to Angeline and me, standing in the middle of the road, our disordered hair escaping from our bonnets and our pelisses hopelessly wrinkled from the accident.

Horror mounted in her eyes.

"Oh, my heavens," she moaned. "Everyone, please, quickly—"

The gilded carriage door opened. A woman – no, a *lady*, there was no other way to describe her – stepped out, laying one hand lightly on her footman's arm.

Her hair was as dark as Angeline's, her eyebrows delicately arched. She looked to be about Stepmama's age, and she wore a carriage gown of bright crimson with a dashingly cut spencer jacket that I remembered Angeline sighing over in last month's issue of *The Mirror of Fashion*.

For a moment no one spoke. A seagull cried overhead, and waves crashed against the rocks below, but everyone on the road stood frozen, staring at her.

It felt like being unexpectedly visited by royalty. I wondered if I ought to curtsey.

Her gaze moved from one to another of us, her eyebrows rising higher and higher. Finally she looked at Papa.

Her lips curved. She shook her head, and her fashionable ringlets danced around her face.

"Why, George Stephenson, of all people," she said. "What an astonishing coincidence."

✩ ✩

I had seen Papa paralysed in social situations, and I had watched him retreat from family arguments more times than I could count, taking refuge in the safety of his books.

But I had never in my life seen him look so shocked – or so horrified – as he did now, staring at the lady from the carriage. He might as well have seen a ghost.

"George!" Stepmama hissed. She hurried to join him, tucking her hand into his free arm and laughing with artificial lightness. "My goodness, our little carriage accident certainly has discomposed you. Aren't you going to introduce us to your friend?"

"Ah." Papa blinked rapidly. "I'm not certain – that is—"

The lady's smile turned feline. "But of course, you won't have heard. I have a different name now. A second marriage, you know," she added confidingly to Stepmama. "But then, I'm sure George understands such matters." There was a decided snap in her tone at those last words.

"George?" Stepmama's eyebrows rose.

"Er," said Papa. His gaze was darting back and forth, as if he were searching for a means of escape.

"Yes, my new title is *la Marquise de Valmont*," the lady said. "My second husband – my late husband, I should say, poor man – was an émigré, you see. He fled France when the revolution came, before he could be executed for his aristocratic title – and, luckily for all of us, he carried all his family's most valuable treasures firmly in hand. Dear Pierre. Always so unrelentingly practical. An unfortunate trait in some circumstances, and yet..." She smiled dazzlingly at all of us, resplendent in her finery. "Well, there are some consolations. But, George, don't you think you ought to present your delightful family to me now?"

Her gaze swung back to his, and held.

For once I couldn't read Papa's face at all. It was decidedly disconcerting.

He let out a sigh and drew himself up. He still supported

the coachman on one arm and Stepmama on the other, but he looked taller than he had before, and really quite stern. It was most unlike Papa.

"My lady, may I present my wife, Mrs Stephenson?"

"Mrs Stephenson." The marquise's eyes narrowed as she held out her hand. An elegant mourning ring, set with rich red garnets around a central, braided lock of dark hair, glinted on one finger. "Fascinating."

Stepmama curtsied as she took it. "My lady."

"My daughters, Miss Stephenson and Miss Katherine Stephenson" – Papa gestured – "and my son, Charles Stephenson."

"Of course." The marquise's voice softened. As I curtseyed, I caught the flash of emotion that crossed her face – was it tenderness? Or only wistfulness? A moment later she was back to dazzling charm, saying, "Miss Stephenson – that must be Angeline, then? I daresay you aren't old enough to remember me, though I shouldn't date myself so dreadfully as to admit it."

Angeline frowned. "I'm afraid—"

"She is not," said Papa, and the firmness in his tone took me aback. "She and Charles were far too young to remember any slight acquaintances of mine from so very long ago."

Charles didn't say a word. But from his position by the horses, he was frowning at the marquise with an entirely baffled expression.

Drat. I wouldn't get any answers from him.

"'Slight acquaintances'?" the marquise repeated, and fluttered her eyelashes at my father. "Well, it has been a very long time, after all, so perhaps my memory is failing me. Regardless..." She looked pointedly at the wreckage of our carriage. "We must save our reminiscences for a more appropriate time. I can see that you are all in need of a conveyance. Luckily—"

"We shall certainly not impose on you in such a way," said Papa. I had never heard him sound so stiff and formal in my life.

When Stepmama kicked his ankle, though, he jumped at least half an inch.

The marquise put one gloved hand to her lips, but she couldn't quite hide her smile.

"Of course we would never wish to impose," Stepmama said, "but I must confess—"

"It would be no imposition at all," said the marquise. "You see – and how marvellous this is – we have the very same destination."

"I beg your pardon?" Stepmama's eyes widened.

"Hepworth Park." The marquise turned to Angeline. "May I say how utterly delighted I was to receive my wedding invitation from your charming fiancé? I met him in town last month, and just happened to mention what a very old friend of your father I am, so..."

Angeline took a step forwards, her face lighting up like a flower turning to the sun. "You saw Frederick?"

"Indeed I did. What a handsome young man, and so devoted to his fiancée. Terribly unfashionable of him, you know, but terribly sweet as well, so I forgave him immediately, especially..." For a moment her smile looked a little fixed and artificial, as if it might shatter at a touch. "Well, you see, his description just happened to match my memories... but never mind all that! As you can see, I was delighted to accept his invitation and meet again with old friends." She turned back to Papa, her smile blindingly bright once more, and held out her hand. "Shall we?"

"I don't think—" Papa began.

But this time Stepmama spoke directly over him. "We should be most honoured to accept, my lady." She adjusted her hold on Papa's arm, and from the expression on his face, I guessed she must have pinched it as well.

Whatever she had done, it worked.

"Indeed," Papa muttered, and turned to help the coachman sit on the ground, mindful of the man's injured leg. Once Papa was upright again, he held out his free arm to help the marquise back up the steps to the gilded carriage.

"We should be grateful for the favour, my lady."

We *should* be, of course... but judging by his expression, he certainly wasn't.

Stepmama more than made up for his lack of enthusiasm. She looked as elated as if she'd just been crowned queen. "Come, girls," she trilled as she started up the carriage steps. Her smile looked unbearably smug as she glanced from our fallen, hired carriage to the marquise's gilded wonder. "We mustn't keep the Carlyles waiting!"

"Quite," Angeline murmured under her breath, and raised her eyebrows at me. With a tiny shrug of her shoulders, she followed Stepmama up the steps.

"I say!" Charles called. The horses strained against their traces, and he tightened his hold on the reins. "I say, Stepmama..."

Her head popped back out of the carriage. "You won't mind staying to mind the horses, will you, Charles? Of course we'll send help from Hepworth Park the very moment we can, but we could hardly ask our poor injured coachman to look after them alone, could we? Especially in such deserted countryside – and when there may be robbers about?"

"Oh. I see. Of course not." Charles set his shoulders in a manly way and frowned sternly at the horses. "Have no fear. I'll see to them."

I rolled my eyes as I followed Angeline up the steps. If I'd actually believed in Stepmama's mythical robbers, I would have kicked up a royal fuss about leaving my brother to deal with them unarmed... but it would only be cruel to enlighten Charles about the real reason Stepmama didn't want him with us when we made our first impression on the Carlyles.

As I stepped into the carriage, though, and looked from Papa's expression of sickly horror to the marquise's creamy smile, I wondered whether Stepmama might have made a serious miscalculation.

꙳ ✡ ✡ ꙳

Worldly magnificence was of no importance at all, of course. At least, that's what Papa's sermons had always claimed. But as we drove through the great, wrought-iron gates that led into Hepworth Park, I had to suppress a gulp. And as the grounds spread out before us – each level of the landscaped gardens more magnificent than the last, with views of arching gazebos, elegant grottoes and even a miniature medieval castle in the distance – I began to feel decidedly uncomfortable.

When the marquise's carriage turned the last corner of the long, shell-lined drive, and Hepworth itself rose before us, I had to grip hold of my skirts to stop myself from letting out a cowardly squeak of horror.

It was the largest house I'd ever seen. Huge and built of golden stone, it stood near the top of a cliff overlooking the sea, massive and solid against the blue sky. Outer stairways rose up on either side of the entryway, building up to a long, graceful balcony above the front doors. Tall windows lined every floor of the building and glared at me like a hundred contemptuous eyes.

I wished with all my heart that Stepmama had left me to mind the horses instead of Charles.

The whole carriage fell silent. Angeline was staring out the window, her dark eyes haunted and her bandaged hand brushing against the rips in her pelisse. Stepmama touched one hand to her disordered hair, biting her lip. I looked down at my scratched hands where they clenched around my skirts.

Then the marquise laughed, and leaned forward to tap Angeline's arm with one gloved finger.

"Well! Mr Carlyle has more than his manners to recommend him, it seems. My goodness, Miss Stephenson. I shall be angling for many more invitations from you after this little wedding party. What a delightful house you are to preside over!"

Angeline gave a breath of laughter. "Thank you, my lady, but... I should say that my fiancé's mother, Mrs Carlyle—"

"Oh, you need have no fear of her. On such a vast estate as this, the dower house must be at least a mile away – why, I can't even see it from here, can you?"

I frowned, peering out the window. "'Dower house'?"

The marquise beamed at me. "Why, yes, my dear. The dower house is a perfectly marvellous invention of modern society – I don't know who first thought of it, but every bride must have thanked them in their prayers for decades afterwards! It is a second house on the same estate, smaller but still reasonably elegant... and every good mother-in-law is expected to move into it the very moment her son is married, to give her daughter-in-law her due as the new mistress of the estate."

Angeline's lips parted. Her eyes widened. For a moment she looked dazzled. Then her eyelids shuttered and she shook her head. "Mrs Carlyle would never—"

"Mrs Carlyle would shock every one of her friends and relations if she did anything else," said the marquise. "Trust me, Miss Stephenson. I only met your future mama-in-law for a few minutes last month, but that was quite long enough to convince me that she is not at all indifferent to the opinion of Society. And if she refused to move out of Hepworth Hall on the occasion of your wedding... well." She shook her head. "She would have to have a very, very good excuse, and I personally can't imagine any."

"Oh, thank goodness." I turned to squeeze my sister's arm. "Angeline, you'll be rid of her in just four days!"

"Kat!" Stepmama snapped. "Remember your manners, if you please!"

But the marquise was laughing. "Does she disapprove of you dreadfully, Miss Stephenson?"

"Well..." Angeline shrugged and looked down ruefully at her twice-mended carriage gown.

"All the better." The marquise's lips curved wickedly. "Then she shan't wish to visit you too often. I advise you to offend her as much as possible to keep her safely out of your way."

"Ahem!" Stepmama was coughing desperately, darting anguished looks at Angeline. "I'm sure that what her ladyship actually *means*, when she isn't indulging in her little jokes with us, is—"

It was too late. The carriage had already rolled to a halt before the grand double doors.

"Don't worry, Stepmama," Angeline said. "I have no plans for offending Frederick's mama." She slid a look at the marquise and winked. "At least, not until after the wedding is safely past."

"Angeline!" Stepmama yelped. "This is no time for jokes. You are about to meet your future in-laws for the very first time. You are about to make your first impression on Frederick's entire family, none of whom will have favourable expectations of you. This is one of the most important moments in your entire life. No matter what, you absolutely must not—"

The carriage door swung open, and she snapped her jaw closed.

A footman in blue-and-gold livery stood outside. The front doors of Hepworth stood wide open.

We had arrived.

CHAPTER SIX

IT WAS ASTONISHING WHAT A DIFFERENCE IT MADE TO TRAVEL with an aristocrat. Servants poured out of Hepworth in a mad rush, hurrying to cluster around the carriages. Hepworth footmen helped the marquise's own footmen pull out her dozens of valises and portmanteaus from the second carriage in a noisy, buzzing hive of activity. Even the marquise's French maid, who'd seemed silent and meek on first impression, turned into a veritable Fury as she lectured the poor, hapless Hepworth footman who'd tried to lift a hat box the wrong way.

Between the five of us, I'd thought my family packed like an entire army, but the marquise single-handedly surpassed us all.

From the look on her face, though, she'd never thought twice about any of the effort involved. She sailed forwards with beaming serenity, ignoring the flurry of activity behind her and her maid's rising shrieks of outrage.

The Hepworth butler, grand in a powdered wig and black coat, gave her a respectful bow, ignoring all the rest of us as if we were utterly beneath his notice. I narrowed my eyes at him menacingly. It was one thing to ignore me, but to ignore his future mistress?

Angeline wasn't even looking at him, though. Her eyes were fixed on the tall windows of the house as intently as if she could burn her way through them with her gaze.

I knew exactly who she was looking for.

"I'm sure he'll be out at any moment," I whispered. "He was probably confused by the carriage."

Angeline didn't look away from the windows, but she let out a muffled snort of laughter. "Yes, it certainly doesn't look like anything we'd be arriving in, does it?" She drew herself up, smoothing down the rumpled skirts of her gown. "And we all look such a disaster... oh well. At least we're arriving with *la marquise*. No matter how much Mrs Carlyle wants to sneer at us, she can't help but be impressed by *her*."

"She is impressive," I agreed. I inched closer and stood on tiptoe to breathe my words into her ear. "Angeline, who is she? Don't you remember her at all?"

Angeline shrugged and slid a discreet look at the marquise under lowered eyelashes. "I wish I did. I had no idea we had any such respectable connections. I certainly don't remember Papa or Mama ever having any fashionable visitors in the house."

"But the way Papa looked when he saw her—"

"Ahem." The butler had turned to greet us with unhurried dignity, "Mr Stephenson, Mrs Stephenson, Miss Stephenson..." His weary gaze rested longest on Angeline, visibly cataloguing every strand of dark hair that had come free from her bonnet and pins. "I must beg your pardon for not welcoming you immediately."

His tone wasn't the least bit apologetic, but Angeline smiled as graciously as if he'd been sincere. I blinked. Of all the oddities I'd seen in the last year, perhaps the strangest was the sight of my own sister, clad in a rumpled and torn pelisse, with blood on her cheek and unkempt dark hair streaming free from her bonnet, accepting the Hepworth butler's bow as if it were her due. For a moment I actually felt dizzy.

This house... All this grandeur and magnificence... The only way I'd been managing until now was to pretend this whole event was a sort of elaborate parlour game, something I could participate in for just a little while before returning to reality and the safety of home. But this was real, not a game, and Angeline was about to become the mistress of this enormous house and all its acres of estate.

It was a good thing I wasn't standing closer to the cliff edge, because I just might have fallen off it.

A footman hurried out of the house to whisper in the butler's ear. The butler nodded. "My lady..." He turned to the marquise. "Mrs Carlyle extends her compliments and hopes you will enjoy your room. If you will allow it, Harris will escort you there now to refresh yourself."

"Thank you. My dears, I shall look forward to seeing you again later, once my maid has made me fit for company. *Au revoir!*" The marquise smiled, blew Angeline a kiss, and was gone, following the footman through the open doorway.

Oh, dear, I thought. Angeline drew a deep, visible breath. I was proud of my sister for managing to retain her polite smile, even as disaster loomed before us. So much for having the marquise by our side when we met the Carlyles for the first time.

"Mr and Mrs Stephenson, Miss Stephenson and Miss Katherine Stephenson..." The butler bowed again and gestured at the doorway. "Mrs Carlyle invites you all to meet the family in the Rose Drawing Room."

Stepmama gave a horrified glance down at her own rumpled and dusty travelling gown. "Surely we should also retire to our own rooms first, to wash our hands and faces? And of course our carriage with all our luggage... and my stepson..."

"Shall be sent for immediately. Have no fear, madam, they will all be retrieved within the hour. But Mrs Carlyle was most explicit in her instructions. As you are so soon to become *family*" – his faint, supercilious smile made the word sound like a distasteful joke – "there can be no need for any formality in your preparations." The butler gave another half bow as he gestured again, more commandingly this time. "If you will please follow me..."

Well, there wasn't really any choice, was there? We walked, as directed, through the grand entryway, shed our pelisses and bonnets and Papa's coat, and followed the butler down a broad corridor lined with ancient family portraits. Our steps echoed ominously on the marble floor, and the portraits glowered with disapproval. I could almost feel their painted eyes fixing with horror on my scratches. I stuck my hands behind my back to hide the worst of the marks, and moved safely behind Angeline to hide the rest of me.

I wasn't being cowardly, I told myself...just *showing common sense*, exactly what everyone was always urging me to do. After all, considering the state I was in, standing in sisterly solidarity at Angeline's side was the worst thing I could possibly do for her first impression on the Carlyles.

But I did lean forwards to whisper in her ear. "Don't worry.

Frederick Carlyle would still think you were beautiful even if you were completely caked in mud."

"I practically am," Angeline hissed back. The fear I'd seen in her face before was gone; it had been replaced by something far more familiar – and more ominous. "Mrs Carlyle must be delighted."

"What do you mean?" I frowned and nearly tripped over her skirts as I thought back to the message the butler had passed on. "She was actually being kind, for once. She said you would be family—"

"She let the marquise refresh herself before she was seen in public; that was kind. When it came to us, though, she made certain that the rest of the Carlyles would meet us looking as if we'd been tossed straight through a haystack! It's exactly the first impression she wanted to make – that I come from a family of country bumpkins, with no idea of fashion or anything else." Angeline kept her social smile, but the words hissed through her mouth. "She thinks she's already won."

"Oh, dear." Of course, she was probably right – but at this moment the fury in Angeline's voice worried me far more than any of her future mother-in-law's schemes. I reached out and squeezed her hand reassuringly. "Well, don't worry. I'm sure Frederick won't let her say anything too dreadful."

"Oh, I won't need Frederick's help for this." A dangerous light glittered in Angeline's eyes. "Trust me, Kat. I can take care of her by myself."

Oh Lord. I gulped as liveried footmen pushed open a pair of elegant white doors at the end of the corridor.

Angeline might not have been nervous anymore... but I certainly was.

"The Stephenson family," the butler announced in thundering tones.

We walked into the lions' den.

The entire Rose Drawing Room was filled with Carlyles – Carlyles sitting straight-backed at the little round tables scattered all around the room; Carlyles leaning indolently against the wallpapered walls; Carlyles lounging on the long settees... but for all their variation in posture and appearance, every single one of them, as my family stepped into the room, gazed at us with eyebrows arched high in arrogant disbelief.

Frederick Carlyle wasn't among them.

Unfortunately, his mother was.

Mrs Carlyle sat in the centre of the long room in a high-backed velvet chair like a throne. A sugary-sweet smile creased her round cheeks but left her brown eyes as hard as polished buttons.

"My dear Miss Stephenson," she cooed, and held out her tiny, plump hands to Angeline. "How delighted I am that you have arrived at last. Why, I have been in such a state of apprehension, you can hardly imagine – only to think of my son's future bride travelling all across the countryside, no doubt staying at the worst of inns, and in a *hired carriage*, of all things the most dreadful and unhealthy..."

She shuddered and traded a meaningful glance with the two ladies who sat on either side of her, both as thin and hungry-eyed as harpies. "Why, I could hardly even bear the notion of it without suffering the most painful palpitations! It is no wonder that paltry carriage fell apart before you could even arrive. My poor, poor child!"

Angeline took Mrs Carlyle's outstretched hands and swept a graceful curtsey. Her own voice cooed just as sweetly in reply. "I am so pleased to be able to set your mind at ease, ma'am. You may rest assured that we stopped in only five of the worst inns available. The others were very nearly respectable... much to our disappointment, of course."

"Mrs Carlyle!" Stepmama lurched forwards, pulling Angeline back as a ripple of disapproving whispers passed through the room, "We are so pleased to be here at last, of course, and so very grateful for your gracious hospitality, especially in the wake of our unfortunate accident." She cast an anguished look at Angeline. "And dear Mr Carlyle?"

"Oh, Frederick cannot be here, I'm afraid," said Mrs Carlyle. "Such a pity, but it had to be done, you know. My dearest niece, Jane, could hardly be left out of the wedding party – and really, one could hardly expect a girl like her to travel across the country in anything but the first style of elegance!" She swept an expressive look across Angeline's rumpled figure and shook her head.

"No, Jane required a proper carriage and a respectable gentleman escort. So when my brother-in-law learned – only a few days ago – that he was unable to escort her, Frederick was forced to act out himself. He was the only one who could possibly have been trusted to look after dear Jane properly, you see. He hopes to return by tomorrow night but, needless to say, I urged him not to hurry at all – I have been so looking forward to having time alone with dear Angeline myself, before he returns to monopolise her."

"You are too kind, ma'am." Angeline bared her teeth in the semblance of a smile. "If only I could repay you in the manner you deserve."

"Oh, my dear..." Mrs Carlyle's voice became even more sickly-sweet, something I would have sworn wasn't physically possible. "Never fear that I would abandon you now, just when you most need a mother to look after you.

Why, after the upbringing you must have had – and I know you won't mind me saying this, Mrs Stephenson, for you know we are all family now – well, as I was only just saying to dear Honoria and Letitia," she gestured to the two harpies on either side, "to let you, of all the girls in England, be thrown willy-nilly into sole responsibility for this vast house and its estate... Why, it would be nothing less than an act of utter cruelty, wouldn't it? Which I could never possibly allow."

What on earth was she talking about? I blinked rapidly, trying to puzzle out the meaning buried in her flow of words. From the malicious gleam in her eyes, I knew it couldn't be anything good, but for the life of me, I couldn't make it out. Stepmama was frowning too, looking just as confused as I felt.

Angeline, though, didn't seem to be having any difficulty with interpretation. As I watched, her skin blanched paler than I had ever seen it. The dried blood on her cheek stood out like fire. "You don't mean—"

"But of course." Mrs Carlyle's smile became an outright smirk. "I know that Frederick... Oh, he is *so* generous! *Such* a good boy, and so concerned for his mother's welfare... Well, of course he had intended me to have the whole of the dower house for my very own once the two of you were married, to grant me much-needed peace and quiet – my nerves, you know, afflict me terribly, and my health!"

"Ma'am," Angeline began. She was breathing quickly.

Mrs Carlyle waved her away. "Oh, you are good to be concerned, but I won't weary you with the list of all the ailments I suffer. No, I have thought it all over very carefully in the last few days. As tempting as it is to have a house to oneself, I simply cannot bring myself to be so selfish. First of all, I had already faithfully promised the dower house to Honoria and Letitia," – the harpies nodded in eager agreement – "but secondly, and far more importantly..."

She looked my sister up and down, from Angeline's dust-laced, loose dark hair and glass-scratched cheek to her wrinkled, two-year-old carriage gown. Her gaze lingered on the rips in Angeline's sleeve, and her smirk deepened.

"Oh, my dear. As a sensible girl, you must agree – I could hardly leave you, of all people, to be mistress of Hepworth, could I? If he had chosen anyone else of course, it might well have been different – for instance, if he had only chosen to marry my dear Jane, whom all of us had expected to be his bride ever since the two of them were mere children, and already so well suited to each other..."

She sighed and waved a hand in front of her face as if she were pushing aside temptation. "But no, we mustn't speak of that. We must simply face the facts, and it would be too, too cruel – not only to Frederick and his name and reputation, but to you as well, to subject you to such a humiliating impossibility. But you needn't fear. I wrote to Frederick's guardian, who of course must still make all the final decisions on such matters, and I received my answer only this morning. He has agreed – I shall continue in charge of Hepworth, and we shall all be the happiest of families."

I had never seen my sister truly dumbstruck. But as Angeline stared at her future mother-in-law, while whispers and tittering laughter rippled across the room, her lips opened and then closed again without uttering a single word.

I knew exactly what I would have said, if I could. But I didn't think Mrs Carlyle would take kindly to being called a wicked, scheming troll... and the last thing Angeline needed now was for me to make her terrible first impression on the Carlyles even worse.

So all in all, it was the worst possible timing for me to sense magic rippling suddenly through the air.

CHAPTER SEVEN

IT WAS GUARDIAN MAGIC, NOT WITCHCRAFT. THAT MEANT it had to be coming for me.

I twisted around, trying to follow the trail. I'd learned to sense the ripple effect of magic being practised nearby, and I could recognise the different kinds. If it was witchcraft, I could even tell who had done it, through their signature scent. Guardian magic was different though. I still couldn't recognise the power signatures of different Guardians, no matter how hard I tried... and not every Guardian in the Order was a friend, to say the least.

Angeline's elbow in my ribs signalled new trouble. I snapped back to attention and found the whole roomful of Carlyles staring at me.

"Must I really repeat myself?" Mrs Carlyle's eyebrows had reached a dangerous height. "I said, is there something amiss, Miss Katherine?"

"No, ma'am," I lied. I felt another flare of magic, this time perilously close. Whoever it was, they were standing outside the house, just by the long windows – and I could swear they were trying to catch my attention.

If there was one thing I was sure of right now, it was that I didn't want anyone from the Order coming in to find me, in front of all the Carlyles. But that meant I had to get out.

Gold spots flickered in the air outside the windows, and I gulped. I had to get out *fast*.

"Are you certain? You seemed peculiarly excited by... something." Mrs Carlyle started to turn her head towards the window.

"It was only the... the wallpaper!" I said, and stepped forwards to recapture her gaze.

She stared at me. "The wallpaper?"

Curses. "Yes. I have a passion for wallpaper," I said, and gave up for good all my fantasies of making a reasonable impression on Angeline's future in-laws, or of pleasing my own family with my behaviour. Even *I* could barely tolerate my own words as I finished, sickeningly: "Yours is particularly fine, ma'am."

She blinked rapidly. "Good heavens. What an unusual fascination for a girl of your age. Might I ask what exactly about my wallpaper captured your attention?"

"Ah..." My mind went blank. It was pink, I could see that much, but I wasn't standing close enough to make out any of the detail. I said, weakly, "The colour?"

Angeline made a choking sound and turned away.

Stepmama cleared her throat. "I beg you will forgive my youngest stepdaughter, Mrs Carlyle. It has been a long journey, and the carriage accident was most unnerving for her. She is merely overtired and forgetting her manners."

"Indeed." Mrs Carlyle's lips twisted petulantly. "I do

recall, now, how unusual I found Miss Katherine's style of address when we first met, last autumn. I had assumed that she would have outgrown her oddities by this spring, but—"

"Kat is uniquely herself, ma'am," Angeline said. "It is, in fact, one of her most appealing qualities." She took a step in front of me, reclaiming Mrs Carlyle's glare.

"Well." Mrs Carlyle snorted, and turned to include the harpies beside her in her astonishment. "I must say, if my mother had raised me with the goal of *being myself*—"

Oh, dash it. "May I please be excused, ma'am?"

"I beg your pardon?"

Mrs Carlyle's tone was icy. The harpies were both glaring at me with pure venom in their eyes. Even Angeline was staring at me now. The gold spots had disappeared from the air outside the windows, but I wasn't reassured. That had only been a first attempt to make contact. The next one might be witnessed by someone else.

"Katherine," Stepmama began in a tone that boded terrible retribution later.

"I left something in the marquise's carriage," I said. "It will only take me ten minutes to fetch it, I promise."

Mrs Carlyle tittered while the harpies beside her glared, stiff-backed and fiery. Rustling and whispers sounded through the rest of the room, among the other watching Carlyles.

Mrs Carlyle said, "What you may not have been raised to understand, Miss Katherine, is that the servants in any respectable household are more than capable of noticing and retrieving any items you may have forgotten in your own haste."

"They won't have seen this one," I said. "I'm sorry, ma'am, but I truly can't wait, so—"

"Katherine!" Stepmama hissed. "Will you please—"

I didn't catch the rest of her command. All my attention was on the horrible apparition that had appeared outside the windows.

This time it wasn't a few specks of glittering gold signalling to me.

It was worse. Much worse.

Standing outside was the one single person who hated me and my family more than anyone else. She was the one person I trusted least in the world... and her lips were curved in a smile of malicious delight.

Lady Lydia Fotherington had brought about my own mama's expulsion from the Order of the Guardians, and she had tried to have me banned from it as well. She had turned Mrs Carlyle against my sister in the first place, and it was only through blackmail that I had finally forced her to gain Mrs Carlyle's consent to the marriage.

As she looked through the window at the roomful of staring relatives, glaring aunts, an outraged Mrs Carlyle, and a lecturing Stepmama, she raised one beckoning hand to me – then, when I still didn't move, she mouthed words I could read all too easily through the window.

Shall I come in to get you?

My stomach clenched.

"I'm sorry," I repeated to Mrs Carlyle and Stepmama and Angeline and everyone else. "I really have to go!"

I darted out of the room before any of them could stop me.

☆ ☆ ☆

I was cursing myself and the whole Order of the Guardians as I ran down the long corridor, my feet thudding against the floor under the appalled gaze of all those ancient family portraits. Even the footmen broke their professionally stone-faced expressions to look shocked as I tore past them and out the front door.

Angeline was going to murder me later, and the worst of it was, I deserved it. *Dash* it again!

I burst around the corner of the house at full tilt and found Lady Fotherington and my magic tutor, Mr Gregson, standing together just by the cliff edge beyond the house, deep in conversation under the blue sky. They were thankfully out of sight of the gathering in the Rose Drawing Room, but I was horribly conscious that the full pantheon of Carlyle relatives must have seen me hurrying past the long windows on the way. There had been too many footmen in the front hall for me to dare to turn myself invisible.

I cringed as I imagined what Mrs Carlyle must be saying to my family. When I'd agreed to take on the responsibilities of a Guardian, this wasn't what I'd had in mind.

"Well?" I demanded, charging towards my summoners across the grass. "What could possibly be so urgent that I had to embarrass myself in front of all of Angeline's new in-laws?"

"Ah, Katherine," Mr Gregson said. "Direct and to the point, as always." He stepped away from the cliff edge, taking off his hat to bow with his usual grave courtesy. The breeze from the sea below blew at his thinning grey hair, and his small, dapper figure looked very slight against the rugged landscape. "It is good to see you, too, of course. I trust the rest of your family is—"

"Forced to embarrass yourself?" Lady Fotherington murmured, before he could even finish. One perfect eyebrow arched meaningfully. "How fortunate that you've had so much practice in the art."

The first time I'd met Lady Fotherington I'd broken her nose in self-defence, when she'd tried to make me her magical slave. Then, eight months ago, she'd tricked me into attacking her in front of Lord Ravenscroft, the hereditary Head of the Order of the Guardians, and he'd expelled me from the Order before I'd even been officially sworn in as a member.

I didn't punch her now, or even clench my fists. I just looked her in the eye and let a reminder shine straight through my glare: that I was the only person in the world who knew that she'd committed treason in Bath eight months ago, when she'd refused to help me fight against Lord Ravenscroft's plot to harness the wild magic in Bath for Napoleon Bonaparte – a plot which would have seen a French invasion of England *and* the murder of my brother Charles along the way.

If I ever opened my mouth to tell the others what she'd done, she wouldn't only be expelled from the Order herself, she would be stripped of all her magical powers and forced to give up her cherished position as a leader of fashionable Society.

If I ever told anyone else the truth about her, though, she wouldn't wait an instant before telling the rest of Society, and especially Mrs Carlyle, the truth about Angeline's scandalous witchcraft. My sister would be ruined. And Lady Fotherington knew just as well as I did that I would never let that happen – especially not now, only four days before Angeline's wedding.

She smiled as smugly as if she'd read my thoughts. "Quite," she murmured. "And may I ask how you came by those" – her calculating gaze swept from my face to my hands – "*interesting* new ornaments on your skin?"

I gritted my teeth and resisted the impulse to hide my hands behind my back. "It was a feral cat," I muttered.

She let out a snort of laughter. "Feral Kat, indeed."

"That isn't what I—"

"Ahem." Mr Gregson coughed as he stepped between us. "I do apologise for the disturbance of your family's visit, Katherine, but it was regrettably necessary. A highly unpleasant discovery has come to light, in relation to your initiation into the Order, and—"

"It's not been put off again, has it?" I could hardly believe it. "You said the Order was finally ready to choose a new Head, so there would be someone to host the ceremony by next week. What else can we possibly be waiting for?"

"It seems a very paltry dilemma to you, does it not?" Lady Fotherington's eyes narrowed. "Your mother was the same. Centuries of tradition, centuries of trust, all seen as insignificant compared to her own selfish, personal desires."

I snorted. "Centuries of stagnation, you mean."

"Ahem!" Mr Gregson cleared his throat loudly. "We have not yet chosen a new Head, no," he said. "There is a great deal to consider, when one is forced to choose a Head by election rather than birth for the first time in four centuries. But that, in this particular case, is not the deciding factor. I'm afraid it is something far more serious. You see, your new portal to the Golden Hall..."

"Yes?" I said. I could feel Lady Fotherington's gaze on me, and I tried to keep my voice steady. But even the mention of it hurt, every single time.

I shouldn't have needed the new portal I'd been fighting so hard to get. I should have still been using Mama's beautiful golden mirror.

71

Sacrificing it had been the right decision, I told myself for the thousandth time. It really had been. I *knew* that to be true.

But it still didn't make the pain go away.

"Well," Mr Gregson said, and cleared his throat again. "That is..."

"Oh, don't be so afraid to say it, Aloysius." Lady Fotherington's green eyes gleamed with pleasure. "It can't be done, after all."

"I beg your pardon?" It was a relief to be able to turn on her and let all my grief funnel into annoyance. "What are you talking about?"

"This shining *new* portal we are meant to be giving you." She accented the word 'new' with relish. "As you tossed aside your own so carelessly."

I filled up my chest with a deep, deep breath to keep myself from speaking. I didn't punch people anymore. And I wasn't going to satisfy her with a display of temper. But I had to take three quick steps to the edge of the cliff to control myself.

Waves lashed at the pebbled beach below. Salt-laced wind whipped up from the ocean to slap against my face and tangle my hair. I said, without looking back at either of them, "Why can't I have my new portal now?"

Mr Gregson used his most scholarly tone as he answered. "Of course, our portals are generally inherited from our own families—"

My words came out through clenched teeth. *"I know."* The vast grey waters blurred before me; I opened my eyes wide against the stinging sea breeze and forced myself to breathe deeply. "That can't be the only way to get one. You said one would be found for me once the rest of the Order agreed to it, so—"

"But not every family that was once in the Order is still in the Order," Mr Gregson continued, as if I hadn't spoken a word of interruption. "Some families simply died out, without any new children to continue the bloodline; other families..." He coughed. "Well, not every child who is born to be a natural Guardian is invited into the Order, even if their ancestors were members. If their parents turned to trade, or some other unsavoury occupation..." He winced. "There is nothing that can be done. The Order does have strict entry standards, as you know."

Lady Fotherington snorted pointedly. I stiffened my back and took deep, salt-laced breaths.

"So what you're saying is that the Order has a collection of leftover portals," I said. "Taken back from the families who aren't allowed in anymore." The words tasted as sour as green apples on my tongue. "I'll have to use one of those."

"No," said Mr Gregson. "That is what we planned for you to use, but unfortunately, we have made a rather unpleasant discovery."

I turned back to face them. My eyes were dry, and if my face looked red, well, the sea breeze was more than enough to explain that. "Tell me," I said, and lifted my chin as I met Lady Fotherington's contemptuous gaze square-on.

"The portals," said Mr Gregson, "are gone. Someone has stolen them."

CHAPTER EIGHT

"STOLEN THEM?" I REPEATED.

"Oh, don't look so shocked," Lady Fotherington snapped. "Half the Order thinks you were the one who did it."

"What?" I stumbled back a step on the grass.

"Why not? You're notorious for tossing away your own portal, and as we all know you don't care about the rules—"

"Lydia!" Mr Gregson snapped. To me he said, "Have no fear, Katherine. Any malicious rumours are merely that: rumours. The Order as a whole is well aware of the debt it owes you after last September's activities in Bath. No one seriously suspects you of this crime."

"Mmm," said Lady Fotherington, and raised both eyebrows in a patently sceptical expression.

There were only two possible courses of action I could take. I could leap for her throat, or I could ignore her. The first option was dangerously tempting... but I reminded myself that I was thirteen now, not twelve, and I turned away from her, breathing hard.

"When were they taken?" I asked Mr Gregson.

He gave me an approving nod, as if he'd seen the decision playing out in my head. "Three days ago. We'd hoped to find and apprehend the thief by now, but it is proving to be surprisingly difficult. The portals were clearly taken by someone with magical powers, but no magical residue was left behind for identification... and that is very odd indeed."

I frowned. "If they were actually taken from the Golden Hall—"

He interrupted me. "No, Katherine. They had originally been kept in the Golden Hall, but during Lord Ravenscroft's tenure as Head, they were moved to a nonmagical location in London."

"So it might not have been a Guardian who stole them," I concluded.

"Well, of course it wasn't a Guardian." Lady Fotherington rolled her eyes. "If you knew more about the Order, you would be aware that none of its members – none of its *full* members, at any rate" – she eyed me meaningfully – "are the sort who would ever commit a theft. Obviously it must have been a witch who did it."

"Of course." I rolled my eyes right back at her. "How could I have forgotten? Because anytime anything goes wrong anywhere in the world, every Guardian has to immediately blame a witch for it."

"Ahem." Mr Gregson cleared his throat loudly. "We are all aware of your, ah, *distinctive* views on witchcraft, Katherine. But Lady Fotherington's theory does, in this case, make a great deal of sense. Every Guardian in the Order has a portal of his or her own already – well, apart from you, that is."

"Indeed," Lady Fotherington murmured.

I narrowed my eyes at her.

"*Therefore*," Mr Gregson continued, raising his voice, "no Guardian would need to steal a portal to the Golden Hall, much less multiple portals."

"Hmm," I said. "What about the Guardians who don't have portals of their own? The ones who haven't been invited into the Order?"

My tutor and Lady Fotherington both regarded me with pitying smiles on their faces.

"Have you taught her nothing, Aloysius?" Lady Fotherington sighed.

Mr Gregson said gently, "Without joining our Order, Katherine, they would never have received any training, and their Guardian powers would never have developed in the first place."

"But—"

"You may take my word for it," said Mr Gregson. "As the Historian of our Order, I would have come across any mention of counterexamples. In all the history of Britain, there have been no recorded cases of any Guardians successfully learning to exploit their powers without mentorship and training by the Order."

"Well—"

"None," he said, and looked at me sternly through his spectacles.

I sighed and let that possibility go. But... "That still doesn't mean it had to be a witch. Lord Ravenscroft was a Guardian, and he—"

"Really, there is no point in empty speculation." Mr Gregson pulled out a silver pocket watch from his waistcoat and frowned down at it. "I am due back in London in less than twenty minutes, so we must make haste. Katherine, Lady Fotherington will answer any questions you may still have, and if you two would please make an attempt, just this once, to work peacefully together..." His voice trailed off, as if even he was losing hope of that.

Lady Fotherington's upper lip curled into a sneer. "'Peaceful' is not a word easily associated with Miss Katherine."

It was easier to ignore her this time, with the promise of a real Guardian assignment ahead of me. Even with the horrid addition of Lady Fotherington as my mentor, it was still an exciting prospect – and surely, if the Order had chosen me for a task, no matter what it was, it must mean they finally trusted me. Mustn't it?

"But what are we meant to be working on?" I said. "What are you talking about?"

My tutor looked decidedly harried. "Well, if the portals really have been brought to Devon—"

"I beg your pardon?"

"Really, Aloysius," Lady Fotherington murmured, "don't you think you've missed a few vital points in your explanation?"

"I daresay." Mr Gregson gave another anxious look at his pocketwatch. "But with the Prime Minister and His Majesty himself expecting me..."

My eyes widened. "The king knows about the missing portals?"

An expression of true pain crossed Mr Gregson's face. "The king," he said, "is most concerned. After the treasonous disaster in Bath, led by the Head of our Order..."

Lady Fotherington shook her head, her face tightening. "I told you it was foolish to let the government know about that. Now that they've found out about the missing portals as well, we'll be lucky if they don't try to dissolve the Order by the time the week is out, as a danger to the country."

"They couldn't do that," I said. "Could they?"

Mr Gregson sighed. "The Order may be a secret to the rest of the nation, but it works under the authority of the king, and has done ever since its first founding. If King George himself should command us to be dissolved..."

"I see," I said.

I took a deep breath. *Well.* I'd thought I had enough of a challenge ahead of me trying to change the Order's mind about Mama and about witchcraft, not to mention getting my own initiation accomplished in the first place. But if the Order itself was dissolved before I'd even managed to become a full member...

"We'll just have to find the portals," I said. "You think they're here in Devon?"

"Last night we sensed one of them being used, for the first time since their disappearance," said Mr Gregson. "Unfortunately, we lost the trace almost immediately, as it wasn't in use for long, but it was certainly in Devon, and near the north coast. So, as you were already planning to spend the week here, in such an ideal location for the search..."

"Of course," I said. I was grinning; I couldn't help it. I felt as if a bubble of excitement was filling me up and nearly lifting me off the ground, the way my magic had last night. I was in Devon already – so why shouldn't I take the lead on the search?

I might not have been officially initiated yet, but I was a real Guardian, and the rest of the Order obviously knew it, if they were putting me in charge of such a vital assignment.

"I won't let you down," I said. "I promise. I'll—"

"That is why Lady Fotherington will be staying with you while she performs the search," Mr Gregson finished.

"What?" All my exhilaration fell away, sending me back to reality with a thump. "Lady Fotherington?"

"Quite," Lady Fotherington said dryly. "I promise you, Miss Katherine, the distaste is entirely mutual. I can think of nowhere I would care less to be than this ridiculous farce of a wedding party."

"Wedding p—" I had to cut myself off before I could parrot the words back at her in pure shock. My head was whirling in the worst possible way. "But you can't stay here! You aren't invited to the wedding!"

"No?" Lady Fotherington arched one eyebrow. "Do you truly think that Mrs Carlyle will turn me away?"

I ground my teeth. Of course, Lady Fotherington was so influential in Society, no hostess would dream of refusing her, but... "You're the reason Mrs Carlyle originally forbade the marriage! You're the one who told her that Angeline was a witch."

"I am also the reason the wedding is taking place," Lady Fotherington said. "Remember?" There was a bitter twist to her lips as she brought up the favour she'd paid me to keep silent about her treason. "If I hadn't promised Mrs Carlyle that I had been wrong about Miss Stephenson, and that the match was to be welcomed..."

We glared at each other in simmering silence. Mr Gregson broke it with a cough.

"Lady Fotherington," he said, "has the ideal qualification for attending this wedding. If you recall, Katherine, what you told the residents of Bath last autumn, when you and your family first arrived?"

"Ah..." I blinked, trying to remember.

We'd been swept to Bath by Stepmama in a rage, after Angeline's betrothal to Frederick Carlyle had been publicly forbidden by his mother. Stepmama's snobby Bath relations had been ready to turn us away at the door, though, until – in a fit of fury against them and against Lady Fotherington herself, in particular, for ruining all of Angeline's hopes – I'd invented the wildest and most implausible story of my entire life.

I'd told them that Lady Fotherington, my own mother's worst enemy... Lady Fotherington, one of the leaders of the fashionable world that sneered down at us... Lady Fotherington, I'd said, was actually my...

"Oh Lord," I said. I could actually feel the colour draining from my face. "You can't mean..."

"Of course," Lady Fotherington said, and curled her lips into the semblance of a tender smile. "You could hardly fail to invite your own godmother, could you?"

I closed my eyes against the contempt on her face.

This time Angeline really was going to murder me.

✩ ✩ ✩

I was trudging back towards the house when Charles arrived riding a sleek black mare I'd never seen before. He jumped off and gave her an affectionate pat on the neck as one of the Hepworth footmen hurried forwards to take the reins. Then he strode over to join me, looking annoyingly self-satisfied.

Charles's thick blonde hair glinted like the most unlikely of halos in the sunlight. Dust covered his wrinkled jacket and trousers, but he looked disgustingly good-humoured as he fell into step beside me.

"What are you doing out here on your own, then?"

he asked. "Run away already? It must be a challenge for you to act like a lady for a whole hour at a time, I daresay."

"Very funny." I scowled, thinking of the scene I really *had* run away from in the Rose Drawing Room.

Between facing the consequences of that and waiting for Lady Fotherington to make her official arrival – by carriage rather than magic, this time – I couldn't think of anything worse than walking back into Hepworth. My pace slowed from a trudge to a snail's pace, and I searched for a good distraction.

"Where did you find the horse?" I asked.

"Oh, the Carlyles sent her, along with a carriage for the coachman. Pretty thing, isn't she? Rides like a dream. I say, if I had Carlyle's stable—"

Rolling my eyes, I cut across him ruthlessly. "So you weren't attacked by robbers, then?"

Considering that Charles was the son of an impoverished vicar, he wasn't likely to ever have any stable at all, much less one that rivalled the stable at Hepworth.

Charles being Charles, he only shrugged as the topic shifted. "No one attacked us. But I can't say I was expecting anyone to bother."

"Oh?" I stopped walking entirely to look at him more carefully. "So who do you think was behind it?"

"Hmm. Let me think," he drawled, and shook his head at me. "Really, Kat, if you had the brainpower of a fly..."

"I beg your pardon!"

He sighed. "Well, who do you think it was? Obviously it must have been that fellow who was watching you last night. He probably went off on some fit about the evils of witchcraft. Moralistic sort, fanatical. I met a few of those at Oxford."

His face stiffened for a moment, as if he were

remembering something unpleasant. For the first time that I could remember, it occurred to me to wonder what Oxford – and boarding school beforehand – had actually been like for Charles when he'd first arrived, as the son of a notorious witch.

Before I could start to feel any sympathy, though, he said, "But there's nothing to worry about, now that I've got you in hand."

My teeth set together with a snap. "You have *not* got me in hand."

"No? Someone needs to," he said. "Just look at you. Not an hour after arriving at Hepworth, and you're already skulking about outside."

"I was not skulking!"

"Skulking," Charles repeated firmly. "Which is just the sort of behaviour that attracted that madman's notice in the first place. So until we get back to Yorkshire, you'll stay safely inside like a proper lady, and I'll keep an eye on matters outside. It'll be for the best, for all of us."

I couldn't speak. I was too outraged to form coherent words.

He reached over and rumpled my hair, sending the last two pins flying. "Now then, Kat, don't sulk. It's only a week." He frowned. "Although if we don't find that fellow before the end of the week... well, who knows?" He shrugged. "Maybe you'll get used to being a proper lady. You might even find you like it, once you give it a real try."

"Get used to it?" I croaked. "*Like it?*"

Before he could utter another word I lunged for Hepworth, moving as quickly as my legs would take me.

I had changed my mind. Lady Fotherington wasn't the worst of my problems after all. Neither were the Guardians' missing portals, my mysterious – and possibly murderous – follower, or even the truly hideous prospect of facing Angeline and Stepmama after I'd embarrassed them in front of the entire Carlyle clan.

Far more urgent and desperate than any of those other challenges was the problem of Charles... because if I didn't come up with a solution soon, I was afraid I might just have to murder him myself.

CHAPTER NINE

HEPWORTH MIGHT BE THE GRANDEST HOUSE I'D EVER SEEN, but even Hepworth had its limits. With the entire Carlyle clan in residence, Angeline and I were left sharing a bedroom again.

When I opened the door, she was leaning over the blue-and-white china washbowl, bathing her hands and face. It should have been a pleasant sight, especially in such a light, airy room, with a window facing out towards the sea. But the moment I opened the door, I knew something was wrong, even though nothing looked out of place. I sniffed tentatively... and then I knew.

Oh Lord. It was the telltale scent of lilacs.

Angeline had cast a spell.

I froze, wondering if I could back out of the room before she noticed me.

"For heaven's sake, Kat," Angeline said without looking up. "Don't just stand there gaping. Close the door behind you, at least."

I gave one last, wistful look at the empty corridor behind me before I followed her orders. Then I sidled in with my back against the pale blue wallpaper, scouting the room with more than my eyes.

It wasn't as if I was in any real danger, I told myself. As a Guardian, I was perfectly capable of quashing any of Angeline's spells... at least, if I found them before they found me.

That was less reassuring than I might have hoped. Angeline had got more and more clever with her spells this past year.

She straightened, water dripping off her face, just as I was sniffing the air by the chest of drawers, trying to pinpoint the source of the spell.

"Trying out for the role of a hunting spaniel?" she asked dryly. "Really, I know you must be nervous about facing me – and you certainly should be, after your behaviour earlier – but pretending to have gone mad is going a little too far in self-defence, don't you think?"

"Erm..." I narrowed my eyes at the room around me, too busy to answer. I knew she'd cast a spell... so where on earth had it gone?

Angeline sighed. "As long as you're lurking over there, will you pass me a towel?"

I tossed her a towel from the pile on the chest of drawers, and waited until she'd buried her face in it. Then I sat down on the canopied bed, folded my hands, and said, "I thought you weren't planning to do any more magic before the wedding."

"Ah." Angeline's hands stilled for a moment. Then she finished wiping her face with careful motions. "You noticed, did you?"

"I do have a nose."

"That explains the hunting dog impression. I suppose I should have known." She lowered the towel and met my eyes. Her own were red-rimmed, as if she'd been crying since I'd seen her last.

The sight made me intensely nervous. Angeline almost never cried. But on the rare occasions she did, terrible, dangerous things happened.

Her voice was perfectly steady, though, as she spoke. "Tell me, Kat. Do you honestly believe you're in any position to judge me, after the way you acted in front of all my future in-laws this morning?"

"Of course I'm not judging you," I said. "Don't be stupid! But you're the one who said it was too dangerous to perform any magic before the ceremony."

"Did I?" She dropped the towel onto the dressing table and looked grimly into her own reflection in the mirror. "How very sensible of me."

"Er...?" I looked at her reflection in the mirror too. Angeline wasn't crying now. But she looked as if she might snap at any moment. I swallowed hard. "You know, if you cast a spell on Mrs Carlyle—"

"Tempting," said Angeline. She sat down and began to brush out her thick hair with quick, vigorous strokes. "Very, very tempting. I think she'd look quite attractive with five or six large warts on her nose, don't you? But I'm not quite that foolish yet. Not when she has friends like your Lady Fotherington on her side to warn her if I did it."

"Lady—?" My voice came out as a squeak. I cleared my throat and said firmly, "She's certainly not *my* Lady Fotherington."

"Whatever you want to call her." Angeline waved a dismissive hand. "She's in your precious Order, isn't she? So she'd be able to sense any spells I lay on her friends, as well as passing on malicious gossip to them. I'm only glad Mrs Carlyle doesn't seem to have invited her."

"Right," I said. "Um. Speaking of which..."

"Of course. Your Order." Angeline's face tightened. "You're all quite committed to stopping any acts of magic that you don't happen to approve of, aren't you? Even if they're perfectly just and reasonable?"

"Well..." I thought of the way the other Guardians reacted to any acts of witchcraft. "I wouldn't put it quite that way, but—"

"Quite," said Angeline. "So you can hint and spy just as much as you like, Kat, but I will absolutely not tell you about the spell that I just cast."

Uh-oh. "How bad is it?" I asked faintly.

"It is not bad at all," said Angeline, and her chin rose an extra half inch higher in the air as she glared at herself in the mirror. "It is completely reasonable and justified."

Oh Lord. I closed my eyes for a moment of true horror as I added that to my list of priorities.

One, distract Charles from his newfound mission in life; *two,* find out who was trying to murder me; *three,* find the missing portals before the Order could be disbanded and *four,* as quickly as I could, find out what on earth Angeline had got herself into this time... before Lady Fotherington did.

⋆✩ ✩⋆

In the end it wasn't Angeline's reaction to Lady Fotherington's arrival that startled me most.

Angeline dipped a very, very slight curtsey as Lady Fotherington was ushered into the crowded drawing room before lunch, and she gave her a frosty but courteous nod, which was exactly what I'd expected. Even better, just as I'd hoped, she didn't cast me a single accusing glance at Lady Fotherington's entrance. I'd taken the coward's route and decided not to warn her ahead of time after all. She knew that Lady Fotherington was a friend of Mrs Carlyle's, so why should she think to blame me for the arrival?

But someone else reacted much more strongly.

"Lady *Fotherington*, did you say?" The marquise looked as if she'd seen a ghost.

Everyone else in the room had been presented to Lady Fotherington, of course, as befit her station; but even Lady Fotherington was below the rank of a marquise. And as Mrs Carlyle presented Lady Fotherington to the Marquise de Valmont, the marquise's delicate eyebrows rose perilously high in a look of outright shock.

"My lady," Lady Fotherington murmured, and dipped a genuinely exquisite curtsey of her own.

There was no hint of recognition in her face, and certainly nothing to explain the marquise's reaction.

Even after only a few hours' acquaintance, though, I knew the marquise well enough to understand that she was never taken off guard for long.

"Well!" Her eyebrows lowered, her lips curved into a smile, and she nodded her head with gracious condescension. "What a delightful surprise! I have heard so much about you."

"Only flattering gossip, I hope," said Lady Fotherington. She was smiling as she said it, her voice abstracted and her attention already turning away...

So she didn't see, as I did, the way the marquise's eyes narrowed for a dangerous moment.

"Mmm," the marquise answered noncommittally.

I blinked and turned to look at Papa. He was looking

faintly green with horror as he gazed at both women together.

Lady Fotherington's own gaze rested on him with what I would have taken as mere casual curiosity if I hadn't – unfortunately – known better. One of the most uncomfortable discoveries of last autumn in Bath – even more awkward than discovering the Head of the Order's treason – had been that Lady Fotherington, of all the most unlikely ladies in the kingdom, had nursed a passion for my quiet, scholarly papa when they'd both been young. It had been part of what made her hate Mama so much.

It was all so profoundly embarrassing that I cringed every time I thought of it. I wished I could scrub the knowledge right out of my mind.

"Well!" said Mrs Carlyle. Her little button eyes were sparkling with pleasure as she gazed from one impressive guest to the next. Between Lady Fotherington's fashionable standing and the marquise's rank, their corner of the room positively glowed with the halo of their social importance. I was only surprised that Mrs Carlyle was refraining from literally rubbing her hands together with hostessing glee.

There was a definite light of triumph in her face, though, as she spoke to the room at large. "Shall we all move on to the dining room for a light luncheon? Angeline, my dear," she cooed. "I am so sorry we don't have enough gentlemen to escort you to the table today, but I'm certain you won't mind being escorted by your younger sister. After all, unlike all the other young ladies here, you two must be used to such privations, mustn't you?"

"But of course." Angeline's sweet smile made my blood run cold. "I do hope you have a few table scraps to spare, so that we may feel truly at home? Perhaps a few squares of burned toast to make us comfortable?"

Mrs Carlyle blinked rapidly as titters raced through the roomful of Carlyles. "I beg your pardon?"

The marquise's lips twitched. "Luncheon," she said. "I can hardly wait. Angeline, you may abandon ceremony and sit with me, if you please." She aimed a dazzling smile at Mrs Carlyle and added, "We have so much to catch up on, I know you will forgive our shocking informality. I quite envy you such a charming daughter-in-law, you know."

"Well!" Mrs Carlyle said. She looked like a startled pigeon, waggling with indecision. "Well..."

The demands of rank won out, and she gave a weak smile. "Of course, my lady. What delightful informality. Of course..."

"Thank you."

The marquise brushed past Papa on her way to the door, and Papa jumped as if he'd been electrified. I rolled my eyes and moved to the back of the long, rustling queue of Carlyle relatives. I didn't mind in the least being last in rank and escorted by nobody. It made matters so much easier.

I stepped aside to let Stepmama and Papa move just in front of me, while Charles politely offered his arm to a giggling Carlyle cousin.

And that was when I saw it: a slip of white peeking out of Papa's closed fist.

The marquise had slipped him a note as she'd passed.

I stared at it, strategies forming rapidly in my head. All I had to do was bump against him, just as she had a moment ago...

Too late. Papa lifted one hand to his chest, as if he were straightening his cravat. When he lowered his hand again, it was open and the note was gone, hidden in some pocket.

Dash it.

I looked from Papa, who wore his usual social expression of pained good humour, to the marquise at the very head of the queue, inclining her head towards Angeline's and laughing at a joke I couldn't hear.

There were definitely secrets afoot.

CHAPTER TEN

AT TEN o'CLOCK – "COUNTRY HOURS, MY DEARS!" MRS CARLYLE
trilled – the party finally broke up for bed.

I could have let out a shout of relief. I'd been sitting
upright with my hands neatly folded for so long my fingers
had locked into place, and my lips had positively gone
numb from my meaningless smile.

For Angeline's sake, though, I restrained myself and
only curtsied to Mrs Carlyle with my eyes modestly
lowered as I passed her on my way to the door. Even when
Charles gave me a commanding scowl from across the
room to remind me of his earlier orders, I only rolled my
eyes a very little bit... and only because if I hadn't, he would
have been immediately suspicious.

I had a plan for the night ahead of me, and it certainly
didn't involve lying quietly in my bed, no matter what
Charles might expect.

First, though, I had to wait for Angeline to fall asleep.

It took well over an hour. When she'd finally stopped tossing and turning in the bed beside me, I pushed myself up on one elbow and took a furtive peek at her through the darkness. I could just make out her closed eyes and hear her even breathing.

I passed an exploratory hand an inch over her face. No response.

Finally. I slid out of bed and reached for my valise. Holding my breath for silence, I eased it open.

My hands closed on emptiness. The rope I'd used to climb out my inn window – then carefully repacked – was gone.

Curses. One of the fearsomely efficient Hepworth maids must have unpacked it. But where would she have put it? I turned in a tight circle in the darkness of the room. Angeline was a famously heavy sleeper, but even so, I didn't dare light a candle.

I could hear the muted roar of the sea through the closed window, wild and tempting all at once. The sound itched against my skin. I wasn't meant to be sitting uselessly inside the house in a quiet, stuffy bedroom. I should be outside, searching for my mysterious follower, getting things done!

We were staying on the third floor of the house, though, and I wasn't yet confident enough in my new magical skills to try flying all the way down to the ground. Without a rope, that meant I couldn't leave through the window after all. There was only one other option.

I closed my eyes and summoned up power through my body. *Can't see me, can't see me, can't see me...*

I waited until my whole body felt light and tingly with energy, then edged the door open.

Charles sat in the corridor outside, looking straight at me.

I almost slammed the door shut in surprise.

"Nice try, Kat," he drawled. His arms were crossed, his long legs stretched across the floor, and he'd propped his boots on the wall beside me. From the look of him, he'd been waiting there for some time. His blonde hair fell halfway across his eyes as he gave me – or rather, my shoulders – a superior look. "But you're not going anywhere tonight. I've even got that bit of rope you packed, so—"

A gasp escaped my mouth. The rascal! I'd never dreamed my careless older brother could be so devious.

At the sound of my gasp, Charles's eyes narrowed and his gaze moved upwards, focusing closer to my face. "So you'd better give up and go straight back to bed."

I ground my teeth. The worst of it was, I couldn't even argue without waking Angeline and half our neighbours.

I took a reluctant step back, then stopped, stifling a groan of irritation at my own stupidity as my brain finally started moving again.

Charles wasn't looking at my face. He was looking slightly to my side. It was surprisingly disconcerting... and enormously helpful, as it reminded me of what I'd been too surprised to remember until then.

He couldn't actually see me. He was only guessing that I was there, hidden in the darkness of the room. My magic-working was still in effect. And since it was...

"Fine," I whispered. "But I think you're being completely ridiculous."

Moving as smoothly and silently as I could, I slid out through the open door. I held my breath as I pulled it closed hard – just as I might have done if I were really retreating inside the room, angrily giving up my plans for the night. Then I stepped carefully over my brother's outstretched legs and flattened myself against the wall.

Only a few inches from my head, candlelight flickered from a brass wall sconce, casting a warm glow of light onto my brother's familiar face. I watched it more nervously than I could ever have imagined before the last few days.

Charles might be prone to horrifying acts of reckless stupidity when he was surrounded by his university friends... but I was finally coming to realise that my older brother was no fool. Even after the door closed, he didn't relax. If anything, he looked even more suspicious. His blue eyes narrowed, and he leaned forwards, his head cocked as if listening for movements inside the room.

I held very still and tried not to breathe. Charles had no way of knowing that I could turn myself invisible. He had never seen me do it. There was no possible reason for him to suspect...

Oh Lord. As his face turned, I followed his gaze to the floor by my feet.

I was standing just by a wall sconce... and the flickering candlelight cast my shadow straight across the floor.

Curses. I whirled round and tore down the corridor.

My brother's legs were longer than mine, and I knew he was a faster runner. So when I came to the broad main staircase, I ran straight past it.

Charles would expect me to take that staircase, the quickest route out of the house. Instead I ran all the way to the far end of the corridor, to the plain, nondescript door I'd noticed earlier, the one that no guest would ever use: the door to the servants' staircase.

I waited by it, panting, while I watched my brother lope down the main staircase. Then I pushed the servants' door open and stepped into total darkness.

The guests' corridor had been lit by candles, but the servants at Hepworth didn't have any such assistance.

The stairway was as black as a pit. Luckily, I had plenty of experience in finding my way in the dark.

I fumbled my way down the steep stairs and breathed a sigh of relief when I reached the bottom. The stairwell opened out onto a long, low-roofed corridor, so narrow I could touch both walls with my hands: the servants' corridor, running behind the grand public rooms of Hepworth's ground floor. Of course, it was unlit too.

I hoped the servants had a good supply of candles to carry with them. But somehow, when I thought of Mrs Carlyle's hard, button eyes, I couldn't quite imagine it.

The air in the corridor was suffocatingly close and stale. It took a full five minutes of fumbling against the walls, stubbing my toes and stifling curses, before I finally found a doorway. I was so relieved, I pushed it open and stepped through without even pausing to think.

Then I froze.

I'd stepped into the Hepworth library. And I wasn't alone.

Candlelight flickered across the glass windows of the bookcases that lined the wall. Two people stood whispering together with their backs to me. One of them was the marquise, wearing an exotic crimson dressing gown; the other was Papa, still dressed in the plain frock coat and breeches that he had worn at dinner.

Their voices were low, but the fury in their hissing whispers could have set the library alight.

I nudged the door closed as gently as possible, biting my lip with concentration. Luckily, they were far too involved in their argument to notice.

"You had no right to come here. How dare you do such a thing?"

I barely recognised my own papa's voice. I had never

heard him sound so coldly furious before. It was very nearly frightening... which was an even more absurd idea than thinking Charles clever.

Wasn't it?

The marquise's voice was just as cold. "When did I ever give you leave to regulate my actions?"

"You made a promise to me thirteen years ago."

"I was a fool to make that promise. You should never have asked it of me. If you had any sense of honour—"

"If you had any sense of responsibility—"

"What harm can it do them now? No one knows who I used to be. No one—"

A soft but perfectly audible click sounded just outside the room. The marquise's voice cut off with a snap. As I watched in mute horror, the handle on the library door began to turn. Grimacing, the marquise hissed something underneath her breath.

I would have cursed, too, if I had been in her position.

My head was whirling with a muddle of suspicions and shock, but there was one thing I knew for certain: Papa couldn't be found alone in the library at night with the marquise. They might only have been having an argument, but the gossip would be ruinous... and not only for their reputations. Papa had nearly lost his position as vicar in our village in Yorkshire after the rumours of Angeline's witchcraft had spread last year. If a new scandal erupted now, nothing would save him.

I didn't dare make him invisible in front of her, but if I could somehow drag him into the servants' corridor...

I started forward.

The scent of bluebells filled the room.

I had to throw my hands over my lips to hold back a cry of sheer surprise.

The Hepworth butler stepped into the library. He looked around, frowning. His hook nose twitched. His frown deepened.

He shrugged and leaned over to extinguish the candle that stood in its silver stand on the secretaire in the corner. No shadow but his own fell across the carpeted floor.

The room plunged into darkness. He left, closing the door quietly behind him.

In the darkness two new shadows formed.

"Was that really necessary?" Papa's voice sounded more weary than angry now.

"Still afraid of magic, George?" The marquise sounded just as weary. "Never mind. This isn't the time or the place to discuss it."

"If you leave tomorrow—"

"I do not plan to go anywhere until after the wedding," the marquise said sweetly. "So you shall simply have to grow accustomed to my odious presence. Because you insisted on 'protecting' the children from their birthright, I've been forced to miss the last thirteen years of Angeline's life. I will not miss her wedding now."

"You have no right—"

"Good night, George," the marquise said.

The library door opened and closed. I heard Papa sigh heavily in the darkness. Then one of the glass doors on the bookcases creaked as it was opened. There was a moment of fumbling before it closed again, and Papa left the room.

Leave it to Papa to notice an interesting new book even in the middle of a most furious debate.

It was the only familiar quality I'd seen in him in the last ten minutes.

As the door closed behind him, all the strength drained out of my legs. I collapsed onto the carpet.

If there was one thing I knew how to recognise, it was witchcraft. But I'd had no idea that any witches were powerful enough to cast invisibility spells. I could have sworn that was only a Guardian power. More than that, her spell had been stronger than my magic-working – even their shadows had disappeared under its influence.

But the marquise's witchcraft wasn't the most shocking aspect of the scene I'd just witnessed.

Thirteen years ago, she had made Papa a promise – a promise to leave us all alone, to protect us from... what exactly? Her magic? Our birthright, she had called it.

Thirteen years was a number I knew all too well. Thirteen years ago had been one of the most important and eventful years in my family's history.

Thirteen years ago I had been born... and Mama had died.

Or...

It hurt to breathe now, as the thought worked its way up through my chest.

Had she really?

CHAPTER ELEVEN

I DIDN'T Go oUT LooKING FoR MY MYSTERIoUS FoLLoWER after all. I couldn't. I could barely force my numb legs back up the servants' staircase.

For hours I lay awake in the darkness, my stomach churning. When bright sunlight woke me, after only a few hours of restless sleep, all the same questions popped back into place, just as unresolved and overwhelming as they'd felt the night before.

No one knows who I used to be, the marquise had said, just before she cast the strongest spell I'd ever come across.

Was it possible? Could it be true?

I'd never known Mama, only seen the miniature portrait of her that sat in our drawing room until Stepmama arrived in the house. I hadn't recognised the marquise from that portrait... but then, who would be recognisable from a two-inch-wide picture painted twenty years ago?

The marquise had thick, dark hair like Angeline... and like Mama, in the portrait.

The marquise was a powerful witch, just as Mama had been.

But most compelling of all, the marquise had promised Papa thirteen years ago to leave us all alone, to keep us safe from the taint of her magic... and as Stepmama was infinitely fond of pointing out, our mother's notorious reputation as a witch had nearly ruined all of her children's prospects forever. It was only Papa's second marriage that had brought the family some respectability and made it possible for Angeline and Elissa to make such eligible matches.

Papa's career in the Church had already been crippled by his first marriage, and it was too late to recover it by the time I was born. But if Mama and Papa had decided, together, that it was best for me, Angeline, Elissa and Charles...

I lurched out of bed as if I could escape the idea if I only moved fast enough. But it didn't work. Even as my bare feet landed on the soft carpet, my stomach rolled with nausea. I ran for the window and pushed it open to take deep, gasping breaths of fresh air. It was cool and salty, and it stung my nose and throat.

But it didn't stop the sickness from rising inside me.

It couldn't be true, I told myself. It *couldn't*. Charles would have recognised her. *Angeline* would have recognised her. And then there was Lady Fotherington – she would never forget her nemesis so easily.

Even Charles, though, the oldest of my siblings, had only been eight when Mama had died. In thirteen years her appearance might well have changed enough that Charles wouldn't take the similarities as anything but coincidence. And it would never occur to Lady Fotherington to recognise her scandalous former rival, who'd worn twice-turned gowns and had no real dowry, in a wealthy marquise's polished guise.

Everything in me wanted my theory to be wrong. Everything in me felt sick at the very idea of it.

I had lived all my life with the knowledge that I would never know my mother. But I did not think I could physically bear it if she had left us all on purpose.

"Kat?" Angeline's voice was thick with sleep. "What are you doing?"

I whirled around with sheer relief. "Angeline!"

Until now I'd almost forgotten: I didn't have to solve this on my own. Nine-tenths of the time I hated being the youngest in my family. This time, though, nothing in the world sounded better than turning over my dilemma to my aggravating, know-it-all big sister. For once, I would let her tell me exactly what to do.

Then I saw Angeline's face, and the words froze in my mouth.

If I hadn't known better, I would have thought she'd stayed awake all night. Her face was pale with exhaustion, and the skin under her eyes looked almost bruised. I couldn't remember the last time I'd seen Angeline look so fragile.

She frowned at me. "Well? What is it? You haven't run into any more feral cats, have you? I'm not sure I'm up to explaining a whole new set of scratches to Mrs Carlyle today." She'd obviously meant that last bit as a joke, but the fatigue in her voice made the joke fall flat.

I frowned back at her. "You look horrible. What kind of spell was it that you cast yesterday?"

Angeline groaned. "I told you already: I'm not telling

you that! Let's not argue about it, please." She closed her eyes and snuggled deeper into her pillows. "I'm too tired for arguments, and I'm already dreading meeting Mrs Carlyle over breakfast. Just warn me, please, if there's anything I need to know before I face her again."

I looked at Angeline's closed eyes and the smudges underneath them. I took a deep breath and let it out. The salty air from the window mixed with the sour taste in my mouth.

Thirteen years ago, Papa had said.

The truth had already waited thirteen years to be discovered. It could wait a little longer... at least, until my sister had to face it.

"No," I said. "There's nothing."

⁂

Angeline might have been dreading her next confrontation with her future mother-in-law, but no one would have guessed it two hours later as we walked together into the breakfast room. From the confident tilt of her head to the cool smile on her face, she was every bit the future mistress of Hepworth, surveying her domain.

But the reply in Mrs Carlyle's hard brown eyes and pursed mouth, as she glared at Angeline from the head of the main table, was: *Not as long as I live.*

I let Mrs Carlyle's glare pass over me. I had far more important matters to worry about.

Papa sat at a small, square table at the back of the room, reading a leather-bound book as he ate: clear evidence that Stepmama was not yet awake and about. She would never have permitted such unsociable behaviour.

Various Carlyles milled about the sideboard, filling

their plates, while others chatted at the scattered tables that filled the long, light room. Lady Fotherington sat at Mrs Carlyle's own table, listening with a condescending smile as the others talked. But the one person I was looking for was nowhere to be seen.

The first hint I had was a breath of perfume sweeping up behind me, exotic and sophisticated. "Angeline and Katherine! My dears." The marquise tucked her hands into our arms and smiled at us both, linking us together. "What a pleasure to see you again."

I smiled back weakly. I had never paid much attention to Stepmama's lessons in social graces. I was fairly certain, though, that *"Are you my mother?"* would be considered far too forward for public breakfast conversation.

Luckily, Angeline was almost never lost for words. "Your ladyship." Her cool, public smile turned into a real one – and even a teasing one – as she continued: "I am astonished! I thought all true sophisticates stayed abed until noon, to preserve their delicate complexions."

"Well, my dear..." The marquise gave a warm, throaty chuckle. "Never let it be said that I am not a true sophisticate – but how could I possibly gather any of the best gossip while sitting alone in an empty bedroom? And even more important, how on earth could I create gossip there myself?"

They laughed together, their voices mingling, and I shivered at the sound.

Was it actually familiar? Had I heard that throaty laugh before, in the first few days of my life? Or was I only imagining it?

"Katherine." The marquise frowned down at me. "Are you cold, dear?" She leaned closer, with what looked like real concern.

The concern in her voice felt *too* good. I jerked back, breathing hard.

"I'm fine!" I said. "Truly."

She was not my mother, I told myself. Or if she was...

But no. That wasn't even a possibility.

Anyone who would willingly walk out of my life when I was only ten days old was no mother at all.

"I'm only hungry," I said, and pulled away. "Aren't you?"

I scooped up a plate and headed for the sideboard. My heartbeat was thudding as hard against my chest as if I'd spent the last few minutes running across a field instead of standing still in a breakfast room. I couldn't stop myself from sneaking glances back at her, even as I selected my eggs and toast.

I was concentrating so hard on the marquise, I didn't even notice Charles until his hand fell on my shoulder.

"Aha!" he said.

I was so startled, I jumped. Then I scowled up at him, snatching back the tongs I'd dropped.

"What do you mean, 'Aha'?" I said. "You sound like the villain in a play."

He scowled right back at me. If I hadn't known Charles so well, I might have found him genuinely forbidding.

"You," he snarled, and jerked his head at the door. "You're coming with me."

"I beg your pardon?" I sighed and held up my half-filled plate for his perusal. "I am in the middle of gathering breakfast, in case you hadn't noticed, so—"

"*Now*, Kat." His hand tightened on my shoulder.

"For heaven's sake," I began... then stopped, as I looked at him more closely.

A muscle was twitching in Charles's jaw. I hadn't even

known that people *had* muscles there. But that wasn't the most startling thing I saw. What stopped my voice in my throat was the look in his blue eyes.

Charles was the only sibling too lazy to be drawn into any of our family arguments. Whenever other people grew angry, Charles fell asleep to escape the shouting. But unless I was completely misjudging his new and utterly unfamiliar expression, my careless, sleepy older brother was in the grip of a white-hot rage.

The world had obviously turned upside down, so it was best to be very careful.

"Ah..." I set down my plate, keeping a wary eye on Charles's face. "I suppose I can always eat later."

"Hmm," said Charles. The muscle in his jaw twitched again.

Oh, dear.

That was anything but reassuring. I snatched a hard-boiled egg from my abandoned plate even as my brother steered me firmly away from the crowded sideboard.

At least I'd have some nourishment, no matter where he took me.

As Charles guided me through the crowd of Carlyles, I looked for Angeline with increasing urgency. It wasn't that I needed rescue, I told myself – but surely someone ought to know that Charles was marching me away, just in case I didn't come back again?

When I finally spotted her, though, Angeline's face was tilted away from me. She was laughing at something the marquise had just said, and was surrounded by a group of young Carlyle women. I started to lift my hand in a frantic wave. Then I felt Lady Fotherington's gaze fall on me. I saw her eyebrows begin to rise.

I straightened my shoulders, dropped my hand, and

walked the rest of the way as casually as if Charles's tight grip on my shoulder was no more than an affectionate touch. I would be dashed if I would give Lady Fotherington the satisfaction of seeing me marched out of the breakfast room in disgrace.

The very thought of her amusement was enough to stiffen my spine and chase away the ridiculous nerves that had taken hold of me. I held my tongue as Charles walked me down the long corridor and out the great front doors of Hepworth, but as soon as we were outside and the doors had closed behind us, I yanked out of his grip – or tried to.

I'd forgotten how strong my older brother really was.

"What is the matter with you?" I demanded. Gusts of salty air whipped past us under a deep grey sky. Stepmama would shriek later on when she saw my hair, but I didn't care. I couldn't yank my shoulder free from Charles's grip, so I stomped on the tiny shells that lined the drive and kicked them up towards his trousered legs. "You're acting like a madman! You—"

"What's the matter with me? With *me*?" Charles bellowed the words straight into my face, even as the wind whipped his thick blonde hair into tufts and billows, like waves atop his head. "I'm not the one who goes running out of the house in the middle of the night! I'm not the thirteen-year-old *infant* who thinks she can take on a murderer by herself, and won't even let her own brother protect her! I'm not the one who—"

Shells spattered against our sides like tiny bullets, kicked up by horses' hooves. We both spun round.

An arriving carriage, pulled by four heavily muscled brown horses, had swept around the curve of the shell-lined drive while we were busy shouting at each other. We traded a furious glance as it rolled to a stop nearby.

"This is not finished!" Charles hissed at me.

"It certainly isn't," I hissed back, and stuck my tongue out at him for good measure.

"Ho there!" The carriage window opened, and a familiar face appeared. Frederick Carlyle's dark blue eyes sparkled with wicked amusement as he looked us both up and down. "I'll thank you two ruffians not to startle my horses, please!"

"Carlyle." Charles took a deep, visible breath and ran his hand through his wildly disordered hair. The smile he gave our future brother-in-law looked decidedly strained. "Right," he said. "Beg your pardon, it was just – that is—"

"Give me just a moment and I'll make introductions," Frederick Carlyle said. He disappeared from view.

As servants swarmed out from the doors of Hepworth, the carriage door swung open. A footman knelt to lower the carriage steps. A woman's booted foot appeared, under sky-blue skirts, and I stiffened, leaning forwards.

Drat. I'd almost forgotten this complication.

"That'll be his cousin Jane," I whispered to Charles. "The one his mother wanted him to marry."

She stepped fully onto the top step, and I groaned. "Oh Lord, of course she's pretty. What a nuisance! You'd better make sure you tell Angeline she – Charles? Charles?"

A strangled sound had emerged from my older brother's throat. I turned and blinked.

My older brother was staring at Jane Carlyle. His mouth had fallen open. His blue eyes were wider than I'd ever seen them.

"Ah," he said. "Ah... gah...."

I'd never seen that expression on Charles's face before, but I knew exactly what it meant.

A feeling of delicious lightness unfurled inside me.

I had to stop myself from laughing out loud with sheer delight.

Frederick Carlyle helped his cousin out of the carriage, and I started forward to greet them both, beaming with all my might.

I had just discovered the perfect distraction for my brother.

CHAPTER TWELVE

JANE CARLYLE'S HAIR GLINTED RED UNDER HER FASHIONABLE straw bonnet, and her eyes shone forget-me-not blue. There were a dozen freckles scattered across her creamy skin, and when she smiled at us, a dimple popped into her cheek.

I was afraid that Charles might disgrace us both by whimpering out loud. So I inserted myself between them as I gave her my best curtsey, as straight-backed and graceful as even Stepmama could wish.

Unfortunately, my dignified first impression didn't last for long.

"Cousin, this is Miss Katherine Ann Stephenson, also known as Kat, also known as a dangerous scandal to Society," said Frederick Carlyle, and he swept me up into a hug that left my feet dangling a full foot above the ground.

"Oh, not fair!" I said. But I wrapped my arms around the broad shoulders of his blue coat and hugged him back anyway, tossing all thoughts of dignity aside. "I missed you!"

"I've missed you, too, rascal." He ruffled my hair as he set me down. "Have you been keeping your stepmama in convulsions, as usual? You'll have to tell me all your horrifying adventure stories later. And Stephenson." He gave Charles an affable nod. "Everything all right?"

"Ah," said Charles, still staring at Jane Carlyle. "Ah. Ah."

"It's a pleasure to meet you both," she said in a soft, husky voice, and she gave us a curtsey that would have made Stepmama sigh with pleasure. "Cousin Frederick has told me so much about all of you."

Oh, dear. I gave my future brother-in-law a wary look. If he'd told her too much about Charles, my wonderful distraction wouldn't last long at all.

Charles wasn't doing his own cause much good either. If he didn't close his mouth soon, he might just start to drool.

Luckily, although Jane Carlyle was at least twice as round as me and far better-endowed in the chest region, she was scarcely half an inch taller, which made it easy to intercept her gaze. I moved between her and Charles, and stepped hard on my brother's right foot as I did it.

"Ouch!" Charles said. "Dash it, Kat!"

I ignored him with the ease of long practice. "Did you have a pleasant trip?" I asked Jane.

She blinked and looked away from Charles to meet my gaze. "It was a very easy trip," she said. "It was so kind of Cousin Frederick to escort me all the way, although I did tell him it truly wasn't necessary. My papa was perfectly willing to escort me himself, at least as far as the edge of Devon. He had a matter of business to take care of by himself in

Somerset before he could start for Hepworth, you see, and he didn't want me to be late for the wedding party."

I frowned. "But I thought Mrs Carlyle said—"

"There was obviously a misunderstanding," said Frederick Carlyle, and grimaced at me expressively.

Aha. So Mrs Carlyle had started her tricks even before Angeline's arrival. I said, "Well, at least you're here sooner than expected. Your mama thought you wouldn't arrive until at least tonight."

Jane Carlyle let out a gurgle of laughter, looking suddenly far less like a prim young lady and much more like someone I might want to know after all. "Perhaps it does usually take that long, when Frederick isn't the one in charge... and on his way to see his fiancée for the first time in nearly six months. How many weeks and days has it been, Cousin? Exactly? I'm sure you gave me a precise number last night when you refused to stop at either of those first two inns I spotted."

"Yes, well..." He shrugged, looking slightly shamefaced, and glanced hopefully through the open doors. "Still, you can't lay all the blame on me. I would have stopped longer at the inn this morning to let you have a real lie-in if you hadn't—"

"Nonsense," said Jane Carlyle, and gave both me and my brother a dazzling smile. "Really, gentlemen can be so foolish, can they not? As if I would have stayed an instant longer in an inn like that." She leaned forward, dropping her voice to a whisper, and Charles nearly knocked me over in his eagerness to lean closer in return.

"If you can believe it," Jane Carlyle whispered to us, "there was *gambling* going on at that inn this morning. In full daylight!"

Oh, dear. "Gambling?" I echoed faintly. I tried not to

let my eyes slip guiltily back to my older brother.

She nodded vigorously. "*And* excessive drinking." Her eyes widened with passionate intensity. "My papa has always said, if there is one type of person no lady can allow herself to be associated with, it is a man who gambles and drinks to excess."

I gulped. Behind me, Charles had gone as stiff as a statue. "Not at all?" I asked. "But what if he reforms? He would be all right then, wouldn't he?"

Jane Carlyle shook her head with a world-weary sigh. "I'm afraid I could never trust a man like that," she said. "My papa says it is always safest to shun such gentlemen entirely."

Behind her, Frederick Carlyle only rolled his eyes, with the look of a man who had heard this lecture many times before. But as I looked into Jane Carlyle's round, pretty face, full of innocent conviction, I could barely restrain myself from cursing out loud in the most unladylike fashion imaginable.

My plan for Charles's distraction was already going terribly wrong.

✫ ✫ ✫

I forgot all my frustration, though, when I saw the look on Angeline's face as the four of us – or, more precisely, as Frederick Carlyle – walked into the breakfast room. It was like watching the sun finally come out after weeks and weeks of endless grey sky.

Being Angeline, she had far too much self-control to run to him in front of his mother and all their relatives... but as she sat watching him from her seat at his mother's table, the glow on her face could have lit the whole of Hepworth.

"Frederick!" Mrs Carlyle dropped her knife as we entered. It hit her plate with an inelegant clatter. "And Jane. Oh, my goodness! We never expected you so soon, did we?" She turned to the harpy aunts on either side of her for clucking confirmation. "You must have been terribly rash on the roads! I shall have palpitations for days at the very thought—"

"Oh, no, Aunt." Jane Carlyle gave her aunt the most respectful curtsey imaginable, but her soft voice cut off Mrs Carlyle with neat efficiency. "Cousin Frederick is an excellent whip, you know. We were perfectly safe."

"It is too kind of you to say so, my dear. But how very like you!" Mrs Carlyle sighed, and held out her be-ringed hand to her son for a kiss. "Well, Frederick, as you are here after all..."

"Mama," he said, and nodded respectfully. But he was already walking past her, his dark-blue eyes intent.

He didn't stop until he'd reached the end of the table. Then he reached out to take Angeline's hands in his.

I could almost see the spark of contact as their hands met. Neither of them said a single word. They didn't have to. The air around them positively sizzled with sudden heat.

I looked away quickly, feeling my own skin flush with embarrassment. There were some moments that shouldn't have to be shared with company.

I must have been the only person in the room who wasn't watching, though. Even Papa had set down his book and was beaming fondly at them both from his far table. Next to Angeline, the marquise was smiling with clear approval, and several of the Carlyles around the room had sympathetic smiles on their faces. One of the older female Carlyles was even dabbing at her eyes with a handkerchief.

Mrs Carlyle was not.

She coughed, loudly and repeatedly, until Frederick Carlyle finally looked up. "*Frederick*." Her tone had turned to ice. "I note that you haven't yet greeted either of your aunts, despite the fact that they arrived while you were gone."

"Haven't I?" He didn't let go of Angeline's hands as he turned, smiling, to the harpies. "Forgive me, Aunts. I hope your journey wasn't difficult?"

"Not *difficult*," said Honoria. "Not by our standards, at any rate."

"When one is already prepared for rudeness and inefficiency at every turn..." Letitia sighed.

"Oh, dear," said Frederick Carlyle. "That is a pity."

But his gaze was already sliding back to Angeline's face, and he didn't seem to be able to stop smiling. "And your trip?" he asked her, leaning closer. "I hated not being here for your arrival. If there had been any other way..."

"Poor Cousin Frederick," said Jane Carlyle. She curtsied to Angeline every bit as respectfully as she had curtsied to Mrs Carlyle a moment before. "Do forgive me for keeping him from you, Miss Stephenson. It was all a terrible misunderstanding, I'm afraid. You see, my papa—"

"Yes, well, never mind all that," said Mrs Carlyle hastily. "I'm sure Frederick could never mind spending more time with you, my dear, no matter what the circumstances might have been. Why, the two of you have always been so fond of each other! I'm sure if your dear papa and I have said it once, we've said it at least a thousand times: the two of you would make a perfect match, in every possible way. Everyone always expected it to happen!"

Angeline's face tightened, losing some of its glow. I ground my teeth and thought about forbidden magic.

Frederick Carlyle turned to look at his cousin, and Jane Carlyle met his eyes.

Her lips quivered. His eyes widened. Then they both collapsed into laughter.

Frederick bent over almost double as he shook with laughter, never letting go of Angeline's hands. Jane Carlyle turned quite pink, she laughed so hard.

Mrs Carlyle's eyes looked smaller and harder with every moment that passed before her son finally recovered himself.

"I do beg your pardon, Cousin Jane," he said, straightening. "That was terribly ungentlemanly of me. It was only—"

"Oh, Cousin," Jane Carlyle said. She was wiping her eyes with her handkerchief, which was small and dainty and pink, and perfectly embroidered with the letters JC. "You cannot be any more horrified by the idea than I am, I promise you. When I think of your notoriously murderous tendencies—"

"His *what*?" growled Charles. It was the first time he'd managed a coherent phrase since her arrival, and his tone was so full of menace that she blinked rapidly and took a step away from him.

Frederick Carlyle only grinned. "Never fear, Stephenson," he said. "My murderous tendencies, as my cousin likes to call them, began and ended with her favourite doll, and only when she'd aggravated me past bearing by throwing my best pair of Hessian boots into the sea... and purely because she found that I'd been playing cards regularly at Eton, just like every other fellow there. My cousin has a bit of a fixation about the evils of gambling, you know."

"Childish fancies," said Mrs Carlyle coldly, and glared at him. "I am sure that you young people find your wit very amusing, but—"

"I did very nearly the same thing to Charles, once," said Angeline, and she gave Jane Carlyle a smile of genuine friendliness. "I'm so pleased to meet you, Miss Carlyle."

"And I you," said Jane Carlyle. "Especially as you've made Cousin Frederick so happy."

"Regardless!" said Mrs Carlyle. She was breathing hard. "Frederick, you still haven't greeted any of your other guests. What can you be thinking?"

"Not very much, apparently," he said affably. He turned to the other guests at the table. "My lady." He bowed to the marquise. "I'm so glad you were able to come. And..." His eyes widened as, for the first time, he seemed to notice who else was sitting at the table. "Lady Fotherington? I am..." He traded a quick look with Angeline. "...surprised to see you here."

"How could I miss it?" She gave him a thin smile. "When my own god-daughter's sister is being married..."

I cringed. Luckily, no one was looking at me.

"*God-daughter?*" the marquise said.

The sharpness in her voice made everyone turn to her. She laughed lightly, glancing at the curious faces around her, then said, "Forgive me, I was only surprised. Did you truly mean to say... that is... do I understand that you, Lady Fotherington, are actually Miss Katherine Stephenson's godmother?"

"Why, yes," said Lady Fotherington. She shrugged gently, every line of her body speaking distaste. "I knew her mother, you see."

I looked at the marquise's face and bit my lip. If she really was my mother... if she was...

"Indeed," said the marquise, in a tone of cool, aristocratic surprise. "I hadn't realised." She turned her gaze to me and gave me a long, thoughtful look. "I think

Katherine and I must have a good talk, and soon. There is so much I need to catch up on in her life."

My fingernails bit into my palm so sharply I could hardly even feel my own head nodding agreement.

CHAPTER THIRTEEN

WITH FREDERICK CARLYLE'S ARRIVAL, A WHIRL OF ENERGY seemed to take over the house party. Within ten minutes, an expedition to the local village had been proposed by Frederick Carlyle and eagerly seconded by Jane Carlyle. And while Mrs Carlyle was still detailing every single one of her objections to her son, from the unhealthy dirt of the village to the greyness of the weather, the entire party – except for Mrs Carlyle and the harpies – was organised into a line of carriages outside Hepworth's front doors.

The marquise tucked one hand firmly into my left arm and smiled past me as Stepmama pulled a reluctant Papa through the open doors to join the expedition. Charles stood a few feet away from us, arms crossed and gazing with smouldering intensity at Jane Carlyle, who was sparkling up at Angeline and another young Carlyle lady. Despite Mrs Carlyle's ominous claims about the weather, the sky had finally cleared. In the bright sunshine,

Jane looked even prettier and more vibrant – and poor Charles looked even more hopeless.

I sighed. If Charles had any common sense, I would leave him to his own devices. But even with all of his recent developments, he was still the same hapless older brother who had let his friends talk him into stupid amounts of drinking and gambling in the first place...and who had only finally managed to give up the gambling when he started winning at it. Clearly, the fact that Jane Carlyle was not a sensible object for his affections wasn't likely to take away any of his interest in her. In fact, I had an uncomfortable suspicion that her impossibility might make his feelings even more intense.

Clearly, he would need my help.

The marquise kept her gaze firmly focused on Stepmama's face as she spoke, ignoring Papa entirely.

"Of course we could hardly steal Angeline from her fiancé, but the rest of you will ride with me, will you not? Do say you will. I couldn't possibly lose my travelling companions now!"

"Well..." Papa began. Even I didn't hold out much hope for him, as I saw the look Stepmama shot him. Still, he did his best. "We appreciate the offer, my lady, but I think we would do better to—"

A second hand took hold of my right arm and pulled. "I'm afraid I shall have to deny you some of your pleasure, my lady," said Lady Fotherington. "You see, my god-daughter and I require a bit of private time together."

Oh Lord. I stifled a groan. If there was one thing I did *not* require, it was privacy with my mother's old nemesis. Still, I had promised Mr Gregson to work with her, so I sighed and stepped towards her... or at least, I tried to.

The marquise's grip had tightened around my arm.

When I glanced up at her, I found her smiling sweetly at Lady Fotherington over my head. "Oh, but surely you must have had a great deal of time together already, my lady," she said. "After all, as her godmother..."

Lady Fotherington smiled back charmingly. Her grip tightened too. "Can one ever have enough time with a favourite god-daughter?"

"You must allow me to claim the privilege of a very old friend of the family," the marquise said, and gave my left arm a surreptitious, quick, hard tug. It nearly pulled me off my feet.

"Ah, but I was acquainted with her mother," Lady Fotherington said, and tugged my right arm just as hard – and just as discreetly. No one watching us could have seen what either noblewoman was doing.

The marquise's eyes narrowed, and she pulled harder. "What a coincidence. So was I."

I struggled to stay upright, and wondered if this was how toffee felt when it was pulled.

"Were you indeed?" Lady Fotherington yanked my right arm so hard it burned, but her rigid smile never left her face. "How odd, then, that we never met."

"Odd, indeed." The marquise drew a deep breath. Her smile was beginning to look decidedly forced. "We must have moved in different circles."

"Perhaps—" Lady Fotherington began. Then she broke off with a little huff of surprise, as the marquise let go of my arm... and I tumbled straight into Lady Fotherington's side, nearly knocking her over.

"Katherine Ann Stephenson!" Stepmama gasped. She let go of Papa to scramble over and pull me away from Lady Fotherington. "How could you be so clumsy?"

"How indeed?" Lady Fotherington said, and let go of my

arm to brush off her skirts. She gave me a look of distaste and heaved a martyred sigh. "Come, Katherine. My carriage is waiting for us."

"Do enjoy yourselves, both of you," said the marquise. Her gaze rested on me with mysterious intensity. "I hope you shall tell me all about it later."

"Hmph," said Lady Fotherington, and set off for her carriage without even bothering to look back to see if I would follow her.

I would have loved to make her look foolish... but I remembered my promise to Mr Gregson and followed with a heavy sigh.

A Hepworth footman assisted her ladylike passage up the carriage steps; I waved him away and climbed the steps on my own, like a capable person. Lady Fotherington arched one eyebrow at me in a look of complete disdain. I bounced on the padded leather cushions of the seat across from her, just to make her wince.

The footman closed the door and shut us away from the bustling crowd of Carlyles. We were completely alone together, for the first time since we'd met almost a year ago.

The luxuriant carriage suddenly felt far too small. I drew a deep breath of stuffy air and repeated silently to myself: *I promised Mr Gregson. I promised...*

"Thank heavens," said Lady Fotherington, and leaned back with a sigh. "I couldn't possibly have kept up that agonising pretence any longer. How is it that you always contrive to make yourself so particularly disagreeable? At least the rest of your family manages to convey the appearance of respectability most of the time, despite how difficult that must be for them – particularly for your sister the *witch*."

Her lips twisted into a sneer on the last word, and my chest burned with instant rage.

That was it. I'd promised Mr Gregson to work with her for the Order's sake, but I'd never, ever promised to sit quietly while she insulted my family.

I crossed my arms in a gesture so unladylike it would have made Stepmama and my sister Elissa both cry out in pain, and I looked around as if I were weighing up the carriage's value, from the thick leather cushions to the green satin curtains drawn back from the thick glass windows. "Do you consider this the height of respectability?" I asked. "I can't say I think much of it. When we rode in the marquise's carriage—"

"The less said about that, the better." Lady Fotherington tapped her fingers in a quick, irritated tattoo on the cushion beside her as her face tightened. "If you had any conscience, you would be ashamed to admit how you've drawn another respectable member of Society into your family's toils. And what exactly was she about, claiming to have known your mother?"

"Well..."

Lady Fotherington turned her head to look out the window with narrowed eyes. "I can tell you from very personal experience that your mother *never* moved in elevated social circles, even before the scandal of her witchcraft came out. The only reason I was forced to know her myself was through the Order, and as the Marquise de Valmont is certainly not a Guardian—"

Oh, *no*. This was *not* a line of thought that I wanted her to pursue.

"The Order!" I yelped. "That was why you wanted me here, wasn't it?"

I was silently snarling every curse I knew as I dropped

my arms and leaned forward to attract Lady Fotherington's attention away from the marquise.

She was a snob, she was a bigot, and she was the woman who'd ruined my mother's career in the Order... but no one had ever accused Lady Fotherington of being stupid, any more than I had ever been accused of having too calm or controlled a temper. And the very last thing I wanted right now was to make Lady Fotherington think hard about where she might have met the marquise before... or exactly who the marquise might have been.

"Really, Katherine." Lady Fotherington turned back to me with a pained sigh. "This carriage is not so large that you must shout for me to hear you. I would have thought that even you might have learned some modicum of self-control by now, after nearly a year of contact with Society."

So would I, I thought glumly. But learning self-control hadn't happened yet, around Lady Fotherington, at least. And that had to change.

As Lady Fotherington rapped the roof above us to signal to the driver, and the carriage rolled into motion down the long, shell-lined drive away from Hepworth, I faced an unpalatable truth.

If we were going to work together, I would have to learn to keep my temper around her no matter how much she irritated me... and not just for my own safety any more. I was keeping other people's secrets too now, and I couldn't afford to let them slip in the presence of my mother's worst enemy.

"But yes," Lady Fotherington said, with heavy patience in her tone, and it took me a moment to remember what she was talking about. "Naturally, I invited you to share my carriage only for the sake of our mission. You may be certain that I would never have done so for the pleasure of your company."

For once I forced myself to bite my lip and hold back the cutting response I wanted to make. Instead I gave her a nod every bit as aristocratically cool and gracious as the marquise herself might have managed.

Lady Fotherington regarded me through dangerously thoughtful green eyes. I restrained the impulse to scratch my nose. Outside the windows the landscaped Hepworth gardens rolled past us like an artist's idyll... but inside the carriage, things felt far from idyllic.

It was a relief when she finally spoke again.

"So," she said. "As the entire party knows, I've joined this little expedition, just like every other guest. However, no matter how great the lure of rural bliss" – sarcasm curdled in her voice like sour milk – "I can hardly fritter away my day looking at provincial ribbon shops when the Order is under threat of being disbanded. The portals have been traced to Devon, and they need to be found immediately."

I straightened, brightening. "What are we going to do?"

"We?" said Lady Fotherington. She raised both eyebrows as she looked me up and down. "We are going to spend the day taking a refreshing walk outside the village by ourselves."

"Um..." I blinked at her. "I thought you said—"

"It is perfectly proper and plausible for a godmother to choose to spend the afternoon walking alone with her god-daughter," said Lady Fotherington, "even if not easily understandable in this particular case."

"But you just said—"

"I," said Lady Fotherington, "cannot imagine a worse way to spend an afternoon than tramping outside in the mud. That is why you are going to be taking that walk on your own, for at least three hours, and taking care to stay well away from any other members of the party who might notice my absence."

"Oh, for heaven's sake," I said. "You can't be serious! The portals need to be found straightaway, don't they? I know you don't enjoy my company, but if they really are here in Devon, it's absurd not to let me help you look. If you would only think clearly about it for a moment..."

Lady Fotherington's icy glare would have chilled me to the bone if I had let it. "I do thank you for your advice," she said. "How fortunate I am, indeed, in having a thirteen-year-old child to instruct me on how to lead my most important investigation. A thirteen-year-old child, I should add, who isn't even a full member of our Order yet. How could I possibly fail to follow your instructions?"

I gritted my teeth. "I'm not trying to instruct you," I said. "I'm just saying..."

"If you wouldn't mind too terribly, I would prefer that you not." Lady Fotherington closed her eyes and set her head back against the cushions. "To be quite frank, the sound of your voice is enough to give anyone a headache, and I simply cannot take another moment of it."

"You – you—"

I slammed my jaw shut to stop myself sputtering.

Lady Fotherington's elegant profile was as smooth and unruffled as if I hadn't said a word.

Grinding my teeth, I sat back in my seat and practised keeping my temper.

CHAPTER FOURTEEN

I WAS STILL SIMMERING TWO HOURS LATER AS I STOMPED down a long, overgrown footpath. On my right, a field full of brown-and-white cows watched me with placid curiosity. To my left, a slow-moving brown river unfurled without any rush.

None of it made me feel any calmer.

It wasn't that I didn't like the countryside. Unlike Lady Fotherington, I would choose a good muddy walk over a tedious shopping expedition any day of the week. The sky had brightened, the sun was shining down on me and it was a perfect day to be outside.

But that was hardly the point.

Somewhere nearby, Charles was pining after Jane Carlyle, and if I knew my hopeless brother at all, he would be so wrapped up in torturing himself over his own Dark Past, he wouldn't have the sense to give her a single decent smile, much less formulate a flirtatious remark or two.

Somewhere nearby, the marquise was charming Stepmama and the Carlyles and dragging a miserable Papa in her wake... and I was too far away to pick up a single clue she might let drop. If she was my mother, shouldn't I know? I had to find out, one way or another.

And of course, most aggravatingly of all, somewhere nearby, the single most important piece of Guardian business in the whole country was taking place without me.

I kicked a muddy stick with all my strength. Even the satisfying distance it travelled wasn't enough to make me feel better.

If those portals weren't found quickly, the Order would be dissolved before I even became a full member. If I was ever going to restore Mama's reputation within it – or carry out the career I knew I had been born for – I couldn't let that happen. But what could I do here?

I had promised Lady Fotherington not to let anybody see me until our walk was officially finished...

...but I hadn't promised not to turn myself invisible.

Ha!

Satisfaction filled me, replacing all the fury that had powered my walk until now. I stopped walking and closed my eyes to focus.

I could hear the river rippling quietly to my left; I could hear the soft swishing sounds of the cows moving through the grass on my right and a seagull calling in the distance. I drew power slowly through my body, from my mud-covered walking boots up to my chest and arms and head.

Can't see me, I thought. *Can't see me, can't see me...*

I waited until my whole body felt light and tingling and weightless. Then I opened my eyes.

A scowling, broad-shouldered boy stood directly in front of me.

✧ ✧ ✧

I was so shocked, I lost my focus. The magic-working dropped away, leaving me visible. He didn't blink. Hadn't he even noticed that I was invisible before?

Then I realised something that made my chest feel tight with more than shock.

If I hadn't seen or heard him coming across this long, flat field, that meant only one thing: he could do magic too. And since I hadn't even sensed any spell or magic-working in the air...

I wasn't just facing an angry boy at least two years older than me, a whole foot taller, and dangerously muscled through his arms and shoulders; I was facing an angry magic-worker who was much more powerful than I was.

"Katherine Stephenson," he said in a voice thick with rage.

I lifted my chin and looked him straight in the eyes, squashing the cowardly little voice in my brain that wanted me to turn tail and run. "Yes," I said. "That's me."

He had curling brown hair and fierce green eyes, and I had never met him before in my life, but I had seen his outline between the trees only two nights before.

My mysterious follower had finally found me alone. Charles was going to be furious.

"Well?" I drawled. "You've been following me for days. Surely you must have something you want to say to me."

He stared down at me as incredulously as if I were speaking Russian. "You aren't even frightened yet, are you?"

Oh Lord. That little whimpering voice in my brain was back again, reminding me of all the reasons I ought to be.

He'd already tried to murder me once by sabotaging my

family's carriage. If he tried again, this time with magic, I didn't think I'd be able to stop him.

If I'd lifted my chin any higher, I would have fallen over backwards. "Of course I'm not frightened," I said. "Why would I be?"

He shook his head and let out a crack of laughter. It sounded as wild and biting as a wolf's bark might sound as it circled trapped prey. "God! They were right about you."

"They?" I said. I frowned. "Who— ?"

Then he lunged, and my words cut off with a squeak.

It only took one stride of his long legs for him to loom over me. His big hands settled around my throat. They more than circled it.

His fingers flexed. His warm breath ruffled the top of my hair.

I felt my pulse beating frantically against his thumbs, putting the lie to every confident word I'd spoken.

"You *should* be frightened," he whispered. "Believe me, Katherine Stephenson. After what you did to me, you should be terrified."

I gritted my teeth. I looked up, feeling his calloused fingers shift against my throat with every movement.

He might be bigger and stronger than me in every way, but I would be *damned* if I would let myself be bullied.

"Until you started following me around like a lapdog, I'd never seen you in my life," I said. My voice was trembling, but I met his gaze square-on. "No matter what stories anybody has been telling you—"

"KAT!" My older brother's bellow whipped across the field like wildfire. "What the *devil* is going on here?"

I slumped with relief. For once, Charles had perfect timing.

My follower's hands fell away from my neck. I gave him my cockiest grin, relishing the look of chagrin on his face.

"Yes?" I said. "Won't you stay and meet my brother? We can have a lovely chat about all that gossip you've heard about me. I'm sure he'd love to hear you repeat it. We can—"

My voice cut off with a gasp as he grabbed my shoulders. His breath was hot against my ear.

"You might think I followed you," he whispered, "but you brought me exactly where I needed to be. And next time, there won't be any conversation. Next time, you're going to find out exactly how much you can lose, in payment for what you took from me."

My voice came out in a shameful squeak. "I told you, I didn't—"

It was too late. He had disappeared. I couldn't even sense a spell or magic-working to explain it.

I stood frozen for a moment. Then I gathered my wits and lunged forwards. Whether he was a witch or a Guardian, I knew invisibility I might not be able to see him, but I could still touch him if I knew where he was.

My hands passed through thin air. I let out a curse of sheer frustration. He couldn't run that fast, could he?

If there was one thing I knew how to do, it was how to break a spell or magic-working. Even if I couldn't sense the one he'd conjured, I knew it had to be in this field somewhere.

I closed my eyes. I waited until my head was buzzing with electric power. Then I let it all explode into the air around me: *NO!*

The power I'd released blew out like a candle. I staggered back, breathing hard. My chest burned with pain. My head was swimming.

A pair of strong hands caught my shoulders from behind. I shrieked and jumped, twisting away.

"Dash it, Kat! It's only me." Charles grabbed me again, pulling me close. The hug felt more comforting than I wanted to admit, but when I looked up, his face was ashen with panic. "What the devil did that fellow do to you?"

"I..." I struggled to catch my breath. I'd never seen my older brother look so afraid. It felt wrong, and it made my stomach hurt as well as my chest. "Nothing," I said, and straightened my shoulders. I forced a reassuring smile for his sake. "I'm fine. Truly. I am."

My smile didn't seem to have had the right effect. Charles's face flushed with rage. "Fine?" he said. "*Fine?* Oh, well, that's all right, then. Next you'll be telling me that that wasn't the very same fellow who saw you the other night, and tried to murder us all the next day because of it!"

"Well," I began. "The point is—"

"The point," said Charles, "is that I've found you running around on your own in the middle of nowhere. Again! When you knew for a fact there was a murderer coming after you. Don't you have any brains at all in your head?"

He didn't even wait for me to answer. "I'll wager the next thing you're going to tell me is that the blackguard wasn't even threatening you. Oh, no. He had his hands wrapped around your neck – *around your neck!* – only to tell you how much he admires your magic, no doubt!"

I rolled my eyes at my brother and pulled away, brushing down my dusty pelisse. "There's no need to be sarcastic."

"No need?" Charles said. His voice rose to a roar. "*No need?*"

There was obviously no point in trying to hold a rational conversation with him in this mood.

"Well," I said, "it was very kind of you to rescue me, but—" I stopped. "What are you doing here, anyway? Don't tell me the whole party's leaving the village already."

If Charles had been sent to gather us up, while Lady Fotherington was still out on her mission, there would be real trouble. I would wager anything that she'd blame me for it, too.

"Of course not," said Charles. "They're all settling in at the pub for a massive luncheon. Quite a decent-looking place, actually. I wouldn't have minded giving it a go myself, except..." His voice shifted to a martyred tone. "I knew, when I saw you go off with Lady Fotherington, you would never have the sense to stay with her for long. I just knew you would have run off from her by now and never even thought twice about the danger. Your blasted temper—"

"Ohhh!" I set my hands on my hips and glared at him. "For your information, that is not what happened at all. Lady Fotherington is the one who left. Not me! And it was Guardian business, so I'm not allowed to tell you about it."

If I'd thought that would settle him down, I was wrong. Charles only rolled his eyes. "Well, of course it all comes down to that dashed Order. Give me some credit, Kat. I knew that much the moment she called herself your godmother."

I winced. "Yes, well, you remember what I said in Bath..."

"Do I?" Charles heaved a sigh. "If you expect me to remember every wild story you've told at one point or another..."

I gritted my teeth. At times like this, it would have been so much easier to be an only child.

Luckily, I had ammunition of my own.

"How lovely it's been to have this conversation," I said

in my brightest and most social tone. "Have you said even one pleasant thing to Jane Carlyle yet, or were you saving all your wittiest remarks just for me?"

A dark flush spread across Charles's face. For the first time in our conversation, his gaze dropped. "I don't know what you're talking about."

"Oh, no?" I raised my eyebrows at him with withering contempt. "Do you know what the only thing you've said to her so far has been? I'll tell you. It was a growl. A growl! Don't you have any idea how to talk to young ladies? Or did they not teach that in any of your Oxford drinking clubs?"

"Dash it, Kat!" Charles jerked away to glower at the river beside the path.

Sunlight glinted off the water, but my brother looked as grim as if he were staring into an abyss.

"What would be the point?" he said. "You heard what she told you. Any men who've ever gambled or drunk to excess are to be shunned. That's what she thinks... and the worst of it is, she's right. I don't deserve to be anywhere near a girl like her, after all the things I've done. So what exactly would be the purpose of me trying to impress her?"

With his arms crossed and his blonde hair glinting in the sunlight, he looked just like a poet, romantic and desperate.

I rolled my eyes in sheer disgust. "Oh Lord," I said. "It's no wonder you were sent home from Oxford so many times."

"I was," Charles said, "and I deserved it. That's why—"

I overrode him ruthlessly. "That," I said, "is why it's lucky you have me as a sister."

"I beg your pardon?" A look of panic replaced the brooding despair on my brother's face. "Kat?" he said. His arms fell to his sides. "You aren't planning any more of

your wild schemes right now, are you? Kat? You wouldn't –
you couldn't—"

"Don't worry," I said, and reached up to pat his shoulder
comfortingly. "I'll take care of everything."

CHAPTER FIFTEEN

CHARLES CONTINUED TO SPUTTER FOR QUITE SOME TIME, but I didn't bother to listen. Now that I'd decided what to do, all that was left was to formulate a plan... and when it came to romantic strategy, there was no point in asking my older brother for suggestions. It would be far more sensible not to let him know what I was planning until it was too late for him to escape.

I let him go on talking as long as I could, in the hope that it would help him feel better. After all, lecturing me had always seemed to give Stepmama great relief. By the time Charles had followed me all the way to the bridge by the edge of the village where I was supposed to meet Lady Fotherington, though, it was time for me to be firm.

"I promised her not to let anyone see me," I explained for at least the third time. Really, it seemed to be taking an inordinate amount of time to imprint this very simple point on my older brother. I spoke as slowly and clearly as

I could. "If she finds you waiting with me, she'll be furious. So yes, I really do mean that you have to go away!"

He scowled down at me. "And if that scoundrel comes back while I'm gone?"

I shrugged, affecting lightness. "I don't expect him to return that quickly."

Next time..., he'd whispered into my ear. I repressed a shiver. The last thing I wanted was for Charles to realise I was actually afraid. It was horrifying enough to realise it myself. And I certainly wasn't going to give into my fear, especially when I was almost certain that I wasn't yet in any danger.

Surely my follower would want me to have more time to worry and to fret before he returned. Anyone who whispered such ominous threats into a person's ear must be hoping to torture them with at least a sleepless night or two before he came back to follow through. That was the whole point of issuing threats, wasn't it?

That was what I was hoping, anyway. And if I ever managed a moment or two on my own, I might even be able to puzzle out what on earth could have made him so furious at me in the first place.

Charles crossed his arms and stuck out his jaw. He looked approximately as movable as a granite cliff.

I groaned. "For heaven's sake! You can lurk nearby if you really must. Just make certain Lady Fotherington doesn't see you."

"You want me to lurk?" He blinked and looked around. "Where do you expect me to do that?"

It was a fair question. The old stone bridge was only wide enough for two slim people to walk side by side, and it was far too low for anyone to hide behind. The field of yellow gorse behind us wouldn't hide anyone over two feet tall, and the thatched cottages of the village beyond the bridge were too far away for him to keep anything like a proper eye on me.

I sighed. It was up to me to sort things out, as usual.

"Remember, you're the one who wanted to be here," I said.

I narrowed my eyes on his face and drew power up from the soles of my feet.

Can't see him, can't see him, can't see him...

Charles disappeared from view.

"Kat?" he said. All I could see were spiny gorse stalks waving in the breeze behind the spot where he'd been standing, but my brother's voice sounded as clear as ever, and just as outraged. "Dash it, Kat, what have you done this time? You haven't used any magic on me, have you? *Kat?*"

"Shh!" I said. I could sense more power coming my way, fast. Guardian power, this time: Lady Fotherington, transporting towards us using her portal. "Don't make any noise!" I hissed. "She can't see you."

"What— ?"

Golden specks swirled in a furious rush between us, and Charles's voice cut off. *Thank goodness.* I didn't know any magic-working powerful enough to keep my opinionated older brother silent.

The specks swirled into a familiar figure, vibrating with rage. Lady Fotherington brushed the dust off the skirts of her gown and her emerald-green spencer jacket in a series of slaps so hard that I was surprised not to see smoke swirling up from the top of her elaborate bonnet.

"How did your search go?" I asked sweetly.

Her head jerked up like a scent-hound who'd just caught the smell of prey. I had to force myself not to take a step backwards.

"I feel a magic-working. One of your magic-workings."

She snapped her head towards me and fixed me with her green gaze. "What are you doing? Tell me the truth. Now."

I rolled my eyes and prayed for Charles to keep silent. "What do you think I was doing? You left me alone for three hours. Is there anything I *could* do except practice? You know I'm supposed to be inducted into the Order as soon as you find those portals."

Her lips twisted. "Ah, yes. Perhaps there is a good reason not to find them after all." She straightened her skirts with one last yank and started across the bridge without looking back.

"Wait!" I hurried after her. Little though I wanted to do it, I knew my responsibilities. "I need to tell you about something that happened while you were gone."

"Out here?" Lady Fotherington cast one swift, dismissive look back at the field of gorse behind me and snorted. "Trust me, Katherine. You may be interested in the little dramas of rural life, but I have rather more urgent matters to attend to."

"It's magical," I said through gritted teeth. "There's a boy, just a few years older than me, who's been following me. He—"

"Really, Katherine." She kept on walking, and not for the first time, I cursed my shorter legs. I had to hurry to keep up with her as she tossed her words back to me like scraps to an over-eager puppy. "If some lout from a nearby farm has conceived an infatuation with you—"

"A *what?*" I was so shocked, I stopped walking.

Unfortunately, Charles didn't.

He crashed into me from behind and knocked me off my feet. With an undignified squeak I went flying forwards, face-first towards the grime-encrusted stones of the bridge.

Then Charles's hands caught my waist from behind. He pulled me backward just in time, an instant before I could hit the bridge. I landed back on my feet, panting. I swallowed hard, dusted off my skirts...

... and found Lady Fotherington staring at me from the end of the bridge.

"What in heaven's name do you think you're doing?" she said. "Have you taken up acrobatics now? I do realise that you are ill-suited for a future in Society, but I don't believe there are any travelling fairs quite desperate enough to hire you."

I took a deep breath. I willed the heat to drain out of my cheeks. For once, no matter how hard I tried, I couldn't quite force myself to meet her eyes.

At least Charles was still invisible. If I'd lost my magical focus, that might have made things even worse.

I said, with as much dignity as I could muster, "I was only surprised by what you said."

"About infatuation?" Lady Fotherington looked me up and down and let out a snort of laughter. "Well, perhaps you were right to react so strongly. After all..."

If I didn't interrupt her, I would have to kick her, and I had promised myself not to do that anymore. "It's not an infatuation. He's angry at me."

"Really? Imagine my surprise." Lady Fotherington shook her head and turned back towards the village.

Curse Charles! I could feel him shaking with silent laughter behind me, but I couldn't do anything to punish him for it, in case he made a noise and gave us both away.

I was starting to think that turning him invisible might have been a bad idea.

I balled my hands into fists and hurried after Lady Fotherington. "That isn't the point! When he came after me to threaten me—"

"My, what a fascinating life you do lead in your imagination," Lady Fotherington drawled. She didn't even slow her pace. "Was this how you entertained yourself the entire time I was gone? Spinning a new wild story just for my enjoyment? It's not that I'm not flattered, Katherine, but I'm afraid I've never taken much of an interest in any of your fictions."

I could feel a red haze creeping over my vision. I battled to hold it back. We were only fifty yards from the first of the cottages now. If I wasted my time shouting at her, I would lose my chance to safely talk about magic.

"The point is," I said, pushing my words at her back, "his magic was strong. Stronger than mine. It was so strong," I added, before she could take the opportunity to say something cutting, "that I couldn't even sense a magic-working or a spell as he did it. It was... oh, my Lord. I hadn't even thought of that!"

I stumbled to a halt as the realisation hit. This time I put one hand back to ward off Charles.

"Just like the person who stole the portals," I breathed. "Mr Gregson said no one could tell what kind of magic had been used to steal them, didn't he? He said there were no traces of magic left behind for identification. Exactly like today. Oh. My. Lord." I shook my head. "No wonder the portals have come to Devon. He was carrying them with him. My mysterious follower is the portal thief!"

☆ ☆

It took me a long moment to emerge from my daze of astonishment. When I finally did, I saw that Lady Fotherington had stopped walking. She stood with her back to me, one hand on her waist, her fingers tapping dangerously against her hip.

"There are so many things I dislike about you," she said. "It really is difficult to know where to start."

"Don't worry about that!" I waved it aside. I was almost staggering with the combination of shock and growing excitement. "Don't you see? He's not just somewhere in Devon. He's right here in this village with us! He followed me here from Yorkshire. All we need to do to get the portals back is—"

"No!" Lady Fotherington swung round. Her face was flushed; her eyes glittered. "Not another word, Katherine. Not one more word!"

I stared at her. "But—"

"You always need to be the centre of attention, don't you? Just like your mother. You always have to be the heroine of the hour." Her words rattled out so quickly, I could barely understand her. "When people think back to that catastrophe in Bath, do they think of those shocking public scenes you were involved in, and how close they came to betraying our Order's existence to Society? Do they even think – just think! – of the irreparable loss to our whole nation when our own hereditary Head abandoned us all?"

"Ah..."

"I'll tell you what they think. They think of Miss Katherine Stephenson and how she *saved us all*." Sarcasm dripped off her voice like venom. "What would we possibly have done without her? How could we possibly have survived?" She swept me with a look that made my whole body flush hot with shame and fury. "You must absolutely love it."

My skin felt as if it were covered with a thousand hot needles, all poking into me at once. I lifted my chin anyway and glared straight back at her. "I know what would have happened if I hadn't been there," I said, "and *so do you.*"

I didn't have to say the rest. We had both been there in that hidden room beneath the Baths when Lord Ravenscroft had revealed his treason. Lady Fotherington hadn't lifted a finger to fight against him, even when I had begged her for help. She had simply gone into shock, unable to take in the truth of his plans even when he stated them directly in front of her. He'd been her friend, and more than just a friend to her; I was... well, we all knew what she thought of me. Learning the truth must have felt like having the world turned upside down around her.

I said, "If you ignore the truth I'm telling you now, just like you did last time—"

"You couldn't bear being left behind this time, could you?" Lady Fotherington's face wasn't flushed anymore. It was white with anger. "You couldn't bear that I would be the one to save the Order instead of you. You couldn't bring yourself to let that happen, not even for the sake of preserving the Order itself. That's why you've created this mad story. You had to bring all our focus back to *you*, just where you've always wanted it.

"And that..." Her upper lip curled into a sneer. "That is why I have always been right about you, no matter what happened in Bath last autumn. *Always.*"

She stepped back. She lifted the skirts of her gown and twitched them as if I were a bug that had brushed against them.

"Enough," she said. "You can ride back in the carriage with the marquise, since she's taken such a fancy to you. You and I have nothing left to say to each other."

CHAPTER SIXTEEN

I WAITED UNTIL LADY FOTHERINGTON WAS OUT OF SIGHT before I let go of my magical focus. Charles appeared two feet behind me on the rough footpath.

"Don't," I said as he opened his mouth to speak. "Don't say anything about it. Please."

He looked at me for a long moment. My eyes felt hot; my chest was tight and prickling. I looked down so I wouldn't have to see his face.

He shrugged. "All right," he said. "It's time to meet the others, anyway. I'll see you there, shall I?"

He strode past me easily on his long legs. On the way, he reached out a hand to clap me companionably on my back. It was just the sort of gesture he would have made to one of his ridiculous Oxford friends. But it felt surprisingly good.

Or maybe it was just that everything else felt so bad.

I let myself sink down onto the footpath after he'd left, curling my legs up underneath me. I tipped my face up to the sky and watched the clouds so I wouldn't have to think.

At the end of five minutes, though, I drew a deep breath and stood up, brushing off my skirts. No matter how I felt or what I wanted, there was one truth that trumped all the rest. If I curled up and hid from Lady Fotherington for the rest of the afternoon, that would mean that she had won... and that she was right about me.

I started down the footpath to the village.

Luckily, it was easy to find the rest of the party. The whole village was tucked into the side of a cliff, along a single cobbled road that wound back and forth, lined by houses, all the way down to the beach and the fishing boats below.

There was only one pub, the Rose and Anchor, and it was set directly at the top of the village square, overlooking rows and rows of slate rooftops and the blue sea below. It was a big, rambling, white building framed by ancient-looking timber, and the landlord had set an assortment of rough wooden tables and benches across the square to take advantage of the bright sunlight

Of course, the only proper way for any lady to eat at a pub was in a stuffy private parlour well removed from the common crowd... but as I took in the scene before me, my lips curved into a decidedly unladylike grin.

It was a good thing Mrs Carlyle had refused to come along on this expedition. The very sight of her son, his fiancée, and all their gathered wedding guests sitting outside in the village square in broad daylight, laughing, eating and drinking in full sight of every passerby would have sent her into strong palpitations.

It was exactly like Frederick Carlyle to have organised it, though... and exactly what made him so perfect for Angeline.

"Kat!" He spotted me across the square and waved me over to their table. "There you are! We've already ordered for you."

Angeline sent me a smile, Charles patted the bench beside him, and I felt some of the knots inside me begin to relax. I walked over to join them, picking my way over the bumpy, beach-stone cobbles and breathing in the tangy, fish-laced breeze.

It was a genuine delight to see the pained look on Lady Fotherington's face as she sat ramrod-straight on her bench at a plain wooden table on the edge of the square, only five feet away from a group of village women who stood chatting together on their way home from the market. All of them, I was pleased to see, were carrying large buckets full of goggle-eyed fish. Lady Fotherington winced every time she caught sight of them.

Her ladyship was obviously not accustomed to such informal dining conditions.

I wasn't quite ready to face her again, though, despite everything I'd told myself back by the bridge. So I was grateful that Angeline, Frederick, Jane Carlyle, and Charles had all gathered at a small table at the opposite end of the square, giving me a perfect excuse to avoid her. I slid onto the bench between Charles and Angeline, facing away from the pub and away from Lady Fotherington, and happily accepted a bowl of soup.

The sea below glittered blue in the sunshine. Fishing boats bobbed along the water in a scattered mass, white and red and yellow and green, while women worked on long nets along the pebbled beach. I took a deep breath and felt the energy of it all rush through my body.

"This is wonderful," I said.

"Isn't it?" Frederick Carlyle turned to gaze down at the

beach below. "I always forget, while I'm away, how much I love it here. And I really shouldn't say this, but..." He lowered his voice and turned back to me, raising his glass. "If you want to experience something really wonderful, you should have just a taste of this house brandy."

"Frederick!" Jane Carlyle said. "How can you say such a thing! As if Miss Katherine would ever dream of drinking strong spirits. A vicar's daughter, Frederick!"

"Miss Katherine," Angeline said dryly, "is prone to all sorts of adventures, but judging by where we are..." She narrowed her eyes at the endless blue water. "How far are we from France?"

"Travelling by boat, on a few cloudy nights, with a good lantern..." Frederick met her gaze with an implausibly innocent expression. "Are you trying to imply something about this delicious brandy?"

"Only," said Angeline, "that I expect it's had even more adventures than Kat."

"What on earth are you two talking about?" I said.

"These cliffs." Frederick gestured with his glass at the rugged cliffs all along the bay, stretching into the distance. "They're full of hidden caves. It's a perfect playground for children – I spent half my life running around them as a boy."

"Oh, I remember that!" Jane Carlyle had been looking disapproving ever since brandy had been mentioned, but now her expression melted into sheer wistfulness. "We spent hours hunting for new caves while Aunt Delilah thought we were playing safely in the gardens. If she'd had any notion what we were really doing—"

"Or if your father had found out his cherished only daughter was crawling up and down cliffs in the most precarious manner..." Frederick gave an exaggerated shudder. "Have I mentioned that my uncle is a former cavalry officer, with a roar to freeze the heart of any ten-year-old boy?"

"I loved those summers," Jane Carlyle said. But her face looked oddly melancholy, for such happy memories.

I didn't have time to wonder about that, though, as Frederick continued.

"Those caves may be bliss for children, but they're an absolute treasure trove for smugglers. The coastal guard's too thinly spread to hunt down even half their hiding places."

"Aha," said Angeline. "And considering that we're not far from France..."

"Exactly." Frederick swirled the brandy in his glass. "My mother – like most of the other landowners – has always chosen to ignore the 'free trade', as they call it around these parts... which is, at least, a step up from the old days, when the family used their old priest holes and passageways to hide some of the smuggled casks."

"Priest holes?" I said. "Passageways?" I sat up straighter. "Do you mean to say you actually have *secret passageways* in your house?"

"Look out, Frederick." Angeline was grinning as she put a warning hand on his arm. "If you let Kat know about those..."

"Too late," said Charles, and sighed mournfully. "We'll never see her again. She'll be lost in the bowels of Hepworth forevermore. A hundred years from now, they'll know her only as the family ghost. She'll torture all your poor descendants by wandering around wringing her hands and moaning, 'If only I'd listened to my family's good advice – '"

"Oh, be quiet!" I swatted him on the arm. But everyone at the table was laughing now, and Jane Carlyle was looking at Charles with a definite glint of interest in her blue eyes.

"I'll show you the secret passageways myself," Frederick promised. "There's one that starts in one of the guest rooms, actually – I believe it's where your sister Elissa will be staying. It leads straight down into the cliffs. I haven't been down there in years, but—"

"It starts in Elissa's room?" I stared at him. "That is so unjust! Elissa would never explore a secret passageway. Why didn't you put me and Angeline there?"

"Probably because you *would* explore a secret passageway," Angeline said. "And the last thing any of us need this week is you running around on midnight explorations."

Charles cleared his throat pointedly. I glared at him.

"Anyway!" I turned back to Frederick, pointedly ignoring both my siblings. "You were talking about how your mother ignores the smugglers?"

"Good try, Kat," Charles murmured. He leaned back, crossing his arms and spreading his legs under the table. "But not quite good enough."

"Have no fear," Angeline said to him. "Elissa and I will keep an eye on her every minute she's in that room."

Jane Carlyle let out a muffled giggle.

I gritted my teeth.

Frederick only grinned and took another sip of his brandy. "My mother ignoring the smugglers?" he said to me. "Yes, that's right. Of course, turning a blind eye to the free trade is the easiest thing to do, and if it were only a matter of smuggled spirits, I wouldn't take too strong a stance against it myself. With the war against France heating up, though, brandy isn't the only thing being smuggled across the water nowadays."

I thought of Lord Ravenscroft and grimaced. It would have been smugglers who carried his treasonous messages back and forth to France. They would have carried him, too, if I hadn't thwarted his plans. "If the Customs officers can't stop them, though..."

"A group of really determined local men might, if I could organise the villagers and the other landowners against them. The smugglers aren't popular sorts around here, just good at frightening people into submission. And now that I'm twenty-one and can finally start taking care of what needs to be done..."

He stopped, his brows drawing together, and looked between me and Angeline. "What? What's amiss?"

"Nothing," said Angeline, and looked down at her soup.

I said, "But what about your mother? Isn't she still in charge?"

"Mama?" He shrugged. "Hasn't anyone explained it to you yet? She'll be moving to the dower house after the wedding, so Angeline and I can take over – what?" He leaned forward, his frown deepening. "There is something wrong, isn't there?"

"*Nothing*," Angeline repeated, and stepped hard on my foot under the table.

Oh, for heaven's sake. "It's hardly a secret," I muttered. "Everyone in the drawing room yesterday heard her say it."

"We'll talk about it later," Angeline said, in a voice like steel.

I rolled my eyes. "Fine. But if you ask me—"

"We'll talk about it now," said Frederick Carlyle. All his easy good humour was gone; his voice sounded every bit as steely as Angeline's had. "What did Mama say to you while I was gone?"

Angeline sighed and looked up. Her colour was

heightened, but her voice was perfectly steady. "Nothing that need worry you," she said.

His eyes narrowed. He leaned closer, putting his soup in serious danger. "And what is that supposed to mean?"

Honestly, if I didn't step in, this conversation would never go anywhere.

"She's not moving out," I told him.

Frederick blinked. "I beg your pardon?"

"It's not—" Angeline began.

I talked over her. "She wrote to your uncle, because he still makes all the important decisions, and he agreed that she would stay in Hepworth to manage things instead of moving to the dower house, because they think Angeline isn't refined enough to – ouch!"

Both of my siblings had stepped on my feet at once. I curled my aching toes and glared at them both. "That was hardly—"

"That's enough, Kat." Angeline's cheeks were decidedly flushed now. She darted a swift glance under her lashes at Jane Carlyle before looking back at her fiancé. "I didn't say anything before because there's nothing for you to worry about. I'm—"

"Nothing to worry about?" Frederick repeated. He let out a sharp, humourless bark of laughter. "First Mama wrote to my uncle without telling me, and no doubt gave him the worst sort of description of you, my future bride. Then she announced their decision to you in the most humiliating way possible, in front of all my relatives, before I'd even been informed – and you think there's nothing for me to worry about?"

His voice never rose to a shout or a bellow. But by his last words, the air around him was positively vibrating with tension. The rest of the wedding guests could sense it too.

The tables around us grew silent and Carlyles craned their necks to take in the confrontation.

Angeline's shoulders hunched. She lowered her voice to a near-whisper. "Frederick, you cannot afford to offend your uncle. He has made his decision, and whether we like it or not, he's going to remain your guardian for the next nine years. There's nothing you can do about it."

If I'd ever doubted that Frederick Carlyle knew my sister, I was proven wrong now.

"There's nothing *I* can do about it?" he repeated. He'd lowered his voice to a whisper to match Angeline's, but it had the odd effect of making his tone sound even more dangerous. "Aha. So there's something you're planning to do about it instead. And it never even occurred to you to ask me for help?"

"Well..." She looked around our tiny group and bit her lip. "You don't have to worry," she said again. "I'll take care of it myself. If there was anything you could do... but there isn't, is there? So what would have been the point of telling you? I didn't want to upset you for no reason, or—"

"You didn't want to upset me?" He shook his head, but his gaze never wavered from her face. "You think I'm too much of a weakling to stand up against my mother."

"That's not—"

"You do," he said. "You think that if I have to choose between you and her, you'll lose. Or worse, that even if I do stand up for you, *I'll* lose. That's it, isn't it?"

"Frederick..."

"After all this time," he said, "you still don't completely believe in me, do you? No matter what you say, no matter what I do, in your mind, it's still Angeline against the world. You still don't trust me to stand by your side."

Beside me, Charles cleared his throat. "Ah," he said.

"Ah, Carlyle. Perhaps we might all just—"

"Isn't the weather fine today?" Jane Carlyle said brightly at exactly the same time. "Why this breeze is positively – oh, I do beg your pardon, Mr Stephenson. I didn't mean to interrupt..."

Charles flushed. "No, no, it wasn't... That is, I didn't..."

They both trailed off in mutual confusion and politeness. But none of it had mattered.

Frederick Carlyle paid no attention to either of them. All his attention was fixed on my sister.

"Believe me, Angeline," he said. "It's too late not to upset me."

He stood up, tossing his napkin aside. "I'm going down to the beach, by myself. I need a walk and some air."

"I'll come with you." Angeline set down her soup spoon and started up, smoothing down her skirts. "Just give me a moment to—"

"No," Frederick told her. "Don't bother. Why should you even want to?"

He looked straight into her eyes and shook his head. "You obviously don't think you can count on me for anything. So I'd rather you didn't come."

CHAPTER SEVENTEEN

"OH, DEAR," SAID JANE CARLYLE.

Five minutes had passed since Frederick Carlyle had stalked off in the direction of the beach. Angeline had lasted only half a minute longer before stalking off in the opposite direction.

Gossip swelled and swirled around the tables. Only our half-empty table had stayed stunned and silent until now.

"It's my fault," I said. I stared down at the broth rippling gently in my soup bowl. Despite the cool breeze, my face was hot and my eyes were burning.

Lady Fotherington had been right about me.

"I shouldn't have told him," I said to the soup. I couldn't make myself raise my eyes to my brother, or to Frederick's cousin. I didn't want to see the accusing looks on their faces.

If I'd listened to Angeline, if I hadn't told Frederick about his mother, they would both still be here now. They would both still be happy and in love and ecstatic to be together. But because of me...

"Don't be stupid, Kat," said Charles. "He would have found out sooner or later."

"Mr Stephenson is right," Jane Carlyle said. She reached across the table to cover my hand with her own. "You mustn't blame yourself, Miss Katherine. Aunt Delilah has always been very good to me, but I have to admit she can be a bit... well, a bit..." She sighed. "Well, you mustn't blame yourself, anyway."

"Come on." Charles nudged my arm roughly. "You might as well eat the rest of your soup before it goes completely cold."

I picked up my spoon and raised my eyes. They were both watching me, looking worried. Neither of them looked angry or accusing.

I wasn't at all convinced that they were right. But I lifted a spoonful of broth to my lips and forced myself to swallow it so they wouldn't worry anymore.

Silence fell over our table again. Gulls cried overhead. Snatches of conversation carried from the other tables.

"... cannot be a good sign, can it?"

"... only three days until the wedding..."

I could see Stepmama looking rigid with embarrassment two tables away, even as the marquise chatted gaily away beside her, as if nothing in the world were wrong. The marquise's voice rose, liltingly, above the rest of the gossip.

"... and then the earl said...!"

The rest of their table dissolved into laughter.

Jane Carlyle said softly, "I always loved my summers here."

She was looking over her shoulder at the rows of slate roofs tucked into the cliff below us, and her lips had curved into a wistful smile.

"Papa sent me here every summer after my mother died. It really was like paradise to me. To have the sea so close and Cousin Frederick to play with..." She hesitated, looking embarrassed. "I suppose Papa must have really sent me here because of that foolish notion he and Aunt Delilah had that we would be married one day... but of course Frederick and I had no idea of that in those days. And as my aunt only wanted us by her side for half an hour a day – and Cousin Frederick was a positive demon at getting free of his tutors..."

The curve of her lips took on a wicked curl, and I heard Charles let out a wistful sigh beside me.

"I spent every day of those summers running about climbing cliffs, building forts, shooting pistols and doing all the other things no young lady is supposed to know how to do," Jane Carlyle said. "Those were the most marvellous summers of my life."

I was afraid my brother might actually forget himself and let out a groan of longing at any moment. So I spoke quickly.

"It's no wonder you're so close to your cousin, then."

"Oh, yes." She paused and nibbled her full lower lip. Under the table, I put a steadying hand on Charles's arm. "I... I don't know exactly how much it would be right for me to say to you – as I said, I do owe Aunt Delilah a great debt of gratitude, and—"

"Never mind all that," I said. "We're practically family now."

"That's true." She brightened and leaned forward, dropping her voice to a whisper. "I don't know if your sister realises just how good she's been for Frederick. He's been under a great deal of pressure for so many years, you see, ever since his father died. My aunt is... well, of course she does dote on him, as everybody knows, but, well..."

"Only as long as he does exactly what she wants him to do?" I supplied.

"Yes, exactly." Jane sighed. "And you know Frederick – he is a most independent-minded man. But he does truly love his mother, and he hates feeling that he's hurt her in any way. And every time he's ever done anything she's disapproved of, she's reacted by swooning and taking to her bed with violent convulsions or nervous distemper for days, and telling him it was all his fault...so, well, you can see his difficulty."

Charles grimaced, and I nodded. It was only too easy to imagine.

"So," Jane continued, "these last months, as he's been forced to fight her every step of the way to finally set a date for the wedding – and then keep it – no matter how unwell the very mention of it made her, every single time..." She shrugged delicately.

Ouch. Of course I'd known that the wedding had been delayed and delayed, but somehow I'd never thought about it from Frederick's point of view. Still...

"Angeline loves him," I said firmly.

"Oh, of course she does!" Jane's eyes widened. "That is perfectly obvious. And if you had seen him springing the horses to get home to her these last two days..." She giggled infectiously. "Well! All I'll say is, I never knew my cousin had it in him. And *that* is why I think your sister is so good for him. Because of her, he's finally steeling himself to do what he needs to do in regard to my aunt, no matter how painful it may be for both of them. But all the same..."

She sighed and glanced down at the beach. Frederick's figure was a tiny spot in the distance. "Well, you can see why he would take it so badly when he thought Miss Stephenson didn't trust him to do it."

"Yes." I sighed and sat back on the bench.

It was too much for me to solve, at least right now. Even thinking about all the angles of it made my head hurt.

But one point had finally, belatedly occurred to me as I'd listened to the last part of her story. As Jane Carlyle had leaned across the table to share her whispered thoughts, Charles had gradually leaned further and further backwards, his expression looking more and more pained, as if he could force himself to physically resist her appeal...

And I had realised exactly what I had before me, right now, at this half-empty table.

It was the perfect opportunity to start Charles's campaign.

I cleared my throat. I batted my eyelashes. I set my plan into action.

"Charles," I said. "May I have a sip of your drink?"

"Ah—"

"Oh, Miss Katherine, you mustn't let my cousin's foolish joke rankle you," Jane Carlyle said hastily. "No one would ever seriously expect you to drink hard spirits! Tell her, Mr Stephenson—"

"Well," Charles began.

"But it's only a fruit cordial," I said. "Isn't it, Charles?"

"Er..."

"You see?" I scooped up his cup and took a long sip. "Mm. Elderflower cordial. Delicious." I beamed at both of them. "Charles never drinks hard spirits, you know."

Charles gaped at me.

Jane Carlyle said, "Really?" and turned to look at my brother. I gave him a helpful nudge, to remind him to close his mouth.

"Oh, yes," I said. "Why, he made the decision to give them up months and months ago – last September, wasn't it, Charles?"

"Well," my brother said, "that is, well, yes, I did, but that was only because—"

"What a remarkable decision to make!" Jane was gazing at him with outright admiration now. "And so rare for any gentleman. Why, even Cousin Frederick *will* insist on drinking a glass or two of brandy or ale now and then, no matter how often I warn him of their dangers."

"Charles made the decision without any persuasion," I said. "It was all his own idea."

"My goodness!" She tilted her head, studying him with deep interest. "Mr Stephenson, I had no idea you were such a moralist."

"Well," Charles said. "Ah. Indeed." He reached for his elderflower cordial and took a desperate gulp.

"Oh, Charles is quite the moralist," I said. "Why, it was only two nights ago that he told me how tedious he finds gambling – remember, Charles?"

Charles choked on his cordial. I politely ignored his coughing and gasping, but I was pleased to see the look of concern grow on Jane Carlyle's face as she watched him.

"My dears." The marquise spoke behind me at the same time that her warm hand descended on my shoulder. "I do hate to interrupt your conversation, but I think it best that we find your sister and Mr Carlyle before the gossip becomes too intense. Of course, lovers' quarrels are perfectly natural, but in these particular circumstances, with so many guests eager to report back to their hostess..."

She shook her head. "I've persuaded your stepmama and papa to remain at their table, so as not to give the impression that the family is worried – but Miss Carlyle, if you wouldn't mind, do you think you might be able to search out your cousin on the beach? Do see if you can persuade him to put on a show of his usual good humour when he returns, no matter how distressed he may be feeling. And Charles, if you could possibly find Angeline and do the same? Katherine, you may come back to my table with me, as I told all my neighbours I was coming here to steal you – and my dears, you will all be sure to act as if nothing were amiss, won't you?"

"Of course," Jane Carlyle said, and set down her napkin with a decisive swish. "I'll find a maid from the inn to accompany me."

Still coughing, Charles waved one hand in agreement to the plan. He swung his long legs over our bench to stand up.

Their gazes crossed. Jane Carlyle smiled. Her eyelashes lowered.

Charles tugged at his cravat as if it had suddenly become too tight.

I smiled in perfect satisfaction.

✧ ✧

Unfortunately, my pleasure didn't last long.

Even after Angeline and Frederick were retrieved, it was obvious that neither of them was feeling any happier. Oh, they both smiled polite, social smiles and joined in with the general conversation like the perfect host and hostess, but neither of them fooled me for an instant. During the few, brief moments when Angeline and Frederick had to speak directly to each other, their eyes didn't meet even once.

It was almost enough to make me regret finishing

my soup. But it was something else that made my stomach really start to churn: the look of gratitude on Stepmama's face, directed at the woman who'd arranged us all so neatly. The woman who'd stepped up to save Angeline's reputation among the Carlyles as easily and as naturally as if it were her own responsibility... or as if Angeline were her own daughter.

And if she was...

My stomach clenched sickeningly as the full implication finally hit me.

If I was right about the marquise, what did that mean for Stepmama? Was her marriage to Papa even valid? Or had she been tricked in the most heartless way possible, just to save all of our reputations?

As Angeline and Frederick Carlyle looked everywhere but at each other, I looked back and forth between the marquise, her dark eyes laughing and dangerously intelligent, and my stepmother, who hung admiringly on the marquise's every word.

Now I really wished I hadn't eaten any soup.

CHAPTER EIGHTEEN

BETWEEN MY CHURNING STOMACH AND MY CHURNING mind, the carriage ride back to Hepworth seemed to last forever. Every friendly word exchanged by the marquise and Stepmama made me feel worse.

It didn't even help that I'd spent my entire childhood wishing my stepmother didn't exist.

I remembered Stepmama slicing every string out of my mother's enchanted harp when she first arrived in our house, because it wouldn't stop singing the name Olivia. I'd been only seven years old at the time. I'd huddled into Elissa's protective embrace, Angeline pale with fury beside us, as Stepmama raged through the house, removing every reminder of our mother and locking them all away in a cabinet none of us were allowed to open.

I had never truly hated anyone before that day.

But that had been a full six years ago. For six years Stepmama had lectured and pried and managed us all, and she had never let us forget how difficult she found it to be our stepmother, particularly when it came to me and Charles and Angeline... but she had never, ever left us, no matter how angry we made her.

Of course, that was only because she considered us her duty – and her burden, as she'd added often enough – but still...

I remembered her unexpectedly standing up for me against her wealthy cousin last autumn, when I had got myself into so much trouble in front of all the most important people in Bath.

She would never be my mother. But if Papa and Mama really had used her so shabbily, I didn't know how it could ever be forgiven.

I didn't blame Papa for pulling out a book to hide behind the very moment the carriage ride began. I only wished that I could do the same.

As soon as the carriage stopped, though, I was ready. I followed the marquise and Stepmama down the carriage steps, then bolted for the front doors.

"Katherine!" Stepmama couldn't shout – not in front of all the other guests – but her hiss carried through the air like a bullet. "What do you think you're doing?"

"So sorry," I called back without turning round. The butler was standing by the doorway looking more appalled than ever, but I headed for the opening anyway, dodging all the wandering groups of Carlyles heading in the same direction. "I really must—"

"Miss Katherine!" A warm hand tucked into my arm, pulling me to a stop. "There you are." Jane Carlyle beamed at me. "I was hoping to find you again. We were having such an interesting conversation earlier."

"Ah..." I shot a quick look back at Stepmama, who was

stalking towards me with danger in her eyes. "We were?"

Jane Carlyle's skin pinkened behind her freckles. "Why, yes. You were telling me – that is, we were discussing strong spirits and, ah, gentlemen who refrained from—"

"Oh, *Charles!*" Now I remembered. *Dash it!* I needed this time alone to think, if I was to solve any of the problems facing me. But I could hardly stop midway through Charles's romantic campaign, could I?

Her flush deepened as I said his name. "Well... that isn't exactly what I—"

"Yes?" Charles spoke directly behind me. "Were you calling me, Kat?"

Jane Carlyle's face could have lit a fire as he stepped up beside me, looming over both of us. I let out a groan of frustration as I looked from the two of them to the crowd of Carlyles who'd got between me and the door, and to Stepmama, who was only a few feet behind me. The marquise had disappeared, probably to change into yet another fabulous gown, but I had missed my opportunity to flee.

So much for time to think.

"Never mind," I said glumly to both of them. "I think it's time for tea."

We followed the rest of the crowd towards the Rose Drawing Room, the site of my public embarrassment the day before. Of course, Papa had managed to escape into the library while Stepmama was occupied with me. Papa always did manage to escape, unlike me.

With every step I took, my mood fouled even more. Then, ten feet from the open doorway, I heard something that broke through my gloom: voices mingling inside the drawing room. Not just voices: *familiar* voices.

Elissa and her husband had finally arrived.

I grabbed my brother's arm. "Charles!"

He grinned down at me. "Well, brat? Aren't you going to go running in there like a madwoman to jump on her?"

"No!" I tried to glare at him, but it didn't work. My own grin couldn't be repressed. My eldest sister was finally here, after all our months apart, and I felt as if I could fly from sheer excitement.

I bounced up onto my tiptoes to peer over the groups of Carlyles in front of me, all moving at a pace that was suddenly much too slow for my liking. "Of course I'm not going to jump on her," I told Charles, as I craned my neck for a better view. "I do have some sense of propriety, you know."

He snorted and pushed me back down until my feet were pressed firmly against the floor. "Not that I've noticed," he said.

Jane Carlyle was looking at both of us as if we'd suddenly gone mad.

I said, "Anyway, she would be horrified if I did that in front of all the Carlyles."

"I know," said Charles. "That's why I was looking forward to it."

"You—!" I punched his arm with my free hand.

He laughed.

Jane Carlyle said, "What are you two—? *Oh.*" She stopped still as we reached the open doorway.

"Papa," she whispered.

I barely heard her. All of my attention was focused on the two beloved people who were sitting together on the rose silk sofa, drinking tea with Mrs Carlyle, and a big, burly, grey-haired man I didn't recognise.

It had been one hundred and twenty-four days exactly since I'd last seen my eldest sister. As I saw her now, her fair hair piled into fashionable ringlets around her face and her head tilted in a perfect semblance of deep interest in whatever Mrs Carlyle was saying, warmth spread through my entire body, accompanied by sheer relief.

Elissa might be the prissiest female in all England, but she always knew the proper thing to do. *Always.* She would know exactly what to think about the marquise and Stepmama, and how to manage awful Mrs Carlyle, and she would find a way to reconcile Angeline and Frederick somehow. All I had to do was tell her everything that had gone wrong in our family without her.

I started forward, pulling Charles with me.

Her husband, Mr Collingwood, saw me first. His face brightened as he nudged her arm.

Elissa's blue eyes met mine across all the Carlyles in between and her face broke into a smile of pure delight. She looked even paler than usual, but she was still one of the most beautiful people I had ever seen, and in her new London clothing she was effortlessly elegant. Pride filled me to bursting as I noticed the Carlyles looking at her with open admiration.

She waited politely until Mrs Carlyle was finished speaking, then rose to her feet and started straight towards us, past the tea table piled high with cups and cakes.

"Kat," she said. "And Charles!"

I barely noticed Mr Collingwood shifting on the couch behind her with an oddly nervous look. I was too busy beaming at my oldest sister as I walked towards her with all the grace and dignity that she'd ever begged me to remember.

I didn't run. I didn't even hurry...

And that was why I wasn't close enough to catch her when her eyes rolled up in her head and she collapsed in a swoon.

✦ ✦ ✦

Gasps filled the room. I was frozen with shock, but Mr Collingwood and Charles weren't. They both lunged towards her as she fell.

They were both too late.

Elissa hit her head with a sharp crack on the over-burdened tea table. One of the table legs buckled and collapsed.

"My best china!" Mrs Carlyle cried.

A second leg cracked, and the table tipped.

The gilded china teapot, silver tea tray, and half a dozen thin china cups, saucers and cake plates slid in an avalanche onto the floor. The sound of shattering china filled the air as tea flooded the Chinese carpet and streamed across the skirts of Elissa's fashionable gown.

Mrs Carlyle put one hand to her eyes and fell back onto the sofa. "Oh, my smelling salts – someone find them, quickly!"

Carlyles came fluttering to her aid from across the room. I ignored them all as I pushed my way to Elissa's side. Charles and Mr Collingwood were already bending over her. Shards of china dug into my skin as I dropped to my knees beside them, mashing slices of cake into the wet carpet.

"What's wrong with her?" I said. "Elissa! Elissa, wake up! Why isn't she waking up? *What's wrong with her?*" I repeated, turning to my brother-in-law. He was cradling her head in his arms, looking as anguished as I felt.

Mr Collingwood had been born to look the part of a dashing Gothic villain, with his dark hair and eyes and great hook nose, but he had the heart of the mildest sheep imaginable. So it was a genuine shock to hear him say: "I can't tell you."

"You can't tell us?" I stared at him. My shock was rapidly transforming into anger. "What are you talking about? You mean you *won't* tell us—"

"Come on, Kat," said Charles. "We need to get Elissa somewhere with a bed and some peace and quiet. And then," he added, turning an unfriendly look on our brother-in-law, "perhaps Collingwood will see fit to tell us exactly what's happened to our sister."

Mr Collingwood swallowed visibly. I didn't blame him. This new Charles was capable of looking quite frightening when he really tried.

Angeline spoke behind us in a cold, controlled tone that told me just how worried she really was. "They should have a bedroom already prepared. Mrs Carlyle?"

"Oh, I can't be bothered with tedious household matters now! Cannot you see how distraught I am? Frederick, my Kashmir shawl—"

"Henshawe!" Frederick Carlyle's tone was surprisingly commanding; it took me a moment to realise he wasn't replying to his mother but addressing the butler, who had followed him into the room. "Escort the Collingwoods to their bedroom, if you please. And send one of the maids for my mother's shawl."

"Frederick!" His mother's gasp was nearly a shriek. "I want you to find the shawl yourself! At a time like this, when I am so unwell—"

"Yes, sir," Henshawe murmured, and inclined his head to our family group with cold courtesy. "Will Mrs Collingwood require a footman to carry her?"

Elissa's eyes were already beginning to flutter open. She started to lift her head from Mr Collingwood's arms, then let out a moan of pain that made my chest hurt.

"She won't need a footman," Charles said, and reached for her.

He was too late. "I have her," said Mr Collingwood.

He rose to his feet, cradling her in his arms. With her head tipped back and her fair hair spilling over his black-clad arm, it was a moment directly out of one of Elissa's favourite novels.

I remembered how some of those novels ended, though, and I wasn't amused.

I took Angeline's hand as we followed the butler out of the room.

Stepmama trailed well behind us, making such anxious, bleating noises that I finally turned to look back at what was worrying her.

Well. At least that was one mystery I could solve without any difficulty. As usual, our stepmother was far more worried about respectability than about any of us.

The burly, grey-haired man beside Mrs Carlyle was glowering at us ferociously, and all the older female Carlyles were clucking around our hostess in deep distress. Stepmama's face looked nearly green with anxiety as she looked back and forth between Elissa's limp body and the social chaos we'd left behind. Even Jane Carlyle was looking as horrified as if she'd seen a ghost, and Mrs Carlyle had wrapped both hands around Frederick's wrist to restrain him from coming with us.

I snorted and tightened my grip on Angeline's hand, turning my back on all of it. I didn't give a hang what any of the Carlyles thought. Elissa mattered more than any of them.

By the time we finally arrived at her bedroom, on the far side of the third floor, Elissa's eyes were open, but her face still looked deathly pale. She smiled reassuringly at Mr Collingwood as he set her down on the canopied bed, but I didn't miss the way her face had tightened with the move. Based on the crack I'd heard when she fell, she must have developed a tremendously painful bump on the back of her head by now.

Standing in the doorway, the butler cleared his throat and looked down his nose at our hovering family group. His gaze passed over Mr Collingwood's elegant figure with just as much disdain as it did over the rest of us, and I realised I'd been wrong about Henshawe when I first met him. He didn't look down on our family in particular; he looked down on nearly everyone, regardless of social rank.

I supposed that was an improvement of sorts.

"A maid will bring Mrs Collingwood a cold compress and a hot posset," he announced.

"Oh, no." Elissa's voice was faint. "You mustn't worry..."

"No, ma'am," Henshawe said witheringly. "I never do."

He turned and glided out of the room with regal grace, closing the door behind him.

"Well, then." Angeline sank down on the mattress by Elissa's knees and reached for our sister's hand. She was smiling, but her dark eyes were watchful. "What was that all about? If you really wanted to make a scene, you know, all you had to do was throw a teacup or two. There was no need to hurt yourself in the process."

Elissa cringed and put her free hand over her eyes. "Oh! I am so sorry for my behaviour, Angeline. And so mortified! I cannot believe I—"

"Don't be a ninny," I said. "We all know you couldn't help it." I climbed onto the other side of Elissa's bed and tugged her hand away from her face. It felt reassuringly warm – but then, my own hands were still cool from the air outside. I peered into her eyes, frowning. "What's wrong with you?"

"Nothing," she said. "Truly, Kat."

"Nothing?" I repeated. I could feel Charles moving to

stand behind me. I hoped he was crossing his arms at her the way he'd crossed them at me that morning, and giving her his impressive new threatening scowl, too.

I drew myself up, squeezing Elissa's hand hard between both of mine, and gave her my own most furious look. "'Nothing' doesn't make you swoon," I told my oldest sister. "'Nothing' doesn't make you see a physician and then send letters that scare the wits out of all your family without even telling them anything useful! 'Nothing' doesn't—"

"Oh, Kat!" she gasped.

She was making the most alarming stifled noises. For a horrible moment I was afraid I'd made her cry.

Then I realised she was trying not to laugh.

"I couldn't possibly explain it in my letter," she said to me and Angeline and Charles and Stepmama. "It would have been far too improper! But now that I can finally say it privately..."

She pulled her hands free from me and from Angeline. She turned away from all of us to her husband, who was standing by her pillow. She took his hands in hers and beamed up at him as lovingly as if he were the only one in the room.

"We are going to have a baby," she said.

CHAPTER NINETEEN

MY MOUTH FELL OPEN. NO WORDS CAME OUT.

But one person in the room wasn't too shocked to speak.

"I knew it!" Stepmama cried. She bustled up to the side of the bed, her face vivid with satisfaction. "Oh, when I saw that letter I just knew what it must be. Elissa, my dear, you have done so well! Already in an interesting condition, less than a year after your wedding – oh, what all my friends will say when they hear the news! Why, Mrs Glossop's daughter has still not shown any signs of increasing after more than three *years* of matrimony! And my own cousin Eleanor's daughter-in-law, who has been married for nearly *five* years, *if* you can believe it..."

Someone had to stop her. I shook myself out of my daze and took action.

"Well," I said. "At least now Mrs Carlyle can't blame you for swooning onto her tea table."

"Oh, no!" Elissa's dreamy smile was replaced by a look of pure horror. "You mustn't tell her, Kat. You mustn't tell anyone!"

I blinked. "But..."

"I couldn't bear the indelicacy of it." Elissa shuddered, still clinging to Mr Collingwood's hands. "To have all those strangers looking at me and knowing that I was increasing..."

Angeline raised one eyebrow. "As opposed to all those strangers looking at you and thinking you're clumsy? Or infectiously ill?"

Elissa lifted her chin imperiously. "I won't have it," she said. "Of course, everyone who sees me will realise... eventually, when it can't be kept hidden any longer... but no one has to know yet, apart from our own family. I want each and every one of you to give me your promise that you won't share the secret with anybody, no matter how tempted you might feel."

Charles snorted behind me. "No worries here. Trust me, Liss. I'm happy for you, but I'm not tempted to go gabbing about it."

I glanced at Elissa's stomach. It looked as slim as ever beneath her high-waisted muslin gown. "Are you really certain you're increasing?"

"Kat!" Angeline snapped.

Elissa's blush lent colour to her cheeks; even the smile she gave me looked embarrassed. "Of course I am," she said. "That was why we saw the physician, silly."

"You must have blushed like a sunset the entire time you discussed it with him," said Angeline. "Or did you make poor Mr Collingwood do all the talking?"

Elissa and Mr Collingwood both answered Angeline at once, but I didn't hear a word they said. I was too busy trying to make myself believe the news.

I had been waiting one hundred and twenty-four days to see my sister again. But somehow it had never occurred to me that she would have changed.

Elissa was – well, she was Elissa, and that was all there was to it. She was the closest thing to a mother that I had ever known. She had brushed my hair in the morning when I was little, she had carried me out to the garden to listen to Mama's enchanted roses sing when I was sad, she had told me stories before I slept at night....

And now she was going to have a baby of her own. The thought of it made my chest feel very strange. But I knew what I had to say.

I took a deep breath and pulled my lips into a smile.

"I'm happy for you, too, Elissa," I said. I forced myself to look up at Mr Collingwood and include him in my smile. "I'm happy for both of you."

"Thank you, darling." Elissa finally detached one of her hands from Mr Collingwood's grasp and reached out to me. "I know you'll be a wonderful aunt."

Aunt? I gulped. That was something I hadn't even considered yet. I hadn't grown up with any aunts or uncles of my own. Papa's closest relatives were a set of cousins out in India. If Mama had had any relatives, I'd never heard of them. What were aunts even meant to do with babies?

That was definitely too much to think about just yet. But I wrapped my fingers around Elissa's warm hand, and I tried to look at least half as happy as I knew I should be at the thought of it.

"We must start making plans," Stepmama said. She perched on the side of the bed and began ticking items off on her fingers. "Of course, there is the christening to consider – your papa will want to do that himself – but even beforehand, there is so much to decide. The clothing, and the silver, and..."

Angeline must have noticed Elissa's sagging eyelids and fading complexion just as I did. We both spoke at once.

"Elissa needs—"

"I think Elissa—"

But for the first time in our whole acquaintance, Mr Collingwood spoke over all of us.

"Elissa needs to rest," he said. As all four of Elissa's relatives turned to stare at him, he squared his shoulders and added, "You see, the carriage ride was awfully difficult for her. And she's tired all the time now. So..."

"Oh! Oh, well, of course." Stepmama rose, smoothing down her skirts. "Yes, of course. We'll leave you to your rest, my dear. Charles? Girls?"

Charles was already halfway to the door, but Angeline and I stayed exactly where we were. We exchanged a look of amused exasperation. Stepmama could be so absurd.

Of course Elissa needed rest. That's why Charles and Stepmama had to leave. But Angeline and Elissa had shared a room and a bed all their lives until Elissa's wedding this past September. And I couldn't even count the number of times that I'd crept in with them on long, dark nights when I was younger.

It was ridiculous to think that her sisters would have to leave the room just so that she could rest. I turned to Elissa, waiting for her to set Stepmama straight.

But Elissa was busy pushing herself deeper into the pillows and turning her face into her husband's palm. "Thank you," she murmured on a yawn. "I do love you all, you know."

"Elissa...," I began.

Her eyes were already falling closed. "Love you, Kat," she whispered.

I swallowed hard and followed Angeline out of the room, leaving Elissa behind.

My eyes felt hot and swollen as I stepped into the hallway, under the gaze of yet more disapproving Carlyle portraits. I would not cry. I would *not*. But if Stepmama dragged me back down to face all the Carlyles again now, I might just explode.

All I wanted was to run outside in the open air, until my lungs were burning and my legs were aching and I couldn't think about anything at all... not even the memory of my oldest sister turning away from me, when I'd been waiting for her for so long.

With my mysterious follower lurking in wait, though, I was trapped inside this house. Even my bedroom would be no refuge, since Angeline shared it. For once, I felt too raw to talk even to her.

Once I turned my mind to it, though, I knew exactly how to escape every social obligation. I'd seen someone else do it every day of my life.

"I'm going to join Papa in the library," I said, and started running before Stepmama could even argue.

I ran all the way down the three flights of stairs and down the hallway, even though the door to the Rose Drawing Room was open and I could hear the guests still mingling inside. Maybe they would see me. Maybe they would whisper. But I couldn't stop running now.

A footman bowed as I barrelled towards him, head down. He reached out to open the library door for me. I didn't wait to let him. I was too afraid of what would happen if I stopped running.

I flung the heavy, wooden door open… and it banged against the wall with a crash that broke through the gold-and-burgundy wallpaper and left a visible dent in the wall.

Papa jumped in his big, wing-backed chair and dropped his book on his lap. "Kat?"

I saw the footman look at the damage to the wall before he closed the door, but he didn't say anything disapproving. Neither did Papa.

They didn't need to. I stood on the black-and-gold Chinese carpet and felt everything inside me crumble.

I'd just gone running through Hepworth like a madwoman, embarrassing Angeline in front of all the servants and all her in-laws… again.

I'd damaged the wall in her fiancé's beautiful library because I was too careless, just as everybody always told me.

My oldest sister was having a baby, and I wasn't even happy for her.

Lady Fotherington was right. I was a horrible person.

"Papa," I said.

My voice cracked. My legs buckled. I landed on the carpet with a thump and pressed my face into my curled-up knees so at least he wouldn't see me cry.

I was trying so hard not to make any noise as I sobbed, I didn't hear anything outside my own heaving breath. But a moment later I felt a hand touch my hair.

Papa was leaning over me, holding out his pocket handkerchief. It was one that Elissa had embroidered, with Papa's initials – GES – swirling across the top corner in dark blue thread. I took it and pushed it hard against my eyes.

Papa sighed and knelt down beside me. He set one hand on my shoulder, but he didn't say a word.

I couldn't stop crying. After a moment, though, I reached up with my free hand and put my hand over his.

I couldn't remember the last time I'd got comfort from Papa. I'd always gone to my sisters for help, not to him.

Papa's hand on my shoulder felt surprisingly strong.

When the tears finally stopped, I wiped my eyes and blew my nose hard on the handkerchief. I folded it up and started to hand it back to Papa, then remembered the nose-blowing and snatched it back.

"I'm sorry—"

"Shh," said Papa. He drew me up, setting one hand at my elbow. "Come and sit down, Kat. You need to rest." He settled me in the big chair across from his own, by the empty fireplace. "Wait here."

I did, even as he walked out of the room and closed the door quietly behind him. My chest was still shuddering, my heart still racing from how hard I'd sobbed. I took long, deep breaths, staring into the empty grate. The servants at Hepworth were efficient; there weren't even any splinters left of the wood that must have heated the room all through the winter and early spring.

It wasn't like our ramshackle vicarage. Nothing around here was.

Papa came back into the room, looking as grave as when he'd left. "I've ordered tea and cakes," he said.

I forced myself to summon up a smile for him. "Thank you."

He shook his head, as if he could shake my thanks away. "Would you like a book? They have..." He frowned at the books behind all their glass cases. "Well, I've primarily been looking through their Classics section, but I'm certain we could find a novel somewhere, or..."

"No," I said. "I don't need anything to read. Thank you,

Papa." I almost laughed, but I didn't; he was trying too hard for that.

There was something else I knew I had to do, though, even if he didn't like it. It might be the only chance I would get to corner him privately before we left Hepworth.

I straightened my back and clenched my hands around the folded handkerchief. "Papa," I said, "can I ask you a question?"

"Of course, my dear." He sat down in the chair across from me. "If it concerns social matters, though, your stepmama might be more useful – or perhaps one of your sisters?"

"No," I said. "You're the only one who knows the answer to this." I took a deep breath and looked into his worried blue eyes. They were the same bright colour as Elissa's and Charles's eyes. I'd seen them almost every day of my life, but it had never before felt so hard to look into them.

"Papa," I said. "Who is the marquise? Really?"

His face went very still. "I'm not quite certain of what you mean."

"Yes, you are," I said. I leaned forward, crumpling the handkerchief in my hands. "Please, Papa! I know that it's a secret. But if you don't tell me, I won't know how to—"

The door swung open, and I broke off. A footman held the door open, while a maid carried in a tray of refreshments. I waited, cursing inwardly, while she poured the tea into two delicate white-and-gold cups and arranged the rich, sultana-stuffed teacakes neatly on our plates. It would be only a minute, I told myself. As soon as they were gone, and I had Papa to myself again...

"Well," said Papa, standing up and starting for the door. "I shall see you at supper, my dear."

"What?" I stared up at him. Even the maid paused in the middle of setting out his teacakes. "But we were just—"

"Forgive me, Kat." Papa turned back to give me a pained half smile, but he didn't meet my eyes. "I think it best that we not continue this particular discussion."

"But, Papa...," I began.

It was too late. Even as I spoke, he slipped out of the room with the speed and agility of many years' practice. The sound of the heavy door clicking shut was all he left behind him.

CHAPTER TWENTY

THE LAST THING I FELT LIKE DOING THAT NIGHT WAS GOING down to supper with the Carlyles. When Stepmama knocked on our door to summon us, I was shamefully tempted to invent a headache as an excuse.

Angeline was already heading to the door, though, looking tense but magnificent in her finest evening gown of dark rose silk. I squared my shoulders and slid off the bed to follow her. If Angeline could face the Carlyles after her public quarrel with Frederick that afternoon, and if Elissa could face them after her china-shattering swoon, then I could certainly face them, too.

Perhaps, though, just for tonight, I might face them from the back of the room, in the most unobtrusive corner I could find.

Tonight, the pre-supper gathering was being held in the Long Gallery, on the first floor. As we stepped inside, I couldn't stifle my groan. Luckily, no one was paying attention to me... or at least, none of the guests were.

The corridors of Hepworth might be lined with ancient family portraits, but the Long Gallery was where they came to roost. The gallery stretched the full length of the house, and the inner wall was lined entirely by scowling Carlyles. Worse still, it wasn't just one row of portraits; there were multiple rows, one on top of another. Each painting I passed looked even older and more outraged by my scruffy, low-bred presence. Even when I looked away, I could still feel all those painted Carlyle eyes glaring down at me.

Tall windows lined the opposite wall, overlooking the cliff and the wild expanse of sea below. I looked across at them longingly as I followed Stepmama through the scattered groups of Carlyles, all sipping wine and gossiping avidly. Every single conversation stopped abruptly as Angeline and I passed. As soon as we were safely past, though, the whisperers started up again, and I could feel their curious gazes following us.

Angeline's chin rose higher and higher. I tried to imitate her, but my skin prickled with embarrassment. If only those windows had been less than half a mile above the beach, it would have been irresistibly tempting to jump straight out of one of them and escape.

I was so busy with my fantasies, I didn't recognise the danger ahead until it was too late.

"My dear Mrs Carlyle," Stepmama cooed. "What a delightful room this is. I must applaud your excellent taste."

Dash it. Why hadn't I paid better attention to where Stepmama was leading us? Now I was trapped exactly where I least wanted to be: directly in front of our hostess, who was standing with the big, grey-haired man who'd arrived at teatime. Jane Carlyle stood nearby, looking oddly pale and subdued.

Mrs Carlyle's smile was a mere stretch of her lips. "How kind of you to approve, Mrs Stephenson." She looked past Stepmama to Angeline, and her smile faded entirely. Her voice turned tart. "And you, Miss Stephenson? Can I dare to hope that you approve of my taste as well?"

Angeline sank into a curtsey. "I cannot imagine you thinking anything else, ma'am."

Jane Carlyle put one hand to her mouth as if she were only holding back a cough... but I could swear I'd seen her lips twitch.

The man beside her didn't look amused. His heavy silver brows drew together. "That sounded remarkably impertinent, young lady."

"Papa..." Jane Carlyle breathed. Her voice sounded thin and stretched.

He shot her a look that made her pale even further, until her freckles stood out on her white cheeks. Then he swung back to Angeline, his broad shoulders blocking the light as he moved forwards. "I don't believe we've been introduced."

Her eyebrows arched. "Indeed not." She looked at Mrs Carlyle. "Ma'am?"

Stepmama said hastily, "Oh, dear, yes, you haven't been introduced yet, have you? Poor Angeline was indisposed this afternoon, you know, so..."

She was? I blinked at my sister. *Hmm.* When I'd come back from the library that afternoon, our bedroom had been empty. I'd assumed that she'd spent the afternoon with the rest of the house party.

Before I could start speculating, though, Stepmama hurried on. "Colonel Carlyle, may I present my two younger stepdaughters? Miss Katherine is my youngest, and Angeline – Miss Stephenson – is, of course, dear Frederick's fiancée."

"Hrmm. Yes. So I hear." He glowered at her. "That's still on, is it?"

Angeline stiffened. "Yes," she said.

Stepmama let out a nervous trill of laughter. "My dear Colonel Carlyle, whatever can you mean? Why on earth wouldn't it be on? The wedding is in only three days!"

"I heard there was a ruption this afternoon." His steely grey eyes narrowed. "According to what I heard, there was a public quarrel – and not just where family could see it, either, but in the middle of the town square. First time in over three hundred years that a Carlyle's been drawn into shaming himself in public, and in our own village no less."

"The town square," Mrs Carlyle moaned. Her voice sounded piteous, but her eyes were positively glittering with pleasure. "Oh, Miss Stephenson, do please tell us that was not the case. Just to think of every curious village gossip—"

"There certainly seem to have been plenty of gossips at work today, even without the villagers' help," said Angeline.

"Well!" Mrs Carlyle drew herself up. "Of all the outrageous things to say!"

Jane Carlyle's eyes were still submissively lowered, but her soft voice cut off her aunt quite as efficiently as a shout. "It was only a small misunderstanding, Aunt Delilah. There was no true quarrel involved."

"Ha." Colonel Carlyle glowered down at his daughter. "That's not what I heard."

"Dear Jane," said Mrs Carlyle. "She is such an angel, she always takes the kindest interpretation of events."

"Indeed," said Angeline. "What an extraordinary concept. It must seem very strange to you."

Mrs Carlyle sighed. "I have always been so impressed by Jane."

Colonel Carlyle grunted and turned his glower back to Angeline. "She certainly deserves better than she's got," he said.

Jane Carlyle stared hard into her lemonade glass, while all the colour she'd been missing flooded back into her cheeks.

A familiar voice spoke behind us. "My, this looks like an interesting conversation," said Frederick Carlyle.

I had never been so glad to see him.

He stepped up next to Angeline and turned a smile onto his mother and uncle. "What have I been missing?"

"Oh, Frederick," Mrs Carlyle sighed, "must I speak to you again about being late for your own gatherings? You are the host, you know, even if only in name, and as your uncle says..."

"Your uncle," said Angeline, "was just asking me whether the rumours were true and our engagement had been called off."

Frederick's face went still for a moment. Then it hardened. He turned to her, and for the first time since luncheon, I saw them meet each other's gaze. "And what did you tell him?" he asked. His voice sounded every bit as cool and disinterested as if they were only discussing the weather.

Angeline's colour heightened, but she didn't drop her gaze. "I said that we were still betrothed."

"Good," said Frederick. "I'm always glad to hear the latest gossip." He slipped her hand into his arm as he turned back to his family. "There," he said. "And now that that question is settled..."

I frowned. Angeline's hand might be tucked into Frederick's arm, but both of their backs looked as rigid as if they'd been cast in steel. Whatever Angeline had been up to this afternoon, she obviously hadn't spent the time making up with her fiancé.

Jane Carlyle said, "Miss Katherine, would you care to take a turn about the room?"

"But, my dear Jane—" Mrs Carlyle began.

"I would be glad to," I said.

From the way Stepmama glared at me, I could tell that I'd sounded too fervent. I couldn't help it. Moving away from the main group felt like taking a deep breath of fresh air. And when Jane led me to one of the tall windows on the other side of the room, I felt the muscles in my shoulders begin to relax for the first time since I'd stepped inside the Long Gallery.

Back in Yorkshire, it would have been nearly dark by now, but here the sun still hung low in the sky. The rough cliff jutted out above the water; grey waves crashed against the beach far below. It was all perfectly magnificent, but I seemed to be the only one in the room who noticed. Jane Carlyle wasn't even looking out of the window.

"I must apologise for my family," she said.

She was gripping her glass of lemonade with both hands. All the vivacity and sparkle she'd shown earlier in the day seemed to have completely drained away from her. She kept her eyes lowered as she spoke.

"Would you please pass on my apologies to your sister? I swear, Miss Katherine, I have never desired to marry my cousin, no matter what my fath... no matter what *anyone* may have thought. I couldn't bear for Miss Stephenson to think – to believe—"

"Oh, you don't need to worry about that," I said. "And you don't need to apologise to Angeline, either."

"No?" Her lips twisted mournfully. "You needn't worry

about hurting my feelings, Miss Katherine. I do love my family, but it would take a very forgiving nature to excuse—"

"Angeline isn't that forgiving," I said, "but she knows better than to blame you for your relatives. Well, if we believed in doing that, we'd all have to shun ourselves, wouldn't we? And that would be terribly uncomfortable."

Jane Carlyle gave a hiccup of laughter and looked up to meet my gaze. "You say the most extraordinary things, Miss Katherine! I must say, I do like it." She took my hand in hers. "Apart from Cousin Frederick, no one ever says such things in my family. I am so glad we are to be relatives soon."

Relatives with the Carlyles... I forced myself not to shudder. I didn't want to offend one of the only two Carlyles I actually liked.

Behind me I could hear rustling begin around the room – the unmistakable sound of the party gathering up for dinner. I leaned closer to the window. There was a small boat bobbing on the water, perhaps a mile out. It looked wonderfully free.

Something nagged at my mind as I looked out at the boat. Something I should have put together earlier. Boats and water and this part of Devon...

"What were we all talking about at lunch?" I asked. "Before Frederick and Angeline's quarrel, I mean."

"Um..." Jane Carlyle's brow furrowed. "I remember we discussed the danger of strong spirits, and how your brother Charles doesn't drink them, or gamble, or – oh!" She let out a squeak and jumped as if she'd been poked with a pin. "Mr Stephenson! I didn't see you."

Aha. Maybe Charles would remember.

But when I turned around, I was too stunned to ask him.

"Miss Carlyle," Charles said, and bowed stiffly. I blinked at the sight of his butter-blonde hair combed firmly into place for the first time in my memory. Then he straightened, and I lost the power of speech entirely.

Charles hadn't only combed his hair. His cravat looked as if it had been tied by a professional valet. His tight-fitting jacket didn't show a single crease. I wasn't surprised that Jane Carlyle's eyes were widening as she took in the startling sight.

My brother looked like the model of an elegant gentleman... at least, if you could excuse the fact that his entire outfit had probably cost less than a single one of the Carlyles' wine glasses. From the look on Jane Carlyle's face, I thought she probably could.

There was only one explanation for such a shocking turn of events. For the first time in our lives, my older brother must have actually intended to take my advice.

Unfortunately, now that he was in Jane Carlyle's presence, the plan seemed to be running into a few obstacles.

"Ah," said Charles. He was still gazing down into her face. He didn't seem to be able to look away. "Um," he said. "That is..." He tugged at his cravat, ruining the perfect creases. "I mean to say... Miss Carlyle..."

"Yes?" Jane Carlyle fluttered her eyelashes up at him. For the first time since we'd returned to Hepworth that afternoon, she had a definite sparkle in her eyes.

"Yes," Charles said. "Miss Carlyle, you look very... very..."

"Very?" Jane said, fluttering her eyelashes even more. Her mouth curved into a knowing smile.

Oh, dear. The smile was too much for him. Poor Charles's mouth dropped open. He leaned forward. She leaned closer.

Before anyone could finish Charles's sentence, a beefy hand landed on Jane Carlyle's shoulder.

"Come, Jane," Colonel Carlyle barked. He didn't even bother to look down at her as he pulled her away. "If you don't hurry up, your cousin won't escort you into dinner. Can't you walk any faster, girl?"

"What?" Jane spoke in an anguished undertone, resisting his pull. "But, Papa, I'm sure Frederick doesn't want to escort me into dinner. His fiancée—"

"What does 'want' have to do with it? That puppy may choose to ignore his duty in every other way, but—"

I cleared my throat. "Colonel Carlyle," I said, "my brother just asked Jane if he could escort her into dinner, and she accepted. You wouldn't want her to go back on her word, would you?"

Charles's jaw dropped. "Ah..."

Jane Carlyle flashed me a look of intense gratitude. "Of course," she said. "I couldn't possibly go back on my word, Papa. You know you have always said how important it is for young ladies to keep their promises."

Colonel Carlyle let out a wordless growl that made the hairs on the back of my neck stand up. He seemed even bigger than I'd remembered as he turned to loom over me, his broad chest filling up my vision and the heat of his glare fixed on my face.

Charles cleared his throat and edged his broad shoulder between us. In a bare thread of sound, Jane whispered, "Papa, please..."

"Well, now," the marquise said brightly from behind the colonel.

Scowling, he made way for her to pass. She stepped up to join us, taking my arm and tucking it into hers.

"It sounds as if this has all been settled very neatly,"

she said, beaming at my brother and Jane Carlyle. "But now, Katherine, I am going to steal you away. As this is only an informal family group, I plan to throw tradition and etiquette to the winds and sit next to you at supper tonight rather than sitting surrounded by gentlemen.

"After all..." She smiled benignly and tightened her grip on my arm until I had no chance of escape. "I think the two of us really ought to have a good talk before things go any further. Don't you, my dear?"

I gulped and turned away from the others. "Yes," I said. "I suppose we should."

CHAPTER TWENTY-ONE

IT WAS LUCKY FOR THE MARQUISE THAT SHE WAS THE highest-ranking lady at Hepworth. As she swept to the front of the dinner queue with me as her escort, Mrs Carlyle looked as if she'd swallowed a rock. I could feel Colonel Carlyle's outrage from all the way across the room, and Lady Fotherington raised one supercilious eyebrow as we passed. But not one single person uttered a word of protest.

Life certainly was different for the aristocracy.

The marquise didn't even seem to notice the embarrassed shuffling at the supper table, as our neighbours reacted to the shocking shift in seating arrangements. She smiled serenely as she sank down into the seat of honour on Frederick Carlyle's left, and she nodded for me to sit down beside her. I sat down obediently, set my napkin on my lap, and waited for Miss Hortense Carlyle, one of Frederick's second cousins, to stop fluttering and dithering and eyeing the empty chair beside me as if it were a poisonous snake poised and ready to attack.

"I just don't know," Hortense whispered loudly to her escort, an older Carlyle in his late thirties. "I truly don't know what my mama would say. If only she were here to advise me! I don't think I really ought – or where I ought – but oh, I can hardly sit next to another female, even if she is only a girl, but still!"

For heaven's sake. It was hurting my head to listen to her, so I cut her off before she could waste any more minutes of our lives. "It really is all right," I told her, and I gave her my most winning smile. "You can pretend I'm a gentleman for the night, if that would make you feel better."

"Ohh!" She gasped and shrank back against her escort.

He glared at me over her head.

"What an impossibly shocking thing to s— that is..." Hortense's gaze landed on the marquise, and she stopped, blinking rapidly with her big brown eyes. "I mean to say... well, of course, my own mama would *never* have countenanced me saying such an improper thing in my life, but I didn't mean to offend – but really... ohhhh," she wailed, "I just don't know!"

Pressing one hand to her cheek, she sank down onto the very edge of the chair beside me. As I leaned forwards to pick up my fork, she leaned as far away from me as she could without falling off her chair. I wondered if I ought to reassure her that I didn't have any infectious diseases. Then I saw the protective way her escort was hovering over her, and I decided against making any moves that could be interpreted as an attack.

If Hortense Carlyle hadn't looked so ready to weep from the social horror of it all, I might have been more offended.

As it was, I sighed and pulled my own chair an inch further away from her, for her sake. She could hardly enjoy the feast laid out before us if she spent the entire time worrying about me breathing on her food.

As I finished shifting my chair, Angeline caught my eye. She was sitting on Frederick's right, directly across from the marquise. Of course, the laws of social etiquette meant we weren't allowed to converse with each other across the table – we could only speak to our neighbours on our left and on our right – but as my sister caught my gaze, she closed one of her own dark eyes in a wink.

I winked back at her and turned to my food, suddenly feeling much, much better.

That didn't last long.

"So, Katherine," the marquise murmured. The long table was covered with a dozen different kinds of food, from big, goggle-eyed silver fish to entire cows' heads propped up on silver platters to bowls of macaroons, nuts and jellied eels, but she didn't even bother to watch as a footman filled her plate. All her focus was on me. "Tell me," she said. "How long have you been acquainted with Lady Fotherington?"

"Lady Fotherington?" I blinked and turned reflexively to look.

Lady Fotherington was seated at the other end of the table, two seats away from Mrs Carlyle, looking infinitely weary and sophisticated as she listened to the eager young Carlyle beside her. I breathed a sigh of relief. She was definitely too far away to hear us over the din of supper conversation and the clatter of cutlery against plates.

I turned back to the marquise... then froze as I met her gaze. Her eyes were every bit as dark as Angeline's, and they were watching every move I made. I swallowed the chunk of fish in my mouth and set down my fork. I couldn't afford any distractions from this discussion.

"Lady Fotherington," I repeated. "Um." I took a breath. "Well, you know that she's my godmother."

"Is she?" The marquise took a sip of the dark red wine in her crystal glass. Her gaze didn't move from my face.

I looked into her face, searching for some sign I could trust. "You heard her say so yesterday."

"Mm." The marquise took another sip and swirled the wine in her glass. "I heard her say it," she agreed. "The only question is... how long, exactly, has she been your godmama?"

I speared another bite of salty fish, as an excuse for a moment of silence. I needed to think my strategy through.

My mother was supposed to have died when I was ten days old. If the marquise was my mother, that meant she must have left us well before my christening ceremony took place. She couldn't know the awkward truth that I was the only one of my siblings not to have a godmother at all. Papa had abandoned that particular detail, too distracted by grief – I'd always assumed – to arrange it.

If she really was my mother, though, she would know better than anyone else that we were only play-acting. Papa would never have chosen Mama's old nemesis as my godmother, and Lady Fotherington would never have agreed to it.

So it was time to abandon my defence and go on the attack instead.

"That's an interesting question to ask," I said, and made my own voice just as soft and steady as hers. "How long have you been the person you are now?"

Her eyebrows rose. "A marquise, you mean? I believe I told you that my second husband was an émigré.

Poor Pierre fled the revolution in France in eighty-nine, but we didn't meet until—"

"That wasn't what I asked," I said.

"No?" said the marquise. "I didn't really think so." She set down her glass, murmuring something I couldn't catch.

I leaned closer. "I beg your pardon?"

She looked me directly in the eyes and spoke in a near-whisper. "You tell me, Katherine. Who do you think I used to be?"

My hand tightened around my fork. Everyone around us was talking and laughing, and footmen were moving around the table refilling glasses, but it all faded into a blur until the only thing I could see or hear was the marquise, looking at me with dark eyes just like Angeline's.

"I think..." I began. But the words felt too big and too dangerous in my mouth. They choked me, closing up my throat, until I couldn't say them.

I took a deep breath and tried again, while she watched me with an expression I couldn't read. "I think," I repeated, keeping my eyes fixed on hers and my voice as steady as possible, "that you used to be my—"

"Yes, Mr Carlyle?" She turned away.

All the noise of the crowded dining room flooded back upon me, leaving me almost deafened. It took me a long moment to come out of my daze and realise what had happened. Frederick Carlyle had asked her a question. She was laughing and leaning towards him to answer, while Angeline conversed with her other neighbour, across from me, and footmen leaned over to refill all their glasses.

I closed my gaping mouth with a snap. On my left, Hortense Carlyle was darting nervous glances at me, in between minuscule nibbles of her food. All along the table,

Carlyles were eating and talking, and a whole row of footmen in powdered wigs stood lined against the wall behind them, watching us all with careful attention.

I couldn't believe I had come so close to revealing the family's most dangerous secret in front of all of them. But I knew one thing: that bubble of silence around us had not been natural, and it hadn't been all in my imagination, either.

Among all the scents of meat and fat and cooking oils and candlewax that rose up from the dining table, I recognised one scent that shouldn't have been there: the faint, lingering scent of bluebells. The marquise had cast a spell, in front of everyone, and even I hadn't spotted it. What's more, I still didn't know the real intention of her spell.

Had she cast it only to keep our conversation private from the others? Or had she cast it to trick my secrets from me?

I breathed in the scent of bluebells as she tilted her head towards my future brother-in-law, and I forced myself to face the truth. I didn't know what the marquise wanted, or what she was really doing here. And whether she was my mother or not, that meant I couldn't trust her.

My plate was covered with food I hadn't eaten yet. I speared a slice of ham, but all I could taste were bluebells, and my throat felt dry and tight. There was too much noise around me, and there were too many people I didn't know or didn't like.

I leaned forward, searching for the one person I could always trust.

Elissa sat at the other end of the long table, with Mr Collingwood on one side and Colonel Carlyle on the other. Her plate, unlike mine, was empty, and although her expression was perfectly amiable, I didn't like the look in her eyes. Something was definitely wrong.

Even as I thought that, Mrs Carlyle's petulant voice rang out, carrying over all the other conversations at the table.

"Mrs Collingwood! You haven't taken a single piece of food."

As the rest of the table fell silent, Elissa's fair skin flushed. She straightened. "I beg your pardon, ma'am. I'm afraid I'm not hungry."

"Not hungry?" Mrs Carlyle looked like an angry frog, chin tucked in and cheeks puffed out with outrage. "Don't be absurd! You can't have eaten since noon, at the very latest. Of course you must be hungry by now."

Mr Collingwood gave Elissa a quick, anxious look. "We ate quite a large luncheon at the inn we stopped at, Mrs Carlyle—"

"Doesn't seem to have altered your appetite," Colonel Carlyle said. "That's a healthy platter in front of you, young man."

"Well, you see, my wife is a little delicate right now," Mr Collingwood began, "so—" He stopped abruptly, with a pained look at his delicate wife. I wondered whether she'd pinched him or just nudged him under the table.

"Too delicate for my food?" Mrs Carlyle glared at my sister. "Really, Mrs Collingwood! We have a French chef, you know."

"Ma'am, I am certain it's all delicious," Elissa said. "I've had enough, though, really, so—"

"Hasn't taken a single bite while *I* was watching," said Colonel Carlyle. "Ridiculous thing, a perfectly healthy young lady pretending to be delicate. All to attract attention, I daresay. Certainly wouldn't allow my Jane to play such tricks."

Mrs Carlyle narrowed her eyes. "Oh, young ladies nowadays may fancy themselves very delicate and important, feigning swooning fits in public and pretending to be ill. But when it comes to refusing to eat perfectly good food that's been prepared by the best chef in Devon, as *everyone* agrees—"

"Mama," Frederick Carlyle began, "if Mrs Collingwood truly doesn't wish to eat, then—"

"Please!" Elissa said. "Don't worry. I will eat. Here." She helped herself to a fish from the closest platter, then winced as she looked down at its glassy eyes. She looked away quickly. Her smile looked strained. "Thank you, Mrs Carlyle, for advising me."

"Well!" The bunch of tall peacock feathers attached to Mrs Carlyle's hair bobbed as she shook her head. "Well." She turned back to her neighbour, and conversation slowly began to resume around the table.

I watched Elissa take a very small bite of her fish. The colour of her cheeks was definitely fluctuating. This was very odd.

Beside me, the marquise had stopped talking to Frederick Carlyle. "Mrs Collingwood," she murmured over my shoulder. "That would be...?"

"My eldest sister," I said, still frowning across the table.

Elissa closed her eyes and breathed deeply. Mr Collingwood had stopped eating. He was watching her nervously.

"Elissa," the marquise breathed.

The tone of her voice caught my attention. I turned back to her. She was gazing across the table with the oddest expression on her face: mingled delight and raw pain.

She caught me looking at her and blinked. Her face

rearranged itself into a social smile, but it was too late: I'd already seen the truth, and it left me feeling breathless and strangely frightened. She looked back at me, her dark eyes wary above her polished smile.

"So, my dear," the marquise whispered. "You were starting to tell me earlier: who is it, exactly, that you think I am?"

My chest was hurting. That look on her face, as she'd watched Elissa...

It didn't matter. It couldn't matter, not until I knew the whole truth. So I shook my head and said, "No one, my lady. It was only a joke."

Her eyebrows rose. Her lips parted. I kept every sense alert for magical trickery...

... and that was why I wasn't looking when my perfectly proper eldest sister was sick all over the Carlyles' dining table.

CHAPTER TWENTY-TWO

"WELL," SAID ANGELINE, "AT LEAST KAT ISN'T CAUSING all the most embarrassing scenes, for once."

We were sitting on Elissa's bed, where Elissa lay propped up by pillows, her slim hands spread across her face. She didn't even seem to hear Angeline's words.

"In front of everyone," she moaned into her hands. "Everyone saw me. *Everyone.*"

"I didn't see you," I said, and patted her leg reassuringly through the bedcovers. "I only heard you."

"It was quite loud," Angeline agreed from Elissa's other side. "Although not quite as loud as Mrs Carlyle's screams, admittedly."

"Or Stepmama's," I said. "She was fairly noisy too."

"Ohhh," Elissa moaned.

"At least you hadn't eaten very much," I said. "It could have been much messier if you'd eaten any of the—"

"Stop!" Elissa shouted the word in the most unladylike

200

tone I'd ever heard from her. She threw out her hands in a warding gesture. "Please, Kat! If you love me, do not mention any of those foods. Even the thought of them..."

"You shouldn't have eaten anything," said Angeline. "For heaven's sake, Elissa, if the smells were bothering you that much, why didn't you ask to be excused?"

"I couldn't," Elissa said. "Mrs Carlyle would have made such a fuss. It would have been too humiliating."

We both looked at her in silence. She said, "Well, I didn't realise what would happen!"

"Has it ever happened before?" Angeline asked.

Elissa winced. "Not in public."

"Hmm." Angeline crossed her arms.

I said, "Are you really certain you're not ill, Elissa? Because between this and your swoon—"

"Of course I'm not ill, darling. I told you earlier, I'm only..." She paused, flushing a deeper pink. "In an interesting condition."

"Breeding," Angeline said bluntly.

"Really, Angeline." Elissa's flush faded as she glared at our sister. "Must you be so crass?"

"Must you be so ridiculous?" Angeline glared back at her. "If you would only admit to the rest of the house party what's happening, no one would disapprove. You could have simply explained that you were feeling ill from your condition and couldn't take the scent of so much food around you—"

"I think not." Elissa shuddered. "Can you imagine the remarks they would all make then? Mrs Carlyle and Colonel Carlyle, particularly—"

"I hope this baby is worth it," I said.

"Kat!" They both gasped at once, turning to me in horrified unison.

"Of course it's worth it," Elissa said. She laid one hand protectively across her flat stomach, staring at me. "How could you even think such a thing?"

I crossed my arms, but I couldn't meet her gaze. "It's making you miserable, and I don't like it."

"Oh, Kat..." Elissa sighed. "That's what happens when you have a baby. It's perfectly natural."

"For heaven's sake, do you think Mama wasn't ill when she was increasing with you?" Angeline said.

There was a horrible moment of silence. My arms fell to my sides. I could actually feel the colour draining from my face.

Mama had been ill when she was increasing with me?

Mama was supposed to have *died* when she had me.

"I'm going to be fine!" Elissa said hastily. "Kat, sweetheart." She pushed herself forwards and gathered me in her arms. "Women have babies every day and remain perfectly healthy."

"Mama didn't," I whispered. I wrapped my arms around Elissa's chest as tightly as I could. I was having trouble breathing.

"Mama had four babies," Elissa said firmly, into my hair. "This is only my first."

"Mama didn't have a witch *and* a Guardian for a sister," Angeline said even more firmly. Her arms closed around us both.

"Angeline..." Elissa's sigh ruffled my hair.

"No," said Angeline. "You may be as scandalised as you like by the whole idea of magic but, like it or not, you are going to have all the magical protection we can give you... for your sake *and* your baby's."

"Well..."

"Definitely," I said. I breathed in Elissa's scent, the most comforting one I knew. "We'll find out how to keep you both safe."

"Well, I suppose, if it really is for the baby's sake..."

"There," Angeline said. "You see? It's not so hard to be sensible instead of proper, is it?"

"Oh, really, Angeline." The door of the bedroom clicked open, and Elissa drew back, disentangling herself from both of us. Her face lit up. "Mr Collingwood!"

I looked at Angeline. She looked back at me. We rolled our eyes at each other. Only Elissa would be prim enough to still call her husband "Mr Collingwood" after nine full months of marriage.

"Darling," Mr Collingwood said, and hurried across the room to hover by the bed. "I'm so sorry I couldn't get away until now. Mrs Carlyle—"

"Oh, no," Elissa said. "You were quite right. Of course I wouldn't have wanted you to offend our hostess."

"Hmmph," said Angeline expressively.

Elissa ignored her. She reached out to take her husband's hand. "Is dinner over, then?"

Mr Collingwood nodded. "Yes. I'm afraid Colonel Carlyle rather wanted me to stay for port while the ladies withdrew to the Lilac Drawing Room, but your father was already on his way out, so..."

"Of course," I muttered. Papa had escaped again.

"Oh, dear." Elissa sighed. "I suppose you really ought to go back for the rest of the evening, but..."

"Don't be absurd." Angeline stood up, smoothing down her skirts. "You couldn't possibly offend my future mother-in-law any more than you already have, so you might as well be practical, for once. Make your poor husband happy by letting him spend the rest of the evening looking after you. Isn't that right, Mr Collingwood?"

"Er..." Mr Collingwood looked pained. "I will go back if you insist, dearest, but to tell the truth, your sister is quite right that I would actually prefer to..."

"Well, then." Angeline nodded decisively. "Come, Kat."

Sinking back onto her pillows, Elissa said, "You will convey my apologies to everyone, won't you?"

"Oh, really, Elissa." Angeline snorted. "Do you honestly think I'm going to subject myself to Mrs Carlyle again tonight?"

"What do you mean?" Elissa frowned, letting go of Mr Collingwood's hand. "You can't just abandon the house party for the rest of the evening."

"Oh, can't I?"

"Angeline!" Elissa pushed herself up on the pillows. "This house party is being held in your honour!"

"I don't think so." Angeline set her jaw in her most mulish expression. "Mrs Carlyle never had any intention of honouring me with this gathering. All that she's doing is trying to prove to her family what an inappropriate bride I am for Frederick. Isn't that so, Kat?"

"Well..." I looked warily between my two older sisters. "I suppose that probably is what she wants, but—"

"And you'll be doing her a favour by proving her point if you can't even behave with common courtesy to your own future in-laws!" Outrage seemed to have brought back all the energy Elissa had been lacking; her blue eyes were positively flaming. "Even if you don't care for your own dignity, can't you think of your poor fiancé? Mr Carlyle chose you despite every protestation of his mother and his guardian. If you embarrass him in front of both of them now—"

"His guardian isn't here," Angeline snapped.

Elissa blinked at her, distracted in midstream. "He isn't?"

"He isn't?" I said at the same time. Then I thought back to all the Carlyles I'd been subjected to over the past two days. Not one of them had been introduced to me as Frederick's Uncle Henry. "You're right, he's not. How odd. Shouldn't he be?"

Angeline sounded as if she were gritting her teeth. "Of course he should be," she said. "His ward is getting married. That should be a momentous event."

"But..." Elissa's voice had softened in confusion. "Why wouldn't he be here?"

"You tell her, Kat. No, wait!" Angeline mimed astonishment with an overly dramatic gasp that made my own teeth grit. "Now I remember. You can't tell her, because you missed Mrs Carlyle's explanation when we first arrived. You'd already run all the way out of the house by then, sending my future mother-in-law into convulsions of outrage, and leaving me to make excuses for you... as usual."

She divided her glare between me and Elissa. "As a matter of fact, I don't think either of you is in any position right now to give me lectures on my behaviour. Do you?"

Mr Collingwood had been making pained noises in the background for some time. Now he finally broke through. "I say, perhaps I ought to leave the three of you alone to—"

"No!" Elissa said, catching his hand.

"No need for that, Mr Collingwood." Angeline gave him a glittering smile. "This won't take more than a moment to explain. The simple fact is that Frederick's guardian is not here because Mrs Carlyle convinced him not to come. After all, if he were actually allowed to meet me, one never knows what might happen. He might even – horrors! – decide that I am not, after all, a mere country bumpkin, unfit to be the mistress of Hepworth. And we couldn't possibly allow that to happen, could we?"

I sucked in my breath as the revelation burst through me. "So *that's* what you've been up to!"

"I beg your pardon?" She tried to freeze me with her icy glare, but I was too busy putting all the pieces together.

"That spell," I said. "You cast it just after that first meeting, after you found out what Mrs Carlyle had done. It's—"

"You've been casting spells?" Elissa shrieked. One hand flew to her mouth as she stared at our sister. "Here? In Hepworth? Have you gone mad?"

"I have *not*—"

"It was to summon Frederick's guardian, wasn't it?" I said. "You're trying to persuade him across the country with magic, so he can meet you and give you the chance to impress him. No wonder you've been looking so drained. What were you thinking? Even if it worked, if he realised what was happening – or if anyone else found out—"

"No one is going to find out," Angeline said through gritted teeth. "And how can you possibly think it any worse than what Mrs Carlyle has been doing, poisoning him against me? Do you really expect me to sit back and do nothing to defend myself against her?"

Elissa and I traded worried glances. When she spoke, her voice was gentle. "I am sorry she's been treating you so dreadfully, Angeline. But don't you see that that makes it even more important for you to be on your best behaviour? If you want Frederick's other relatives to think well of you—"

"Frederick," Angeline said, "doesn't want my help, as he made perfectly clear this afternoon."

Elissa's eyes flared wide with panic. "You had a quarrel with him this afternoon? Did any of his relatives see? What on earth could have possessed you to—"

"It is terribly charming of you to be so concerned," Angeline said, "but I wouldn't dream of bothering you with any more of my problems when you're feeling so unwell." She was already sweeping towards the door. "Kat! Come with me."

"Perhaps... perhaps Kat ought to stay," Elissa said. "I think—"

"Nonsense." Angeline gave me a hard look. "We don't want to worry Elissa when she's feeling so delicate, do we?"

"Actually..." Elissa began.

I sighed. As much as I hated to give in to Angeline in a tyrannical mood, this time she was right. Elissa really was too ill to solve our problems, no matter how much I wanted her to. "I'll tell you all about it later," I promised.

"No, you won't," said Angeline, and held the door open for me to leave.

I crossed my eyes and stuck my tongue out at her as I passed.

She stuck her own tongue out at me.

Elissa's plaintive voice followed us out. "Please do try to behave, both of you!"

Angeline closed the door with a thud.

The corridor outside was empty and shadowed; all the servants must have been in attendance downstairs. Only a few candles flickered in their wall sconces, spaced along our end of the corridor and leading only as far as the main staircase. The far end of the corridor was a well of darkness. It was one of the first times since we'd arrived at Hepworth that we hadn't been in full view of at least five servants, so it seemed like a good time for plain speaking.

I said, "If you don't want Mrs Carlyle to think you're afraid of her, you'll have to stop hiding from the rest of the company."

Angeline stalked towards the staircase and the light. "I'm not hiding."

"No?" I hurried to keep up with her, peering into her shadowed face. "It certainly looks like hiding to me, and I'm sure that's how she sees it. You hid from them this afternoon, and now—"

She slammed to a halt. "I've already had more than enough lecturing for the evening, Kat."

Something shifted in the corner of my eye, in the deepest shadows at the other end of the corridor, but I barely noticed it. I was too busy trying to read my older sister's face, lined by tension and something more – a deep weariness that made her look almost fragile.

"You have to give up this spell," I said. "It's too dangerous and it's wearing you out."

She snorted. "Of all the people to lecture me about danger—"

"Of all the times not to listen to m—"

An explosion deafened me. Something flew past my cheek in a whistle of air. Angeline let out a short, sharp cry of surprise and staggered back. I smelled smoke; I heard a door open and then slam shut in the darkness at the end of the corridor.

"Kat?" Angeline said in a small, strained voice.

Then she crumpled and fell to the floor.

CHAPTER TWENTY-THREE

"ANGELINE!" I DROPPED TO MY KNEES BESIDE HER, struggling to pull her up. My hands touched something wet. I jumped back, swallowing a moan.

My head was still ringing from the sound of the explosion, but it wasn't that that made me feel faint as I looked at my sister's right shoulder.

Red blood seeped through the bodice of her gown in an increasing flood, coming from just inside her right shoulder. My hands were wet with her blood.

Angeline had been shot.

Faintly I registered the sounds of doors slamming and feet thundering up the steps and down the corridor. But it wasn't until Elissa pulled me to my feet and shook me hard that I could tear my eyes away from the blood pouring out from Angeline's limp body.

"Kat!" Elissa looked wild, her face deathly pale. "What happened?"

Her voice, and the shake, broke me out of my daze. I swallowed hard, looking past her. Mr Collingwood knelt at Angeline's other side. Three footmen hovered around us, looking panicked, and the butler, Henshawe, stared at us in open-mouthed shock from the head of the staircase. It was the first time I had ever seen him without an expression of lofty disdain.

I looked straight at him, ignoring all the rest. I was already cursing myself for the precious seconds I'd wasted. "We need a physician," I told him. "Quickly. Tell Frederick Carlyle and the marquise. But don't tell Mrs Carlyle yet, for heaven's sake!"

I was ready for him to argue. Instead Henshawe nodded with what looked like pure relief.

"Yes, miss." He hurried down the stairs with the first speed I'd seen him use since our arrival.

Elissa was staring at me. "The marquise? What on earth...?"

Angeline let out a low moan, and Elissa dropped down to her side, abandoning the interrogation. My eldest sister's face was grim, but she ran gentle hands over Angeline's dark hair. "Dearest. Can you hear us?"

"I..." Angeline's eyes flickered halfway open. Her voice was stretched and taut with so much pain, it made my stomach clench. "My shoulder..."

"It's going to be all right," I said, and clenched my fists until the nails bit into my palms, anchoring me against the dizziness in my head. "You're going to be all right. I promise."

"What—?" Angeline stretched her neck and winced. "Oh..."

The blood was running all the way down her arm and chest now, swirling onto the wooden floor.

Mr Collingwood said, "Can't we move her somewhere more comfortable? Perhaps—"

"Carry her onto our bed," Elissa said. "But do be careful!"

"I... don't think... want to move anywhere," Angeline whispered.

I thought of the marquise and the reason I'd asked for her. "Yes, you do," I said. "Trust me. We want privacy."

She took a slow breath and nodded. Her lips twisted into the semblance of a smile. "Suppose... last thing I want... Mrs Carlyle coming to gloat."

"That isn't going to happen," Elissa said firmly, and she nodded to her husband.

Mr Collingwood stooped to lift Angeline. I could tell he was trying to be gentle, but as he scooped her up into his arms, she let out a sound between a cry and a moan. Her eyes rolled back in her head. Mr Collingwood froze.

"She's swooned again," he said to Elissa. "Should I—?"

"Just get her inside," Elissa said.

A footman hurried to open the door. Elissa took my hand, and I squeezed my fingers tightly around hers as we followed Mr Collingwood into their room.

As I passed through the door I cast one last look back at the darkness at the other end of the corridor. Every muscle in my body wanted to run after the villain who'd done this, but I knew it was too late. He would be long gone by now, escaped down the servants' staircase. Right now Angeline needed me exactly where I was. But later...

Later, I promised myself, I would find him, and he would find out exactly what it meant to hurt my sister.

Mr Collingwood was laying Angeline on the bed when I heard the sound of running feet in the corridor outside. The door burst open, and Frederick Carlyle arrived, panting and wide-eyed.

"What's amiss? Henshawe mumbled something about – oh, my God. Angeline!" He lunged across the room. "What the devil's happened to her?"

"Careful!" Elissa said. She was standing on the far side of the bed, but she put out one hand to warn him back. Her other hand was already pressing a clean, folded chemise against Angeline's wound, trying to staunch the blood that just kept flowing. "Don't touch her yet. Her shoulder—"

"Frederick?" Angeline's whisper cut Elissa off. Her eyes were still closed, but her left hand lifted off the bed, reaching towards him.

He dropped to his knees on the floor beside the bed and took her hand. "I'm here," he said. He took a deep breath and squared his shoulders. When he spoke again, his voice sounded perfectly steady. "You chose a bit of an extreme way to escape a tedious evening, don't you think? I know you and my mother don't get on, but you could have simply claimed a headache if you didn't want to come back down."

Angeline's lips curved in a smile. "Sorry... didn't think of that in time."

He smiled and lifted her hand to his lips. Then he turned round, and I saw that his blue eyes were bright with fury.

"Now," he said. "I want to know exactly who did this to her."

Elissa and Mr Collingwood both turned to me. I opened my mouth. Before I could answer, there was a light knock on the door. It swung open, and the marquise stepped inside.

"Do forgive me for intruding," she said, "but the butler told me... good God!" She closed the door with a snap and hurried across the room. "I would have come faster if he'd been more explicit." Her eyes were sharp and cold as she looked from the blood-soaked makeshift bandage on Angeline's shoulder to Frederick Carlyle. "Is it common for your fiancées to risk their lives by coming to your house, Mr Carlyle?"

Frederick Carlyle gave her an equally cold look. "I appreciate your concern, my lady, but I'm afraid I can't quite see why Henshawe would have taken it upon himself to summon you. If you'd like to retire, we'll see that—"

"No!" I said. "I sent for her." As the rest of the room turned to face me, I stiffened my back. "Angeline was shot," I said. "I couldn't see who did it, but since the village is half an hour away, I was afraid the physician would take too long to get here."

Frederick Carlyle shook his head. "So you thought the marquise would examine her instead? Kat, of all the nonsensical things you've done..."

"It was not nonsensical," I said. "It was necessary." I looked past Elissa's and Frederick's bewildered faces, directly at the marquise, who was watching me with cool, dark eyes. "I called for the marquise because Angeline needs a witch."

✠ ✠

There was a moment of appalled silence. The sound that finally broke it came from the bed. Even with her eyes shut against the pain, and her voice drained to a whisper, Angeline was laughing breathlessly.

"Oh... Kat," she said. "You... do... keep things interesting."

"Interesting?" Elissa drew a long breath. She exchanged a horrified look with her husband before turning to the marquise with a curtsey fit for a queen. "My lady. I'm afraid we haven't been introduced yet, and I don't have the time for introductions now, but please let me quickly say how very, very sorry I am for any offence my sister may have inadvertently caused. She is still very young, and I'm sure she did not really intend to – to—"

"To call me a witch?" The marquise raised one eyebrow. It made her look even more disconcertingly like Angeline. "Oh, I'm sure the word simply slipped out of Katherine's mouth, quite against her will. Or was it perhaps a joke?"

"Do you think I would joke at a time like this?" I pointed at Angeline. "Look how much blood she's losing! I know how shocking witchcraft is. I know no one else can ever be allowed to find out. But for heaven's sake..." I threw my arms out to encompass everyone around me. "Everyone in this room was born a natural witch except for Frederick, and he's marrying one!"

"Oh Lord," Frederick said, and tipped his forehead against Angeline's hand. "Well, that's torn it. Kat, has anyone ever explained to you the concept of discretion?"

"Kat!" Elissa's voice came out in a piercing squeak that overrode him. "How could you? Mr Collingwood and I would never—"

I cut her off. "Witchcraft is passed to *all* of a witch's children, whether they're too squeamish to use it or not, and that means both of you inherited it too. So." I turned back to the marquise. "I don't care who you used to be, or who you are now. Which is more important to you: to keep your magic safely secret, or to save Angeline's life?"

The marquise looked back at me for a moment that seemed to last for hours. Then she nodded, and her expression turned grim.

"Lock the door," she said.

I ran to the door. As I turned the latch, Elissa said, "Perhaps – perhaps we ought to wait just a bit, before anyone does anything rash. There may still be time for the physician, if—"

"I'm not waiting," said Frederick Carlyle.

"Very wise." The marquise sat down on the bed next to Angeline and ripped through the shoulder of her gown with one neat tug. "To be perfectly truthful, I was already planning to find a way to do this, well before Katherine suggested it. I'd just thought to dismiss the rest of you before I began, for discretion's sake." She looked across the bed at Elissa. "Would you truly prefer your sister to die than be healed by witchcraft?"

Elissa flushed. "Don't be absurd. I only meant—"

"Well, then." The marquise peeled away the cloth and sucked in air through her teeth. "Katherine, bring me water."

There was a china pitcher still half full of water by the washstand. I brought it over.

"Hold her still," the marquise said.

The sounds Angeline made as the marquise washed out her wound were the most horrible I had ever heard. I was shaking by the end of it.

I wasn't the only one. Frederick Carlyle had held her down by her uninjured shoulder, looking as if he might be sick at any moment. Now he cradled her left hand inside both of his own and glared at the marquise.

"Was that really necessary? I thought you were going to heal her with magic."

"Magic can't do everything." The marquise's face was tight, her eyes focused on the wound itself. It looked horrible, a maw oozing blood. "There's no use removing the bullet if an infection kills her instead."

"It was an infection that killed Mama." Elissa's voice was so quiet, I could barely hear her. I looked back over my shoulder and saw her standing in the circle of Mr Collingwood's arms, staring at Angeline with eyes that looked suddenly enormous in her pale face. "It wasn't the birth itself but an infection afterwards that made her ill. The physician said there was nothing to be done."

"Physicians can be fools." The marquise snapped off the words. "If I had been there..." She jerked back, as if her own words had slapped her. I watched the colour flush, then ebb from her face. She shut her eyes, as if she could stop herself from witnessing something terrible.

"I wasn't there," she whispered.

I stared at her, feeling a flutter that felt like terror behind my chest bone. If she really was Mama, why would she feel such anguish over an invented illness? She had to be Mama. Didn't she? Nothing else made sense. She *had* to be.

Because if she wasn't...

Angeline let out a sobbing breath. Her head fell to one side on Elissa's pillow. Every other worry fled my mind.

"Angeline?" I said. "Angeline! Can you hear me?"

She didn't speak. Elissa pulled away from Mr Collingwood and ran to the bed.

"Angeline!"

"Her hand's gone limp," Frederick Carlyle said. "If you are planning to help her, my lady..."

The marquise's eyes flashed open. They looked dark and familiar and very, very dangerous.

"Everyone get out of my way," she said.

CHAPTER TWENTY-FOUR

The marquise's whispered spell began deep in her chest, so low it felt like a thrumming in the air. As I stood three feet back from the bed, holding Elissa's hand on one side and Frederick Carlyle's hand on the other, the room compressed around us. My vision warped. Angles shifted dizzyingly on every side, from the straight lines of the cupboard to the curving outline of the porcelain washstand. It was as if we were all being squeezed into different dimensions.

I pressed my eyes shut and swallowed hard, trying to break the pressure in my head. It didn't work.

"Kat?" Elissa whispered. I opened my eyes and saw her looking almost as green as she had at supper. "Is it normal for magic to feel so – so—"

"Shh," I whispered, and tightened my fingers around hers.

The last thing the marquise needed right now was

a distraction, even if that distraction was Elissa being sick. Curse it, why hadn't I learned any useful magic for situations like this? It was all very well to be able to break spells and turn invisible or even fly... but none of that would help either of my sisters right now.

What was the use of being a powerful Guardian if you had to stand and be quiet at the back of the room while someone else fought to save your sister's life?

Tears were burning behind my eyes, but I wouldn't let them out.

The marquise's voice rose from a whisper to a low-voiced growl. Her face was glittering with perspiration, though she sat perfectly still, not even touching Angeline. She was chanting the spell so rapidly, I couldn't make out a single word, even when her voice rose to a near-shout.

Then Angeline screamed. Her back arched off the bed. Frederick Carlyle lunged forwards.

"No!" I grabbed his arm, holding him back.

The tip of the bullet, black and ugly, was showing through the wound. As the marquise chanted, it wriggled its way upward, accompanied by Angeline's sobbing breath.

I was holding Frederick's arm so tightly, it must have hurt, but he didn't say a word. Elissa clutched my other hand as we all watched the bullet pop out and roll across Angeline's chest, onto the bed and then onto the floor. It finally rolled to a halt at my feet.

Elissa turned away. I could hear her being sick, but I didn't turn. The marquise was still chanting.

But the rhythm of the words had changed.

The angles of the room gradually shifted back into place. I was too uncomfortable to care. My skin was itching all over, from my scalp to my ankles. It felt like insects crawling all across me, clustered and pushed by the marquise's magic.

Everything in me wanted to make the itching stop. I could feel the Guardian power pushing itself up through me, waiting to explode and shatter her spell.

I gritted my teeth. I gripped Frederick's arm, anchoring myself against the urge as it grew more and more impossible to resist. The marquise's voice chanted on and on...

And then stopped, so suddenly that I almost fell over. The relief from the itching was so intense, it was all I could feel for a moment. Then I remembered and lurched forwards.

"Angeline!"

She wasn't sobbing or moaning anymore. She made no sound at all as she lay still on the bed, her face deathly pale. I couldn't even see her chest move. My whole body went numb with terror.

"She was supposed to be healed!" I said.

The marquise lifted her head to glare at me. "She *has* been healed. Look at the wound."

"It's been mended." Frederick traced his fingers over Angeline's skin. "There isn't even a scar. But—"

"She is breathing," Elissa said. "Look, Kat." Elissa herself looked dreadful, wan and frail, but she smiled waveringly as she held her hand over our sister's lips. "It's a miracle."

"It is magic," said the marquise, harshly. "But magic can't do everything. I told you that."

She reached out as if to stroke Angeline's hair. Her hand stilled in mid-air. She pulled it back and set it on her lap. "I removed the bullet and healed the wound, but I can't put back all the blood that she lost."

"What does that mean?" I said.

"It means that she is still in great danger," said Frederick Carlyle. "Doesn't it, my lady?"

The marquise nodded. Lines of exhaustion were etched deeply into the skin around her eyes and mouth. "When a body loses too much blood..."

"It can't be too late yet," said Elissa. "There must be something we can do."

The marquise sighed. "When she wakes up – if she wakes up..."

"*When* she wakes up," I said.

"... She'll be dreadfully cold," the marquise finished, ignoring my interruption. "Make certain she drinks as much as possible – hot tea with sugar would be best, if you can force her to drink it."

"*We can*," said Elissa in a tone I knew well.

It was the same tone that had forced a hundred foul-tasting concoctions down my throat when I was ill; the same tone that had forced me into apologising to Stepmama after a score of shouted arguments, even when I knew that I'd been in the right. It was her eldest-sister voice, and hearing it now, in this horribly unnatural situation, made all the panic I'd been suppressing come flooding up through me, ready to explode over everyone and everything.

I turned away from Elissa's pale, determined face. I marched past the bed and Angeline's body and the fear that filled the air around it, even as the marquise continued with her list of instructions. I marched all the way to the window and pressed my face against the cool glass until the darkness outside filled my vision and the cold within me matched the cold against my skin.

I could hear Frederick Carlyle asking questions and Elissa and Mr Collingwood adding interjections of their own. I could hear the marquise answering them in a voice that was rapidly growing hoarse from her earlier chanting.

And all the while, Angeline might be dying behind me.

I pressed my hands against the glass. I stared into the darkness until my eyes burned with effort instead of tears. I stared into the darkness until the shadows outside began to take shape and sense.

Elissa's room didn't face the ocean. Elissa's room faced the shell-lined drive and the gardens beyond. I could see the rows of hedges spreading out into the distance. I could just make out the flat expanse of flowerbeds before them.

And as my vision finished adjusting to the darkness, I finally saw the still, unmoving shadow that stood not fifty feet outside Hepworth, looking up at Elissa's window and at me, highlighted within it.

My mysterious follower was watching me again.

All the pieces of the night's puzzle clicked together with perfect, murderous precision.

I barrelled across the room and out the door with fury pounding in my ears.

⁂

I heard voices calling out to me, glimpsed angry, agitated figures gesturing at me as I passed, but none of them slowed me down as I ran through the house. I burst through the front doors of Hepworth, and light spilled out into the darkness. I hurtled across the shell-lined drive, heading for the shadows beyond.

A strong hand clamped down on my arm and hauled me back.

"Good God, Kat!" said Charles. "Every time I think you've learned a smidgeon of sense..."

I kicked back at his legs. "Let – me – go!"

He dodged and grabbed my shoulder with his other hand to hold me still.

"The devil I will. I may not know what's happened this time, but I'm dashed if I'll let you go running off into the night just because Angeline's said something to aggravate you, or—"

"Angeline—" I stopped myself, panting with effort and frustration. There wasn't time for anything but the truth. "Angeline didn't say anything," I said. "Angeline was shot. Angeline might *die*. And I'm going after the murderer who did it."

"What?" Charles's grip loosened. I wrenched my arm out of his grip, but he grabbed me back before I could get away. "Damn it, Kat. You can't just throw out a piece of news like that and then tear off! If Angeline's been hurt, why aren't you with her? What—"

"She doesn't need me there," I said, choking on the words. The tears I'd been holding back for so long had finally escaped. They ran down my face and trickled into my mouth as I scowled up at my infuriating older brother, willing him, for once, to understand. "Don't you see? She has Elissa and Frederick Carlyle and Mr Collingwood with her. She has the marquise telling them how to look after her. There's nothing I can do for her, except this."

"Go after a man with a pistol on your own?" Charles snorted. "Oh, yes, that'll certainly help her. I can see how that would make her feel better straightaway. You—"

"You fool!" I yelled right into my older brother's face. I was crying so hard, I could barely see him, even in the light spreading out from the open front doors of Hepworth. "Can't you see it? She was shot because of me!"

"Kat..." Charles began. Then he yelled over my head

to someone else. "You, there, close those doors! And I want the curtains on the windows pulled tight. We need privacy out here!"

The light from the house disappeared as the doors swung shut, casting us into total darkness. I couldn't even see Charles anymore, only feel his hands on my arm and shoulder.

"Right," he said. "Now, what exactly have you done this time?"

I stomped my foot on the ground. Sharp shells bit through my thin evening slippers. "I have no idea!"

"Oh Lord." Charles groaned.

"It's true!" I said. I forced my tears down, smearing one fist across my face. I had to be reasonable, had to make him understand. "He hates me, but I don't know why."

"Are we talking about that madman who's been following you? Damn it! I knew he was more dangerous than you would admit. He was actually in the house?"

"I didn't see him," I said. "But it must have been him. At first I thought maybe he'd been trying to shoot me and missed, since Angeline and I were standing just beside each other. But then—"

"Right," said Charles. "You can tell me the rest later." He turned me around by my shoulders and started pushing me across the drive, back towards the house. "You're going inside right now, and you're going straight to the most crowded room you can find. I mean it, Kat. If I find out you've gone off on your own or—"

"What are you doing?" I said. I dug my feet into the drive, but that only sent shells skittering around me as he forced me forwards. "Charles! What—"

"What do you think I'm doing?" he said. "I'm going after the villain who shot our sister."

The news was like an electric current racing through me, giving me a jolt of power. I hurled myself forwards, breaking his grip. I landed on my hands and knees and rolled away in the darkness before he could catch me.

Then I pushed myself to my feet, panting. "Don't you see? That's exactly what he wants."

"Kat—"

"He didn't shoot Angeline by accident," I said. "He told me this morning that I would find out, soon, exactly how much I could lose. That's why he started by shooting my sister. He's not even trying to kill me yet. First he wants to take away everybody I love." I drew a deep, steadying breath. "I won't let you go after him to be killed too."

As my eyes adjusted to the darkness, I could just make out Charles, a few feet away. He said, "Do you really think I'll agree to just stand here and let you go after a madman with a grudge against our family?"

"No," I said. "That's why I have to *make* you do it."

I focused on Charles's shadow in the darkness. I summoned the power up through my body until I vibrated with it. My finger shook with the strain as I pointed at Charles.

"Dash it, Kat, whatever you're thinking of doing—"

Air, surround him.

His voice broke off in a yelp. "What the devil – ?"

Air, hold him firm. Don't let him move.

"I'm sorry," I said to my brother. "But I have to keep you safe."

I turned away from him, shutting my ears to his protests. I started into the darkness, towards the first expanse of gardens.

Magic slammed into my body, seizing me and lifting me two feet from the ground. I tried to cry out. My voice

wouldn't work. My feet kicked uselessly against thin air.
I reached for the power inside me. I couldn't find it.
My mysterious follower had found me first.

CHAPTER TWENTY-FIVE

"KATHERINE ANN STEPHENSON," MY MYSTERIOUS FOLLOWER SAID.
I heard his footsteps crunch across the drive, coming closer and closer to where I was suspended in mid-air. "I certainly didn't expect you to come walking out here tonight."

"Kat!" Charles yelled. "What's going on over there?"

Charles. A new level of panic swept through me. I couldn't sense my own power anymore. Did that mean that my magic-working had been broken? Or had it been frozen into place? If Charles was still trapped there in the darkness, at a murderer's mercy...

This time when I tried to speak, my voice came out. My mysterious follower must have wanted a reply.

"I don't know what else you expected," I said. I could hear my voice shaking pathetically. I tried to steady it, but I couldn't. I was trapped and I was helpless, and if I couldn't think of the right thing to say, my brother would be killed while I listened. I couldn't even breathe properly, much less make my voice sound calm. But I wouldn't stop talking, not while I had any chance of saving Charles's life. "I'm not a coward like you."

"I am no coward!" He was much closer than I'd realised; I jerked back as he spat the words directly into my face. I couldn't make out his features in the darkness, but I could hear the rage in his voice. "How dare you? After what you've done—"

"You won't even tell me what I've done!" I twisted frantically in mid-air, but he was just an inch too far away for me to reach. "You're too scared even to listen to my side of the story."

"I don't need to hear your side," he snapped. "I've seen all the evidence I need."

"So that entitled you to try to murder my whole family in our carriage? Then shoot my sister, who never did anything to you?" I couldn't stop the sob from leaking into my voice. "She's lying there unconscious right now, do you realise? She might never wake up! And even if she does..."

"Even if she does?" he said. "What then? Perhaps her mind will be damaged – that's happened before, to people who had the courage to stand against you. But then, you don't care about the consequences of your own actions, do you?"

"I... I beg your pardon?" I peered at him through the darkness, thrown out of my train of thought. My eyes were starting to adjust, but I could still make out only his outline, not his expression. "What are you talking about?"

"You'll find that out soon enough," he said. "But first, there's something you should know. I'm not the one who shot your sister."

"What?"

My shout mingled with Charles's. He said, "What the devil are you talking about?" at the same time that I said, "Of course you are. You have to be! And you sabotaged our carriage axle at the inn, and—"

"And?" said my mysterious follower. I could just make out the shape of his arms crossing as he stepped back.

"And..." I stopped struggling against my invisible bonds. I thought hard about everything he had said and done to me since we'd met.

"Oh Lord," I whispered. Cold dread coiled in my stomach. "It really wasn't you."

"Don't be a fool, Kat," Charles said. "You know the blackguard's lying to you. He's been following you and threatening you and—"

"And using magic every time," I said. "He wouldn't have needed to hack at a carriage axle or fire a pistol. He would have attacked us with magic... and it would have worked."

"Apparently I'm not the only one with a grudge against your family." My mysterious follower uncrossed his arms, but it wasn't a reassuring movement. His shadowy outline looked like a predator in the darkness, uncoiling himself and preparing to leap. "But I don't resort to attacking innocent victims, unlike you."

I ignored the taunt. "Angeline's lying unconscious," I said. "If you're not the one who shot her..."

"Carlyle and Collingwood are both with her," Charles said. "Nothing's going to happen while they stand guard."

I could hear the fear in his voice, though, and I knew he didn't believe his own words, either.

"You have to let us go," I said. "Please! I need to be there to protect her."

"Don't you dare ask for sympathy," my follower hissed. "Not from me."

"You don't understand!" I was almost weeping with frustration. "My other sister doesn't know how to use magic. If I'm not there—"

"I wasn't there when you attacked my father!" His voice exploded into a roar as he lunged forwards and grabbed my shoulders. "I wasn't there to stand by his side or protect him from you when you destroyed his mind! Don't you dare talk to me about family. You took away the only family I had!"

His big hands bit into my shoulders so tightly, I knew they would leave bruises. His breath was hot against my face. But it was the words he had spoken that filled me with true horror.

"I know who you are," I breathed. "Your father was Lord Ravenscroft."

✩ ✩

"Will someone please tell me what the devil is going on?" Charles bellowed.

I couldn't answer. I was too busy coping with the disaster in front of me.

I'd seen earlier that day that my follower had green eyes, like Lord Ravenscroft. But my follower's were fierce and clear and nothing like the muddy green eyes that had glared down at me through Lord Ravenscroft's elegant quizzing glass, first as he'd expelled me from the Order of the Guardians, and then as he'd cast the blame upon me for all the crimes that he'd committed.

Lord Ravenscroft had been a fop and a deuced dandy, flashing rubies and diamonds on his smooth, aristocratic fingers. It had been his thirst for money and for grandeur that had persuaded him to give his allegiance to the French and turn traitor to the Crown. I couldn't imagine him even consenting to be seen beside my mysterious follower. I'd felt his fingers around my neck earlier, and they were strong and calloused. Like his clothes, they showed signs of hard work and not much money.

My follower had one thing undeniably in common with the former Head of the Order of Guardians, though: they were the only two people I had ever met whose magic overpowered mine in every single way.

"But Lord Ravenscroft wasn't married," I said. The words popped out before I could think them through. "He was planning to take Lady Fotherington with him to France, not – that is..." I stumbled to a halt, feeling my cheeks grow hot in the darkness. "That is, he never mentioned a wife, so I assumed..."

"He couldn't marry my mother." The words sounded as if they were being ground out through my follower's teeth. "Your precious Order wouldn't let him. She wasn't wealthy enough for the Head of the damned Order, and she didn't come from the right kind of family, according to *them*. She explained it all to me."

"Oh," I said, and closed my mouth tightly to hold back any more observations.

I had only met Lord Ravenscroft for the first time last year, and of course he might have been different when he was younger. But I couldn't imagine the man I had met condescending to take orders about his marriage from any of his less-powerful colleagues within the Order... any more than I could believe that he had ever seriously considered marrying any woman who wasn't well-bred enough for his snobbish tastes – or wealthy enough for his empty coffers.

But even I wasn't rash enough to say that out loud while

hanging in mid-air with Lord Ravenscroft's son holding my shoulders in an iron grip.

"'Oh'? Is that all you have to say about it?" He shook me by my shoulders until my teeth rattled in my head. "You destroyed my father's mind! Are you so shameless you can't even pretend any remorse?"

"No," I said. My chest burned with lack of air and the inside of my head felt like a bowl of jellied eels, but the truth rose, clear as flame, inside me. "He tried to kill my brother and betray my country. I would do it again."

"You *liar*! You shameless – wicked—"

"Kat, you idiot!" my brother yelled. "For God's sake, don't antagonise him!"

Too late for that, I thought. And as Lord Ravenscroft's son was still struggling to come up with an insult appalling enough to suit me, it seemed like the right moment to do something even worse.

I pulled my right foot back in the darkness, and then I kicked with all my might.

He howled and let go, dropping down to grab his knee. The magic released me, and I fell to the ground, landing half-sprawled across the drive. Crushed shells crunched against my palms as I pushed myself to my feet.

"Kat!" Charles yelled.

Apparently my magic-working had broken too. Charles came bounding across the drive even as I ran for the house. We collided with a thud. Before I could even regain my balance, Charles thrust me behind him.

"Stay away from her!"

"Get out of my way." Lord Ravenscroft's son didn't move, but his voice was full of menace. "I don't want to hurt you."

"Your father did," I said, peering around Charles's

shoulder. "He didn't even know Charles, but he was going to murder him to harness the wild magic in Bath and hand it to the French."

I heard a harsh breath hiss out through the boy's teeth. "They told me that was the story you'd given the rest of your Order. But that you would have the barefaced gall to repeat it to me, his own son—"

"'They' told you?" I said. "Who are 'they'?"

"Friends who cared about my father. Friends who cared about what would happen to me without him... unlike your precious *Order*." He spat out the word.

"Ah," I said. "Right." I moistened my lips, remembering what Mr Gregson and Lady Fotherington had said about the Order's entrance requirements. "Lord Ravenscroft never admitted you to the Order, then, even though you were his own son?"

"It wasn't his choice! He wished he could. He didn't have the power to."

I didn't say a word, but he must have heard the scepticism in my silence. He said, "He didn't! He explained it to me."

"Hmm," I said.

"You don't know—" Lord Ravenscroft's son stopped, panting. When he spoke again, his voice was raw with pain. "My father never abandoned me, even though he could have. He *trained* me, even though he had to do it in secret so the Order couldn't stop him. He was proud of how powerful I was becoming. He called me his right hand. I was the only person he could trust!"

"So he made sure that no one else knew about you, and then he didn't even tell you the truth about his plans." I shook my head. "That doesn't sound like pride or trust to me."

232

"Kat..." Charles edged backwards, pushing me with him. "I think you've said enough, don't you?"

"More than enough," said Lord Ravenscroft's son. He raised his right arm, and I froze. But he only pointed at me, where my head poked out from behind Charles's shoulder.

"You made me lose my temper," he said. "I almost forgot that I don't want to kill you yet."

"Um... good?" I blinked.

Charles took a threatening step forwards. "Not *yet*?"

Lord Ravenscroft's son shook his head. Even through the darkness, his gaze pierced me. "Not yet. First I'm going to do to you what you did to my father. After tonight, you're going to see everyone around you lose faith in you and the Order turn against you. You're going to wish you had never dared to enter my father's presence. You are going to weep with remorse for what you did to him, and I'm going to watch your own Order destroy your mind the same way you destroyed my father's."

"Very dramatic," Charles said, and pushed my head back so I was completely shielded by his body.

I felt cold as ice, tingling with the certainty in my follower's voice. "I told you, your father tried to kill my brother and betray our country. I never wanted to attack him. I was only trying to defend—"

"Tonight," said Lord Ravenscroft's son, and disappeared.

CHAPTER TWENTY-SIX

"WELL," SAID CHARLES. HE TURNED TO THE HOUSE AND set one hand on my back to push me towards Hepworth's big front doors. "What a thoroughly unpleasant fellow."

"*Unpleasant?*" I twisted to stare up at my older brother. "He thinks I destroyed his father. He wants to destroy me!"

Charles nodded. "I told you he'd turn out to be a fanatic, didn't I? If you'd only listen to me once in a while—"

"Oh, for heaven's sake!" I dug in my heels and glared at him. "You thought he'd be an anti-magic fanatic like the ones you knew at Oxford. After what he just *did* with magic, you can hardly claim— oh, dash it." I lurched forwards, remembering. "Angeline!"

There was no time to waste arguing with my aggravating brother. I ran for the doors. Charles reached them first and swung them open.

Lady Fotherington stood just inside, waiting for us. The broad front corridor was darkened. There wasn't a single servant in sight.

"What," she said, "has been going on?"

"I'll tell you later," I said, and started past her.

She flung one arm out to block me. "You'll tell me now," she said, "or I'll go straight to Mrs Carlyle and tell her all about the scandalous witchcraft I sensed in Mrs Collingwood's room not half an hour ago."

I circled around her outstretched arm, heading for the grand staircase. "You can't do that and you know it. You promised me—"

"I promised to deceive her about one sister's witchcraft," said Lady Fotherington. "I made no such promises about the other."

Oh, *damnation*. I stopped, casting a frantic look towards the staircase. "There's no time!"

Charles's hand brushed my shoulder. "I'll look after Angeline. Just promise to come as soon as you can. *No delays.*" His tone was heavy with meaning as he glanced pointedly at the doors behind us.

"Fine." I gritted my teeth and watched him lope past me towards the staircase, looking infuriatingly overconfident. He probably didn't even realise he needed my help. It would serve him right if Angeline's would-be murderer came back while Charles was in charge.

No, it wouldn't. Nausea circled through my stomach at the image. Charles might be tall and strong, but he was unarmed. If the murderer still had his pistol...

"So," Lady Fotherington said in a tone like poison. "Which of your sisters was dabbling in witchcraft this time? And how exactly did you plan to keep it secret, when they were letting out such blasts of power directly above the drawing room?"

"Oh Lord!" I wanted to tear my hair out. Instead

I stalked past her to push open the library door. Thankfully, no light shone inside – Papa must have either retreated to his own room or been herded back to the drawing room by Stepmama. "If you're going to start hurling ridiculous accusations, you could at least have the decency to do it in private."

"Are *you* giving me lessons in propriety now?" She swished past me into the darkness of the unlit room.

"Maybe you need lessons," I said as I shut the door behind us. Tension was rippling through me, but I forced my voice to sound careless and confident. Around Lady Fotherington, I couldn't afford to let my guard down. *Take the offensive before she can,* I told myself, and squared my shoulders. "When you first arrived at Hepworth, you transported yourself to a spot directly in front of the drawing room windows, in front of all the Carlyles. I had to go tearing out of the house just to keep anybody else from noticing what had happened."

"Is that really what you imagined? That you were protecting me from exposure?" She let out a bark of contemptuous laughter. "No one else would have noticed me, Katherine. I'd set a magic-working on myself – I was invisible to everyone but you."

I blinked, shaken out of my confidence. "You can do that?"

"I can do many things," she snapped. "But you cannot distract me from my purpose. If I discover that you've been playing with witchcraft yourself, after all your promises—"

"It wasn't me," I snapped back. "And it wasn't either of my sisters."

"Then who was it?"

I opened my mouth, then froze. "Ah..."

"Quite." A flash of Guardian power swept the room;

every candle in the library burst into flame, and Lady Fotherington faced me with one eyebrow arched imperiously. "Perhaps you'd like to think through your story more carefully. Which innocent victim would you like to accuse of witchcraft? Your brother-in-law, Mr Collingwood? Or Frederick Carlyle himself? They were the only ones in the room with you, weren't they?"

"Um..." I moistened my lips, trying to collect my scattered thoughts. "If you want to talk about magic—"

"Ohhhh," Lady Fotherington breathed. "*Oh*. They weren't the only people in the room with you, were they? There were others missing at the same time. Your father was gone – but he's no witch, so he couldn't have been the one; Jane Carlyle had stepped out earlier on some excuse, but she was back by the time I sensed the witchcraft; Colonel Carlyle and the other gentlemen had all returned by then; and the only other person missing..." Her lips curved into a smile of pure, malevolent delight. "My, my. Can you guess who made her excuses only a few minutes ealler, after the butler had sought her out particularly? I presume he must have been carrying a message from you?"

"No!" I said. "You're imagining things. She didn't have anything to do with it! That is..." I gulped as I realised my mistake. "I don't know who you're thinking of, but—"

"Too late," Lady Fotherington purred. "So *that* was how she knew your mother. We certainly did move in different circles, indeed. What a delicious scandal this will be! When Society learns that the Marquise de Valmont is a practising witch..."

My stomach clenched so hard I had to clap one hand against it to stay upright. "You can't tell anyone," I said. "Please. She didn't do anything wrong. I made her—"

"Oh, I don't doubt that you were at the bottom of it. You always have had a positive genius for causing trouble." Lady Fotherington wasn't looking at me anymore, but into a middle distance that seemed to contain visions of an enthralling future, judging by the dreamy look on her face. "When I think of the haughty way she spoke to me... oh, it will be a pure delight to bring her down. She may be the queen of Edinburgh Society right now, but just a few hints dropped in the proper ears, and—"

"Stop!" I said. My head was ringing with panic; I remembered the marquise's husky voice talking about discretion, and then the anguished look in her eyes as she'd spoken about my mother's death. "She saved Angeline's life," I said. "Someone shot Angeline. She would have died if the marquise hadn't used her magic!"

"Very philanthropic of her," said Lady Fotherington, "and certainly nothing the Order could use as an excuse for pacification. But you know as well as I do the price for having your magic discovered. Social ruin – just as your own mother found out." She spoke the words with satisfaction, her green eyes half-closed. "I don't think our fashionable marquise will enjoy paying that price. Do you?"

I stared at her. Tingles raced up and down my skin: first hot, then cold, until I was dizzy with them. *The price Mama had paid.* Mama had lost everything when Lady Fotherington exposed her witchcraft: her membership and her life's vocation in the Order, her place in Society, and all her friendships. Even Papa's career had been destroyed. It was one of the first things I'd learned when I was old enough to understand: Mama had lost everything, and doomed us all through her exposure.

If the marquise actually was Mama, this would destroy

everything she'd worked for. *Again.* Everything she'd sacrificed – even walking away from her children – would have been an utter waste.

And if she wasn't... I remembered again the look on her face as she'd spoken of Mama's death. *I wasn't there.*

I wanted to believe she was Mama. I wanted it with every fibre of my being, even if it did mean she had chosen our futures over our love for her.

But even if she wasn't, one thing shone true: if she was ruined now, it would be my fault.

I looked at Lady Fotherington, my mother's worst enemy. I lifted my chin and I said, "It was me, not the marquise. I did it."

She frowned at me, coming out of her daze. "What are you talking about? You said the marquise—"

I held her gaze and clenched my fists, willing her to understand as I gave up everything I'd worked so hard to gain. "If you leave the marquise alone," I told her, "you can tell the Order this, and I won't deny it: I am the practising witch. Not her."

✧ ✧

Lady Fotherington blinked rapidly, several times in a row. Then she said, as slowly and carefully as if she were speaking a new language, "I could tell them that you are a practising witch?"

"Yes." I held myself stiff with my shoulders squared and my chin up, like a soldier on parade duty. It was the only way I could do what I knew I had to. Still, the words burned my tongue as I spoke. "Tell them that you discovered me secretly practising witchcraft... just like Mama."

"Just like your mother," she repeated softly. The words

tingled down my spine like ice. "They'd cancel your initiation if I did that."

"Yes."

She paced around me in a slow circle, watching me from every angle. "You would never be a member of our Order."

"No."

"Everyone would say that I had been right about you all along."

I gritted my teeth. "Yes."

"And you wouldn't deny the accusation?"

I shook my head, my lips pressed tightly together.

Her green eyes were wide and shining in the candlelight. "Just who is the marquise to you, to make you care so much?"

"That doesn't matter!" I ground out the words through my clenched teeth. "Do you want to do it, or not?"

Lady Fotherington looked at me without speaking for a long moment. Then she began to laugh.

"Oh, this is too perfect," she said. "This is better than I ever dreamed. When I think of how you sneered at me last autumn in Bath... When I think of how you dared to threaten me... how you humiliated me by forcing me to tell those ridiculous stories to Mrs Carlyle and Mrs Wingate to save your disgusting witch of a sister from ruin..."

My fingernails were biting so deeply into my palms, my fists burned. "Just tell me what you're going to do!"

Lady Fotherington stepped back. She smiled and looked me up and down. "You have caused me so much trouble over the past year, Kat Stephenson. Do you know, believe it or not, I think I actually despise you even more than I despised your wretched mother."

"Then do it!" I said. "Tell the others. Have me thrown

out of the Order, just like you always wanted. I won't stop you."

"I know," she said. "And *that* is why I can't quite decide. You must care about the marquise very, very much, if you're willing to give up everything for her."

"It was my fault she was caught," I said. "That's all. It wouldn't be fair to let her suffer for my mistake."

"No," said Lady Fotherington. "It wouldn't be fair at all. And you would suffer a great deal over that, wouldn't you? You would blame yourself very bitterly, indeed."

I didn't trust myself to reply.

She waited a moment, then shook her head, her smile deepening. "Lost for words?" she asked. "What a rarity. In fact, how positively delightful. Katherine Stephenson, completely in my power."

Rage simmered inside me, but there was no way to let it out. I couldn't even argue. All I could do was stand there, waiting for her to decide my future.

"I like it," she said softly. "Oh, I like this very much. And do you know what else? I'm not going to make my decision now. I'm going to wait, and let you wonder."

"What are you talking about?" The words burst out of my lips. "You have to make a decision. You can't just—"

Lady Fotherington's voice snapped out like a lash. "Oh, I can. And I will. For once, Katherine, I am the one in control over you – and believe me, I plan to make full use of it."

I closed my eyes before I began to beg. The words felt like sand grating against my throat. "Please," I said. "Please, just tell me what you've decided. *Please*."

I heard the familiar click of the library door opening.

I opened my eyes just in time to see Lady Fotherington lift her hand in farewell as she walked out of the room.

Guardian magic swept behind her in a wave.

The library door shut, and all the candles went out, leaving me alone in the darkness.

CHAPTER TWENTY-SEVEN

ANGELINE NEEDS ME.

That was what I told myself when my legs wanted to give way and drop me to the carpet of the pitch-black library.

Angeline needs me.

That was what I repeated to myself over and over again as I walked out of the room and up the curving flights of stairs, ignoring the interested gazes of all the footmen who'd reappeared in the ground floor corridor and all the guests who were streaming onto the staircase from the second floor drawing room.

Angeline needs me.

I could let myself panic later about what Lady Fotherington was going to do, and just how horrible it would be no matter what she chose. Later, I might even let myself remember my follower's threats, and wonder what he might be doing now, while I was distracted by Angeline's would-be murderer.

Tonight, he'd said. *Tonight...*

But if I started thinking about that, I really would start shaking. So I shut off my mind completely and just focused on pushing my way up through the crowd of guests, keeping my senses alert for any magic in the air as I hurried to the only place I needed to be right now: Elissa's room.

I wasn't the first one to arrive.

"What can be the meaning of this? How dare you!"

I heard Mrs Carlyle's voice all the way from the staircase, even before I turned the corner and saw her standing outside Elissa's room.

Now that the guests were on their way to bed, three footmen stood spaced along the length of the corridor, awaiting any orders. They all had their eyes trained respectfully away from their mistress, but Mrs Carlyle's guests were less reserved. Every Carlyle around me was openly staring, and Mrs Carlyle's face turned redder and redder as more and more of her relatives gathered around her.

"I said, *let me in!*"

"I can't do that, ma'am." Charles blocked the doorway, his arms crossed and his blonde hair sticking up in all directions, as usual. He'd closed the door behind him, and his shoulders rested lightly against it as he loomed over her. "I'm afraid my sisters can't receive any visitors at the moment."

"Cannot receive visitors? Don't be ridiculous! I am about to become Angeline's mother-in-law."

"Yes, but you see, Angeline's not well," said Charles. His gaze fell on me as I pushed my way through the crowd, and his expression eased into pure relief. "Ah, there you are, Kat. You'd better come in."

"Not well – not – of all the nerve!" Mrs Carlyle's jaw

dropped open as she glared between the two of us. "You can hardly let *her* come in and not me!"

I gave her what I hoped was an appeasing smile. "Truly, now isn't a good time for a visit," I said. "Angeline isn't feeling well at all."

"Ha." Mrs Carlyle crossed her arms. She glanced back at the crowd of watching Carlyles, and her voice grew even louder. "Something very odd is going on in this house, and I know it. I saw the local physician's carriage arrive not ten minutes ago, then turn around again before I even had time to demand an explanation. Well, you may all think yourselves very clever, but I will not be kept in the dark in my own house!"

She was almost screaming now, and the sound grated straight down my spine, making me wince. This couldn't be the restful atmosphere Angeline needed. Unfortunately, none of the other Carlyles looked interested in stepping in to help. Like it or not, I seemed to be the only one available to settle Mrs Carlyle down.

"Of course you can't be kept in the dark," I said. "Angeline was... well, the truth is, Angeline was..." I traded a frantic glance with Charles as I paused, hoping for inspiration. But then, was there any point in keeping the truth a secret? Several of the servants had heard the gunshot, after all, including the butler... and for all I knew, her murderer might be standing in the crowd of Carlyles watching me right now.

No, I decided. There was no point in lying. So I took a deep breath and said, "Angeline was shot."

Unfortunately, my brother took a deep breath at exactly the same time – and it seemed that we hadn't done a good job of silent communication after all. "Angeline fell over and hit her head," he said.

Oops.

Charles's eyes widened. "Ah, that is...," he began.

"I mean..." I said.

"What?" said Mrs Carlyle. "*What?* Fell over? Shot? *What is going on in my house?*"

The door swung open, catching Charles off guard. He stumbled back, losing his balance.

Jane Carlyle caught him in her arms. For a moment, his back was pressed against her.

"I say!" Charles pulled himself upright and turned round. When his gaze landed on his rescuer, his mouth dropped open. "Oh, I say!" His cheeks reddened. He reached up to tug at his cravat. "I do beg your pardon, Miss Carlyle. I didn't – that is, I hardly—"

His gaze landed on her small hand, still holding his right arm. His voice cut off as sharply as if he'd received a blow. I thought he might actually swoon.

Jane dropped her hand, flushing. "Please don't worry, Mr Stephenson. It was completely my fault."

"Oh, no," he said. "No, no, no. It was mine. Stupid place to lean, really. But... you saved me from falling." He took her hand back in his, leaning closer.

Her eyelashes fluttered down. She leaned closer to him. It was as if the wooden floor had developed a sudden slope, pushing them both off balance. "Oh, it was nothing. Truly. I was only glad to—"

"Will someone please tell me what my niece was doing in that room?" Mrs Carlyle shrieked.

For the first time in our entire acquaintance, I was actually grateful to her for an interruption. It would have been too humiliating if my brother had actually forgotten himself so far as to kiss Jane Carlyle in front of me.

Jane Carlyle didn't look grateful for her rescue, though.

In fact, she looked decidedly disappointed as Charles let go of her hand and stepped away from her. After a quick sigh, though, she straightened her shoulders and turned to Mrs Carlyle.

"Of course, Aunt Delilah. You certainly deserve an explanation."

"I certainly do," Mrs Carlyle said. She was frowning back and forth between Jane and Charles, looking confused. "But..."

"I know how distressed you must feel," Jane said. "You must have been terribly concerned when you saw the physician's carriage."

"Of course I was," Mrs Carlyle agreed. I doubted that even the dimmest of the Carlyle relatives could have believed her, though... especially when she added, "And no one thought to ask whether I might want to see him myself before he left!"

"Oh, dear." Jane took her aunt's arm. "I imagine you must be in want of a good cup of tea, mustn't you?"

"Well..."

"And perhaps a reviving plate of biscuits. You have suffered a great shock, after all."

"Yes, but—"

"You must let me look after you," Jane said. "We couldn't possibly let your health suffer so shortly before the wedding."

"I suppose not," Mrs Carlyle agreed, and let her niece move her forwards. Her voice drifted back as Jane guided her down the corridor. "But I deserve an explanation!"

"Of course you do," Jane said. "Of course..."

Their voices drifted into the distance as they turned down the stairs. As the crowd of watching Carlyles disintegrated into small groups and moved away, I was left staring after them in awe.

"Do you think Jane Carlyle might actually be a magic-worker?" I whispered to Charles.

He was gazing down the corridor with a positively sickening expression on his face. "I think she's the most magical girl in the world."

Well, that was more than enough to snap me out of my daze. "Come along," I said, and took his arm in a firm grip, shaking my head. "We'd better check on Angeline."

When we stepped inside, the room felt almost empty. Only Elissa remained with Angeline, leaning over the bed and pressing a damp cloth against our sister's forehead. Her face brightened as Charles closed the door behind us. "Oh, thank goodness," she said. "You managed to send Mrs Carlyle away."

"Not us," I said. "It was Jane Carlyle who did it. She was..." I looked at our brother and rolled my eyes, "positively *magical*. Wouldn't you agree, Charles?"

"I'm so glad." Elissa sat back, missing Charles's answering grimace. She'd drawn up a chair between the bed and the window, by the side table with the china washbowl. Setting down her cloth, she leaned back in the chair, closing her eyes and massaging her forehead. "It was very kind of her to help us."

"How did she know you needed help?" A little coil of guilt twisted through my stomach as I asked. The big, airy room felt awfully empty now, without Mr Collingwood and Frederick Carlyle and the marquise to fill it up, and with only Elissa, pale and ill-looking, left to take care of our sister. When I'd run out of the house earlier, I'd been so certain I was doing the right thing....

"She came up with Charles," Elissa said.

"She caught me on my way upstairs." Charles shrugged, avoiding my gaze. His cheeks were still faintly flushed.

"Well, she'd seen you tearing out through the house like a wraith, so she knew something must be amiss."

"She was wonderful," said Elissa. "She even persuaded Mr Carlyle to leave for a few minutes to clear his head and fetch food for all of us. He took Mr Collingwood along for help."

"Hmm," I said. "So they left you here alone to manage everything?"

"Don't be absurd." Elissa opened her eyes and frowned at me. "Jane and Charles were here too. And anyway, who else should look after Angeline but her own sister? If you hadn't gone running off—"

"Never mind," I said, and finally let myself look down at the still figure lying on the bed between us. My throat clenched. I had to force the question out: "How is she?"

I'd asked, but I didn't really want an answer. Not when I could see that Angeline's face was a deathly chalk-white, her lips pale. She hadn't moved since I'd entered the room, but her chest rose and fell evenly. That had to be a good sign... didn't it?

"She's calmer now," Elissa said. "But when Mrs Carlyle was making such a fuss outside, she grew terribly restless." Elissa's lips tightened; for a moment she looked older and almost like a stranger. Then she said, "I know she must wake up soon. The marquise said she needs broth and sugared tea to strengthen her and help with the blood loss. But oh, Kat... the pain she was feeling..."

My chest tightened. I had to cough before I could speak again. "What about the physician? What did he say?"

"We sent him away," Elissa said. "We couldn't let him see her."

"What? But—"

"For heaven's sake, Kat!" She sighed. "Do be sensible.

What would he have thought? We could hardly tell him she had been shot when there was no wound for him to see. And the marquise told us above all else not to let anyone take any leeches to Angeline. She's lost far too much blood already without the physician's leeches draining her of more."

I turned to Charles, who was leaning bonelessly against the wall. "So that was why you told Mrs Carlyle that Angeline had only hit her head."

Charles snorted. "Not that it did much good." He pointed at me and raised his eyebrows at Elissa. "Guess who told Mrs Carlyle and half the Carlyle guests that Angeline had been shot?"

"Oh, Kat!" Elissa cried. "You didn't!"

"I couldn't help it!" I crossed my arms and glared between them. "No one had told me we were meant to keep it a secret."

"How could we when you'd gone tearing off in the middle of the marquise's instructions?" Elissa shook her head. "You're thirteen years old, not a child anymore. How could you let yourself behave so impetuously, and with so little consideration for the rest of us? What could you have been thinking?"

"I was trying to save Angeline's life!" I hissed.

I could see Elissa preparing to launch into one of her standard eldest-sister lectures, the kind she'd delivered to me all her life. I knew all the signs, and how to divert her. But this time I couldn't bring myself to try a diversion. This time I was suddenly so furious, I could have sent magic rocketing around the room like fireworks.

"Don't talk to me as if I were a fool!"

I would have bellowed at her, if it hadn't been for Angeline's limp figure between us. Instead I spat my words out like bullets, aiming straight for Elissa's primly disapproving expression. "You have no idea what's been happening to us without you. You wouldn't let me tell you earlier, when I needed your advice. You don't even care!"

"Kat?" Elissa stared at me. "What in the world – ?"

"I say, Kat, steady on," said Charles. "There's no need to—"

"Of course there's a need!" I almost laughed at their blindness. But the laughter might have torn something inside me. "Someone tried to kill our sister! They've already tried once before. Don't you think they're going to come back to finish the job, now that Angeline's too weak to even fight back?"

"They tried before?" Elissa whispered. Her eyes were on me, but she curved one protective hand around Angeline's arm.

"We won't let them," Charles said, speaking over her. "Don't worry, Kat. She's protected now."

"That's not enough," I said. "We have to find out who did it. Otherwise, all they have to do is distract us, or separate us, just long enough to... oh Lord."

My arms dropped to my sides. My mouth dropped open in true horror. "Oh," I said. "Oh, no. Oh, *no*."

"What?" said Elissa. "What is it now?"

I swallowed hard. I looked at her so I wouldn't have to look at Charles. Even thinking about Charles was making me feel sick. "What if they already came back to try again," I said, "and it was only Mrs Carlyle's arrival that prevented it?"

"What do you mean?" Charles said. "There was no one here but us and Miss Carlyle, and – wait." He shook his head. "You couldn't possibly imagine—"

"But what if it's true?" I asked him. "What if Jane Carlyle did it?"

CHAPTER TWENTY-EIGHT

"No," CHARLES SAID. "ABSOLUTELY NOT. DASH IT, KAT!"
He pulled away from the wall he'd been leaning against, his blue eyes flaring wide. "That's a damned poor excuse for a joke."

"I'm not joking," I told him. "I wish I were." The look in his eyes made pain flare through my chest, but I looked back at Angeline on the bed, pale and still, and I forced myself to continue. "We have to think it through. Don't you see? It makes too much sense to ignore."

"Why?" said Elissa. Her expression was troubled, but her voice was soft. "Tell us, Kat. Why would you possibly suspect Miss Carlyle?"

"She was too intent on getting into this room," I said. "The rest of the company was still in the drawing room when Charles came back into the house, but she was waiting for him by the stairs. She made a point of catching him on his way up here and persuading him to bring her along." I turned back to Charles. "She told you she'd seen me running out of the house and guessed that something was wrong – but what if that was just an excuse? If she really was so concerned, why did she wait half an hour to ask one of us about it?"

"There could be a dozen reasons," Charles said. "There's no reason to think she was speaking anything but the truth – only your wild imagination at work, as usual."

Elissa was frowning, though, so I aimed my words at her.

"Once she was here, what did she do? She talked Frederick Carlyle and Mr Collingwood into leaving the room. Frederick would never have left Angeline's side if she hadn't talked him into it. Why?"

"She said... oh, she thought he should have some time away, to clear his head. And Mr Collingwood..." Elissa frowned harder. "Well, I can't quite remember why she thought he should go along, but—"

Charles let out a grunt of frustration. "It was to help Carlyle carry everything. Damnation, Elissa! Don't tell me you're actually letting yourself be influenced by Kat's nonsense."

"It isn't nonsense," I said. "It was Jane's idea, wasn't it, that you should go outside to deal with Mrs Carlyle? Even though she would clearly have been better at it herself?"

"No," Charles snarled, and set his jaw together with a snap.

It was Elissa who said the rest. "As soon as she arrived she suggested that Charles should wait in the corridor to keep any gossips from trying to come in."

I looked at Charles. He glared back at me. "Don't look like that, Kat. Mrs Carlyle arrived not five minutes later. Miss Carlyle was right to be concerned."

"Hmm," I said. I looked back at my oldest sister. "Elissa?"

Elissa looked down at her hands, twisting together in her lap. Her voice was so soft I could barely hear it. "After Charles left, she suggested that I go to her room and take a rest. She said she could look after Angeline by herself for a time."

"Yes," I said as all the pieces of the puzzle fitted together. They didn't feel good... but they fitted, in a horrible, cold way that made me feel sick and suddenly much, much older. "Yes, that makes sense."

"Of course I refused," Elissa said. "I couldn't possibly have left Angeline, no matter how weary I felt, but—"

"But she kept trying to talk you into it," I finished for her. "And if Mrs Carlyle hadn't arrived and refused to leave..."

"No," Charles said. "No. No. No!" He grabbed his hair with both hands, as if he would yank it out by the roots. "I don't care how you put it or what a case you make. Everything she did could have been perfectly innocent, and you know it. Every single thing that you're making out to be so suspicious—"

"All of them, though?" I asked. "Put together? And there's more. Lady Fotherington said Jane had left the drawing room earlier on some excuse – she came back just before the marquise healed Angeline."

"That could be pure coincidence." Charles glared at me. "She could have needed to step outside for some fresh air. She could have needed to visit the convenience. She could have—"

"She could have been shooting Angeline," I said. "It was perfect timing."

"But why?" Elissa was shaking her head. "I just don't understand, Kat. What possible reason could Miss Carlyle have for wanting to murder Angeline?"

"If you'd been here," I began... and then cut myself off, feeling a flush of shame as I met her steady gaze across the bed and remembered what I'd said to her earlier. "Well, you weren't here," I said, "so you wouldn't know, but everyone in the Carlyle family wanted Frederick to marry Jane. It's been expected ever since they were children. Colonel Carlyle sent her here every summer as a child, just to further the plan. Mrs Carlyle is furious that it didn't work."

"But Miss Carlyle didn't want to," Charles said. "You heard her, Kat. She laughed and laughed at the idea when Mrs Carlyle brought it up. So did Carlyle, for that matter."

"Yes," I said. "I heard her laugh. And isn't that exactly what she should have done, to divert any suspicion once Angeline was murdered?"

"No!" Charles said. "I mean, yes, I suppose, if she were a completely heartless villainess, it might have been – but she's not. Deuce take it, you're talking about her as if she hadn't a conscience!"

"Whoever shot Angeline doesn't," I said. "And Jane Carlyle told me this afternoon that she'd grown up doing everything a boy does during those summers, from climbing up and down cliffs to building forts... and shooting a pistol. Frederick taught her."

There was a nasty silence in the room. Elissa started to say something, then stopped, biting her lip.

"So she knows how to shoot a pistol," Charles said. "So? So does Elissa. I taught her, remember? It's not a crime. And do you really think Miss Carlyle got down in the dust at our coaching inn to saw the axle of our coach half off? Or – aha!" Charles shot out his finger accusingly. "She couldn't be the murderer! She was with Carlyle the morning our coach was tampered with. So where exactly does that leave you and your theories, eh?"

"Oh, thank goodness," Elissa said. "Charles is quite right. If she was with Mr Carlyle when the first attack happened, she could hardly have—"

"She could have hired someone," I said. "She must have enough money for it. If she weren't an heiress, Mrs Carlyle wouldn't want her as a bride for her son."

"And *that* is why there was no need for her to do it in the first place." Charles paced to the other side of the room and back, as if he couldn't contain his restless energy any longer. "Deuce take it, Kat, you know as well as I do that Jane Carlyle could marry anyone she wanted. She's got money, beauty, brains, a sense of humour..." He swung round to glare at us both, propping himself up with one hand fisted against the wall. "There is no reason she should be so desperate to marry Frederick Carlyle!"

There was a soft clicking sound. Charles staggered and lost his balance as the wall that he'd been propped against opened up into darkness beside him.

I would never have guessed there was a hidden door. There were no telltale marks in the wallpaper, and there was no door handle on our side that I could see. But a tall rectangle opened up out of the wall and swung wide open into darkness. Frederick Carlyle stepped through it, holding a plate of sandwiches and followed by Mr Collingwood.

It was the secret corridor he'd told me about earlier. At any other time, I would have been thrilled to discover it.

"Well," he said. "Here we are at last. We came back this way to avoid awkward questions – we were barraged by quite enough of them on the way down. Entertaining though that was..."

He was half smiling, but it was only a shadow of his

usual affable grin. His gaze went straight to the still figure on the bed. When he turned back to the rest of us, even his strained attempt at a smile had faded, although his tone was light.

"So tell me." He raised his eyebrows. "I only overheard part of your conversation, but it was fascinating. Who is so desperate to marry me? I'm afraid the position of fiancée is already taken. Angeline may be desperate enough to get herself shot by a burglar, but that's not going to get her out of it."

There was a dead silence. Elissa and Charles and I traded glances.

"What?" Frederick Carlyle said. "I was joking. Obviously. I just..." He wiped one hand over his face with a look of pure exhaustion. "I should put these sandwiches down... somewhere..."

"Here," Elissa said, and rose to take them. She directed a stern warning glance at me and Charles as she set them down on the dressing table. "Why don't we all take a sandwich before we say anything more? It will —"

"Kat's had her maddest theory yet," Charles said. "She thinks your cousin Miss Carlyle is the murderer."

I gritted my teeth.

Frederick Carlyle stared at Charles. He began to laugh. Then he stopped, as everyone else in the room stared at him.

"Wait," he said. "Are you actually serious?" He turned to me, shaking his head. "Kat?"

I steeled myself. "Everyone in your family expected you to marry her."

"Everybody but the two of us!" he said. "Honestly, Kat, it would have been like marrying my own sister. It was only an absurd notion that Mama and my late aunt cooked up between them back when we were infants. Neither of us ever paid any attention to it."

He shook his head. "Anyway, why would you even imagine that this was a deliberate murder attempt? The only reasonable explanation is that a burglar somehow—"

"That was no burglar," I said. "The person who shot Angeline was waiting for her in the darkness at the end of the corridor when we stepped out of the room. They'd blown out all the candles at that end, in preparation. This was planned. And this is the second time someone's tried to kill her in the last two days."

Frederick blinked. Then he sat down on the very edge of the bed and set one hand on the bedcover over Angeline's legs as carefully as if she were made out of glass. "I see," he said. "Angeline didn't mention – well." His face twisted. "No, she wouldn't have mentioned it to me, would she?"

"Mr Carlyle..." Elissa began.

"No." He looked up. His face had smoothed into expressionlessness, but it hurt to look at his eyes. "Don't try to pretend it isn't true. Angeline still doesn't think I can protect her."

"She doesn't think anyone can," I said. "She never has. It's just—"

"Just Angeline, against the world." He nodded, unsmiling. "Well, that's for the two of us to sort out between ourselves. Later. But for now..." He squared his shoulders. "Tell me exactly what happened yesterday, in the first attempt."

There was a second click. We all jumped.

"Sorry," Mr Collingwood said. "Didn't mean to startle you." He'd closed the hidden door behind him and was holding out a tray with a jug of fresh milk and an assortment of cups. "Thought we might all appreciate a drink, too, while Kat tells her story. Especially Elissa, as she didn't have any supper."

"Thank you, darling," Elissa said. She started to move towards him, but he waved her back.

"You need to rest," he said. "Just sit and listen while Kat talks."

Charles snorted. "Hardly a recipe for restfulness."

Everyone did drink and eat while I described the carriage accident, though, even Charles. He swallowed down his cup of milk in a single gulp, and then glared at it as furiously as if it were to blame for not being brandy. At the end of my story he leaped in before anyone else could speak a word.

"The point is, Miss Carlyle wasn't there to damage the carriage. Kat can spin as many wild theories as she likes to explain that part, but she hasn't got a drop of proof."

"No," Frederick Carlyle said. He was frowning down at Angeline's limp hand, lying on top of the bedcovers. "I can see why you're suspicious, Kat, but... no. No, I'm with Charles. I just can't believe it either."

Elissa looked at Mr Collingwood. He shrugged, and she sighed. "If only we had some proof..."

"Fine," I said. "You all think we need proof?" Everything had gone cold and clear inside me. I looked down at Angeline's pale face, and I saw a plan laid out, dangerous but perfectly aimed. "Then let's find some."

CHAPTER TWENTY-NINE

OF COURSE, IT WASN'T QUITE THAT SIMPLE. NO PLAN ever could be once my family got involved. But half an hour later, after I'd argued myself hoarse, they all finally filed towards the bedroom door, casting a fair number of dubious and unhappy glances behind them.

"Do be careful, Kat," Elissa said. "And don't forget, if Angeline wakes, or if she shows even the faintest sign of a fever or a chill—"

"I won't forget," I said. "And don't worry. I can certainly overpower Jane Carlyle, even if I am right about her."

"You aren't," Charles said. He fixed me with a cold look. "It's a good thing Carlyle and I are keeping guard outside the room. When the real murderer comes, someone ought to be prepared for him."

"Fine," I said. "I truly hope you're right. I do."

But I didn't believe he was... and from the look on my brother's face, he knew exactly what I was thinking.

"Cheer up, Charles." Frederick Carlyle slapped his shoulder encouragingly. "Think of how you'll enjoy triumphing over your sister once we prove her wrong. And anyway..." His expression darkened. "We have to do something. We can't just wait for the scoundrel to try again when we're offguard."

"No," Charles agreed. He took a deep breath and braced himself as stiffly as if he were facing a firing squad. "Go ahead and do it, Kat."

Elissa made a soft sound of distress and turned away. Mr Collingwood put his arm around her shoulder; I only rolled my eyes. She could worry all she liked about propriety later, once our sister was finally safe. In the meantime, magic was the best defence we had.

I focused on Charles and Frederick, who were standing side by side, both in plain black-and-white evening dress, though Charles's was distinctly rumpled. Frederick was gazing towards the bed, his face pale and determined; Charles was glaring at me. As I drew the power up through my body I stared at them so hard, the two of them nearly blended together in my sight.

If Lady Fotherington could do this sort of magic, so could I.

In my imagination, I drew a transparent cloth around them, wrapping them together – and linking them to me.

No one else can see you. No one can see you except each other... and me.

Power emptied out of me in a wave. Mr Collingwood gave a start of surprise.

"I say! That really is rather peculiar, isn't it? They are still here, aren't they?"

Elissa turned, wincing, to look. From my perspective, Frederick and Charles were both still solidly present and looking back at her with raised eyebrows, but her gaze passed straight over them. My magic-working had succeeded.

Despite everything, I felt a little burst of pleasure.

Take that, Lady Fotherington.

Elissa only sighed, her tone subdued to a dull whisper. "Well done, Kat. I suppose."

"For heaven's sake." I frowned at her. "You don't have to speak as if we were at a funeral!"

There was a painful moment of silence. Everyone looked at Angeline's still figure. She looked even paler than she had earlier, her face chalk-white against her dark hair. Panic worked its way up my chest until it was nearly choking me.

"I didn't mean...!" I swallowed hard, fighting down the knot that wanted to close off my throat. "There's not going to be a fu—"

"It's all right, Kat." Frederick's lips twisted, even as the others jolted at the sound of his voice coming from thin air. "We all know what you meant." He nodded at the closed door, though only Charles and I could see him. "Shall we?"

No one else said a word as they all filed out the door. It shut behind them, and I sank down into the chair Elissa had vacated. My hands were trembling.

My plan was going to work. It was.

But the room suddenly felt very quiet... and terribly empty. I couldn't hear Angeline breathing. I watched her chest rise and fall until my vision blurred.

With everyone else arguing and filling up the room, I'd almost been able to forget that Angeline was here... or rather, that the still, limp figure lying on the bed was the same person as my vibrant, overconfident elder sister.

It was wrong for Angeline to be so quiet and still. She

should have been arguing with me and Elissa, flirting with Frederick, filling up the room with the force of her personality. Angeline was never silent.

If she wakes up..., the marquise had said. I'd been trying to forget that part.

It was easy to argue with my brother. I knew how to do that. It was infinitely easier to scheme and plan to catch a would-be murderer than to confront the fact that we might already be too late. That Angeline might not ever wake up.

I stood and almost ran to the window. I started to push it open, to draw in the fresh air. Then I stopped. Angeline might develop a chill, Elissa had said. I relocked the window with clumsy fingers that slipped on the latch.

My breathing sounded loud and laboured. It was so loud, I was surprised it hadn't woken Angeline. Then again, if all the sounds of a Stephenson family argument hadn't woken her...

No. No, I wasn't going to think about that.

I walked to the end of the room and back. The hidden door was closed again, and I couldn't even see where it had opened in the wall. A secret passageway in the house, running all the way down through the cliffs, Frederick had said. In any other circumstance, I would have been on fire to explore it.

I walked back and forth, counting my steps across the floor. I timed my breaths to coincide with my steps.

The figure on the bed didn't move.

The sound of voices outside alerted me just in time. Elissa had fulfilled her part of the plan.

Her voice drifted through the door. "If you're really certain..."

"Of course! You must take some rest, Mrs Collingwood. I'll be absolutely fine."

The door handle began to turn.

Blast! I'd been so distracted, I'd almost forgotten my own part in this scheme.

I drew the power up through me in a mad rush. *Can't see me, can't see me, can't see me...*

"I'll look after Angeline," Jane Carlyle said, and pushed the door wide open. "Leave everything to me."

Her bright gaze passed over me without a blink. She stepped inside – and Charles slipped through the door before it could close behind her. He had to skip backwards to keep her arm from brushing against him. It didn't stop him from glowering threateningly into the room, though he was looking in quite the wrong direction.

I'd carefully set the magic-working on him and Frederick so that no one else could see them, but they could still see each other, and so could I. I hadn't thought to be so specific with my own magic-working, though. No *one* could see me, not even my brother.

Judging by Charles's expression, that was probably a good idea.

I'm going to see for myself, he mouthed, and gestured to make his meaning even more obvious. He might have been facing the wrong direction, but the message was still perfectly, depressingly clear.

I bit back a groan. Charles was supposed to be waiting outside with Frederick Carlyle to stop anyone else from coming in. We'd agreed on that – we'd *all* agreed on that, for heaven's sake.

The last thing I wanted was for my brother to have to watch as Jane Carlyle tried to murder our sister. Did he have so little sense that he couldn't even imagine how much that would hurt him? Or did he actually think I might lie to him about what happened here?

I wasn't sure which I would prefer right now: to push him out the door for his own protection, or to throttle him for being so stupidly untrusting.

Unfortunately, I couldn't do either without ruining the plan entirely.

Jane Carlyle crossed the room at a brisk walk, frowning to herself. As Charles took up position by the tall chest of drawers on the far side of the room, I stood by the bottom of the bed, close enough to leap into action.

"Oh, poor thing," Jane Carlyle murmured as she leaned over the bed.

Ha! Charles mouthed.

I gritted my teeth. I would not let him distract me.

Jane laid her hand on Angeline's forehead. She made a soft tsking sound. She set one hand on Angeline's lips.

My muscles tensed.

Jane reached for the pillow underneath Angeline's head.

Oh, my God. She was going to smother Angeline while my sister lay unconscious!

Not while I'm here, I vowed.

I lunged around the bed. Panic and fury combined to give me a burst of speed. Two steps away – one –

Jane fluffed up Angeline's pillow and stepped back. "There," she said. "At least now you'll be a little more comfortable."

I slammed to a halt only inches away from her, pressing my lips closed to hold back my panting breath. I could actually *feel* Charles smirking across the room as he saw his point about Jane being proven. I didn't turn to look at him. I couldn't bear it.

Thank goodness he couldn't see me. It was the only thing saving me from exploding with sheer embarrassment.

Jane sighed, turned around, and walked straight into me.

"Oh!" She stumbled back. "What in the world – ?"

Charles started forwards. I leaped to the side like a cat. Jane put out her hands, testing the air. She blinked and shook her head.

"But I felt..." She stopped, looking back at Angeline, and sighed. "*Quiet, Jane*," she said to herself in a barely audible – but startlingly vicious – tone. For a moment, I didn't even recognise her voice; then I realised that that was because she was mimicking someone else, someone I felt I ought to recognise but didn't. "*Your imagination's running away with you again, girl. No one's interested in what you think.*"

I winced. I still wasn't sure who she was mimicking, but one thing came through perfectly: the pain in her voice.

Charles had come to a halt halfway across the floor, frowning. For a moment I wished that he could see me after all. I would have quite liked to swap a puzzled look with him right at that moment.

Jane sighed again and smoothed down Angeline's bedspread. Then she walked around the bed to sit down in Elissa's chair, between the bed and the window. Sitting there, she looked entirely different to the bright, vivacious girl I'd met that morning, full of sparkling energy and fun. This Jane Carlyle only looked weary and sad.

As I watched her I felt all my certainty begin to trickle away.

She didn't look as if she were plotting to kill Angeline. She looked as if she was doing exactly what she'd offered to: looking after her cousin's fiancée out of simple kindness.

But in that case, why had she been so determined earlier to get everyone else out of the room? Of course she knew Elissa wasn't well; everyone knew that after tonight's fiasco at the dinner table. But Frederick was a twenty-one-year-old man with boundless energy, and he'd spent barely an hour by Angeline's side before Jane had persuaded him to leave 'to clear his head' and to take Mr Collingwood with him.

Charles would have snorted at me and told me to control my wild imagination. But the more I thought about what I'd just heard her say, the more uneasy I felt, and the more my imagination wanted to run wild.

I would have gambled a great deal on the wager that Jane Carlyle had heard those insulting words – and that vicious tone of voice – addressed to her many times before. I'd been too distracted by my own family worries ever since Elissa's arrival that afternoon to think much about Jane's family; but once I started, I remembered all the things I'd noticed without thinking about them at the time... like the horror in Jane's voice when she'd recognised her own father's arrival so much earlier than expected... and the change in her demeanour from the moment he'd arrived.

Summers at Hepworth had been the best parts of her childhood, she'd told me. I'd thought that was because she loved Frederick so much. It had made me suspicious of her claim not to want to marry him.

But what if that hadn't been because of Frederick? What if she had loved those summers so much because they were an escape from someone else?

I swallowed hard. My mind was suddenly racing.

What if I had completely missed the real murderer after all, just as Charles had claimed?

A soft click sounded nearby. I turned around slowly, dread thickening my throat.

The hidden door in the wall swung open. Colonel Carlyle stepped through it, his bulky shoulders filling the doorway, his fierce gaze turning straight to the bed.

"Good," he said. "You got rid of the others."

Jane Carlyle stood up. Every line of her body signalled unhappiness and defeat.

"Yes, Papa," she whispered. "I did as you asked."

CHAPTER THIRTY

"I'VE BEEN LOOKING AFTER HER MYSELF, JUST AS YOU TOLD me to," Jane said. Her eyelashes were lowered submissively, and her voice was a near- whisper. "Mrs Collingwood is resting in my room, and Frederick—"

"I know all that, girl. Why the devil do you think I'm here? Collingwood's down in the billiards room with the rest of the men. He told us all about it, so you don't need to natter on about it now."

"I'm sorry, Papa." Jane's shoulders hunched closer together.

He didn't bother to reply. He strode straight to the door that led to the corridor – and to Frederick Carlyle, outside – and turned the key in the lock. Then he crossed to the bed in a predatory, rolling swagger. He leaned over the bed, looked down at Angeline – and spat onto her bedcovers.

My breath caught in my throat. Charles started forwards. I put out one hand and caught his arm, holding him back. We needed more evidence before we could act. But the air felt heavy with rage and violence, and I was intensely grateful to have my older brother inside the room with me after all.

"Papa?" Jane said. Her eyes had opened wide at her father's action. Her voice was tentative, but she ducked her head away from him as she spoke, as if she were frightened to even say the words. "I did what you asked. Frederick and Mrs Collingwood will be grateful to me, I'm sure. That was what you wanted, wasn't it? You came to see that I'd done it, but—"

Colonel Carlyle didn't even look up. "You've done your job," he said. "Now get out. Wait for me in the secret passageway."

"Papa?"

"I said get out." His voice didn't rise, but his words came out as a snarl that shivered down my spine. "Do you still understand English, girl? Or do I need to remind you how to follow orders?"

"But..."

He looked up and met her gaze. As I watched, Jane Carlyle's face paled.

"You have five seconds to get out of that door," Colonel Carlyle said. "Five... four... three..."

"No," Jane whispered.

He straightened, slowly and deliberately, rolling out the muscles in his back. "What... did... you... say?"

She stared at him from across the bed. She was only an inch taller than me; she looked tiny compared to him, and positively sick with fear. But she straightened, too, stiffening her shoulders until she looked as if she were braced against a storm.

"I'm not going to leave, Papa," Jane said. "Not until

I know what you want with Angeline Stephenson. I can't. It wouldn't be right."

Charles stirred, trying to pull away from me. I closed my other hand around his arm, holding him still. We needed to hear Colonel Carlyle's answer too.

Colonel Carlyle's voice came out in a low growl. "Are you actually daring to question your own father?"

Jane wrapped her arms tightly around her chest. I could see her whole body shaking, but her voice was firm. "I'm not questioning you, Papa," she said. "But I can't leave you alone with her. I told Frederick I would look after her. You wouldn't want me to go back on my word."

He stared at her for a long, heavy moment. Then he gave a humourless bark of laughter. "Fine," he said. "Stay and watch. Don't say I didn't warn you."

He reached for Angeline's pillow.

Jane gasped and started forwards. "What are you doing?"

"What do you think I'm doing?" he said, and yanked the pillow out from under Angeline's head. "Finishing the job I started earlier, before your fool of a cousin can ruin us both."

Angeline's head lolled back against the mattress. Her eyes half opened. A weak moan emerged from her throat before she sank back into unconsciousness.

I gritted my teeth. One more moment... just a single moment longer, to make absolutely certain...

"Papa!" Jane lunged across the bed and grabbed his thick wrist. "What are you talking about? You can't mean to—"

"For God's sake, don't snivel," Colonel Carlyle snapped. "Blame your idiot of a cousin if you don't have the stomach for what we have to do. He was supposed to marry you.

If he'd only done his duty to the family instead of letting some shabby-genteel trollop distract him—"

"But I don't want to marry Frederick!" Jane said. "I swear, Papa, I never wanted to marry Frederick, and he never wanted to marry me."

"What do I care whether you want to or not?" Colonel Carlyle shook her off as easily as he would have shaken off a puppy. "The only good you've ever done me was being born a girl, so you could marry your cousin. If it weren't for him, Hepworth would be mine now. Hepworth should have been mine, and your aunt knows it. That's why she promised Frederick to you."

"Frederick never promised anything to me," Jane said. "And Aunt Delilah had no right to make such promises for him."

"No?" He snorted. "Then how about this – if your cousin doesn't marry you, you and I will both end up in debtors' prison."

Jane's mouth dropped open. "What? But – but your business investments—"

"Failed," Colonel Carlyle snarled. "Failed, all of them."

"But all the money from your inheritance, and Mama's dowry – *my* dowry!"

"Gone," he snapped. "Just like we'll be, if we don't act now. So, are you going to help me, or are you going to run and hide in that passageway while I do it, so you can soothe your pretty little conscience like the brainless fool you always have been?"

I could feel Charles vibrating with fury. I hung on to his arm, watching Jane Carlyle. I had to see what she would do.

She looked at her father, and she shook her head. "No, Papa," she said softly. "I'm not going to hide in the passageway."

"Good girl." He nodded. "In that case—"

"I'm going to stop you," Jane Carlyle said.

She stepped back, opened her mouth wide, and let out a piercing scream.

It only lasted an instant. Colonel Carlyle was around the bed in a bound, clapping one massive hand over her mouth and fastening his other around her neck.

"You – stupid – disobedient – disgrace!"

The door handle rattled – Frederick Carlyle trying to get in from the corridor outside.

Colonel Carlyle let out a wordless snarl. He tightened his grip around Jane's neck. "I'm going to take my hand off your mouth," he whispered, "and then you are going to reassure whoever's out there that everything is absolutely fine. Do you understand me?"

She nodded. He lifted his hand away from her face.

Jane let out a second scream, even louder than the first.

Her father slapped his free hand back over her mouth with a smack that resounded through the room.

I let go of Charles's arm just as he lunged forwards, yanking himself free.

"Get your hands off her!" he bellowed.

Oh Lord. The last thing we needed now was public proof that we'd been working magic. I dropped the magic-working that had held Charles invisible and started after him. Luckily, Colonel Carlyle had been facing away from him. As he swung around, the rattling of the doorhandle turned to heavy thuds against the door – Frederick Carlyle throwing himself against it.

"What's going on in there?" Frederick shouted.

Dash it, did *no one* understand the rules of invisibility?

I spun round and lunged for the door. Charles would have to deal with Colonel Carlyle on his own for the moment.

I had to let Frederick in before all the other Carlyles in this wing of the house could come tumbling out of their rooms to find out what was wrong – and discover their host turned magically invisible.

I heard Jane gasp behind me. "Mr Stephenson – Papa, *no!*"

There was a meaty thud of a fist hitting flesh. From Jane's moan of horror, I didn't think it had been Charles who'd thrown the punch.

I grabbed for the key – and it slipped straight out of the lock, falling onto the floor with a clatter. *Curse it!*

"Damn it, let me in!" Frederick shouted through the door.

I could have screamed with frustration as I knelt, scrabbling to pick up the key with shaking hands. I heard Charles let out a grunt of pain behind me.

My brother could box and wrestle as well as any Oxford undergraduate. But Colonel Carlyle was massive compared to him, bulky with pure, bull-like muscle, and more than that, he had spent twenty years fighting in the heat of true battle, not just sparring with university friends.

And from all the sounds coming behind me, this was another battle he was winning.

I wanted to help Charles, but first I needed to get Frederick safely inside the room. If the other Carlyles saw him turn visible and realised we'd been using magic, we would all be ruined.

I finally managed to turn the key in the lock. As it clicked into place, the door burst open... and slammed straight into me, smashing me against the wall. Frederick Carlyle overshot the entrance, stumbled, and fell to his knees. I pushed the door shut even as I heard other doors slamming open all the way down the corridor, and more footsteps pounding up the stairs.

My face was burning with pain. My stomach ached where the door handle had smashed into it. I was panting. But I lunged towards the bed without even bothering to drop Frederick's magic-working first. I'd worry about that later. Now I had to save my brother.

Unfortunately, Frederick pulled himself to his feet at just the same time. We knocked into each other and fell in a tangle onto the hard floor, just as Colonel Carlyle yanked my brother up from the bed where he'd fallen across Angeline's legs.

There was a growing bruise on the colonel's chin, but it didn't slow him down. Charles's blue eyes looked glassy, and he was swaying on his feet. As I watched, though, I realised at least part of that was intentional; he was manoeuvring Colonel Carlyle away from Jane, who had her hands clapped over her mouth, watching them both with horror as she huddled by the head of the bed, near the side table that held the sponge and bowl of water for Angeline's face.

"You have no right to interfere between a man and his belongings," Colonel Carlyle snarled. "What I do with my own daughter is my concern, and nobody else's."

Charles glared at him through rapidly swelling eyes. "You are never going to touch her again."

"Damn you, boy, she's my legal property!"

Charles drew himself up. Bruises covered his face. His hair was a rumpled nightmare, his cravat was twisted out of all recognition, and I had never been so proud of him in my life.

"Your daughter," he said, "is *not* your property. She is your superior, in every possible way."

"That's it!" Colonel Carlyle grabbed him by the neck. As Charles struggled in his hold, he marched him towards the window. "You're going to take a terrible fall, boy, in your grief over finding your sister dead. And nobody – *nobody* – will regret your passing."

I lunged to my feet, even as Frederick started forwards. But Colonel Carlyle was already unlocking the window and wrestling Charles towards it.

There had to be a magic-working I could cast to stop him. But my mind was whirling with such panic, I couldn't think it through.

I couldn't let my brother be killed in front of me. I wouldn't. I took a deep breath, cleared my head...

... and Jane Carlyle spoke. I'd been so intent on watching Charles, I hadn't paid any attention to her until then.

"You're wrong, Papa," she said. "*I* would miss him."

"Quiet!" Colonel Carlyle snapped. He didn't even look round as he pushed the window wide open. "I'll deal with you later."

"No," Jane said. Her lip was already swelling, but her voice came out with ringing clarity. "I'm sorry, Papa, but you will never, ever deal with me like that again."

Something in her tone must have alerted him. He began to turn...

Just as she lifted the big, ceramic bowl full of water and broke it against his head.

Colonel Carlyle's eyes rolled back. His hands fell away from Charles. He collapsed like a mountain tumbling to earth.

I let out my held breath and dropped the magic-workings that held Frederick and me invisible.

Jane Carlyle didn't even notice. She was too busy steadying Charles on his feet, her eyes shining with admiration.

"Oh, Mr Stephenson," she said. "I can never thank you enough. You were so brave, so kind – the things you said—"

Charles grabbed her hand. "I?" he said. "I? *You* were amazing! Your courage – your strength – your—"

Frederick raised his eyebrows expressively, shook his head, and turned away from both of them to check on Angeline. I couldn't move anywhere, not yet, not until my breathing slowed down a bit. But if I had to listen to too much more of this...

Sudden pain lanced through my head, and my vision blurred.

Words raced through my head like thunder, shaking my whole body with their power.

"*Now*," Lord Ravenscroft's son whispered into my mind.

I gave a violent start. A gasp tore itself from my throat.

Frederick turned, frowning. "Kat? What is it?"

There was no one else in the room with us, I was absolutely certain. But I could hear my follower's words all too clearly as he finished, whispering straight into my head.

"*I'm going to destroy you now, and there is nothing you can do to stop me.*"

A picture floated straight into my vision, obscuring everyone in the room with me: the ocean, dark and wild, waves lashing against the beach. Above it, a cliff, with Hepworth towering overhead. And on the beach...

"Oh Lord," I whispered.

I knew exactly where my follower was, and what he was about to do. And if he succeeded...

If he succeeded, he wouldn't destroy only me. He would destroy the entire Order, and all of Britain with it.

"Kat?" Frederick said. "What in the world – ?"

"I'm sorry," I said. "I have to go, I have to... Tell Lady Fotherington to find me on the beach below Hepworth. *Now!*"

"What are you talking about?" he said. "You can't just – Kat! Kat, come back!"

But it was too late. I was already throwing myself through the hidden door into the darkness of the secret passageway beyond.

CHAPTER THIRTY-ONE

I HURRIED DOWN NARROW, TWISTING STEPS IN THE darkness, feeling my way with hands pressed against the wall on either side. I couldn't see before me, I could only feel that I was going down, down, down into the heart of Hepworth, my evening slippers sliding dangerously against the curved steps at every turn.

I couldn't bear to slow down, though, not even to protect my own neck. The image my follower had projected into my mind had been too clear and too terrifying to allow for any delay. On the beach there had been a boat, with a lantern muffled by a dark cloth to hide its light from any observers. And I had listened to every word Frederick Carlyle had told me earlier about the boats that drew up at night here in Devonshire.

That was why Lord Ravenscroft's son had wanted to come to this part of Devon. He'd told me earlier, though I hadn't understood him at the time: *You brought me to exactly where I needed to be.* After stealing the Order's portals, he had needed to come to the coast because that was where the smugglers were – smugglers who carried things back and forth from France.

There was only one reason Lord Ravenscroft's son would be meeting with smugglers tonight, in the shadow of Hepworth itself. He was going to give them the portals he'd stolen from the Order, giving Emperor Napoleon's own magic-workers free access to the Golden Hall and all the secrets of the British Order that lay within....

And he was going to make the Order believe that *I* had done it.

After tonight, he'd told me, the Order would turn against me as they had turned against his father. After tonight, he'd said, he would watch them destroy my mind...and as much as I didn't want to believe it, if he succeeded in tonight's plan, that was exactly what would happen. Magical pacification would be the Order's immediate punishment for any Guardian who committed treason, and the process of forcibly taking my powers away would destroy my mind every bit as thoroughly as the wild magic of Bath had destroyed Lord Ravenscroft's.

More than that, the king would disband the Order in a heartbeat, the very moment he discovered the loss of the portals to the French. I wasn't going to let that happen.

Lord Ravenscroft's son might think himself very clever, but he'd made one vital mistake when he let me see what he was planning. He might have thought I'd be trapped in the house by my family, or slowed down by the difficulty of finding a path down the cliff until he was safely finished... but he'd wagered without the secret passageways built into Hepworth..

I could tell exactly when I'd left the house behind and

descended into the cliff itself. The air around me turned cold and damp. The scent of the sea filled my nostrils. The steps beneath my feet turned slick. The walls pressed tighter and tighter around me, suffocatingly close and heavy until I felt the pressure of the entire cliff above me and my chest tightened to gasping point. If the walls collapsed on top of me...

They hadn't collapsed in the last two hundred years, I told myself. So why should they collapse now?

Still, I half-ran, half-slid even faster down the stairs. Then my foot skidded off the corner of a step, and I fell forwards into the dark.

I hit my knee first, then my shoulder, and then all I could do was wrap my arms over my head and tuck myself up like a hedgehog as I tumbled down the last ten steps, bruising every inch of my back and legs along the way.

I landed at the bottom of the steps with a crash that rattled all through my bones. My heartbeat was racing so fast, I felt like my chest might explode. Every bit of me hurt. Rocks poked up into my side as I lay curled up on the rough earth, gasping for breath and shuddering all over.

I was still alive. That was the first coherent thought I could come up with. All the way down the steps I'd expected to hit my head or break my neck at any moment. Instead, I'd survived. It was a miracle....

But one that would be utterly wasted if I lay here feeling sorry for myself any longer. Lord Ravenscroft's son wouldn't wait for me, and neither would the portals.

Slowly, tentatively, I stretched out my legs, wincing with pain. As I pushed myself up, straightening my back, every muscle in my body shrieked in protest.

I took a deep breath. I focused on the pain and then I shut my mind to it. My muscles could shriek all they wanted, but I wouldn't pay attention. I couldn't.

First I had to save the Order, save England, and then save myself.

I reached out in the darkness, orientating myself. The stairs had definitely come to an end, and I was standing in the middle of a small circle of earth, roughly four feet across and bounded by cool, rough stone on every side. I could hear the sound of waves crashing nearby.

Nearly there.

I fumbled until I found a vertical crack in the wall. *The door.* Another minute of frantically scraping my hands against the wall, and I'd found what I was almost certain was the handle. I dug my fingers into the crevices to open it, but I caught myself just in time.

No. I couldn't just leap out into the middle of danger, not when Lord Ravenscroft's son had already proven himself to be stronger than me. I had to be sensible, had to think things through. Magic wouldn't be enough for this battle; I needed all my wits about me... and most of all, I needed the element of surprise.

I closed my eyes and drew power through my aching body.

Can't see me, can't see me, can't see me...

I waited until the power was shimmering through me and I knew I was safely invisible.

There. For once no one could accuse me of being too impulsive or too thoughtless.

Perfectly invisible, I opened the door. It opened into half darkness – a cave, lit only by the gleam of moonlight shining through a narrow entrance. Men's voices drifted in from the beach outside.

Aha.

I slid through the door and carefully closed it behind

me, holding my breath. I stepped softly forwards, towards the opening to the beach and the smugglers and my only hope of saving everything...

And my magic-working shattered like broken glass.

Light blossomed around me. A familiar voice spoke just behind me.

"Finally," said Lord Ravenscroft's son. He stepped forwards, holding the lantern he'd just unveiled in one hand and a dark velvet pouch in the other. "I've been waiting for you, Katherine Stephenson."

✩ ✩

Light encircled the two of us, leaving the rest of the cave in shadow. I tasted the sharp, salty smell of the sea as I turned to face my enemy. Out of the corner of my eye I glimpsed dark, square shapes that could have been crates, stacked around us a few feet away from the sloping, damp walls of the cave. But what drew my gaze with a magnetic attraction were my enemy's eyes, fierce and raw with emotion. The lantern cast its light directly up into his face so that he looked nearly demonic.

I should have hated him the way I'd hated his father. But I couldn't.

Lord Ravenscroft had never looked vulnerable to me. If I hadn't heard this boy's story, I might have seen only arrogance in his eyes, the way I'd seen it in his father's. But how could I blame him for hating me when he believed I had stolen his father from him?

"You're wrong about me," I said. "Someday you're going to realise that I was telling the truth, and you're going to regret this."

He sneered down at me, taller and stronger in

every way. "It's too late for you to lie your way out of this. I knew I could lure you down here easily and I was right. Wasn't I?"

I sighed. My whole body hurt, my head ached from being rattled all the way down the stairs... and he was right. I had run directly into his trap, too frightened by his plan to think clearly. The sound of water relentlessly dripping nearby felt like a dull reminder of every mistake I had ever repeated.

I really was too impulsive, just as Charles always said. But it was too late to change that now. There was no use pretending to either of us that I could defeat him with magic. All that was left was honesty.

"Well?" I said. "What now? You have me here where you wanted me. Those smugglers are waiting to take the portals to France, aren't they? I worked out that much on my own. But why do you need me here just to pin the blame on me? If you're going to betray the whole kingdom just to pay me back for what you think I did—"

"I'm no traitor," said Lord Ravenscroft's son.

I raised my eyebrows at him, almost laughing. "You stole the portals from the Order of the Guardians. You're giving them to a gang of smugglers to be passed on to French magic-workers. How exactly do you define treason? I may not have gone to Eton or Harrow, but—"

"Neither did I," he snarled. "And I know exactly how treason is defined, thank you."

"Then what on earth do you think you're doing?" I pointed at the cave opening and the smugglers moving around outside. "Your father betrayed his country for money. Is that what you're after too? Or—"

"My father did nothing of the sort!" he said. "He... No." He stopped, and drew a deep breath. "I'm not going to be drawn into arguing with you. You're not important enough."

I snorted. "You've put an awful lot of effort into getting me here, for someone you think so unimportant."

He clenched his fist around the lantern's handle until it tipped off-kilter, flashing the light back and forth around us. Stacks of wooden crates flickered in and out of sight as the light swept across them. "I," he said, "am going to do to you exactly what you did to my father. And I'm going to do a good deed for my country at the same time – to prove to everyone that my father was innocent after all."

"Hmm." I crossed my arms, shifting my stance on the rocky ground. "That will be a good trick, considering that Lady Fotherington, my father, and I all saw him confess to what he was doing."

He stared at me. "What does Lady Fotherington have to do with anything? You were the only one there when it happened. That's why the rest of the Order had to take your word for what he'd done."

I stared back, forgetting the discomfort in my feet. "How could you know what I had done and not know that Lady Fotherington was there? How did you even find out about it in the first place? You're not a member of the Order, so they wouldn't have told you. And—"

"I told you," he said. "Friends of my father found me. True friends. Friends who cared about me and wanted me to know—"

"Friends who wanted you to believe the worst," I said. "Friends who lied to you to get you to do exactly what they wanted. And they needed you because... *oh*. Oh, yes," I breathed.

The sounds of the dripping water and the men's voices outside all faded in my ears as the puzzle pieces finally put themselves together, neat and shining in the darkness.

I shook my head in wonder as the last piece slipped itself into place. "My tutor told me the portals weren't kept in the Golden Hall. They'd been moved to London under Lord Ravenscroft's direction. That means... that means that Lord Ravenscroft was one of the only people who knew where they were. But Lord Ravenscroft had told you."

"I saw them," said Lord Ravenscroft's son. His face looked suddenly younger, and achingly vulnerable. "He took one out and showed me once, when I'd impressed him. He said that one day, when the time was ready, he would give me one. One day..."

"So in other words," I said, "these friends of your father needed you to get the portals. And to get the portals, they had to persuade you that I was to blame for your father's fall, to make you so angry you'd set out for revenge. So that's why—"

"They told me the truth!" He glared at me. The moment of vulnerability was gone; or rather, he'd hidden it beneath his father's arrogant glare. "You can't pretend—"

"I'm not pretending anything," I said. "For heaven's sake. Do you really think the Order would have believed Lord Ravenscroft, their own Head, was a traitor, only because I said so?"

"You told them—"

"They wouldn't have believed a word I told them without undeniable proof," I said. "Didn't your friends tell you that part? Your father expelled me from the Order. He ordered my tutor to pacify me and destroy my mind. Your father told all the other Guardians that I was a dangerous menace who couldn't be trusted under any circumstances."

He blinked at me. "Well... yes. That was why you hated him. That was why you wanted revenge, and why—"

"That," I said, "is why I couldn't possibly have done what they've accused me of. Do you think anyone in the Order would have believed me? They would have laughed in my face at the whole idea – that is, if they hadn't been too busy pacifying me first. The only way they could have ever been persuaded was by real, solid evidence – and not from me. From other people who were there and saw everything. Including Lady Fotherington, your father's friend – who hated me far too much to try to save me from him."

"But..." He shook his head, and the lantern shivered in his hand. "That's not right. They told me – he swore to me—"

"Indeed I did," said a voice several feet away. The voice was deep and masculine and tinged with an unmistakable French accent. It came from the entrance to the cave, blocked now by a tall, cloaked figure. "And I can see that I've arrived just in time. Miss Stephenson, you've been extremely useful. But my dear boy..." He turned his gaze to my companion, and his voice gentled with regret, "I'm very much afraid that you may finally have come to the end of your usefulness to us. Your father would have been so disappointed."

CHAPTER THIRTY-TWO

LORD RAVENSCROFT'S SON SPUN ROUND SO QUICKLY, the lantern rattled in his grip. "Moreau! You weren't supposed to – you said you'd wait while I—"

"So this is your 'true friend'," I said, and shook my head in disgust. "For heaven's sake. You knew your father had been convicted of treason, but you still trusted a French spy's word on what had happened?"

"Moreau's not a spy! He's an émigré – so he fled the Revolution, he didn't support it – and he was Father's friend and – and anyway, I'm not listening to anything you say." Lord Ravenscroft's son was panting by the end of his speech, looking back and forth between me and the man in the entryway. "Moreau, tell her. She *was* the only one there when Father lost his wits, tell her – explain!"

I looked past him to the man in the entryway. "Yes," I said. "Do tell me exactly what happened to me and what I did. That should be an interesting story. Do you want to tell me exactly what you told him?"

"Oh, I think you've worked that out for yourself already, Mademoiselle." Moreau shook his head. His face was hidden by shadows, but his tone sounded genuinely regretful. "It is a pity, too. You are far too convincing for our friend's best interests. If it hadn't been for you, I could have found a great deal more use for him, and it would all have been far more pleasant and less painful for everybody concerned."

"I don't understand," said Lord Ravenscroft's son. The lantern was definitely wobbling in his hands now. "Why are you talking this way?"

"Oh, I know you don't understand quite yet," said Moreau, "but you would have soon enough, I assure you. I can read the signs quite well, you know – and I was rather afraid that something like this might happen when you insisted on confronting her by yourself, like the perfect young hero. That was why I decided to drop in on your tête-à-tête before it could go too far – and I arrived none too soon, it seems."

He sighed. "It is a great shame for any promising friendship to end so soon... but now, *Mademoiselle* Stephenson and my dear Alexander, I don't believe we can delay any longer." He stepped into the cave, as graceful as a dancer, and held out his hand in mock-courtesy. "Alexander, the portals, please."

Lord Ravenscroft's son – Alexander – only stared back at him. In the light of the lantern, his eyes looked huge in his pale face. "But that was only supposed to be a ruse! We were only going to pretend to pass them on to the smugglers so the Order would see Katherine and – and... oh, my God." He shook his head. "It was never a ruse. You really were planning to send the portals to France the whole time. And I thought – you made me think..."

He closed his eyes. "I've been such a fool," he whispered.

For a moment the only sound in the cave was the drip of water.

"Poor boy," said Moreau. "You mustn't blame yourself. The loss of your father, following so soon after your mother's death... it was hardly to be expected that you should be capable of thinking clearly. You may stand firm in your own conscience after this, knowing that you meant only the best all along." He took a long, gliding step closer. "And now, Alexander..."

"And my father?" Alexander asked. His eyes were still closed; his voice sounded raw. "Was she telling the truth about that, too? He really was a traitor, after all?"

"Rest assured," said Moreau, "he would not think badly of you for helping us now. I truly was his friend, you know. We worked together for some time."

"And you didn't have to trick him into helping you." Alexander's face tightened. "Not like his stupid son." He opened his eyes.

It hurt to look at his face, which was lined with pain. But he wasn't looking at me, or even at Moreau, as he spoke.

"He wasn't even planning to take me with him to France, was he? After everything he said..."

"My dear boy," said Moreau, "this is all ancient history. Why torture yourself over it any longer? All you have to do is hand over the portals to me now, and then you may forget all about this unpleasant interlude. Pursue a new life, separate from all these painful recollections. In fact..."

He stepped closer, until his outstretched hand was only inches away from Alexander's arm. The lantern cast just enough light across Moreau's face for me to glimpse the smile curving his lips. "You can even come with me, if you like, just as your father planned to. For all we know, he may have planned to send for you once he arrived. Why not? Emperor Napoleon is not so particular as these snobbish English aristocrats, demanding gentle birth from all in their Order. In France, you may find the career you were born for."

"As a traitor?" Alexander's voice was dull. "As the useless rubbish the Order always thought I was?"

"As the practical young man", Moreau said gently, "that I know you to be."

Alexander lifted his chin. I watched his green eyes narrow, and the skin on my arms prickled. I knew that look. I had seen it on Lord Ravenscroft's face every time he looked at me.

"You," he said, "knew my father. You do not know *me*." He threw out his arm.

A surge of wind billowed up around us in a roaring wave that hurt my ears. It flung itself at Moreau, lifting him off the ground...

And disappeared, as the Frenchman landed neatly back on his feet and dusted off his cloak. Alexander gaped at him, looking as bewildered as if he'd been the one knocked off-balance.

"That," Moreau said, "was very foolish. Do you think just because your English Guardians are too frightened to combine witchcraft and Guardian magic that you are the only one who ever tried? Do you truly imagine that you can stand against me on such a battleground with only the training of your own father, a man with no witchcraft in his veins?"

Alexander gaped at him. His mouth opened and closed. The lantern swung back and forth in his hands. "You stopped – you broke—"

"Yes, Alexander, I broke your working. As I shall break every working you bring against me." Moreau straightened; his voice shifted. "I have been patient with you until now, but I shall be patient no longer. Give me the portals, or I will show you what a true magic-worker can do."

Tension filled the air. Alexander and Moreau locked gazes like two stags locking antlers. It was as if no one else existed in the world but the two of them.

It was the perfect moment to make my move.

I darted forwards, snatched the lantern from Alexander's hand, and smashed it to the floor. Blackness fell around us. I grabbed Alexander's arm and pulled him backwards.

It was like trying to pull a cabinet full of stones.

"Come *on!*" I hissed, and pinched his arm for good measure.

Finally he started moving. I breathed a sigh of relief and dragged him over to the corner of the cave where I'd first emerged. I slid my free hand across the damp wall, searching for the door handle. The surface was rough and dotted with sharp stones that scraped against my palm every inch of the way, but I didn't let the scratches stop me.

All we had to do was get back through the door into the secret passageway. Then we'd find a way to block it somehow, get up the stairs to Hepworth, find a way to summon the rest of the Order, and then –

"Very cleverly done, Mademoiselle Stephenson." Moreau's voice sounded less than perfectly cool for the first time since I'd met him. "You took me quite off guard."

I ignored him, running my hand across the wall with increasing urgency. There had to be a door handle on this side too. Didn't there? All I needed was one more moment to find it. If I could only think of a distraction...

Alexander let out a grunt behind me. A flash of light exploded around us, blinding me. When my eyes cleared, I was in darkness once more... and my hand was no longer holding Alexander's arm.

"Alexander?" I spun round. "Alexander! Where are you? What—"

"Do not be alarmed." I couldn't see Moreau as he spoke, but I could tell from his voice that he was moving further away. "He is perfectly unharmed. You see, I am not a total villain. However..." For a moment he stood silhouetted against the entryway, looking back at me. "I warn you not to test my generosity. Go ahead and do exactly as you were planning, Mademoiselle Stephenson. Retreat into the safety of the house, where you belong. There is no more you can do here tonight, and you may trust me when I say you would sincerely regret making any further efforts."

He bowed sweepingly and disappeared through the entryway. "Farewell."

"Wait!" I started forwards.

I only managed one step before tripping. I had walked straight into Alexander's crumpled body.

Oh, damnation. Moreau had said he hadn't hurt him!

I ground my teeth together. Moreau had the portals – but I could hardly leave Alexander lying injured and helpless in the dark. It might have been what he was planning for me... but if I was honest with myself, I couldn't blame him. If anyone had done to Elissa or Angeline what he thought I had done to his father, I would have reacted in exactly the same way.

I dropped down to my knees and ran my hands across his limp figure, biting back my impatience. "Are you all right? Are you—"

"Moreau," Alexander mumbled. "The portals."

"Yes, I know. I'm not completely unobservant." I rolled my eyes in the darkness. "But I was afraid you were—"

"We have to get them back!" He leaped up.

His head knocked straight into my nose.

"Ow!"

I clamped my hands to my face as tears sprang to my eyes. My nose was burning and swelling up under my fingers.

"I beg your pardon," he said. But he was already moving, lunging for the entryway and the moonlit beach beyond. "Come on!"

Gritting my teeth, I stumbled after him. I was only a foot behind him when he hit the entryway and rebounded as if he'd run into a wall. He slammed straight into me, knocking me backwards. I fell onto the hard stone floor. He landed directly on top of me.

I bit back the worst curse I had ever heard Charles utter during his drinking days.

Next time, I was definitely going to leave any angry, arrogant, male companions on the ground while I went off and managed the rescue missions myself.

I shoved at Alexander's back until he rolled off onto his hands and knees. Then I pulled myself up to a sitting position, breathing hard. "Will you please slow down and start acting like a rational human being, for once in your life?"

He didn't answer. He was staring past me towards the cave entrance.

I scooted around to follow his gaze, wincing with discomfort. Then I saw what he'd been staring at, and I forgot all about the pain in my limbs.

White smoke was swirling and billowing up through

the air. As I watched, it separated into two columns... two columns that swirled into human shapes, one much taller than the other.

"What in the world – ?"

"It has to be something Moreau left behind," Alexander said. "I set it off by trying to go through, and then..." His voice cut off in a strangled gasp.

The taller figure was moving towards him. The smoke had solidified into a solid human form, pure white but perfect in every detail, from the form-fitting evening clothes to the carefully pomaded hair, to the all-too-familiar quizzing glass held up to its eye as it inspected the boy who knelt beside me.

"Father?" Alexander whispered.

But I didn't have time to pay proper attention. The column on the left was moving too.

This figure was smaller – only a few inches taller than me. Her pure white form held no hint of colour, but I knew her hair was dark. I knew the smile of delight that spread across her face as she saw me, and I knew that the gown she was wearing was red.

I knew, because it was the same gown she had worn in her miniature portrait, the only picture of her I had ever seen.

"Mama," I whispered as she held out her hand to me.

And I knew it was her.

CHAPTER THIRTY-THREE

MY MOTHER'S GHOST HELD OUT HER HAND TO ME, AND I lunged for it, shuffling on my knees across the cold cave floor. Our hands reached for each other, clasped – and her bright white fingers passed through mine like smoke, chilling me through and through.

"Mama!" I curled my icy fingers against my chest, but I couldn't look away from her.

She smiled at me as tremulously as if I were the miracle, not her. "Katherine," she murmured.

Her voice sent a thrill through my body.

It shouldn't have – couldn't have – been familiar. I hadn't heard her voice since I was ten days old. But every bone in my body resonated with it... *recognised* it.

I had been waiting for my whole life to hear her voice again. I just hadn't realised it until now.

My face was wet with tears. I didn't bother to wipe them away even as they streamed down my cheeks and onto my neck and chest in a silent, unquenchable flood. I couldn't take the time to wipe them away. More than that, I couldn't spare the effort. I was too busy memorising every inch of the woman who was smiling down at me for the first time in more than thirteen years.

She shone in the darkness, glowing white. "My Kat," she whispered. "But where are your sisters?"

"Elissa – Elissa's resting. She's going to have a baby," I added, and I felt my tears stream even faster as I saw the joy spread across Mama's face at the news. "She's going to be a wonderful mother."

She shook her head wonderingly. "And Angeline?"

"Angeline..." I swallowed down the sob that tried to burst up through my throat. I wanted to throw myself forwards into my mother's arms, but they were only white smoke and wouldn't hold me. "Angeline's resting too. She's – she was shot. She's very ill. Frighteningly ill. I found the person who did it, but—"

"She was shot?" Mama's eyes widened in horror. "How could you have let that happen?"

Her words hit me like a blow. I almost doubled over. It hurt to speak. "I couldn't stop it. I thought I was the one in danger, not her—"

"So you let her be attacked? How could you, Kat?" Mama shook her head. Sparkling white tears appeared in her eyes. I felt sick as I watched them trickle down her cheeks.

"I'm so sorry, Mama," I whispered.

Male voices were speaking nearby in agitated, rising tones – Lord Ravenscroft and Alexander, only a few feet away – but I couldn't take in a single word. All of my world was my mother's face, and the disappointment in her eyes as she looked down at me.

"Oh, Kat," she said. "But what about the Order?"

I swallowed hard. "What do you mean?" I asked. But I had a horrible feeling I already knew.

Her face softened into wistfulness. "I knew," she said. "I knew the moment you were born that you were the one who had inherited my powers. I knew, even then, that I could count on you. I knew you would prove to them how wrong they were to expel me. I knew you would prove yourself to the Order, and restore my reputation in it. You have done that, haven't you, Kat? Haven't you?"

If the cave's floor had reared up and slammed into me, it could not have hurt me more than her words and the look on her face as she said them.

The look on her face – and the memory of Lady Fotherington, not two hours earlier, as she'd laughed at me and left me alone in the unlit library to await her decision. There was every possibility that my place in the Order – and all our family's future eligibility for it – had already been ruined forever.

I wanted to let out a wail of misery, like the baby I had been when I first lost my mother. But I wasn't an infant anymore, and I couldn't ask my mother for comfort. Not for this. Not when I knew the truth and couldn't ignore it any longer.

It didn't matter what I did the rest of this night, whether I saved the portals or not... because either way, by the morning, my career in the Order would be over, and so would every hope I'd ever had for restoring Mama's reputation.

No, worse: I would drag her reputation through the mud all over again, leaving it more soiled than ever. When the rest of the Order heard that I'd been playing with witchcraft, they wouldn't just remember my mother and sneer; it would be the final piece of evidence they had needed to prove that her entire family line was tarnished.

They wouldn't only feel glad they had expelled her; they would never admit a child from her line ever again.

I looked up at my mother's hopeful, loving face. I opened my mouth to speak. I couldn't make the words come out.

In the end I didn't have to. She must have read the truth in my face.

"Kat," she breathed. She put a hand to her mouth, shaking her head, first slowly and then as wildly as if she could shake away something too horrible to be believed. "Kat, I trusted you! I believed in you! Didn't that mean anything?"

"It did," I said. The tears were coming so hard, now, I was nearly blinded by them. "It does. It means everything. I tried, I truly did. I just—"

"You didn't care," she said softly. "You didn't care about me after all. I died because of you, and you never even cared."

The wail I'd been trying to hold back finally burst out of my throat, and there was nothing I could do to stop it. All I could do was curl up into a ball of misery, wrapping my arms around my legs and rocking back and forth.

The other voices in the cave grew louder and louder, but the only words I heard were my mother's, repeating over and over again in my head.

I died because of you, and you never even cared.

It was the one reproach my brother and sisters had never uttered, even in the worst of our arguments. The one reproach Papa had never even hinted at. The one that nobody in my family would ever, ever say.

But it was the one I had always known to be true.

My mother *had* died because of me... and now I had failed her all over again.

"Just go," she whispered to me, and her voice cut through my piercing wail and the raised male voices beside us as easily as if she were speaking directly into my heart. "Go now, Kat. I can't even bear to look at you."

My wail cut off as abruptly as if I'd been slapped. I hiccupped. My nose was pressed into my legs; my mouth was full of damp muslin from my soaked gown. The cave floor was cold underneath me.

"Yes, Mama," I said. My voice came out as a croak, hoarse with exhaustion and too many tears. "If that's what you want, I'll do it."

I pulled myself up as painfully as an old woman, feeling every joint creak.

"I need to—"

"Just go!" Mama said. "Go back to your sisters. At least you can try to keep them safe... if you truly care about them at all."

"Yes, Mama," I whispered. I turned away. The muscles in my back stung with every step as I hobbled towards the hidden door. I could feel her reproachful gaze burning against me.

It wasn't so hard to find the door handle, this time. I fitted my fingers into the grooves in the wall, drew a deep breath, and looked back.

Mama stood beautiful and shining white, watching me with tears in her eyes. My own eyes dropped; I couldn't hold her gaze.

"I love you, Mama," I whispered.

She turned away from me.

I pulled the door open. It was harder from this direction than it had been from the other side. I had to grit my teeth with effort as I dragged it towards me.

The energy of it cleared my head for a moment from

the haze of grief and exhaustion. If I really wanted to know the truth about the past, the parts Papa refused to tell me...

I couldn't. She wanted me gone. At the memory of her words, the haze started to descend again, and my eyes burned with fresh tears. I wiped them away with the back of my hand. *No*. I would never make it back up all those stairs if I let myself collapse again.

I would do what my mother had asked me to do – the only thing I could do for her anymore. But first I would find out the truth.

I turned back to her. "Mama," I said. "Who is the marquise?"

In my haze, it took me another moment to realise I hadn't been clear. After all, the marquise hadn't had that title yet when she'd known Papa; she'd said that at our first meeting.

"I mean..." I began.

But Mama was already answering. "Oh, Kat." She shook her head at me. "You've ruined her life too. How could you let Lady Fotherington find out about her witchcraft? What were you thinking?"

After all the blows of the last few minutes, this one was only an extra knife wound. "I know," I said. "I know. I wasn't thinking."

"To be so thoughtless..."

"I know!" I said. Then I slammed my lips shut in horror. I hadn't just snapped at my own mother, had I?

I had. Her face was full of shock. "Kat, how could you?"

It took everything I had not to lunge through the door and escape. But I had come this far, and I couldn't stop now. "I'm sorry, Mama," I said. "I am. But who is the marquise?"

She blinked at me. "I don't understand."

"You know who I'm talking about," I said. "You must. Otherwise, how could you know what I'd done? And what I talked about with Lady Fotherington?" I frowned. "How did you know what I'd talked about with Lady Fotherington?"

"What you did...," my mother began.

"But who is she?" I said.

Mama didn't answer.

I took a step forwards, letting go of the door. "Mama?"

"I don't know," she said. "Oh, Kat. How could you hurt me this way?"

Her words were a blow. But I had withstood too many blows tonight already. This one barely hurt at all.

"You don't know?" I repeated. "But you must know. She knew Papa. She knew Elissa. She knew you." I took a step closer. "She said she would have saved you, if she could. How can you not know who she is?"

"Why are you pestering me?" Mama said. She lifted one trembling hand to her mouth. "How can you speak to me this way? Don't you care at all?"

"I care," I said automatically. And it was true.

But for the first time in the last ten minutes, I had noticed something else, beyond Mama's beautiful, eerily familiar face.

I noticed how far she had advanced from the cave door where she had started. And I finally remembered something Alexander had said, something that had been driven out of my mind by everything else that had happened.

I said, "You know what I discussed with Lady Fotherington. I know that too."

Mama's face creased. "Is that meant to be a riddle? Are you trying to play games with me, Kat?"

I couldn't stop my shoulders hunching against her words, but I forced myself to continue as steadily as I could. "Everything you've said was something I knew already. Or..." I put one hand to my churning stomach, "something I was afraid of. Something I felt guilty about already."

"Do you?" Mama looked at me and shook her head with infinite disappointment. "Do you truly feel any guilt? I only wish I could believe it."

"Oh, I do," I said. "And you've brought up everything I feel most guilty about, in the way that hurts the most. Because..." I looked past her at the cave entrance, and I drew a painful breath. "Because that's your purpose, isn't it?"

"Kat?" Mama blinked. "What are you talking about?"

"You look exactly like your portrait," I said, "because that's the only picture of you I ever saw. You sound like yourself because..." I drew a ragged breath. "Because somewhere inside me, I remember your voice. And you know all about my sisters because I do, too."

"Kat—"

"But you don't know who the marquise is because I don't either." I looked her straight in her shining, tear-filled eyes. "And because the truth is, *you are not my mother*."

CHAPTER THIRTY-FOUR

THE SHINING WHITE FIGURE BEFORE ME GASPED. "Kat!" she said. "How can you deny me? How can you...?"

But I shut out her voice even as she continued. I clenched my jaw and clenched my fists and shut her out with every fibre of my being.

"You are not my mother," I repeated. And I knew it to be true.

Moreau had cast an illusion. He had warned me not to walk through the cave entrance. He had promised me I would regret it.

He had been right.

Less than five minutes ago, as I had lain sobbing on the floor, I had thought that nothing could hurt worse than the loss of my mother's faith in me. But now I had lost something even worse, after all – something I'd never even realised I had until it was gone.

I had lost the hope of ever seeing my mother again.

I'd tried to believe that the marquise might be my mother. I'd closed my ears to everything she'd said that contradicted it.

But after this, I'd had enough of grasping at straws.

I closed my eyes. I drew power up through my body until I tingled with it.

I couldn't sense any magic-working or spell in the air. Moreau was like Alexander in that way. But I knew something else I could do.

I opened my eyes and looked at the illusion of my mother, weeping and reproaching me.

I can't see you, I thought with all my might. *I can't hear you. I cannot sense you here.*

She was gone.

I let out a shuddering breath. My eyes burned, but I had used up all the tears inside me. My fingers itched to reach out and touch the empty air where I knew she still stood, but I clasped my hands together to hold them back. I held my magic-working firm and steady, even though everything in me wanted to drop it and let myself believe in the illusion for just one last moment.

Turning away was one of the hardest things I had ever done.

Male voices had been battering at the edge of my hearing for the past ten minutes, but it was only now, with my mother's illusion gone, that I could finally take in the other confrontation that was happening in the cave.

It wasn't going well for Alexander. Unlike me, he hadn't been reduced to weeping; his shoulders were squared and his chin held high. But he had backed up further and further from the entryway, and in the half-light cast by his father's white glow, his eyes looked huge and panicked.

"Did you ever truly believe I was proud of you?"

Lord Ravenscroft sneered down at his son, advancing on him until Alexander's shoulders were pressed against the pile of crates that lined the back wall of the cave. "I wouldn't even marry your mother and taint my name with her witchcraft. Why on earth would I ever choose to acknowledge you?"

"Alexander!" I said. "Don't listen to him."

But Alexander wasn't listening to me. When he spoke, he didn't sound like the angry, powerful magic-worker who'd followed me across England and broken all my magic-workings. He sounded like a frightened boy.

"Father," he said. "Please..."

"I never cared about you," his father said. "You were only useful, as a servant could be useful to me. I trained you as my servant, not my equal."

"Alexander," I said, and I pushed past the chill of Lord Ravenscroft's illusion to grab Alexander's arm. "Listen to me. That is not your father."

The muscles in his arm twitched under my hand, but he didn't look away from the illusion of his father's contemptuous sneer. "Father—"

"Think about it!" I shook his arm. "Your father isn't even dead. How could this be his ghost?"

Alexander shot me the briefest possible glance, his face despairing. "He is dead, though. Everything about him that made him himself. All that's left is his body. Why shouldn't this be his ghost?"

"You didn't keep me safe," Lord Ravenscroft said. He advanced inexorably, sending chills across my skin. "You weren't there to protect me. You couldn't even bring yourself to take revenge on the worthless girl who ruined everything for me."

"I couldn't," Alexander said. The words sounded

torn from his throat. "It would have been wrong. It would have—"

"Wrong? *Wrong*? What do you know of wrong? You're no gentleman. You're not even a Ravenscroft. You are nothing and nobody, only illegitimate rubbish I should have kicked onto the streets years ago. You're—"

"He's only an illusion," I said. I dug my fingers into Alexander's arm, trying to break through the trance that held him. "Moreau left a trap for us in the entryway, remember? This isn't a real ghost. He's using your memories against you. Anything you were scared of, anything you felt guilty about—"

"Not... my father?" The words emerged slowly from Alexander's mouth, as if they were being dragged out against his will.

"No," I said. "It isn't real. It's only—"

"It is real, though," Alexander said. He turned and looked me in the eyes for the first time since the illusions had first appeared before us. "This is what my father really thought of me, all along."

I swallowed, caught between compassion and honesty. "That's... we don't know that that's true."

"Yes, I do," he said. "I just never wanted to admit it to myself."

The illusion of Lord Ravenscroft hadn't spared me so much as a glance – it must have been completely tied into Alexander – but even for me, it was eerie how true the semblance felt. It made me itch with discomfort and the old fear I'd always felt in Lord Ravenscroft's presence.

I couldn't imagine growing up as his son.

"He must have valued you," I said. "He trained you, didn't he? And you inherited his Guardian powers. That has to mean something."

"*That* meant he could never have an heir." Alexander's voice was tired and bitter. "Guardian powers only descend to one child in a generation. Because of me, he was never going to be able to pass on his rule over the Order to a legitimate son. Who knows? Perhaps I'm the reason he turned traitor. What did he have left to lose?"

"Yes!" Lord Ravenscroft said. "You are the reason I betrayed my country. Because of you, my future was ruined. Because of you—"

"You're wrong," I said. I pushed myself between Alexander and the cold, white illusion of his father. I stood on my tiptoes and grabbed Alexander's head to force him to look down and meet my gaze.

"He did have something to lose," I said. "His honour. He gave that up in the end... but you didn't. And that makes you a better man than your father."

Alexander's eyes widened. He opened his mouth, but he didn't speak. So even as Lord Ravenscroft's contemptuous, sneering voice rose higher and higher in outrage behind me, I kept going.

"You," I said, "are not your father. And you are not going to let him stop you from doing the right thing now." I shook him by his broad shoulders. "Are you?"

As Alexander looked down at me, his face slowly transformed from a mask of pain and bewilderment to a look of bemused wonder. He shook his head.

"I think Moreau was right about you, after all," he said. "You are dangerous."

"Thank you," I said. I dropped back down to the soles of my feet, but kept a firm glare fixed on him. "Now, can you break Moreau's casting? Or do I need to—"

Alexander cut me off with a glare at least as scathing as any his father could have managed. "Thank you," he said, with heavy sarcasm, "but I am perfectly capable of breaking any casting whose creator isn't here to fight back."

He narrowed his eyes. Cold air swirled around us... and then there was silence and only the memory of a chill against my back, where Lord Ravenscroft's illusion had stood. I let go of Alexander's shoulders and dusted off my gown. "Well," I said. "Shall we rescue the portals?"

He blinked. "That's all you're going to say?"

I blinked back. "Is anything else required?"

A man's cry of alarm sounded outside. More shouts followed, further down the beach, both male and female.

"Oh Lord," I said. "We'd better hurry." I picked up my skirts and ran for the door.

This time Alexander let me go first... so I was the one who stumbled to a halt in the entryway when I caught sight of the scene outside, and he was the one who walked into me, knocking me forwards.

He caught me before I could fall.

"What the devil?" he said.

He wasn't asking why I'd stopped. He could see that perfectly well over my head. What he was asking was why the beach was suddenly full of men and women in elegant evening clothes, shouting and running towards the water.

At first all I could make out was an indistinguishable mass of people in the moonlight. But as balls of glowing light sprang up in mid-air all along the beach, white, bright, and clearly magical, I began to pick out individual figures and features... and I didn't recognise any of them.

I recognised the other magic that swirled against my senses, though: giant waves of Guardian power rolling past me towards the great black water, and rebounding off it as if it were bouncing off a wall.

"It's the Order," I whispered. Wonder filled me as

I gazed at the group: at least twenty men and women in immaculate evening dress, all gathered together in full strength. My colleagues... at least for a few more hours. "They're all here."

"But how?" Alexander was still holding my arms, as if he'd forgotten to let me go. "Moreau was the one who was going to summon them for our plan. So they could see you... um..."

"See me giving the portals to the French," I finished for him, rolling my eyes. "Yes, I see what you mean. Moreau wouldn't have actually summoned them. So it must have been someone else."

I peered through the mass of people and caught sight of a familiar profile standing high up the beach next to my own magical tutor, Mr Gregson.

Aha.

"Lady Fotherington," I said, and sighed. "I sent for her on my way down. She must have sent for the others."

I should have been grateful and relieved. But all I could think as I saw her was that it must have been the greatest moment of her life... or rather, the greatest moment since she had seen my mother expelled from the Order all those years ago. She'd wanted so badly to be the heroine of the hour this time, saving the portals for the Order and for England, and it looked like she had managed it after all. No wonder she had summoned the whole Order to witness her victory.

In a few hours I would be expelled in shame and disgrace, and she would be feted as the woman who had saved us all.

I was happy for the Order and for England. I was. But all the accumulated exhaustion, grief, and aches of the past few hours settled against me like a weight pressing down against my shoulders, trying to flatten me to the ground. I was grateful for Alexander's big hands on my arms, holding me upright.

"Well," I said. "I suppose they don't need us after all."

"I wouldn't say that." Alexander's tone was grim. "Haven't you looked at the water? Moreau's getting away."

"What?" For the first time I looked past the Guardians on the beach to the frothing water of the ocean, black in the darkness. I could just barely make out a rowing boat a hundred feet away, pulling steadily across the water.

"He can't be stronger than all of them together!"

"I'm sure he isn't." I felt Alexander shrug behind me, his hands flexing on my arms. "But you can't break a combined Guardian-witch magic-working with only one type or another. So no matter how many Guardians try to break his casting—"

"Can you break it?"

His hands tightened on my arms. There was a simmering silence. I couldn't sense the magic he was using, but I felt the intensity of his focus... and when I heard him let out a shuddering sigh, I knew what the answer would be even before he said it. "Moreau was right. He is more powerful than me."

"We have to tell them." I shoved aside the smothering exhaustion and pulled out of Alexander's arms. "Come on!"

I set off across the beach. Sharp rocks bit through my thin evening slippers, and magic buffeted me from every turn. Even though none of it was aimed at me, it felt like trying to run through a hurricane.

I'd only made it halfway to Mr Gregson when I heard a familiar voice.

"Kat! Dash it, slow down!" my brother shouted.

When I turned, I found it wasn't just Charles running down the beach towards me. Elissa followed after, running just as hard, while Mr Collingwood ran beside her, hovering over her as much as a man can hover while running across a pebbled beach. He looked ready to fling himself between her and the rocks at her slightest misstep.

I didn't have time to wonder at either of them being there. A much more worrying danger had suddenly presented itself.

I knew the exact moment Charles recognised Alexander, only a few feet behind me. My brother's eyebrows lowered. His face turned murderous. He changed direction to run straight at Alexander.

"Wait!" I turned back, stumbling as another wave of Guardian power rushed past me, knocking me off balance. "Charles, no – it's not what you think – Charles!"

But I was too late.

Charles had already lunged forwards and knocked Alexander to the ground.

CHAPTER THIRTY-FIVE

"No!" I FLUNG MYSELF FORWARDS. "CHARLES, ALEXANDER wasn't chasing me, he was *helping* me. He hasn't done anything wrong."

"Devil take it, Kat!" Charles stood over Alexander, his fists cocked in a boxing pose, but he looked at me with an expression of sheer exasperation. "I was there when he threatened you, remember? You can't fob me off with one of your wild stories now."

"It was all just a misunderstanding. We've cleared it up now, so please don't hit him again. And Alexander..." I looked down at him nervously. He lay sprawled on his back with one hand cupped over his nose, and to an ignorant observer, he might have looked at a disadvantage. I knew better. "Please don't hurt Charles. He didn't mean—"

"Oh, yes, I did," said Charles. "Chasing my sister all over England, threatening her and frightening her—"

"I *told* you—" I began.

But Alexander cut me off. "I understand," he said. He dropped his hand from his swelling nose and took a deep breath. When he spoke again, his voice sounded oddly nasal, but steady. "It's all right, Kat," he told me. "I deserved that."

"You certainly did," said Charles. But with another dubious look at me, he reached down and took Alexander's hand, helping him to his feet. "So you finally realised you'd been a fool, did you?"

"Charles..." I began.

Alexander drew back his shoulders as stiffly as a soldier presenting himself to his commanding officer. "I owe your sister an apology," he said.

"You certainly do," said Charles.

I rolled my eyes at them both. "There's no time!" Elissa and Mr Collingwood finally reached us, Elissa gasping for breath, and I shook my head at them. "What are you all doing here, anyway?"

All three of them looked at me as if I were mad.

"You were in danger," Charles said. He enunciated the words as carefully as if he were speaking to an infant, or someone who didn't speak English very well. "You went tearing off and told us to send for Lady Fotherington, of all people, to help. Not to mention, I'd just heard you being threatened by a dangerous lunatic the last time you went outside – I beg your pardon," he added as an aside to Alexander.

"Granted." Alexander nodded, sighing.

"But Elissa is... erm." I remembered Elissa's rule just in time to stop myself from blurting out the word 'increasing'. Instead I looked pointedly at her stomach. "She should be resting."

"That's what I told her," Mr Collingwood said gloomily. "I said I would come and look after you myself—"

"And I said not to be absurd." Elissa crossed her arms. "I may not feel well, but there is nothing wrong with me. And I could hardly rest in bed when I knew Kat was in danger, could I?"

I looked from my eldest sister's familiar pose of command to Charles's equally familiar exasperation and Mr Collingwood's resignation, and a warm glow of happiness built inside me, easing all the aches and pains of the evening.

My family was impossible and interfering... and I suddenly felt better than I had for ages.

"Well, come on, then," I said. "We don't have much time."

I turned and started off again across the beach, letting my family follow behind.

When I reached Mr Gregson and Lady Fotherington, they were both focusing so hard on their magic-workings, they didn't even notice me. I had to reach out and tap my tutor on his shoulder. He jumped, and Lady Fotherington jerked out of her own trance.

"So you've finally deigned to arrive, have you?" she said. Her eyebrows rose. "And you've brought your family to observe? How... unusual."

I ignored her. "We can't break this with Guardian magic," I told Mr Gregson.

"Don't be absurd," Lady Fotherington snapped before he could answer. "You may think yourself very clever, but every Guardian on this beach has more experience than you. So if you'll please stop distracting us—"

"She's telling the truth," Alexander said, and stepped to my side, his arm brushing against my shoulder.

Lady Fotherington looked at him, blinked, and looked harder. "And who exactly are you?"

Alexander cleared his throat. I could feel the muscles in his arm stiffening.

"This is Alexander," I said, and added, so he wouldn't have to be the one to say it, "Lord Ravenscroft's son."

"His *what*?" Lady Fotherington's mouth dropped open.

At a different moment I might have enjoyed the look of pure, horrified shock on her face. But with Alexander standing stiff with humiliation beside me, it wasn't in the least amusing.

"Katherine," Mr Gregson said. He sighed and took off his glasses to rub his eyes wearily. "I believe you have some explaining to do, at some point when we have more time for conversation."

"That's fine," I said. "But you need to hear this now. Moreau – the spy with the portals – isn't just a Guardian. He's a witch, too, and he's casting both kinds of magic in combination."

"That's not possible!" Lady Fotherington said. I was almost certain she was talking about combining magics, but her eyes were still fixed on Alexander. She could have been referring to either of them.

"It is possible," Alexander said. He lifted his chin. His expression remained as haughty as his father's, but I could feel the tension radiating off him. "I do it every day. My father trained me."

"That's. Not. Possible!" Lady Fotherington repeated. This time I knew exactly what she meant.

"It is," I said, "if your mother is a witch. Lord Ravenscroft wouldn't marry Alexander's mother, but he taught him how to use both of their powers together. It makes him stronger than any Guardian. And you can't break a combined Guardian – witch casting with only one type of magic."

"Not possible," Lady Fotherington repeated faintly. But she was beginning to look sick.

Mr Gregson frowned intently. "And you say this Moreau is doing the same thing?"

"He's stronger than Alexander," I said. "He's been practising a long time. And I don't think he's the only one. He said the French Guardians aren't as frightened by witchcraft as the English Guardians are."

Lady Fotherington let out a snort. "Not as disgusted by it, you mean!"

"Not as prejudiced," I said, and glared back at her.

Mr Gregson said, "In that case, we will need a witch."

"What?" Lady Fotherington whipped around to stare at him. "Aloysius, you can't mean—"

"We need those portals back," said Mr Gregson. He put his spectacles back on, arranging them with neat precision. "If saving the Order means working with witches for the first time since the Civil War..." He looked at me. "How much witchcraft did you learn before you gave it up to join the Order?"

"Not enough," I said. "I only learned one spell."

Alexander said, "It's the power that's most important, not the training. If we can gather enough witches together, funneling all their power through a casting..."

"That's not as easy as it sounds." Mr Gregson looked across the beach, frowning. "There might be one or two Guardians on the beach with witchcraft in their veins, but it will take time to persuade them. And we don't have much time left."

The boat was only a speck of darkness on the darker waters now.

Mr Gregson looked at me, and I looked back at him. We both turned to my family at the same time.

"I say," Mr Collingwood said. "Er. I mean..."

Charles backed up a step under the weight of our gazes. "Collingwood's right," he said. "Kat and Angeline are the ones who play at magic, not us."

"Oh, I couldn't," Elissa said. Her hands went to her stomach. She said, "The impropriety of it—"

"That's a French spy out there," I said. "If he gets away, all of England will suffer for it. Do you really think it would be improper to save your country?"

"I understand your concern, Mrs Collingwood," said Mr Gregson, "but this is a matter of national urgency. His Majesty himself has authorised the use of any and all magical force to retrieve the portals before the emperor can make use of them. The government will owe you a great debt of gratitude for any assistance you can render."

Elissa shrank back towards her husband's chest. "I don't know..."

"All right," Charles said. He swallowed visibly. "You took a risk to save me last autumn, Kat. I'll do this for you."

"Thank you," I said. "And Elissa, please. No one would think badly of you for it. It can't be improper to defend England!"

She bit her lip and closed her eyes for a moment. Then she looked at me. "If this man gets away, will you be in trouble?"

"We'll all be in trouble," I said. "He'll be able to get into the Guardian's Golden Hall. He'll be able to use our magic against us and—"

"Then you will be in danger." She drew a deep breath and nodded. "Very well. I won't do it for England, Kat... but I will do it for you."

"Thank you." I reached out and squeezed her hand.

It was warm and strong in mine – my oldest sister, stepping in to protect me one more time.

She leaned closer to whisper in my ear. "Can you promise it won't hurt the baby?"

"Don't be ridiculous," I said. "Mama used witchcraft all the time while she was increasing, didn't she?"

"Well..." She smiled weakly. "Just this once, then. But you musn't tell anyone. Especially not Angeline! She would never let me hear the last of it."

"I won't," I promised. I looked past her at Mr Collingwood, whose mother had also been a witch. "And you'll help too?"

"Well, of course," he said. "If Elissa doesn't mind, then why would I?"

"Thank you." I turned to Alexander. "So, if you can just tell us what to do..."

He looked uncomfortable. "The one difficulty is, I've never done it just as witchcraft. I always did the spell and the magic-working together. I can try and work something out, but—"

"But there's no time for experimentation," a new voice finished for him.

We all gasped, even Mr Gregson, as the marquise appeared beside us, smoothing down her skirts as serenely as if nothing out of the ordinary had happened.

"I do beg your pardon for not arriving earlier," she said, "but I do seem to always be the last person the butler tells whenever anything goes wrong."

"The butler?" I stared at her. "What does the butler have to do with it?"

But no one was paying any attention to me.

"Miss Ann?" Mr Gregson said. He was staring at her as if he'd seen a ghost.

She smiled back at him. "The Marquise de Valmont now," she corrected him. She gave a distant, cool nod to Lady Fotherington. "Your colleague and I are house guests together at Hepworth."

Lady Fotherington was shaking her head frantically, as if she could make the last five minutes disappear by sheer force of will. "You know her, Aloysius? You already knew she was a witch?"

"We can discuss all of this later," the marquise said firmly. "Right now, I believe there is a situation to resolve." She turned to Alexander. "Fortunately, I have had a great deal of experience with witchcraft on its own. If you and Kat will act as the lynch pin of our working, connecting the Guardians with the witches, I can manage the witches for the rest of you." She nodded to my siblings. "Link hands, please."

They did, looking nervous but determined. Mr Gregson turned back to face the dark water, as did Lady Fotherington, though her whole face was twitching with frustrated outrage.

Alexander looked down at me and gave a slight quirk of his lips; the first almost-smile I had seen from him. He held out his right hand to me. "Kat?"

I took his hand. His warm skin was rough and calloused, and my hand felt small in his big grip. I closed my fingers around his. Our palms pressed against each other... and I felt a shocking jolt, like a burst of electricity, run up my arm at the contact.

He must have felt it too; his eyes widened, and his smile dropped. For a moment, as we stared into each other's eyes, I felt very odd indeed.

Then I shook myself out of it, breathing quickly. "We'd better begin," I said.

CHAPTER THIRTY-FIVE

"Indeed," said Alexander, and shook himself as he turned away from me.

The power built up through both of us together this time. I could feel Alexander's magic as it passed through the connection of our clasped hands; I could hear the spell he was chanting under his breath even as I felt his will directing the Guardian magic inside him.

Behind me I heard the marquise directing my siblings. "Now, say this with me, and be certain to repeat my words exactly, my dears..."

Around us I felt the rest of the Order aiming all their gathered Guardian magic as one.

My head felt light and giddy as I reached out and joined my power to all the others'... and felt all our magic come together to become one great, living, breathing creature.

It reared back, up over the beach, with a rush that sent a tingling breeze racing over my head; and then it roared forwards, crashing through the barrier Moreau had set across the sea.

Yes. Now, I thought, and I felt every other Guardian and witch on the beach thinking the same, all of us as one in that moment.

Moreau's boat, that tiny speck in the deep, faraway water, lifted up into the air like a bird taking flight. As the smugglers aboard shouted and their oars waved helplessly in the air, Moreau flung his magic back at us... and our power enveloped his, dissolving it like steel melting in a blacksmith's forge.

Our magic carried his boat over the sea, an unwieldy bird with oars waving like a dozen wings, soaring back to the beach against the background of the star-specked sky.

In my heart I was flying with it too, along with everyone else – Elissa, Charles, Mr Collingwood, every Guardian on the beach, the marquise and Alexander.

The boat slid gently to a halt on the beach in front of us, landing without a single bump, and I came back to myself, landing just as smoothly. There were tears in my eyes, but I didn't feel sad. My body felt tinglingly empty of power and of thought... but pure joy thrummed through every inch of me.

It didn't matter what happened after tonight. It didn't matter if I never stepped into the Guardians' Golden Hall again.

I'd had this moment of magic, and it was everything.

CHAPTER THIRTY-SIX

I WAS STILL LIMP AND TINGLING TEN MINUTES LATER, as Moreau was magically confined and the smugglers were tied up for Frederick Carlyle and the local magistrate to deal with. After the long evening I'd had, for once I was perfectly happy to let other people take care of the finalities and flop down on the rocky beach, leaning into Elissa's side.

But when Mr Gregson started towards Alexander with a purposeful air, I jumped back to my feet and hurried to Alexander's side.

My tutor came to a halt in front of us, dividing a long, dangerously speculative look between us. "Now," he said. "I believe there are only a few last details to wrap up before I report back to His Majesty. Katherine, I don't believe you ever mentioned how this young man came to be involved... or, indeed, how you came to meet him in the first place?"

Alexander squared his shoulders. "I made a terrible mistake, sir. I thought—"

I grabbed his arm and pinched him hard before he could go any further. "Alexander came to me when he realised the portals were missing," I said.

"Did he indeed?" said Mr Gregson. Disconcertingly, his gaze was resting on my hand. I had a nasty feeling that he might have seen the pinch.

"He did," I said. "I mean, he'd been tracking the portals for some time, but when he realised that I was in the same area, and that I was a Guardian and therefore really ought to be dealing with the matter..."

"Quite a useful coincidence," Mr Gregson murmured.

"I— Mmph," said Alexander as I stepped on his foot.

"Well, at first Alexander thought that I had taken the portals myself," I said. "But then he realised it must have actually been Moreau, one of Lord Ravenscroft's old friends – probably the one who tempted Lord Ravenscroft into treason in the first place. Oh, and you should know that Moreau was furious at Alexander for trying to get the portals back, so I wouldn't be surprised if he tells you all sorts of malicious lies about Alexander when you interrogate him later."

I stopped, swallowing hard, as Mr Gregson raised his gaze to look steadily into my face.

"Indeed?" Mr Gregson said gently.

He looked at me for a long moment, and then at Alexander, who was looking horribly proud and just like his father... Or in other words, as I'd come to realise, feeling intensely awkward and uncomfortable. Mr Gregson didn't know Alexander, though. He wouldn't be able to see through the mask.

I bit my lip, searching for the perfect persuasion. In the

end all I could think of was the truth. "We could never have saved the portals without Alexander's help," I said.

"That is certainly true," said Mr Gregson. "The Order owes you a debt of gratitude, young man... as does your country." He nodded to Alexander, who nodded jerkily back to him. Mr Gregson sighed. "Still," he said, "it cannot be helped."

"Sir?" said Alexander.

"What?" I said. "But you can't punish him! He—"

"Yes, yes, Katherine, I know." Mr Gregson lifted one hand to hold me back. "You needn't persuade me of the young man's abilities and intelligence." Relief flooded through me as he continued. "Even his loyalty..." He gave Alexander an enigmatic look, "is now aimed in the proper direction, I see. But I am very sorry to say that we still cannot invite him to be a member of our Order at the moment."

My momentary relief dropped away, and outrage took hold. "How can you not? He saved England! He—"

"He is Lord Ravenscroft's son," Mr Gregson said. "His – ahem – *natural* son. After Lord Ravenscroft's treason, his entire family line was barred from the Order. And you know we have never invited any members from backgrounds which are not genteel."

"I understand," Alexander said. I could feel the tension radiating off him, but his voice was steady. "And Miss Katherine is being overly generous, sir. It wasn't I who saved England. Without her, the portals would still be in Moreau's possession."

"I believe you," Mr Gregson said. "And I believe her, too, oddly enough. What's more, I hope very much that, in time, we will be able to extend you an invitation after all."

I blinked. "But you said—"

"I said, 'at the moment'," Mr Gregson repeated. "However, with so many changes coming into place, I hope I may eventually be able to work that amendment as well, when it comes to a young person who has proven his worth in such a deserving manner." He smiled as I stared at him, and added gently, "We have finally managed to appoint a new Head of the Order, Katherine. You are looking at him."

"Oh, thank goodness!" I threw myself forwards and wrapped my arms around him. "The Order finally showed some sense, for once!"

After a moment of surprise, he hugged me back. But Lady Fotherington's voice spoke sharply behind us, cutting off anything he might have said in reply.

"Changes, Aloysius? What changes?"

She had approached us so silently I hadn't heard her until now. Mr Gregson straightened without any sign of discomposure, though, setting me gently aside.

"Well, Lydia, after tonight we can hardly bar the use of witchcraft in our Order, can we?"

"What?" She stared at him. "But – but it's disgusting! It's foul! It's—"

"It is going to be used against us as a weapon by our enemies, before long." Mr Gregson sighed. "As they are already working to develop it, we can hardly help but do the same. I do not believe anyone in the Order or the Government would desire us to be helpless against such a weapon when it comes."

"But – but..." Lady Fotherington spun round and pointed at me. "This is all her fault!"

I rolled my eyes at her. "Do you really think Emperor Napoleon was listening to *me*?"

"You – you..." She glared at me, pressing her lips together.

Her fury was so clear, I could tell exactly what she was thinking. Everything in her wanted to use the bargain we'd made earlier, to accuse me of practising witchcraft... but that threat had suddenly lost all its venom.

I smiled back at her cheekily. "Yes?" I said. "Was there something you wanted to say?"

"Yes!" she said, and pointed at the marquise, who stood a few feet away chatting to Elissa and Mr Collingwood. "That woman is a witch!"

"A witch," I said, "who just helped to save England."

"And whom we shall be asking for a great deal more help in the future," said Mr Gregson, "as we look for a teacher to train those of our own members who carry witchcraft in their veins."

I narrowed my eyes at Lady Fotherington. "So no one had better spread any scandalous rumours about her in Society."

"No, indeed," said Mr Gregson. "No, as Head of the Order, I may safely promise that none of our members will breathe a word about the marquise's witchcraft after tonight's good work. Isn't that correct, Lydia?"

Her words emerged through gritted teeth. "You are the Head of the Order, Aloysius. We must all do as you say in the matter."

"Perfect," I said, and crossed my arms. "It's only a shame that none of you realised this a long time ago. Mama was right, wasn't she? She said it was only ignorance and prejudice that held the Order back from exploring all their powers."

"Well...," said Mr Gregson.

"I can't take this any longer!" snapped Lady Fotherington. With a whirl of her silk skirts, she turned on her heel and stalked off across the beach.

The eyes of all my family members were on Mr Gregson as he gave a slow, distinct nod of acknowledgement.

Lightness unfurled through my chest as the burden I'd been carrying for so long fell away.

I did it, Mama, I thought.

I didn't think of the false illusion that had wept at me under Moreau's direction; I thought of the girl who'd written her magic spells in looping curlicues and sworn in her diaries never to let 'Ignorance, Prejudice or Pride' hold her back from exploring all the talents she'd been given.

I would never be able to meet my real mother or hear her voice again, but I had seen the new Head of the Order of the Guardians admit that Mama had been right after all. And soon all the rest of the Guardians would know it too.

"Thank you," Elissa whispered behind me, and I knew she wasn't speaking only to Mr Gregson.

I turned back to my family... and jumped as the Carlyles' butler stepped out of a shadow on the beach.

"Henshawe!" I yelped.

"Ah, there you are," the marquise said. "I wondered when you would turn up."

Henshawe looked down his nose at all of us with regal contempt. "I beg your pardons," he said. "But I thought you might care to know that your activity has been kept hidden from all the inhabitants of Hepworth. As none of your Order remembered to take care of that matter, I saw to it myself."

"Thank you, Henshawe," the marquise murmured.

"You did what?" I stared at him.

Mr Gregson was staring at him too. "What do you know of our Order?" he said. "And may I ask who I am speaking to, exactly?"

"This is Henshawe," I said. "The butler." Then I stopped, because there was clearly so much more to him than I had ever realised... but I didn't know any of it.

Henshawe nodded condescendingly. "Thank you, Miss Stephenson." He turned to Alexander. "If I might have a word with you, young man, now that you've finished your business here?"

"I... I suppose so," said Alexander. "But why?"

"There is more than one Order of natural Guardians in England, and not all of us" – Henshawe raised his eyebrows pointedly in Mr Gregson's direction – "are so misguided in our entrance requirements."

"*What?*" This time it was my quiet, dapper magic tutor whose bellow echoed down the beach. Even Mr Gregson seemed startled by his own vehemence; he cleared his throat and asked in a more muted tone, "What on earth can you mean, sir? I was the historian of our Order prior to becoming Head, and I can assure you that no such alternative Orders have ever existed in our isles."

"Ours has never chosen to make itself known to your Order, certainly," said Henshawe. "Our members, you see, have very little interest in associating with those of your Order's birth and station outside of our necessary working hours... and we have certainly never wished to be interrupted in our rather more important business of protecting the harder-working parts of society.

"But as I happened to overhear what you said about changes..." His mouth creased into a slight, dubious smile. "I thought perhaps it might be the right historic moment for our two Orders to finally make contact."

Mr Gregson only stared at him. For perhaps the first time since I'd met him, he was at an obvious loss for words.

Henshawe turned back to Alexander. "And now, young man? Do you truly wish to be of further use to England?"

"I... yes," Alexander said. "Yes. I do." He started forwards. Then he turned back and grabbed my hand in a quick, urgent movement. "I owe you thanks," he said. "As well as apologies."

I swallowed, caught in the intensity of his gaze. "Oh, well," I said. "Now that it's all finished safely..."

"It's not finished, though," he said, so softly that I barely heard him. "I promise you that. I will see you again."

He lifted my hand and kissed it, his gaze holding mine.

My mouth fell open. My skin tingled. My face turned hot. I couldn't breathe.

He pressed my hand and strode away, tall and arrogant and looking far too much like his father, following Henshawe into the shadows... away from me.

"Watch out, Kat," Charles said. "A seagull's going to fly straight into your mouth if you don't stop gaping soon."

"Shh!" said Elissa. "Don't tease her."

But I could hear the muffled giggle in my sister's voice.

I slammed my mouth shut and jerked my gaze back from the shadows. Mr Gregson was still staring after them. He didn't seem to have even noticed the hand kiss.

Thank goodness.

I lowered my hand and hid it in the folds of my skirt. I lifted my chin until I looked authoritative and sensible and completely undistracted by any foolish, girlish trivialities.

"There's just one favour I need to ask from you," I said to the Head of the official Order of the Guardians. "I know I haven't been initiated yet, but I need one more magic lesson first. We've tried everything witchcraft can do to heal a person, but we haven't tried Guardian magic yet."

"Another Order," Mr Gregson breathed. "Another..." He shook his head and turned back to me. "I beg your pardon? Another magic lesson, you say? Right now? Is it really so urgent, Katherine?"

I thought of Angeline, lying unconscious back in Hepworth, and I nodded. "Yes," I said. "It truly is."

And I was standing by my tutor's side, surrounded by my family, as I watched Angeline's eyes open half an hour later.

CHAPTER THIRTY-SEVEN

FREDERICK AND ANGELINE WERE MARRIED ONLY ONE day later than originally planned. Angeline was still paler than usual and moving slowly and carefully as she walked down the aisle behind me and Elissa, but her face shone with happiness as she took her place at the altar beside Frederick.

Even Mrs Carlyle, sitting in the massive Carlyle family pew, managed a strained smile for the occasion. None of the villagers could ever have guessed when she'd swept into the church, in full lady-of-the-manor mode, that she had spent so much of the last few days shouting and weeping and uttering threats to her son... threats which he had utterly ignored.

I hadn't been in the room with him when he had confronted her with the truth about Colonel Carlyle. But I, along with all the Carlyles who had gathered in a seemingly casual group outside the door, had heard her shriek of outrage when he had issued his ultimatum: either his uncle would be turned over to the local magistrate... or Mrs Carlyle would agree to move to the dower house and turn over the running of Hepworth to Frederick and Angeline.

Only if Mrs Carlyle agreed to Frederick's terms would his uncle be allowed to quietly leave the country and never return... thus saving the precious Carlyle name from shocking scandal.

"You unnatural child! How could you think to exile your own mother? I sacrificed my health for you, and how do you repay me? By flinging me into the wilderness!"

Frederick Carlyle's voice rose to speak over the sound of her sobs. "The dower house is only half a mile away, Mama, and it is furnished in the height of luxury. We shall see each other regularly."

"Have you no respect for my health? If I fall ill—"

"Then we shall call for a physician immediately. But the air in the dower house is no more unhealthy than the air in Hepworth."

There was a pause and the sound of muffled weeping. Then Mrs Carlyle spoke again with a tone of distinct triumph. "I have just remembered," she announced, "that none of this matters in the slightest. The fact is, I already promised the dower house to your aunts. Now, what do you think of that?"

All the Carlyles who'd gathered in the corridor outside the library listened avidly, as did I. Frederick's voice was steady through the door.

"Then I am sure we can find you an excellent townhouse in London, instead."

Mrs Carlyle's wail nearly deafened me even through the library door. But I and all the other Carlyles drifted away at that point, because it was clear that the argument was over. Frederick – and Angeline – had won.

Mrs Carlyle's bags were packed by the Hepworth maids over the course of the next two days, even as she wept pointedly, shot venomous looks at her son over every meal, and made remarks about ungrateful children at every possible opportunity. Luckily, Frederick Carlyle spent most of his time in Angeline's sickroom, where he was made far too happy by her recovery to worry about anything else.

Best of all, I had been invited into the library for the last confrontation that took place in Hepworth before the wedding.

"You may think me a coward for asking, Kat," Jane Carlyle had said, "but I would feel better for a female companion in the room. Frederick is up in arms, of course, berating himself for never having noticed anything amiss and ready to make it all up to me now, but that isn't what I need or want at the moment. And as wonderfully... protective... as your brother is..."

A flush spread across her cheeks, clashing with her red hair, as her eyelashes fluttered down to cover her eyes. I watched the transformation with interest.

"Yes?" I said. "Is that what all your walks together in the gardens have been about? Him protecting you from harm?"

Her lips curved into a mischievous smile; her blue eyes sparkled as she looked back at me. "Not... entirely," she said. "But I think, for this particular meeting, I don't actually want any man there to protect me. I only want a friend by my side."

So I was the one who went with her into the library where her father waited, an hour before he was due to leave England under the escort of half a dozen of Hepworth's strongest footmen.

"So you've turned your back on your own father," Colonel Carlyle said. He stood by the window, his massive shoulders blocking out the sunlight and his head lowered like a bull prepared to charge. "Thrown in your lot with a ragtag lot of nobodies when you could have been the mistress of this estate."

Jane Carlyle glided to a halt in the middle of the room, her hands folded and her face composed. "I have, Papa," she said. "I hope you will find your own happiness."

"Not likely." He snorted. "And what have you to look forward to, yourself? Your aunt may take you in out of pity, but now that you haven't any dowry, you're not likely to find a suitor to take you – certainly none of the kind you've been raised to expect. And if you think to give in to that fool who mouthed so much nonsense the other night..."

Jane stiffened. "Mr Stephenson is no fool, Papa."

"I know all about *him*. Oh, yes, I looked into him when I first found out about this farce of a marriage. Nearly sank his whole family with his drinking and gambling debts after his first two years in Oxford."

"Mr Stephenson doesn't drink *or* gamble," Jane said. "If any malicious rumours have said otherwise—"

"Rumours, eh? Tell her!" He swung to face me – the first time he'd taken any notice of my presence since I'd walked into the room behind his daughter. "Tell her the truth about your loose screw of a brother."

"Charles is not a loose screw," I said, and glared back at him. "And he doesn't drink or gamble. Not anymore."

"But he used to?" Jane's voice was soft, her face losing colour as she took in the news. As her father smirked, she turned to face me. "Tell me honestly Kat. Did he really drink and gamble your family to the brink of ruin?"

I bit my lip. Every inch of me wanted to say no. Every part

of me that had watched Charles through the last few days of happiness wanted to lie to her and win my brother the woman he wanted.

But there had been too many lies told in the Carlyle family already. I wanted real happiness for Charles, and a future built on truth.

So I said, "He did, and he regrets it terribly. That's why he gave up alcohol and gambling altogether, despite how difficult it was for him. And that's why he's working so hard to take care of everyone else now, to make up for it."

Jane Carlyle took a deep breath... and released it. "I see," she said. "Thank you for telling me the truth."

"You see?" Her father strode across the room to loom over her. He didn't lift a finger, but his whole pose declared triumph and domination, and I saw her flinch back from him. "I told you—"

"You've told me many things in my life," Jane said. "You told me that gamblers and drinkers can never reform, and you've told me now that Charles Stephenson is a fool. But you've also told me that I am a fool, more times than I can count."

She lifted her chin and looked back at him without a single twinge of visible fear. "I don't believe I'll live by your rules any longer, Papa. If Charles Stephenson is a fool, then so am I. Because no matter what his mistakes were in the past, I trust him now far more than I ever trusted you."

She gave him a cool, distant nod and turned away. "I am sorry to disappoint you, but I do wish you all happiness in your new life. Goodbye."

Her father was still bellowing as she walked out of the room ahead of me. Even though I was giddy with relief, I remembered to be the friend Jane Carlyle had asked me to be... so I didn't stick my tongue out at her father, despite my desperate temptation.

A true friend would never ruin a perfect exit.

But that night, when I was finally initiated into the Order, I thought of Jane as I stretched my arms out and flew.

✡ ✡

I stood behind Angeline in church the next morning, wearing the amethyst ring that was my very own new portal. Elissa stood beside me, glowing with pride, and Jane Carlyle sat in the Carlyle family pew beside her aunt. Jane's hands were folded primly on her lap, and a beaming smile for Frederick and Angeline lit up her face... but as I watched, her gaze slid again and again across the church to my brother. And every time Charles met her gaze, they both seemed to forget about the wedding altogether.

It was all so entirely satisfactory, I had to restrain myself from bouncing on my toes with glee. But an elegant bridesmaid at such an important wedding – and a fully-fledged Guardian – would never make such a spectacle of herself.

So I only grinned like a fool as Frederick Carlyle slipped the wedding ring onto Angeline's finger and Papa finally pronounced them man and wife.

They didn't kiss, not in front of so many people; they would never have been so scandalously improper. But as Frederick Carlyle raised my sister's hand to his lips, I saw the look in Angeline's eyes... and it made my own face burn with reflected heat. When I saw Stepmama wiping away tears with her handkerchief, I couldn't blame her.

My eyes were wet too as I ran with all the others out of

the church to fling rose petals over the newly married couple. Angeline laughed out loud with pure joy as the petals rained down around her, as magical as any spell. I sniffed inelegantly as I watched her and Frederick run hand in hand through the rain of petals, running away from me into their new life together.

I wasn't the only one affected by the sight. Beside me, Elissa took her own husband's hand and smiled up at him with shining trust and love. Charles was still laughing and throwing rose petals with Jane Carlyle by his side... but before long he would be leaving too, going back to Oxford to finally finish his education so that he could take up the profession Papa had always wanted for him – the very last one I had ever imagined coming to pass.

My hopeless scapegrace of an older brother was going to become a clergyman. The very idea would have made me laugh out loud in disbelief only a few weeks ago, but now, as I watched him beam with protective pride at Angeline, Elissa and me, it sounded oddly right after all. And there was no doubt in my mind that Jane Carlyle would make a perfect vicar's wife... especially as Frederick Carlyle had already mentioned that he would be looking for a new vicar for Hepworth's own church in a year's time.

It was all going to work out with extraordinary neatness... for everyone but me.

The marquise drifted over to my side as a crowd of well-wishers surrounded Frederick and Angeline.

"Your sister is a beautiful bride," she said. "And she seems to have sorted out her disagreement with her betrothed."

"That was only a silly quarrel," I said.

My eyes were on Frederick's and Angeline's faces. Neither of them seemed able to stop smiling. Even as they accepted the congratulations of all the people around them with equal enthusiasm, from local villagers to Carlyles in their London finery, the two of them leaned closer and closer to each other, pulled by irresistible attraction.

Frederick's guardian had not attended the ceremony. The spell that Angeline had cast to draw him to Hepworth had been shattered by her injury. Something infinitely better had taken its place. By the time Angeline had recovered enough to think about a new spell-casting, Mrs Carlyle's bags were already being packed... and that fact had finally opened my sister's eyes to the truth: in marrying Frederick Carlyle, she was marrying a man just as strong as she was, and just as able to solve their joint problems.

It was exactly what I'd wanted for her. So I didn't know why I couldn't stop crying now.

The marquise glanced down at me, but she was too polite to mention the tears that streaked unceasingly down my cheeks. Instead she said lightly, "It is a pity your godmother could not stay for the ceremony."

I snorted. Lady Fotherington had fled Hepworth with such inelegant speed the very night of the portals' rescue, I was surprised she hadn't tripped over a servant on her way out. Last night she had sent only her excuses to my initiation ceremony, claiming to be too ill to attend.

I hadn't minded her absence in the slightest. But now, as I watched my sister and her new husband, I said to the marquise, "Are you absolutely sure of that?"

"I beg your pardon?" She looked down at me, her eyes dark and dangerously intelligent beneath her fashionable bonnet.

I turned away from Angeline to meet her gaze. "I think," I said, "that my godmother *is* in attendance, actually. Standing just beside me."

The marquise's eyes widened. Then she began to laugh. "My goodness," she said. "You are very like your mother, aren't you? How exactly did you manage to work that out?"

I shrugged. "Your name is Ann. I heard Mr Gregson say so, the other night."

"And?"

I rolled my eyes. "I do know my own name," I told her. "Katherine Ann Stephenson. I never knew who I'd been named for, before."

"Ah." Her eyelashes dropped to half cover her eyes. "But you've realised it now?"

"I have," I said, and I looked at the dark-haired, dark-eyed woman beside me, so unmistakably similar to Angeline... and to the illusion who had wept at me three nights ago. "But I still don't understand. Why did no one ever tell me that I had an aunt? And why did you never visit us after my christening ceremony?"

The marquise pressed her lips tightly together. When she spoke again, her voice was low and full of regret. "I should never have agreed," she said. "And your father should never have asked it of me. But after my poor sister's death, he went a little mad, I think. He was furious that I hadn't arrived in time to save her.

"No, let me be honest... *I* was furious that I hadn't," she added, in a half whisper. "It was all too easy for him to blame me, when I already blamed myself. So when he asked me to stay away afterwards – when he said he would order Charles and the others never to speak of me again, until they all forgot I had ever existed – I could not argue.

"It was my sister's deathbed wish that I be named your godmother, and he did not betray his promise to her... but he wanted no more reminders of magic to ruin all your lives as hers had been ruined. And I..." She swallowed convulsively, as if forcing down a sob. "I listened to him and fled. I married once and married again, and by now, no one even suspects that I was ever the sister of the scandalous witch, Olivia Amberson."

Her dark eyes glittered with tears. "But I remember. And I could no longer stay away."

I reached out and took my aunt's hand. Her long, slim fingers closed tightly around mine. Her mourning ring bit into my fingers, but I didn't mind. I knew, now, whose dark hair was plaited inside it.

I looked across the crowd and saw Papa watching me from the church door.

His familiar, handsome face was filled with so many emotions that I couldn't read them all: pride and shame and resignation... but more than anything else, love.

It had been love for my mother and grief over her loss that made him tell me I had no godmother all those years ago. It had been love for me and my siblings that had led him to marry again later, to give us another mother, even if Stepmama was one we would never have chosen for ourselves. And it was love, now, that showed most of all in his face as he nodded to me across the crowd.

I took a deep breath and I nodded back.

"You will come to stay with me, won't you?" the marquise said. "I believe your father may finally be persuaded, now – especially with your stepmother's approval. I believe you would enjoy Edinburgh society, and I know..." She slid me a mischievous smile. "I would certainly enjoy teaching another rebellious Guardian how to be a witch."

I opened my mouth but I couldn't speak. Instead laughter bubbled out of me, irrepressible as a fountain. At the sound of my laughter, Angeline looked across the crowd of wedding guests. As her dark eyes met mine she laughed too, pressing one hand to her lips and blowing me a kiss. Without letting go of Mr Collingwood's hand, Elissa stepped towards me to cup her hand around my face, and Charles grinned across at me in the bright sunshine of our sister's wedding day.

A line of carriages drew up in front of the church to take us all back to Hepworth for the grand wedding breakfast that awaited us. Rose petals covered the ground, and the fresh, wild scent of the sea filled my senses. Angeline and Frederick climbed into the first carriage, shouted off with rowdy enthusiasm by the crowd of waving villagers. Elissa and Mr Collingwood stepped in after them, Charles helped Jane into the second carriage...

And I squeezed my godmother's hand in mine as I stepped forwards into my future.

-THE END-

ACKNoWLEDGEMENTS

I first started writing this book just two months after my son was born, and I honestly could not have finished it without the help of these people:

I owe huge thanks to my husband, Patrick Samphire, for endless brainstorming sessions, patient support through all my different drafts, brilliant website design (I'm very lucky to be married to a website designer!), and priceless help untangling the plot whenever I got stuck. (Not to mention equal parenting of our son and vastly superior amounts of housework!) Even more than any of that, though, what really made all the difference in the world was that he always fiercely believed in this book and in me.

My parents, Richard and Kathy Burgis, my brother, David Burgis, and my mother-in-law, Beth Samphire, all did heroic amounts of babysitting to give me more time to write. Justina Robson, Tricia Sullivan and Ysabeau Wilce traded stories, advice and support with me as we all worked to balance writing and mothering. Karen Healey and Jenn Reese cheered me on as beta readers all throughout the first draft. I am so grateful to all of you!

Thank you so much to everybody who read and critiqued the novel for me: Patrick Samphire, Tiffany Trent, Tricia Sullivan and Justina Robson.

I continue to have The Best Agents in the World, Barry Goldblatt and Nancy Miles Stott. I thought I was lucky when Barry first sold the Kat books in America and Nancy sold them in the UK; since then, I've learned just how lucky I really am, as they've supported me through this trilogy and the ups and downs of publishing life.

I'm so lucky to work with not one but two wonderful editors, Namrata Tripathi in America and Emma Goldhawk in the UK. Thanks so much to both of you for believing in me and in Kat, and for making my novels so much stronger!

I also feel really privileged to have worked with copyeditor Jenica Nasworthy, who saved me from so many embarrassing mistakes along the way. Thank you, Jenica!

In America, Emma Ledbetter at Atheneum has also gone way above and beyond the call of duty for Kat and for me, too many times to count, and I appreciate it so much. In the UK, Jayne Roscoe, Leonora Mary and Philippa Perry have guided me through publicity with grace and enthusiasm. Thank you all!

I owe huge thanks to Luisa Plaja and Delia Sherman, who both helped me with my Devon research. (Any mistakes that I made anyway are purely my own fault!)

I'm also incredibly lucky to have a brother who is a talented filmmaker. Dave, thank you so much for the wonderful book trailers!

And last but not least, I am infinitely grateful to everyone who's followed Kat's adventures in these books, and/or my own adventures on my blog www.stephanieburgis.com/blog – I love being part of such an amazing community of readers!

ABOUT THE AUTHOR

LIKE HER HEROINE KAT, STEPHANIE BURGIS COMES FROM A BIG, noisy, loving family. She grew up in Michigan, USA, where as a little girl she became addicted to reading and writing stories. At the age of ten, Stephanie's favourite books were *The Lord of the Rings* and *Pride and Prejudice*, and, in her own words, "Writing the Kat books was my chance to finally combine fantasy adventure and nineteenth-century romantic comedy – the two kinds of story I love best."

Before Stephanie became a full-time writer, she was a student of music, playing the French horn. She won a prestigious Fulbright Scholarship to study in Vienna, Austria, and earned a Master's degree in music history. Stephanie has had lots of different jobs, including teaching English to teenagers in Vienna and editing the website of an opera company in northern England.

Stephanie now lives in Wales with her husband, toddler son and their sweet border collie dog, Maya.

Visit **www.stephanieburgis.com** to find out more about Stephanie, Regency England and The Unladylike Adventures of Kat Stephenson.

If you haven't read Kat's first Unladylike Adventures,
why not catch up on what you've missed...

At twelve years old, any proper young lady should
be sitting quietly at home, practising her embroidery
and keeping her opinions to herself.

But Kat Stephenson is no ordinary young lady.

Kat's father may be a respectable vicar, but her late
mother was a notorious witch, her brother has gambled
the whole family into debt, and Kat herself is the newest
target of an ancient and secretive order.

In the first thrilling instalment of The Unladylike
Adventures of Kat Stephenson, Kat sets out to win her older
sisters their true loves, battling highwaymen, practising
magic and breaking all of Society's rules along the way.

ISBN 978-1-84877-007-2 Paperback £6.99

Also available as an ebook

After Kat's sister Angeline's betrothal
to Frederick Carlyle is forbidden by his mother,
Stepmama drags the Stephenson family to the city
of Bath in search of a new suitor. But, unbeknownst
to most of its fashionable, gossipy visitors, Bath
is a place brimful of wild magic.

When Kat uncovers a plot to harness the
wild magic of the Roman Baths, she discovers her
hapless brother Charles is unwittingly involved.
Will Kat's newfound magical powers be
snatched away from her as she defies the
Order of the Guardians to foil the plot
and clear her brother's name?

ISBN 978-1-84877-470-4 Paperback £6.99

Also available as an ebook